Exodus from the Long Sun

"If you have been following this series, be assured that all of the plot threads are woven together, and that there are surprises; if you have not yet begun, do so at once. Right now, Wolfe may be the best science fiction writer in the world."

—*Interzone*

"In this fourth volume of his *Book of the Long Sun*, Wolfe concludes one of the major SF series of the decade. . . . The complex language is lovingly crafted. The culture of the Whorl, particularly in its religious manifestations, is presented in rich and fascinating detail. Silk makes for an engaging protagonist. . . . The series as a whole is a bona fide masterpiece."

—*Publishers Weekly*

"Wolfe's command of language, his empathy with and understanding of his characters, and his narrative mastery are all brilliantly evident as his long, hypnotically compelling saga ends."

—*Booklist*

It is the far future, and the giant spaceship, The Whorl, has travelled for forgotten generations toward its destination. Lit inside by the artificial Long Sun, The Whorl is so huge that whole cities can be seen in the sky. And the gods of The Whorl have begun to intervene in human affairs. An entirely unexpected future awaits as Patera Silk and the other inhabitants are confronted with the world of an alien race. Wolfe's great work is complete, with the mysterious fullness of life itself.

EXODUS FROM
THE LONG SUN

Gene Wolfe

A TOM DOHERTY ASSOCIATES BOOK
NEW YORK

This is a work of fiction. All the characters and events portrayed in this
book are either products of the author's imagination or are used ficti-
tiously.

EXODUS FROM THE LONG SUN

Copyright © 1996 by Gene Wolfe

Cover art by Richard Bober

A Tor Book
Published by Tom Doherty Associates, Inc.
175 Fifth Avenue
New York, NY 10010

Tor Books on the World Wide Web:
http://www.tor.com

Tor® is a registered trademark of Tom Doherty Associates, Inc.

ISBN: 0-812-53905-2
Library of Congress Card Catalog Number: 96-24518

First edition: November 1996
First mass market edition: August 1997

Printed in the United States of America

0 9 8 7 6 5 4 3 2 1

For Paul and Vicki Marxen
—we go way back.

Gods, Persons, and Animals Mentioned in the Text

N.B. The names of Trivigauntis, Fliers, and gods do not adhere to the Vironese conventions. As in *Caldé of the Long Sun,* the names of major characters are given in CAPITALS.

Colonel ABANJA, SIYUF's spymaster.

Aer, SCIATHAN's lover, a Flier.

Aster, a former classmate of NETTLE's.

AUK, the prophet of TARTAROS.

Maytera *Betel,* the big dark woman with sleepy eyes whom SILK was shown during his first enlightenment, now dead.

Colonel *Bison,* MINT's chief subordinate.

Blood, ROSE's son and MUCOR's adoptive father, a crime lord; he was killed by SILK.

Bluebell, one of the women at Orchid's.

Bongo, the trained baboon SILK noticed when buying OREB.

CHENILLE, Tussah's natural daughter.

Chamomile, Swallow's assistant.

Doctor *Crane,* a subordinate of ABANJA's; his death caused SIYUF to send Saba's airship to Viron.

Dace, a fisherman killed by one of Urus's gang.

Dahlia, a student at the palaestra on Sun Street long ago.

Desmid, one of POTTO's spycatchers, now dead.

ECHIDNA, the goddess who conspired to murder PAS, her husband.

Eland, a convicted murderer.

Feather, a small boy who attended the Sun Street palaestra.

Patera *Feeler,* a proverbial carper.

Fulmar, a member of Incus's circle of black mechanics.

Councillor *Galago,* a surviving member of the Ayuntamiento.

Gib, the giant who bought Bongo.

Ginger, a young woman who lost a hand in the insurrection.

Goldcrest, a former classmate of NETTLE's.

Grian, the Flier who escaped the Trivigauntis.

Guan, the man with the slug gun, a subordinate of SPIDER's.

Major *Hadale,* the officer who places SABA under arrest.

Corporal HAMMERSTONE, INCUS's dearest friend.

Hart, a friend of HORN's, wounded in the fighting.

Hide, one of NETTLE's twin sons.

Hierax, ECHIDNA's younger son, the god of death.

Holly, a former classmate of NETTLE's.

Hoof, one of NETTLE's twin sons.

HORN, the colonist who undertook to write *The Book of Silk.*

Hossaan, see *Willet.*

HYACINTH, the estranged wife of Serval.

HYRAX, the dead man in the doorway.

Patera INCUS, the augur who supplants REMORA.

Patera *Jerboa,* the augur of the Brick Street manteion.

Kerria, a boy of four.

Councillor *Kingcup,* the new member of the Ayuntamiento chosen by MINT.

Kit, a former pupil at SILK's palaestra.

Kypris, PAS's mistress, the goddess of love.

Councillor *Lemur,* the presiding officer of the Ayuntamiento, killed by Crane. (Also the bio of the same name.)

Sergeant *Linsang,* one of MINT's volunteers.

Lijam, the Minister of War of Trivigaunte; she is a political ally of SIYUF's.

Lion, the largest of MUCOR's lynxes.

Councillor *Loris,* Lemur's successor.

Macaque, a former classmate of HORN's.

Maytera *Maple,* the youngest sibyl at Jerboa's manteion.

Maytera MARBLE, formerly the maid-of-all-work Magnesia.

Marl, Fulmar's elderly manservant.

Marrow, the greengrocer who becomes a leader of the colonists on Blue.

Private *Matar,* one of SABA's pterotroopers.

Cornet *Mattak,* a young officer who was attacked by an inhumu.

Mear, one of the Fliers killed by the Trivigauntis.

Maytera MINT, the Sword of Echidna, also known as General MINT.

Maytera *Mockorange,* MINT's preceptress long ago.

Molpe, Echidna's mad daughter, the goddess of the winds.

Moly, HAMMERSTONE's lost sweetheart, a housemaid. (Short for Molybdenum.)

Moorgrass, the woman who prepared the body of Orchid's daughter for burial.

MUCOR, the young woman grown from a frozen embryo purchased by Blood.

Murtagon, a famous artist, now dead.

Musk, Blood's lover and chief subordinate, killed by MARBLE.

NETTLE, HORN's wife, a former student at SILK's palaestra.

Councillor *Newt,* the new member of the Ayuntamiento chosen by POTTO.

Private *Nizam,* a young pterotrooper who is fond of animals.

Generalissimo *Oosik,* the commander of the armed forces of Viron, appointed by SILK.

Orchid, the madam of a brothel on Lamp Street.

OREB, a night chough, SILK's pet bird.

The OUTSIDER, the god of gods.

Paca, the dead man in the tunnel.

PAS, the digitized personality of a tyrant.

Peeper, a turnkey at the Juzgado.

Petal, see *Titi.*

Phaea, Echidna's fat daughter.

Patera *Pike,* the elderly augur whose acolyte SILK was, now dead.

Poppy, a friend of CHENILLE's at Orchid's.

Councillor POTTO, a surviving member of the Ayuntamiento.

Patera QUETZAL, a male of the inhumi, native to Green.

Patera REMORA, the lanky augur who expected to succeed QUETZAL.

General *Rimah*, SIYUF's chief of staff.

Rook, one of MINT's subordinates.

Maytera ROSE, the elderly sibyl whose personality has merged with MARBLE's, now dead.

General SABA, the Trivigaunti possessed by MUCOR at SILK's dinner party.

Sergeant *Sand*, HAMMERSTONE's squad leader.

Sard, a pawnbroker; his shop is on Saddle Street, not far from Orchid's yellow house.

Private *Schist*, a soldier in Sand's squad.

SCIATHAN, the Flier captured by the Trivigauntis.

SCLERODERMA, the author of a much briefer account of the exodus from Viron and the events leading up to it.

Scylla, ECHIDNA's eldest child, the goddess of water.

Captain *Serval*, the officer who pretended to arrest SILK in Limna, usually called "the captain."

Sewellel, the dead man in the abandoned guardroom.

Private *Shale*, a soldier in Sand's squad.

Patera *Shell*, Jerboa's acolyte.

Shrike, SCLERODERMA's husband, a butcher.

Sigada, see *Crane*.

Silah, a daughter of the Rani of Trivigaunte.

Caldé SILK, the young augur grown from the frozen embryo purchased by Tussah.

Sinew, NETTLE's eldest son.

Major *Sirka*, the officer in charge of the Trivigaunti advance party.

Generalissimo SIYUF, the commander of the armed forces of Trivigaunte.

General *Skate*, a subordinate of Oosik's, the nominal commander of the Caldé's Guard.

Major *Skin*, a subordinate of Bison's.

Skink, one of MINT's subordinates, crippled in the fighting.

Private *Slate,* a soldier in Sand's squad.

Sphigx, ECHIDNA's youngest daughter, the goddess of war.

SPIDER, POTTO's chief spycatcher.

Sumaire, one of the Fliers killed by the Trivigauntis.

Director *Swallow,* the head of the manufactory that builds taluses.

Councillor *Tarsier,* a surviving member of the Ayuntamiento.

TARTAROS, ECHIDNA's older son, the god of darkness.

Teasel, a girl who was attacked by an inhumu.

Thelxiepeia, ECHIDNA's third daughter, the goddess of learning.

Tick, the catachrest SILK rejected before buying OREB.

Titi, one of SPIDER's spycatchers, now dead.

Thyone, a minor goddess, invoked by those who tell fortunes by throwing the lees of wine.

Commissioner *Trematode,* the Vironese city official overseeing diplomacy, ceremony, and protocol.

Trotter, the owner of a drinking den near the Juzgado.

Caldé *Tussah,* SILK's predecessor, thought to have been murdered.

Urus, a former confederate of AUK's.

Villus, the small boy who scratched MARBLE's face with Musk's needler.

Violet, the second tallest woman at Orchid's.

Willet, the floater driver who brought Hyacinth to Ermine's to meet SILK.

Maytera *Wood,* the oldest sibyl at Jerboa's manteion.

Wool, a subordinate of MINT's, now dead; he was in charge of the oxen used to pull down the Corn Exchange.

Master *Xiphias,* SILK's self-appointed bodyguard.

Chapter 1

BACK FROM DEATH

An eerie silence overhung the ruined villa. Listening for the closing of a slug gun's bolt, Maytera Mint heard only the groan of the wind and the irregular snapping of the flag of truce she held.

"On Phaesday they were *in situ,*" Patera Remora conceded. "The Ayuntamiento, eh?"

They had come abreast of a dead talus, its painted steel sides blistered by fire and blackened by smoke; she caught a whiff of fish oil, despite the wind.

"Might be repaired, eh, General?" Remora pushed back a lock of lank black hair that had fallen over his eyes. "Not like we biochemicals, hey? Still we—ah—dispatch their spirits to Mainframe. Not identical in the, um, revivified one, perhaps. Amongst the new parts."

"Or they really haven't any," Maytera Mint murmured. She had stopped to wait for Remora, and was taking the opportunity to study the windows of the house that had been Blood's.

Her remark bordered on heresy, but Remora thought it

most prudent to return to his earlier topic. "If they're not here, eh? Loris and the rest? Will, ah, Buffalo—"

"Bison." She turned back to Remora, her face pinched and the tip of her delicate nose red with cold. "Colonel Bison."

"Um, precisely. Will Colonel Bison," Remora waved vaguely at the ruined wall, "and his—ah—troopers await our return back there?"

"You heard my instructions, Your Eminence."

"But if we're some time, eh? The front door is broken. Shattered, in fact."

Maytera Mint, who had noted it as they passed through the ruined gateway, nodded.

"So it's not a matter of knocking, hey? Not a mere matter of knocking at all." Remora brightened. "Knock on the frame, eh? We could do that. Wait a bit, Polite."

"I will go inside," she told him firmly, "and search. I would not presume to dictate Your Eminence's course of action. If I can get in touch with the Ayuntamiento, I'll ask them to send for you. If I can't, I may be able to learn where we can. As for Colonel Bison, he's completely loyal, my best officer. My only concern is that he may send in a patrol to look for us, though I have forbidden it."

"I, um, apprehend your position," Remora said, rejoining her. "If one does not expect obedience, one will not, ah, be obeyed. Memorized it in schola, all of us did. Still, if he were to depart? Decamp. Our, um, withdrawal to the city could be hazardous, hey? Laborious, likewise."

"That's not the question." She forgot for a moment that Remora was the second highest dignitary of the Chapter. "The question is whether the enemy's back. There are no bodies."

"These, ah—"

"These taluses. It would take ten yoke of oxen to drag them away, I suppose. No dead bios or chems."

"The, ah, Army, eh? To the Caldé. So I understood."

"Some soldiers went over to him, yes. Others who hadn't heard about him didn't, and were fighting their comrades here."

Remora nodded. "Unfortunate. Um, tragic."

"When this man Blood's bodyguards learned Caldé Silk had killed him, some attacked him and his soldiers. That's when Generalissimo Oosik and General Saba stormed the house."

"Lovely, hum?" Remora harbored a sneaking admiration for architecture as others cherish a vice. "Even, ah, despoiled. Pity. Pity. More so, possibly. No pretensions now. No more vulgar display. Wreckage more—um—romantic? Poetic." He favored Blood's torn lawns with a toothy smile.

Maytera Mint drew her soiled habit more tightly about her and for the hundredth time wished for her coif. "If we were to walk a little faster, Your Eminence, we could get out of this wind, whether the Ayuntamiento's come back or not."

"Of course, of course."

"And though I don't concede that Bison—"

"Those—um—corpses, General." Catching up, Remora strode along beside her, his lanky legs making a single step of two of hers. "You were about to, er, um, propose that we afford them an—ah—sanctified burial? It would be most inconvenient, I fear. Most inopportune!"

"Granted. But there must have been bodies, and I'd think more than a few. The Ayuntamiento's soldiers and this man's bodyguards would have been shooting from these windows."

Maytera Mint paused, drawing on her recent experiences to visualize the scene. "Floaters would have rushed the gate, and Guardsmen and General Saba's pterotroopers must have swarmed through every break in the wall. Then my troopers from the city, thousands of them. Some must have been killed, I'd think at least a hundred. Some of the bodyguards and soldiers must have been killed too. See that line of pockmarks? Buzz-gun fire. A floater's turret gun raked the front of the house."

"I, ah—"

For once she interrupted him. "We would have taken away our dead, or I hope we would. But what about theirs? They were retreating under fire, going down into the tunnels Sand talked about. Would they have dragged bodies along with them? I find it hard to believe, Your Eminence."

"If I may." Remora cleared his throat. "It seems to me that you have, ah, disposed of the, um, dead yourself, though I confess that I am no great hand at matters military."

"Nor I. I was appointed by Echidna, you must have heard of that. What little I know I've picked up as I went along."

"Defeating commanders vastly more—ah—schooled. I would conjecture, leastwise, that there must be something like our schola for the officers of the, er, Caldé's Guard. As we call them now, eh, General? The Civil Guard we used to phrase it, hey? Admirable, I, um, insist."

"I've lost to them, too, Your Eminence. Lost nearly as often as I've won." They were passing Scylla's fountain, now sheathed in ice.

"Though no great hand," Remora repeated, "I offer the, um, this hypothesis. Would not well regulated troops inter their dead? The generalissimo's men are, ah, proficient, to be sure, and we—ah—furnish a chaplain to each brigade. The, um, desiderata of that. Conduct military obsequies. Subsequently, please to follow me here, Mayt—General. Would not such, er, troopers compel the, ah, your own, though not then under, as it were, your eye—"

"Make them bury the rest? Possibly." Maytera Mint, who was very tired, forced herself to stand straighter and square her shoulders. "More likely no compulsion was needed. If they had not thought of it themselves, seeing the Guard and Saba's pterotroopers loading their dead to take back to the city would suggest it. But what about the enemy dead? Where are they?"

"Within this desolate, ah, mansion. I dare say. They would not have abandoned its shelter, hey? Shot through its windows. You—um—proposed it yourself."

She pointed with the stick that held her white flag. "See where the wall's fallen? You can look into several rooms, and there's not a single body in any of them."

"Yet, ah—"

"Through the doorway, too." They had nearly reached the steps of Blood's portico. "That door would have been defended more strongly than any other point, and I can look right into the sellaria. There's not a one. Where are they?"

"I would, er, hazard that the victorious troops disposed of them afterward."

She shook her head vigorously. "Troopers who've won are never anxious to get the bodies of those they've killed out of sight, Your Eminence. Never! I've seen that much more often than I like. They're proud, and it's good for their morale. Yesterday Major Skin was begging, literally begging me, not to have bodies that had lain in the streets for days carted off. If the bodies are gone, it's because their friends came back for them. It would be interesting to see if there are graves behind the house. That's where they'd be, I imagine. By the wall, as far as possible from the road. Do you know if there are gardens in back?"

"I have never, um, had the pleasure." Remora started up the steps. "Nor has His Cognizance, I think. He, um, confided it to me a year or two past. We had been—um—dissecting? Decrying this, er, Blood's influence. Was never a, um, visitor within these—ah—despoiled walls."

"Neither have I, Your Eminence." Maytera Mint hiked up her skirt and started up the steps.

"To be sure. To be sure, General. I regret it. Regret it now. I will not dissemble, nor, um, ever. Seldom. To have seen this in its days of prosperity would—prosperity and peace, eh? The contrast 'twixt memory and the, um, less happy present. Do you follow me? Whereas one can now but picture . . . See that picture? Fine. Very fine indeed, eh? Torn. Might be refurbished yet, in skillful hands. Like the tali, eh?"

"I suppose." She had glanced at the ruined furniture, and was studying the shadowy doorways of further rooms. "He kept women here, didn't he? This bad man Blood who owned the house. Women—women who . . ."

"Enough, enough! Do not, um, perturb yourself, Maytera. General. A few such. An, er, select contingent. So I was given to understand upon the occasion of our—um—my tête-à-tête, eh? With old Quetzal. Do I, um, scandalize you? With His Cognizance. I am, ah, betimes inclined to be overfree. To

presume upon an old friendship. A failing, I concede."
Remora advanced to study the damaged Murtagon.

"Was this where it happened?"

"Where the women—ah?" He glanced back at her with a
half smile. "No indeed."

"Where Caldé Silk killed this man Blood, and Sergeant
Sand killed Councillor Potto."

"We've finer ones at the Palace, hey? Still it's nice and
might be—ah—emended. In an, um, one of the anterooms as
I understand it, General. May I ask why you wish to know?
A, um, monument of some kind, possibly? A dedicational
tablet of, er, bronze?"

"Because we know that the man who owned this house died
in it, Your Eminence," Maytera Mint explained. "This Blood,
with Councillor Potto. If their bodies aren't here, they've
been removed by someone, and I'd think that if Generalissimo
Oosik or even General Saba had done it I'd have heard. A
councillor's body? Everyone would be arguing about what
should be done with it, and I would certainly have heard."

Her tone grew crisp. "Now if you'll oblige me."

Remora, who was not used to being asked for favors in that
peremptory fashion, looked around sharply.

"There seems to be no one here, though my informants . . .
Never mind. Do you agree?"

"There is certainly no one in this room at present except—
ah—ourselves. With regard to the, er, remainder of the, um,
building, I—hum—further investigation."

"I've been listening carefully and heard nothing. The bodies may be in plain view or hidden by furniture or whatnot."
Rather tardily Maytera Mint added, "Your Eminence. I'll
search the rooms on this side. I'd like you to search the other.
We needn't bother with the rest of the house, I think."

"If there are no, er, bodies, General," Remora smoothed the
truant lock into place, "shall we return to the city—ah—forth-
with? Might be wise, eh? We have no way of knowing what
has transpired in our absence, hey?"

She nodded. "Agreed. We'll know then that they've been
here and may return later. I'll leave one of Bison's officers to

watch, with a few troopers. If we *do* find a body, either one, it should be safe to assume that the Ayuntamiento's troops have never come back at all. We can go back to the city at once and forget about this house."

"Wisely, er, spoken." Remora was already hurrying toward the first of his assigned rooms. "I shall inform you promptly should I discover a—ah—the mortal remains."

The anteroom Maytera Mint entered had, it appeared, been the owner's study. A massive mahogany desk, lavishly carved, stood against one wall, and there were shelves of books, mostly (she scanned the titles on a shelf at the level of her eyes) erotic if not pornographic: *Three Maids and Their Mistress, The Astonishing Exploits of a Virile Young Man and His Donkey, His Resistance Overcome* . . .

She turned away. What had it been like to be here under such a master? She tried and failed to picture the lives of the women who had endured it. They had been bad women, as the whorl judged, but that only meant that they had commanded defenses greatly inferior to her own.

Strange, how she had come to think in military metaphors during the past few days.

The desk drawers seemed apt to tell her a good deal about the owner, who counted for nothing now, and nothing about the Ayuntamiento and those who served it. She opened a drawer at random anyway, glanced at the papers it had held— all of them concerned in some fashion with money—shut it, and made sure no corpse lay concealed in the leg hole.

"General!"

Turning so quickly that the long, black skirt of her habit billowed about her, she hurried out of the study and across the sellaria. "What is it, Your Eminence?"

He met her at the doorway, visibly struggling to conceal his pleasure. "I have the—ah—it is my unhappy duty—"

"You've found a body. Whose?"

"The, um, late councillor's, I believe. If, perhaps, you would not care—"

"To see it? I must! Your Eminence, I've seen hundreds of bodies since this began. Thousands." There had been a time when she had found it nearly impossible to cut the throat of a goat; as she pushed past Remora, she reflected that she would find that difficult still, and find it literally impossible to cut a man's, even an enemy's. Yet she had made plans and given orders that had clogged entire streets with corpses.

"I took the, um, responsibility? The—ah—presumption of, er, tidying him up. On his back now, eh? Folded the arms, prior to calling you."

Potto lay almost at her feet, his arms crossed in such a way as to hide the wound Sand's slug had made just below his sternum. The graying hair that he had worn long trailed over Blood's lush carpet, and Maytera Mint found herself muttering, "He looks surprised."

"Doubtless he—ah—was." Remora cleared his throat. "Caught unawares, hey? Shot by one of his own. All in a, um, trice. So my prothonotary tells me. He—ah—Incus is his name, General. Patera Incus. He has, um, fallen prey in some—ah—wise to the notion that he's old Quetzal—"

She knelt beside the corpse, traced the sign of addition, and opened its card case.

"Mad, I fear. Deranged. Bit of rest, eh? He'll come to himself soon enough. General—ah—?"

"In the first place," Maytera Mint explained, "There may be papers of value in here. In the second, there's money, ten cards or so, and we need that very badly."

"I, ah, see."

Cards and papers vanished into her wide sleeve. "Where's the blood? Did you clean up his blood before you called to me, Your Eminence?"

"Through the heart, eh?" Remora's nasal tones sounded slightly strangled. "Not much bleeding then, eh? So I am—ah—apprised."

Gently at first, then with increased vigor, Maytera Mint rubbed the councillor's cheek. "This's a chem!"

"I—um—"

She looked up at Remora. "You knew."

"I—ah—suspected."

"You rolled him over, you said, Your Eminence. You folded his arms. You must have known."

"Then? Oh, yes, I—ah—confirmed, eh? I had, um, and—ah—Quetzal, eh? Old Quetzal. Wouldn't tell. Asked him once. More, actually. He, ah, er, wouldn't. Confides in me, eh? Nearly everything. Very, ah, delicate points. Sensitive matters, finances. Everything. But he—ah—wouldn't."

Suddenly Remora was on his knees beside her. "General—ah—General. Alone here, hey? No one but, er, ourselves. May I call you Maytera?"

She ignored it. "There'll be the question of burial. A dozen questions, really. You must have realized I'd find out."

"I—ah—did. Indeed. Not so swiftly, however. You are most—er—perspicacious."

"Then why didn't you say so? Why all that nonsense about blood?"

"Because I—Incus. Patera Incus. And old Quetzal, eh? My position is, er, delicate. Imperiled. Maytera, hear me, I—ah—beg you. Yes, beg. Implore."

She nodded. "I'm listening. What is it?"

"Incus, my prothonotary. Was. You know him?"

She shook her head. "Just tell me."

"He's been appointed Prolocutor. By, um, Scylla. He says it, I mean. Credits it himself, eh? Convinced. Spoke to him yesterday, but he—you . . ."

"Me?" For a second, Maytera Mint felt she was missing some vital clue. It dawned upon her, and she rocked backward to sit cross-legged on the carpet, her head in her hands.

"Maytera? Er, General?"

She looked up at Remora. "I was appointed by Echidna, in front of thousands of people. Is that it, Your Eminence?"

Remora's mouth opened and shut silently.

"So you know it happened. All those witnesses. And I've been successful, as you say. The victorious commander, chosen for us by the gods. Even Bison and the captain talk like that, and then there's Patera Silk."

Remora nodded miserably.

"Everyone says he's been appointed by Great Pas to be our

caldé, even Maytera Marble. He's been successful, too, so it looks like the gods have decided to choose leaders for us, and if this Patera Incus is going to be the new Prolocutor, he'll want to pick his own coadjutor."

"Nor—ah—um—worse. If he—ah—old Quetzal, you know. Resourceful. Cunning. Seen it myself, hundreds of times, eh? Ayuntamiento had the force, but he'd get 'round them. Get 'round Lemur and Loris, all of them. Old man, hey? Foolish old man. What they think. His Cognizance. Quetzal. But sly, Mayt—General. Very sly. Deep."

She made a small sound of encouragement.

"Compromise. I—ah—sense it. I am not, um, clever, General. Try to be, indeed. Try. Some have said—well, it pares no parsnips. But not like old Quetzal. Experienced, though. My—ah—self. Conferences, negotiations. And I wind it. Wind it already. Be coadjutor, Incus. Obvious, eh? First thing anybody would, er, formulate. Old Quetzal would—ah—visualize? Comprehend the whole before Incus finished. Old man. Die soon, hey? A year, two years, to—ah—fit yourself into the position, Patera. I'll be gone. I can, um, hear him as I—we—speak. So I didn't dare, eh? Tell you. You see my predicament? The—ah—Loris. Galago. All the rest. Chems, every one of them. I suspected it for years. Meeting with this one, that one, entire days, sometimes. Saw them up close. Quetzal knows, he must."

"But His Cognizance wouldn't talk about it?"

"No. Ah—no. Too sensitive. Even for me, eh? He, Incus. I told you?"

"You told me he says Scylla's made him Prolocutor."

"He, um, offered me . . ."

One bony hand pushed back the straying lock, and Maytera Mint saw how violently that hand shook. "He offered you . . . ?"

"An—ah—appointment. A position. He was," Remora swallowed, "not abusive. It was not, I judge, his intent to be—ah—disparage. He said that I—I refused, to be sure. His prothonotary. His, ah, I—I—I . . ."

Maytera Mint nodded. "I see."

"We have been, er, companions, Maytera. Coworkers—ah—partners in peace, hey? Son and daughter of the Chapter. We have conferred, and the same—um—consecrated vision has inspired us both. I well—ah—recollect our first meeting. You averred with—um—coruscant eyes that peace was your, er, sole desire once you had—ah, um—executed the will of the gods. I affirmed? Avowed that it was mine likewise. In concert we have conferred with Brigadier Erne and the caldé. You are a hero, um, heroine to the—ah—populace. There is talk of a statue, hey? A word from you, your support . . ."

"Be quiet," she told him. "I haven't had a moment to get used to the idea that the Ayuntamiento's made up of chems, and now this."

"If I, ah—"

"Be quiet, I said!" She drew a deep breath, running the fingers of both hands through her short brown hair. "To begin with, no, you may not call me Maytera. Not in private, and not any other time. If His Cognizance will release me, I mean to return to secular life. I," another breath, "may marry. We'll see. As for you, if this Patera Incus has in fact been named Prolocutor by Scylla, then he *is* Prolocutor, regardless of any arrangement that he and Patera Quetzal may make. I can readily imagine a younger man of great sanctity deferring to a much older one. Viewed in a certain light, it would be an act of noble self-renunciation. But it wouldn't alter the fact. He would be our Prolocutor, though he wasn't called so. Since he proposed that you become his prothonotary, plainly you're not to be coadjutor any longer. No doubt Patera Quetzal is, in solemn truth, coadjutor. That being so, I'll call you Patera."

"My dear young woman!"

Her look silenced him. "I'm not your dear young woman, or anyone's. I'm thirty-six, and I assure you that for a woman it's no longer young. Call me General, or I'll make your life a great deal less pleasant than it has been."

A door at the far end of the room opened, and someone who was neither Mint nor Remora applauded. "Brava, my dear young general! Simply marvelous! You ought to be on the stage."

He waddled over to them, a short, obese man with bright blue eyes, a cheerful round face, and hair so light as to be nearly blond. "But as for accepting an Ayuntamiento of chems, you need not trouble. I'm no chem, though I confess that the object before you is something of the kind."

Remora gasped, having recognized him.

"This augur and I are old—I really can't say friends. Acquaintances. You, I feel sure, are the rebels' famous General Mint." The stranger giggled. "Presumably you aim at supreme power, which would make you the Govern-Mint. I like that! I'm Councillor Potto. Curtain. Did you wish to speak to me?"

For a fleeting moment in which his heart nearly stopped, it seemed to Silk that he had seen Hyacinth among the cheering pedestrians. Before he could shout to his bearers, the woman turned her head and the illusion ended. He had been ready, he realized as he settled back among the cushions, to spring out of the litter.

I need my glasses, he thought. My old ones, which I can't possibly get back, or some new ones.

Oreb fluttered on his shoulder. "Good Silk!"

"Crazed Silk," he told his bird. "Mad and foolish Silk. I mistook another woman for her."

"No see."

"My own thought exactly. Several times I've dreamed my mother was alive. Have I told you about that?"

Oreb whistled.

"For a minute or two after I woke up, I believed it, and I was so happy. This was like that." Leaning from the right side of the litter, he addressed the head bearer. "You needn't go so fast. You'll wear yourselves out."

The man grinned and bobbed his head.

Silk settled back again. Their speed was increasing. No doubt the bearers felt it a question of honor; when one carried the caldé, one ran. Otherwise ordinary people who had never had the privilege of carrying the caldé's litter might think him on an errand of no importance. Which would never do; if his errand were of no importance, neither were his bearers.

"I've got twenty Guardsmen looking for her," he told Oreb. "That's not enough, since they didn't find her, but it's all we could spare with the Fourth Brigade holding out on the north side, and the Ayuntamiento in the tunnels."

Mention of the tunnels made Oreb croak unhappily.

At what amounted to a dead run, the litter swayed, yawed, and swerved off Sun Street onto Lamp. Leaning out Silk said, "Music Street—I thought I made it clear. A block east."

The head bearer's head bobbed as before.

"If twenty Guardsmen can't find her, Oreb, I certainly can't; and last night I didn't. We didn't, I ought to say. So we need help, and I can think of three places—no, four—where we may get it. Today we're going to try them all. Most of the fires are out, and Maytera Mint and Oosik can actually fight better without me in the way; so although the physician says I should be in bed, and I'm not supposed to have a minute to myself, I intend to take as many hours as necessary."

Yawing as before, the litter turned onto a still narrower street that Silk did not recognize.

"It's up to the gods, I'm afraid. I don't trust them—not even the Outsider, who seems to trust me—but they may smile on us yet."

"Find girl?"

He had lost his desire to talk, but the intensity of his emotions drove the words forth. "What did he *want* with her!" As he spoke, the litter sped past a shop with a zither and a dusty bassoon in its window.

But Caldé Silk of Viron did not see them.

"This is the kitchen?" Maytera Mint looked around her in surprise. It was the largest that she had ever seen.

"There are, ah, alternatives," Remora ventured. "Still entire, eh? Equally, hum, unsigned by Sabered Sphigx."

"I find it cozy," Potto declared. "For one thing, there's food, though your troops, my dear young General, made off with a lot. I like food, even if I can't eat it. For another, I'm a good host, eager for the comfort of my guests, and it's easy to heat. Behold this noble stove and laden woodbox. I'm happily immune to drafts, but you aren't. I'm determined to make you comfortable. Those other rooms offer the chilly attractions of a society beauty. This will provide warmth and tea, even soup." He giggled. "All the solid virtues of an old nurse. Besides, there are a great many sharp knives, and I'm always encouraged by the presence of sharp knives."

"You can't be here alone," Maytera Mint said.

Potto grinned. "Do you propose to attack me if I am?"

"Certainly not."

"You have an azoth, the famous one given you by Silk. I won't search you for it now."

"I left it with Colonel Bison. If I had come armed after calling for a truce, you'd be entitled to kill me."

"I am anyhow," Potto told her. He picked up a stick of firewood and snapped it between his hands. "The rules of war protect armies and their auxiliaries. Yours is a rebellion, not a war, and rebels get no such protection. Patera there knows that's the truth. Look at his face."

"I—ah—assert the privilege of my cloth."

"You can. You haven't fought, so you're entitled to it. The General has and isn't. It's all very simple."

When neither replied, Potto added, "Speaking of cloth, I forgot to say that the rules apply only to soldiers and those auxiliaries who wear their city's uniform, as General Saba does. You, my dear General, don't. The upshot is that though I can't offer violence to your armies as long as the truce holds, I'm entitled to break both your leggies if I want to, and even to wring your necky. Sit down, there's a cozy little table right over there. I'll build a fire and put the kettle on."

They sat, Remora tucking the rich overrobe he wore around his legs, Maytera Mint as she might have in the cenoby, her delicate hands folded in her lap, and her head bowed.

Potto filled one of the stove's fireboxes and stroked a stick of kindling. It burst into flame, not merely at one end like a torch, but along its entire length. He tossed it into the firebox and shoved the firebox back in place with an angry grinding of iron.

"He, um, intrigues to separate us," Remora whispered. "A—ah—hallowed? Elementary stratagem, General. I shall, um, cleave to you, eh? If you in, ah, analogous fashion—"

"Maytera. Call me Maytera, please, Your Eminence, when we're alone."

"Indeed. Indeed! *O, ah, soror neque enim ignari sumus ante malorum. O passi graviora, dabit Pas his quoque finem.*"

Potto was filling a teakettle. Without turning his head, he said, "I have sharp ears. Don't say I didn't warn you."

Maytera Mint looked up. "Then I'm spared the necessity of raising my voice. Are you really Councillor Potto? We came to negotiate with the Ayuntamiento, not with anyone we chanced to meet. If you are, whose body was that?"

"Yes." Potto put the kettle on the stove. "Mine. Have you more questions?"

"Certainly. Are you willing to stop all this bloodshed?"

"It bothers you, doesn't it?" He pulled out a stout stool and sat down so heavily the floor shook.

"Seeing good and brave troopers die? Watching someone who was eager to obey me a few seconds ago writhing and bleeding in the street? It does!"

"Well, it doesn't me, and I don't understand why it should you. I never have. Call it a gift. There are people who can listen to music all evening, then go home and write everything down, and others who can run faster and farther than a horse. Did you know that? Mine's a less amazing gift, though it's brought me success. I don't feel pain I don't feel. Is that what you call a tautology? It's what life has taught me. I give it to you for nothing."

Remora nodded, his long face longer than ever. "I, er, vouchsafe it might be included under that—ah—rubric."

"Councillor."

"Why—ah—indeed. I had no, um, intention—"

"Thanks. I'm the only member who forced his way in, or had to. Did you know that, either of you?"

Maytera Mint shook her head.

"We're all related, as you can see from our names. Lemur and Loris were brothers. Lemur's dead. You don't have to look surprised, I know you know. He packed the Ayuntamiento with relatives, back before Patera here was born. I came to him. I approached him forthrightly and fairly. He'd brought in Galago, a second cousin by courtesy. I was much closer, and I said so. He said he'd take it under advisement. A week later—there'd been this and that, you know, nothing serious—he tried to have me killed. I saw to it that the man's flesh was served to us at dinner, and dessert was his head in lemon sherbert. Lemur jerked away from it, and I scooped up a little sherbet with my fingers and ate it. I took the oath next day. Councillor Potto. My cousins soon discovered that I was a useful friend, not just an unpleasant relative."

Maytera Mint nodded. "You're proud of being useful, as everyone who is, is entitled to be. Now you have a chance to be of great service to our whole city."

"We have, ah, ventured forth in good faith," Remora put in. "The general has come unarmed. My—ah—vocation prohibits weapons. Such, at least, is my own opinion, though the—our caldé's may differ. I ask you, Councillor, whether you, er, similarly. Are we intermediaries? Or, um, captives?"

"You want to go before your tea's ready?" Potto waved in the direction of the door. "Make the experiment, Patera."

"My duty, um, confines me."

"Then you're a prisoner, but not mine. Dear young General Mint, wouldn't you like to know how I manage to be alive in the kitchen and dead in the drawing room?"

"There were two of you, clearly." She had taken her big wooden prayer beads from her pocket; she ran them through her fingers, comforted by their familiar shapes.

"No, only one, and that one is neither here nor there. As we aged, Cousin Tarsier made us new bodies out of chems. Lemur got the first one, and the rest of us later as we came to need them, bodies we can work from our beds. I can't enjoy food, but I eat. I'm feeding intravenously right now."

"What became of the chems?" Maytera Mint managed to keep her voice steady. "Of their minds?"

"I thought you were going to ask me whether he made the others more than one."

"No. Clearly he did, or someone did. But you got this body from another person. And—and changed it to look like you? You must have. Did he consent to any of that?"

"The logical question is whether there are two of all of us." Potto struck the table with his fist. "You didn't even ask how I got the wood to burn. How am I supposed to deal with someone who won't stick to the point?"

Remora began, "I, ah—" But Potto was not through. "By sticking with the point myself. That's it! I may soon stick with one so well that it sticks out your back." He turned to Remora. "Yes, Patera. You were about to say . . . ?"

"I was, um, speculating, Councillor, upon how you ignited that wood so, er, effortlessly. I, um, hope that you will, um, consent to—ah—illuminate that matter for us."

"I am not going to sit here teaching a butcher chemistry. Can't either of you understand that once I've told you what I want, I don't want it? What are *you* doing here anyway? Dear General Mint's the leader, after Silk. Why are you here?"

"To, er, mediate. We, um, His Cognizance and, hum—"

"To bring peace," Maytera Mint declared. "Caldé Silk has offered to let all of you keep your seats under the Charter. Considering all that's happened, I think it very generous."

"For life?"

Remora touched her arm, and she found it easy to interpret the gesture. "Is there a provision for life tenure? If so, I imagine it might be invoked." Remora shook his head; the motion was slight, but she saw it.

Potto smiled; it was so unexpected that she wondered for a moment whether she had unwittingly promised a return to power.

Seeing it, Remora positively beamed. "Better! Oh, indeed! Must be friends, eh? Friends can make peace, foes, er, unable."

"You misunderstand my expression, Patera."

"I, um, hail and approve it. Time—ah—sufficient for understanding, er, presently. Maybe I put forward a proposal,

Councillor? General? My wish, a heartfelt suggestion. That we—ah—solemnly convene at the present moment, offering our prayer to the Nine. Our petition, if you will, that—"

"Shut up," Potto snapped. "I've got the key, and you go on blathering. Caldé Silk sent you, General. Is that right?"

"He would approve of my coming, certainly. For days we've been trying to reach you councillors on our glasses. I thought we might try this."

When Potto did not reply, she added, "His Eminence was chosen as an intermediary by your Brigadier Erne and our caldé. Soon after, as I understand it, His Cognizance offered his help as well. We were and are overjoyed. I would hope—"

"You can't speak for him," Potto told her. "You may think you can, or that Patera here can, but you can't. I've known him a long time, and there's not a more malicious and unpredictable person in the city. Not even me. You're a general, General?"

She nodded. "Appointed by Divine Echidna in a theophany. My instructions," she amended them mentally in the interests of peace, "were to tear down the Alambrera and see to it that Viron remained loyal to Scylla. If you're asking my position in the command structure, Caldé Silk is the head of our government, civil as well as military. Generalissimo Oosik is our supreme military commander. I am in charge of the armed populace, and General Skate commands the Caldé's Guard."

Potto tittered. "Then you've a firm grasp of the military situation. I don't. Lemur was our military man. Explain our circumstances to me, General, so we can start together."

"You're serious?"

He rocked with silent merriment. "Never more."

"As you wish. After Ophidian Echidna's theophany, we had about thirty thousand troopers. Not that there were that many witnesses, or half that many, but a great many who heard what had happened from others joined us. Some were Guardsmen, none, I think, above captain. You, the Ayuntamiento, called out the Army, giving you something like seven thousand soldiers, besides the twenty-four thousand troopers of your Civil Guard."

"Go on," Potto told her. "None of this is quite right, but it's interesting."

"My figures for the Guard come from Generalissimo Oosik, who was certainly in a position to know. Those for the Army, from Sergeant Sand, the leader of those brave soldiers who saw that true loyalty lay in siding with the caldé."

Potto was still grinning. "Excuse the interruption."

"I was about to say that since then we've gained strength, and you've lost it. By shadelow, we had nearly reached our present total of about fifty thousand. I'm referring to my own troops here. That night, every brigade of your Civil Guard went over to the caldé except the Fourth. The Fourth and the Third, which was the generalissimo's, had been holding the Palatine. The Fourth, commanded by Brigadier Erne, was driven from it next day, and into the northern suburbs."

"Where it still is."

"That's correct. We had fires all over the city to fight, hundreds of them, and we've been busy trying to get ourselves organized. When the Alambrera surrendered, we got thousands of slug guns and hundreds of thousands of rounds of ammunition. We had to see to it that they went to people of good character. Furthermore, there's a feeling that the Fourth Brigade might come over to our side in another day or two. Caldé Silk and Generalissimo Oosik think so, and so do I. I'm told that His Cognizance is of the same opinion."

Remora cleared his throat. "It was, hmp!, Brigadier Erne who, um, entreated me to—ah—initiate? To set in motion these negotiations. I, er, thereafter—shortly thereafter—sought out the caldé, whom, um, approved likewise. I can—am able and—ah—authorized. The Brigadier's viewpoint."

"Not now," Potto told him. "General, could you crush the Fourth Brigade? Suppose Silk ordered it."

"Certainly, in two or three hours. Less if I had a few taluses and floaters, as well as my people. But we'd rather not, obviously, in view of the loss of—"

"Not to me!" Potto chortled. "It's not obvious to me! Is the bloodshed really what's bothering you?"

"I should think it would bother anyone."

"Well, you're right, but you're wrong too. The bloodshed wouldn't bother me, but why shouldn't you take five thousand prime troopers if you can get them? We would. Are those the only reasons, General?"

"I'll be frank. There's another aspect. You, by which I mean the Ayuntamiento, are down in the tunnels with most of the Army and a few troopers."

"Nearly a thousand."

"Setting them aside, you must have about seven thousand soldiers down there."

Potto's grin widened.

"More? Very well, if you say so. Seven thousand was our estimate. In any case, if we got deeply involved in an attack on the Fourth, which shouldn't be our primary objective anyway, you might make a sortie from the tunnels and strike us from behind. According to reports I've had, it takes at least four of my troopers to match a soldier, which means that your seven thousand—that's the figure we discussed—are equivalent to twenty-eight thousand of mine. We didn't feel we could risk it. I should say that we don't feel we can as yet."

Potto nodded rather too enthusiastically. "Someplace in all that verbiage was a morsel that seemed intelligent, my dear General. You said our Guard, or what's left, wasn't what you really wanted to destroy. That it was us. Why don't you come down after us?"

Remora looked deeply distressed. "Do you, er, Councillor . . . Is this—ah—productive?"

"I think so. You'll see. Answer me if you can, General."

"Because the tunnels are too defensible. I haven't been in them, but they've been described to me. A dozen soldiers could hold a place like that against a hundred troopers. If we've got to, we'll find a way, digging shafts and so on. But we'd rather not, which is why I'm here. Also there's another consideration. You spoke of destroying the Fourth. Clearly, we don't want to. Still less do we want to destroy the Army, which is of immense value to our city. We know that—"

"You are an amazing woman." Potto pushed his stool back and crossed the big kitchen to the stove. "A woman who talks sense whenever it suits her but can't hear a kettle boil."

"Women generally talk sense, if men will listen to it."

"Those who are generals generally do, anyway. You're right about the Fourth, and right about the Army and not tackling the tunnels, though you really don't understand the situation at all. I'm our head spy, did you know that? I was in charge of Lemur's spies, and now I've got Loris's." Potto tittered. "Who are generally the same, General, and mine. Do you really think all the troopers in the city are yours or ours? You simply can't be that simple!" He lifted the big copper teakettle off the stove; it was spurting steam.

Maytera Mint pursed her lips.

"There are, um, an—ah—minuscule? Likewise. Token, eh? An—ah—few hundred . . ."

"Two hundred, more or less," she supplied. "Two hundred Trivigaunti pterotroopers commanded by General Saba, who also commands the airship. Two hundred's a very small force, as His Eminence says, though with supporting fire from the airship even a small force might accomplish a great deal. General Saba has offered her help when we move against the Fourth, by the way."

"How kind." Potto had carried the steaming teakettle to their table.

"Not to you, Councillor. I realize that. But to us it is. It's a gesture of good will from the Rani to the new government of Viron, and as such is greatly appreciated."

"Your diplomacy flourishes." He raised the teakettle.

"It does. It's in its infancy, but it does." Maytera Mint stood. "We need a teapot, and tea. Sugar, milk, and a lemon, if His Eminence takes lemon. I'll look for them."

"I was about to ask you if my face looks dusty."

"I beg your pardon, Councillor?"

"Whether it's dusty. Look carefully, will you? Maybe we should go to a window, where the light will be better."

"I don't see any dust." She was struck, unexpectedly and unpleasantly, by the lack of warmth in that face, which seemed so animated. Maytera Marble's familiar metal mask held a whorl of humility and compassion; this, for all its seeming plumpness and high color, was as cold as Echidna's serpents.

"It's been packed away for years, you see." Leaning back at an impossible angle, Potto scratched the tip of his nose with the steaming spout of the teakettle. "I'm the youngest member of the Ayuntamiento, dear General. Did you know that?"

Maytera Mint shook her head.

"Just the same, they thought this seemed too young, and asked me to replace it." He contrived to lean even farther backward. A trickle of boiling water escaped the spout. "You don't know about the Rani's horde, either. Do you?"

"What about it?"

"My face?" Potto jabbed the spout toward it. "It was in storage. I said that, why didn't you listen? Now I can't see as clearly as I did. I may have dust in my eyes."

Before Maytera Mint could stop him, he raised the teakettle and tilted it. Seething water cascaded down onto his nose and eyes. Remora exclaimed, "Oh, you gods!" as Maytera Mint jumped back from the hissing spray.

"There. That ought to do it." Straightening up, Potto regarded her through wide blue eyes again, blinking hard to clear them of boiling drops. "That's much better. I can see everything. I hope you can, too, my dear young General. The Rani's horde has already set out, and there's sixty thousand foot and fifteen thousand cavalry. I haven't the luxury of an airship to keep watch on Viron's enemies, but I do the best I can. Seventy-five thousand battle-hardened troopers, with their support troops, a supply train of fifteen thousand camels, and a labor battalion of ten thousand men." Potto turned to Remora. "Trivigaunte's men are of your school, Patera. No weapons. Or anyway they're supposed to be."

Remora had regained his composure. "If this extensive and, ah, formidable force is—ah—marching? Marching, you said, eh? Then I take it that it can't be marching here, or you—um—the Ayuntamiento, more formally. Terms of surrender, hey?"

Potto tittered.

Maytera Mint squared her shoulders. "I wouldn't laugh, Councillor. His Eminence is entirely correct. If the Rani is sending us a force of that size, your cause is doomed."

"It's just as I feared," Potto told her. He held up the teakettle. "Do you think it's cooled too much?"

"To make tea?" She took an involuntary step backward. "I doubt it."

"To wash eyes, so they can see. I think you're right. Boiling water stays hot for a long time."

"I came under a flag of truce!"

He reached for her, moving much faster than so fat a man should have been able to. She whirled and ran, feeling his fingertips brush her habit, reached the door a hand's breadth ahead of him, and flung herself through. An arm hooked her like a lamb; another pinned her own arms to her sides. Her face was crushed against musty cloth.

Sounding near, Potto said, "Bring her back in here."

Not so near, words failed Remora. "You cannot—I mean to say simply cannot—woman's a sibyl! You, you—"

"Oh, be quiet," Potto told him. "Bend her over backwards, Spider. Make her look up at this."

Abruptly there was light and air. The man who had caught her was as tall as Remora and as wide as Potto; he held her by her hair and dropped to one knee, pulling her across the other.

"My son." Looking up at his heavy, unshaven chin, she found it horribly hard to keep from sounding frightened. "Do you realize what you're doing?"

The man, presumably Spider, glanced to one side, presumably at Potto. "How's this, Councillor?"

She rolled her eyes without finding him, and the thick fingers would not let her turn her head.

His voice came from a distance. "I'm putting the kettle back. We can't have it cooling off while I give you the rules."

Remora entered her field of view, seeming as lofty as a

tower when he bent above them. "If there is—ah—Maytera. General. Anything I can do . . . ?"

"There is," she said. "Let Bison know what happened."

"Go back to your seat," Potto told Remora, and he vanished. "Didn't you wonder, my dear General," it was Potto's cheerful, round face opposite Spider's now, "how I happened to be so near my own corpse? Or what became of Blood's? Blood was stabbed by your friend Silk. Let's not call him Caldé. We're no longer being so polite."

"Let me up, and I'll be happy to ask you."

"It won't be necessary. Blood's body has been hauled away already, you see. And you do see, don't you? At present. I ordered that my own wasn't to be touched, because I think we may be able to fix it. I came in person to pick it up, with a few of my most trusted spy catchers. Spider's their jefe. I'd use soldiers, but they're awfully sensitive, it seems, to mention of a caldé, though you wouldn't think it to look at them."

From a distance, Remora called, "Councillor? Councillor!"

She shut her eyes. If she was never to see again, the last thing she saw should not be the high smoke-grimed ceiling of the kitchen in this ruined villa. Echidna, rather, her face filling the Sacred Window. Her mother's face. Bison's, with its quick eyes and curling black beard. Her room in the cenoby. Children playing, Maytera Marble's group because she had always wanted them instead of the older girls this year and the older boys before Patera Pike died. Auk's face, so ugly and serious, more precious than a stack of cards. Bison's. Cage Street, and the floaters firing as the white stallion thundered toward them.

"Did you hear that, my dear General?"

"Hear what?" Maytera Mint opened her eyes, remembering too late that scalding water might be poured into them.

"Tell her, Patera! Tell her!" Potto was giggling like a girl of twelve, giggling so hard that he could hardly talk.

"I—ah—um—proposed an, er, substitution."

"He wants to take your place. Really, it's too funny."

She tried to speak, and found that her eyes were filling with hot tears, irony so cheap and obvious as to be unbearable. "No, Your Eminence. But . . . But thank you."

"He, um, Potto. Councillor. He wishes to, um, secure your—ah—collaboration, hey? I, um, endeavored to point out that to, er, spare me you would, eh? Whatever he wants."

"I can already make you do anything I want." Potto was back. He held the teakettle over her. "What I'm trying to do is what she's done for years. Educate." Giggling, he covered his mouth with his free hand. "Wash the dust out. Clarify her vision. Have I explained the rules?"

"Er—no."

"Then I will. I have to. You want to save her, Patera?"

She could actually hear Remora's teeth chatter. She had always supposed the business about chattering teeth was a sort of verbal convention, like hair standing on end.

"You made your offer, and I said no. But you can save me the trouble of washing her eyes."

"I, um, every effort."

"I'm going to ask questions. Educational questions. If her answers are right, we postpone the eyebath. Or if yours are. Ready? Spider, what about you? When you see the kettle tip, you'll have to hold her tight and keep your hands clear."

"Any time, Councillor."

"I'll start with an easy one. That's the best way, don't you think? If you really want children to learn. If you aren't just showing off. Did you know Silk's friend Doctor Crane?"

She shut her eyes again, finding it difficult to think. "Know him? No. Maytera Marble mentioned him once, the nice doctor who let her ride in his litter. I don't think I ever saw him. I'm sure I haven't met him."

"And you never will. He's dead." Potto sounded pleased. "Your turn, Patera. What about you?"

"Crane, eh? A doctor? Can't, um, place him."

"He was a spy. Let's give the poor fellow his due. He was a master spy, some say the Rani's best. Trivigaunte had more spies in Viron than any other city. It still does, though they have no jefe now. Why do you think that is, Maytera? More spies than Urbs or Palustria?"

"All I can do is guess." Her mouth was dry; she tried unsuccessfully to swallow. "The Rani's a woman, but all the other cities near ours have male rulers. She may have been more sensitive to the danger you and your cousins presented."

"Not bad. Can you improve on that, Patera?"

"I, ah, cheating."

Potto giggled. "Double credit for it. Go ahead."

"His Cognizance, eh? He told me. Not in so many words, eh? No mountains. First, um, er—"

"Objective," Potto supplied.

"Indeed. Next, ah, year. Spring. Not long now, hey, Councillor? Winter has, um, commenced."

"General, this is your area of expertise. Say another force is opposing yours, which is larger. Would you rather fight your way across a mountain range or a desert?"

"I'd want to see the desert," she hedged.

"You can't see either one, and if you won't answer you won't see anything." The teakettle tilted a little.

"Then I prefer the desert."

"Why?"

"Because fighting in mountains would be like fighting in tunnels. There would be narrow passes, in which we'd have to go at the enemy head-on. In a desert we could get around them."

"Correct. Patera, I haven't been giving you many chances, so you first. Two cities I'll call Viron and Trivigaunte are separated by a lake and a desert. A big lake, though it's been getting smaller and turning brackish. That's the situation, and here's the question. If the easiest city for Viron to attack is Trivigaunte, what's easiest for Trivigaunte? Think carefully."

"For, ah, them?" Remora's voice quavered. "Us, I should say. Viron."

"Do you agree, my dear General?"

She had begun a short prayer to Echidna while Remora was speaking; after murmuring the final phrase she said, "There could be other answers, but that's the most probable. Viron."

"I'm putting the kettle on again," Potto told her. "Not because you've passed, but because you may fail right here, and I want the water hot enough to do the job. Listen carefully, because we're going from geography to arithmetic. Listen, and think. Are you ready?"

She compelled her mind and lips. "I suppose so."

Potto tittered. "Are you, Patera?"

"Ah . . . I wish, Councillor—"

"Save it for later. It's time for arithmetic. The Rani of Trivigaunte has seventy-five thousand crack troopers in Viron. The so-called caldé's general has fifty thousand untrained ones, and the traitor commanding the Caldé's Guard has about eighteen thousand fit for duty, of doubtful loyalty. If these numbers have you mixed up, I don't blame you. Would you like me to stop here and repeat them, General?"

"Let me hear the rest."

"We're getting to the crux. Rani, seventy-five thousand. You, fifty thousand. Oosik, eighteen thousand. All these are troopers, armed bios. Now then, the Ayuntamiento, which opposes all three of them, has eight thousand two hundred soldiers and a thousand troopers underground, and another five thousand on the surface. The question is, *who rules Viron?* Answer, Patera."

"The—ah—you do. The Ayuntamiento."

"One drop for that," Potto said. "I'll fetch the kettle."

Maytera Mint squeezed her eyes shut, clenching her teeth as a single scalding drop struck her forehead. Locked in a private nightmare of fear and pain, she heard the opening of the door as if it were leagues away. A new voice spoke in the reedy tones of an old man: "What's this?"

Remora, overjoyed: *"Your Cognizance!"*

Almost carelessly, Potto said: "This is a nice surprise, I had men posted. Another prisoner's welcome, just the same."

She squinted upward. The sere old face over hers was one she had seen only at a distance; she had not realized then how its eyes glittered.

"Release her!" Quetzal snapped. "Let her go. Now!"

She tried to smile as Spider inquired, "Councillor?"

"Class dismissed for the present. It may resume soon, so think about the material." He sounded angry.

Spider stood, and she fell to the floor.

"I've talked to your cousin Loris," Quetzal told Potto, "and I've come to give you the news I brought him. If you decide to detain me afterward, it's the risk I run."

Potto spoke to Spider. "This old fox is the Prolocutor. If that's going to bother you, say so."

"Anything you want, Councillor."

"He's worth two of the general and ten of the butcher. Don't forget it. Old man, what tricks have you cooked up?" Maytera Mint scrambled to her feet, trying not to step on the hem of her habit.

"No tricks, Councillor. There was a theophany during my sacrifice at the Grand Manteion." Simultaneously, Maytera Mint received the impression that Quetzal was never excited, and that he was excited now.

Potto snorted and set his steaming teakettle on the table. "Another one? Who was it this time? Sphigx?"

Quetzal shook his head. "Pas."

"Pas is dead!"

Quetzal turned from Potto. "Great Pas, Maytera. Lord Pas, the Father of the Seven. If it wasn't him, it was his ghost. Which in point of fact is what the god himself said."

Chapter 2

HIS NAME IS HOSSAAN

He himself had shut this door from inside and shot the bolt; it had been the final action of his exorcism. But if this door (the obscure side door of what had been a manteion, and what many passers-by no doubt assumed was a manteion still) was used to admit patrons who did not want to be seen entering Orchid's, there should be someone to answer his knock. By summer habit, he squinted up to gauge the width of the narrowing sun; it was masked by clouds dark with rain or snow, and the awe-inspiring mummy-colored bulk of the Trivigaunti airship.

He knocked again. His bearers had put down the litter and were making themselves comfortable. Did he dare risk their seeing him pound on a door to which nobody came? What would Commissioner Newt have to say about the effect on his prestige and popularity? What would Oosik say? Would it replace the fighting as the talk of the city?

He was smiling at the thought when the door was opened by a small and markedly unattractive woman with a faded rag over her graying hair. "Come—uh. It ain't anymore, Patera."

"I am Orchid's spiritual advisor," Silk told her firmly. "Admit me." The woman backed away; he stepped inside and bolted the door behind him. "Take me to her."

"I'm cleaning up in here." She eyed Oreb with disfavor.

Silk conceded privately that the former manteion could use a cleaning. He glanced up at the stage to see whether the new backdrop was as blasphemous as the one he had cut down, and was illogically pleased to find that it was merely obscene.

"She'll be in her room. She might not be up yet."

"Take me to her," he repeated, and added, "At once!"

"I won't knock." The small woman sounded frightened.

"Never mind. I remember the way." He pushed past her and strode across the former manteion with scarcely a twinge from his ankle. Here was the step on which he had sat to talk to Musk. Musk was dead now. The memory of Musk's tortured face returned.

The courtyard beyond the manteion was deserted but by no means empty, littered with scraps of food over which crows and pigeons squabbled, spilled liquors, bottles, and broken glass. Oreb, bigger than the biggest crow, watched fascinated, cocking his head this way and that.

Orpine's naked corpse had sprawled on this wooden stair. There was no point in looking for bloodstains today, or in trying not to step on such stains as might be present. Silk climbed, his eyes resolutely fixed on the gallery above.

What faith he'd had then! That Silk would be praying now, as confident as a child that the gods heard each word, a prayer to Molpe as patroness of the day, and one to Pas, who was as dead as Crane, Orpine, and Musk. Most of all, that earlier Silk would have prayed devoutly to the Outsider, though the Outsider had warned that he would send no aid.

Yet the Outsider had come with healing when he had lain near death. And to be more accurate (Silk paused at the top of the steps, remembering) the Outsider had not actually said that he would get no help, but warned him to expect none—which was not precisely the same thing.

Buoyed by the thought, he walked along the creaking

gallery to the door that Crane had opened when he came out to examine Orpine's body, and was about to open it himself when it was opened from within.

He blinked, gasped, and blinked again. Oreb, whom few things surprised, whistled before croaking, " 'Lo, girl."

"Hi, Oreb. Hello, Patera. All the blessings on you this afternoon and all that."

Silk smiled, finding it easier than he had expected; there was nothing to be gained by berating her, surely. "Chenille, it's good to see you. I've been wondering where you were. I have people searching for you and Auk."

"You thought I was finished with this." The expression of her coarse, flat-cheeked face was by no means easy to read, but she sounded despondent.

"I hoped you were," Silk said carefully. "I still hope you are—that last night was the last night." If the gods did not care, why should he? He thrust the thought aside.

"Nobody last night, Patera. There wasn't enough to keep the other dells busy. You're thinking how about rust, aren't you? I can tell from the way you look at me. Not since the funeral. Come on in." She stepped back.

He entered, careful not to brush her jutting breasts.

"Now you're wondering how long it'll last. Me too. You didn't know I was a regular mind reader, did you?" She smiled, and the smile made him want to put his arms around her.

He nodded instead. "You're very perceptive. I was."

Oreb felt he had been left out long enough. "Where Auk?"

"I don't know. You want to come to my room, Patera? You can sit, and we could talk like we did that other time."

"I must speak to Orchid—but if you wish it."

"We don't have to. Come on, she's probably about dressed. Her room's up this way." Chenille led him along a corridor he recalled only vaguely. "Maybe I could come by tomorrow to talk? Only you're not at the place on Sun Street anymore, are you?"

"No," Silk said, "but I'm going there when I leave here."

Would you like to come?" When Chenille did not reply, he added, "I have a litter; I've been trying to spare my ankle."

She was shocked. "You can't let people see me with you!"

"We'll put the curtains down."

"Then we could talk in there, huh? All right."

Silk, too, had come to a decision. "I'd like to have you with me when I speak to Orchid. Will you do it?"

"Sure, if you want me." She stopped before Orchid's door. "Only I hope you're not going to get her mad."

Recalling the small woman's fear, Silk knocked. "Were you leaving just now, Chenille? We can arrange to meet later, if this is inconvenient."

She shook her head. "I saw you out my window and put this gown on, that's all."

Orchid's door had opened. Orchid, in a black peignoir that reminded Silk vividly of the pink one she had worn when she had admitted him with Crane, was staring open mouthed.

He tore his own gaze from her gaping garment. "May I speak with you when you've finished dressing, Orchid? It's urgent; I wouldn't have troubled you otherwise."

Numbly, the fat woman retreated.

"Come on, Patera." Chenille led the way in. "She can put on a, you know, more of a wrap-up." To Orchid she added, "He's gimp, remember? Maybe you could invite him to sit."

Orchid had recovered enough to tug at the lace-decked edges of the peignoir, covering bulging flesh that would reappear the moment she released them. "I—you're the caldé now. The new one. Everybody's talking about you."

Oreb offered proof. "Say Silk!"

"I'm afraid I am. I'm still the same man, however, and I need your help."

Chenille said firmly, "Have a seat, Patera."

"Yeah, sit down. Do I call you Caldé or Patera?"

"I really prefer to stand as long as you and Chenille are standing. May I say it's pleasant to see you again? Pleasant to see you both. I've been looking for Chenille, as I told her, and I've met so many new people—commissioners at the Juzgado and so forth—that you seem like old friends."

"Good friends." Chenille dropped onto the green-velvet couch. "I'll never forget how you stood up to the councillors at Blood's." She turned to Orchid. "I told you about it, right?"

"Yeah, but I never thought I'd see you again, Caldé. I mean to talk to."

He grasped the opportunity. "You saw me when Hyacinth and I were riding through the city, and we saw you. Have you seen Hyacinth since then?"

Orchid shook her head as she sat down beside Chenille.

Gratefully, Silk sat too. "I mean her no harm—none whatsoever. I merely wish to find her."

"I'm sure you don't, Caldé. I'd tell you if I knew."

Chenille said, "You're going to ask me in a minute. I can't remember how long it's been since I saw Hy. A couple months. Maybe longer than that."

"No girl?" Oreb inquired.

Silk looked around at him. "Chenille is only one of the people we've been trying to find, actually. Now I'm hoping to find out something about the others."

"I'll call you Caldé," Orchid announced. "It feels easier. A hoppy was here asking about Hy. Did you know that?"

"I sent him, indirectly at least."

"He wanted to know about Chen, too. And Auk." Orchid glanced at Chenille, afraid that she was revealing too much.

"But you told him nothing. I can't blame you. In your place I would probably have done the same."

Orchid struggled to her feet. "I'm forgetting my manners. Maybe you'd like a glass of wine? I remember that time when you said you were sorry you only had water, but water was what I wanted right then. You got some for me, and good water too. You've got a good well."

"No wine, thank you. You told the Guardsman who came here that you didn't know where Hyacinth, or Chenille, or Auk was. I know you must have, because any information you provided him would have been reported to me, with its source. As I said, I would very likely have acted just as you did, if I had been in your place. This afternoon it occurred to me that you might tell me more than you'd tell someone you didn't know or trust, so I came in person. I take it that Chenille was already here when he arrived to question you. Was that yesterday?"

Orchid nodded. Chenille said, "It's my fault, Patera. I asked her not to tell anybody." For perhaps five seconds she was silent, nibbling at her lower lip. "Because of that other man. You know who I mean, Patera? He was at Blood's, too, and he didn't get shot like the fat one. The tall one. He saw me, and he heard my name."

Silk's forefinger drew small circles on his cheek. "Do you think he knew enough about you to search for you here?"

"I don't know. I've tried to remember everything Blood said, and I don't remember anything about that. Only he might have said something before or after or maybe even something I've forgotten. He'd seen me, and knew who I was."

"In that case," Silk said slowly, "I'm surprised that you came back here."

Orchid poured a pony of brandy. "It isn't as dumb as you think, Caldé. If somebody came around, we'd tell her so she'd have time to hide. We did with the hoppy, didn't we, Chen?"

"That's right, Patera. Anyhow I pretty much had to. I didn't have any money—"

"I must speak to you about that; remind me after we leave."

"Except a little here, and my jewelry's here, except for this ring." She held up her hand to display it, and the ruby glowed like a coal from the forge. "I think it's worth a deck, and so does Orchid."

Orchid nodded emphatically.

"Only Auk gave it to me, and I told him I'd never sell it. I won't, either. Remember when you and me talked in the front room of your little house, Patera?"

"Yes, I do. I'm surprised that you do, however."

"I didn't to start, but after a while it came back. What I was going to say is I had my best pieces on, my jade earrings and the necklace, only it got lost when my good wool gown did."

Silk nodded. "Patera Incus said Maytera Marble had made Blood give you the chenille one you had on there."

"Uh-huh. I'll tell you about losing the other one and my

necklace some other time. What I was going to say is they hurt my ears, down in the tunnel. I took them off and gave them to Auk, and he put them in his pocket." She fell silent, her chest heaving dramatically.

"When I find Auk, I'll remind him to return them to you."

"There's something I've got to tell you about him, too. You won't believe me, but I've got to tell you just the same. Only not now."

"All right. Tell me when you feel ready to do so." Silk turned back to Orchid. "Permit me to ask again. Do you know where Hyacinth is? Do you have any idea at all?"

Shaking her head, Orchid passed her brandy to Chenille. "Drink it, you'll feel better." Freed of the stem, Orchid's beringed fingers clenched. "Patera, I need a favor and I need it bad. Ever since I saw you in the hall I've been trying to think of a good way to ask. If I knew anything that would help you find Hy, I'd tell you and ask for my favor. I don't, but I got connections and they know places the hoppies never heard of. I'll get them on it as quick as I can."

Oreb flew from Silk's shoulder to Chenille's. "Where Auk?"

"My question exactly," Silk said. "You told the Guardsman you didn't know where Hyacinth was, and you were telling him the truth. You lied when you told him that you didn't know where Chenille was. What about Auk?"

Orchid shook her head. "I've got a couple culls asking. He's got Chen's bobbers, like she says. We know he's around. We've talked to bucks that saw him. Isn't that right?"

Chenille nodded.

"But nobody seems to know where he dosses. A friend of mine told him I wanted to see him, and he said maybe he'd come later, but he hasn't." Orchid tapped her forehead. "He's cank, they say. Talking clutter."

"Let me know if he comes, will you please? Immediately."

"Absolutely, Caldé. You can count on it. Want me to keep him here until you get here?"

"He'll stay," Chenille interposed. "He'll be in my room."

"Yes, I do," Silk told Orchid. "You've offered me several

favors, and I want them all. I want very much to learn where Hyacinth is. I want to learn where Auk is, too, and I want you to keep him here if he comes. He used to come here often, I know. You said you required a favor from me. I'll help you if I can. What is it?"

"Blood's dead. That's what Chen says, and it's all over town anyhow. They say—am I stepping in it?"

Chenille swallowed a sip of brandy. "They say you killed him, Patera. That's what some people told me out at his house before the fighting was over."

Orchid took a step toward Silk. "I own this." Her voice was husky with emotion. "This house of mine. But I bought it with money Blood gave me, and I had to sign a paper."

Belatedly, Silk rose too. "What did it say?"

"I don't know. It was at his place in the country. Once in a while he'd come to town and see people, but mostly he sent word and you went out there to see him. If he liked you, he'd send his floater for you. That was the first time in my life I got to ride in one."

Recalling his trip from Blood's villa to the manteion on Sun Street, Silk nodded. "Go on."

"We talked about, you know, what sort of house I'd found, where it was and how big and the girls I'd got lined up. Then he pulled out a paper and said sign this. I did, and he stuck it away again and gave me the money. I got the deed, and it's in my name, but now he's dead and I don't know about the paper. I want to keep my house. It would kill me to lose it. That's lily. With him gone, I don't know where I stand, but I'd feel a lot better knowing I had the caldé in my corner."

"He is." Silk started toward the door. "You have my word, Orchid; but I must go—we must, if Chenille's coming."

"I've got to get my coat." She was already on her feet. "Your litter's around back? On Music? I'll meet you."

As he rattled down the wooden steps, Silk could not be sure he had told her it was, or that he had replied at all.

"If you don't want to, they won't make you," Auk told his listeners. "You think the gods are a bunch of hoppies? They don't push anybody around. Why should they? When they want to do you a good turn, they say do this and this, 'cause it's going to be good, you're going to like it. Only if you say it's a queer lay, they say dimber by us, we'll give it to somebody else. Remember Kypris? She didn't say go uphill and solve all those kens. She said if you want to, go to it and I'll keep the street. This is like that. I'm not here to make anybody do anything. Neither's Tartaros."

One of his listeners asked, "What've we got to do now?"

The blind god whose hand was upon Auk's shoulder whispered, "Tell him to make ready."

"To start with, you got to get yourself set," Auk said. "Get used to it. You'll be going to a new place. It'll be better, real nice, but all the stuff you're used to will be down the chute. Even the sun'll be different, a short sun that won't ever go out. You got to think about it, and that's why I'm here, to start you culls thinking. You want to think about what to take, and who to take with you, and talk to 'em. If you're like me, you're going to want pals. Tell 'em. Every man's got to have a woman, too, and every woman's got to take a man. Just sprats don't have to have anybody."

A big-nosed woman shouted, "Over here!" and Auk's listeners drifted away, forming two long lines, slug guns at the ready.

"That went well," Tartaros whispered.

"They didn't believe me." Wearily, Auk started back down the tunnel; this one was open to the sky, as most were on this level. The walls were walls, but had doors and windows in them. He was still trying to make up his mind whether that made things better or worse.

"Men come slowly to belief," the god whispered, "nor is that to be deplored. Some have taken the first step already, because you urged it."

Auk felt a glow of satisfaction. "If you figure that was enough, what we did back there, dimber with me. Think I ought to steal something for her to eat? I said I would."

"You must steal more cards, as well."

Auk steered the blind god around a hoppy's corpse, its

eyes and mouth black with cold-numbed flies. "You won't let me spend 'em, Terrible Tartaros."

"We will have need of many cards, and quickly. Have I not made it clear to you?"

"Yeah, to fix up a lander." Auk smiled at the thought. "I guess you did."

"That is well. Your mind is mending. Steal food, if you wish, Auk, and more cards where you can."

As their litter jogged down Sun Street Chenille said, "I'd like you to shrive me. Will this take long enough?"

"That will depend on how much you have to tell me." Silk was acutely aware of her hip pressing his own. He recalled a rule forbidding sibyls from riding in a litter with a man; he was beginning to feel that there should be another—strictly enforced—against augurs riding with women. "Certainly it would be more regular to do it in the manteion, where we would not be pressed for time."

"You know what I'm afraid of? I'm afraid of some goddess getting in me again. You don't know about Scylla, do you?"

"I've spoken with Patera Incus. He told me that Scylla had possessed you—it was one of the reasons I was anxious to find you—and that she, through you, had appointed him Prolocutor."

Chenille nodded, the motion of her head almost ghostly in the tightly curtained litter. "I remember that a little. Only he talked about it so much after she let me go that I can't be sure exactly what I said. Auk could tell you."

"I'll ask when we find him; but the Prolocutorship is a concern of the Chapter's, not the civil government's. In other words, I have no more say in the matter than any other member of the clergy, and none at all as caldé. Was Auk the only other person present?"

"Dace, but he's dead."

"I see. I refrained from asking Patera about witnesses. As I said, it's a matter that concerns me only as one augur among many. It may be that I'll no longer be an augur at all when the matter comes before the clergy."

Silk was silent for a moment, his eyes vague. "If what Patera reports is true, and I'm inclined to credit him, it's unfortunate that Scylla didn't make her wish known at a time when other augurs, or sibyls, were present. Most of the—"

Chenille interrupted. "I wouldn't mind if it was Kypris again. It might be nice. Only Scylla was really rough. That's how I lost my gown and my good jade necklace. I'd go out to the lake and look for it, only I'm pretty sure somebody's found it by this time. Anyway, isn't there someplace where we could do it besides in the manteion? Kypris got me when I was in there, and Scylla when I was in her shrine at the lake. I'm going to try to stay away from places like that for a while."

"I see. If you don't look at the Sacred Window, you can't be possessed—so Kypris implied, at least." Too late, Silk recalled that there was no Window in Scylla's shrine. "It may be that there are other means, of course," he finished lamely, "or that only she is limited in that fashion."

"Don't you bucks ever get possessed?"

"Certainly we do. In fact, it's much more usual, or so the Chrasmologic Writings imply. Men are normally possessed by male gods, such as Pas, Tartaros, Hierax, and the Outsider, or such minor male gods at Catamitus. That is true of enlightenment as well. I myself was enlightened by the Outsider, not Pas, though it would appear that common report attributes my enlightenment to Pas." Silk forbore mentioning that Pas was dead.

"The reason I was asking—"

Their litter stopped, lowered gently to an uneven surface. Oreb pushed the curtain aside with his beak, and was gone.

"I'll be here a while," Silk told the head bearer. "It might be best if I were to pay you now."

The head bearer made an awkward bow with one eye on his men, who were helping Chenille out of the litter. "We'll wait, Caldé. No trouble."

Silk got out his cardcase. "May I give you something so you can refresh yourselves while you wait?"

"We'll be all right." The head bearer backed away.

"As you wish."

The garden gate was unlocked; Silk opened it for Chenille. "I was afraid you'd give them too much," she whispered as she passed. "They'd get drunk."

That explained the head bearer's refusal, Silk decided as he reclosed the gate; it would not do for the bearers of the caldé's litter to be drunk. He made a mental note to allow for the propensity of the lowest classes to drink too much.

"Is anybody here?" Chenille looked about her at the arbor and the wells, the berry brambles and wilted tomato vines under the windows of the manse, the seared fig and the leafless little pear, and the spaded black soil that had been Maytera Marble's struggling garden.

"At the moment? I can't say. I assume that Patera Gulo's still off fighting—or at any rate off watching what's left of Erne's brigade. Maytera Marble's probably in the cenoby; we'll find out when I've shriven you."

"You won't hold us long with a handful of men," Maytera Mint told Spider. "Colonel Bison has five hundred."

Spider chuckled. He was, as she had concluded a half hour before, rather too well suited to his name, a man who made her think of a fat, hairy spider watching its web in a dirty corner.

Quetzal said, "He's taking us down into the tunnels."

Spider opened a door as Quetzal spoke, revealing a flight of rough steps descending into darkness. "You know about those, old man?"

"I just came up from them. Did you hear me tell Potto I'd talked to Loris?"

"Councillor Potto to you." Spider gestured with a needler; he was two full heads taller. "Now get down there before I kick you down."

"I can't walk fast, my son." Quetzal tottered toward the steps. "I'll delay you and the others."

There had been a note in his quavering old voice that gave Maytera Mint a surge of irrational confidence. "The Nine avenge wrongs done to augurs and sibyls," she warned Spider, "and their vengeance is swift and terrible. What they might do to someone who maltreats the Prolocutor, I shudder to think."

Spider grinned, showing remarkably crooked teeth. "That's lily, General. So don't you shove him down and run. Stir it, now. The tall cully behind you, and me behind him. We're all going to wait nice till Councillor Potto and my knot fetch along his dead body."

She started down the steps, one hand on a wooden rail that seemed both grimy and insecure. Behind her, Remora said, "This is where, ah, the caldé, eh? The cellar, in which, um—"

"Sergeant Sand," she told him. The dull gleam that had been Quetzal's hairless head had disappeared into the darkness; she quickened her pace, although the steps were steep and high, and she was afraid of falling. "Sergeant Sand held the caldé down here for six hours or more. He told me about it."

Remora bumped her from behind. "Sorry! Ah—pushed."

"Keep moving," Spider growled.

The sound of their voices had kindled a dull green light some distance down the steps; in the dimness she could make out ranked shelves of dusty jars, and what seemed to be abandoned machinery. Involuntarily she murmured, "He's gone."

Spider heard her. "Who is?"

"His Cognizance." She halted, speaking over her shoulder. "Look for yourself. He should be on the stair in front of me, but he's not." At the last words, the bright bird called *hope* sang in her heart.

"There you are!" Maytera Marble exclaimed as Silk emerged from the chilly privacy of the vine-draped arbor. "There's a man here looking for you, Patera. I said you weren't here, but he says you've got a litter on Sun Street."

Silk sighed. "It's been like this since Phaesday. No doubt it's extremely urgent."

"That's just what he said, Patera." Maytera Marble nodded vigorously, her metal face luminous in the gray daylight. "And it must be. He came in a floater."

Chenille's smile turned to a stare. "Hello, Maytera. What happened to your hand?"

"How good of you to ask!" She displayed her stump of arm. "My hand's fine, my daughter. I've got it in a drawer, wrapped up in a clean towel. It's the rest of—we should go, Patera. He's waiting for you in front of the cenoby. He came in through the garden and knocked at your manse. I thought he was looking for Patera Gulo."

"I was shriving Chenille," Silk explained. "I'm afraid we didn't hear him."

"I did," Chenille declared, "only I thought it was on the street. It was while I was telling you about—" He silenced her, a finger to his lips.

"His name is Hossaan," Maytera Marble continued. "He's foreign, I think, but he says he knows you. He gave you a ride once, and he was on a boat with you out on the lake. Now where are you—? Oh, I forgot. He can't go through there."

The last words were spoken to Silk's back. At a limping run, he vanished into the narrow opening between the northwest corner of the manteion and the southwest corner of the cenoby.

"There's a gate," Maytera Marble explained to Chenille, "That opens onto the children's playground from Silver Street. But you and I can go through the cenoby."

She mounted the back step and opened the kitchen door. "My granddaughter's in here. I had just fixed her a bite when I saw that man. Do you know her?"

"Your granddaughter?" Chenille shook her head.

"Perhaps you'd enjoy a little boiled beef too?" Maytera Marble lowered her voice. "I think it's good for her to talk with other bio girls. She's been, well, sheltered, I suppose you could call it. And I have something to say to Patera before that man makes off with him. I have a favor to ask him, a great big one."

On Silver Street, Silk was already speaking to "That man." "I haven't been looking for you," he said. "It was stupid of me, incredibly stupid. I've had Guardsmen out combing the city for Hyacinth and some other people, but you had slipped my mind completely."

"We can talk in my floater, Caldé." Hossaan was slight and swarthy, with vigilant eyes. "It'll be more private and get us out of this wind."

"Thank you." Stepping into the floater, Silk let himself sink into its black-leather upholstery.

The translucent canopy went up with a muted sigh, and the freezing gusts that had been punishing Viron ended, if only for them.

"If your Guardsmen had looked, they would've found me." Hossaan smiled as he took his place in the front seat. "These things aren't easy to hide."

"I suppose not. I ran to see you as soon as I realized who you were because I want to ask where Hyacinth is. You brought her to Ermine's on Hieraxday to meet me."

Hossaan nodded.

"From your name—Maytera Marble told me that—you're a Trivigaunti. Is that right? Doctor Crane said once that you were his second in command. Most of the spies he employed seem to have been Vironese, but it would be natural for him to have a few from his own city, people he could trust completely."

"Only me, Caldé. You're right, though. More of us would have made us a lot more effective."

"Do you know where Hyacinth is?"

"No. I wish I did." Hossaan drew a deep breath. "You know, Caldé, you've taken a load off my shoulders. I thought I'd have to find out how much you knew and make sure you didn't learn more than you had to. It turns out you knew everything."

Silk shook his head. "Not at all. Doctor Crane and I made an agreement. I told him all I'd learned or guessed about his activities, and in return he answered my questions about them. I had guessed very little, and he told me very little more, not even his real name."

"It was Sigada." Hossaan smiled bitterly. "It means he was supposed to be handsome and humble."

"But he was neither. Thank you." Silk nodded. "Sigada. I'll always remember him as Doctor Crane, but I'm glad to know how he remembered himself. You weren't called Hossaan when you were at Blood's, I'm sure."

"No. Willet."

"I see. You didn't give that name to Maytera Marble; you gave her your real one. You can't have known that Doctor Crane had told me about you, because you can't have talked to him between our conversation Tarsday afternoon and his death on Hieraxday morning."

"I told you I didn't know how much you knew, Caldé."

"That's right." Futilely, Silk groped in a pocket of his robe. "Do you know, I don't have any prayer beads now? When I was a poor augur, I had beads in my pocket but no money. Now I have money, but no beads."

"An improvement. You can buy some."

"If I can find the time when the shops are open, and get into one without being mobbed. You said you were going to tell me no more than you had to; but plainly you intended to tell me you were a Trivigaunti spy."

"That's right. I was going to tell you because you would have known it from the news I came to give you. Generalissimo Siyuf is coming to reinforce you, with thousands of troopers. I just found out about it myself." Hossaan twisted in his seat until he was face-to-face with Silk. "It means your victory is assured, Caldé. If you're not defeated before she arrives, it will be impossible for you to be defeated at all." There was a timid tap on the canopy, and Hossaan said, "It's the sibyl."

Turning, Silk saw Maytera Marble's metal face, hardly a span from his. "Let her in, please. I can't imagine myself saying anything I wouldn't want her to know—or hearing any such news or confidence, except in shriving."

The canopy retraced, and Maytera Marble entered, her long black skirt and wide sleeves flapping in the wind. "I spoke to you, Patera, but you couldn't hear me."

"No," Silk said. "No, Maytera, I couldn't." He motioned to Hossaan and the canopy enclosed them as before.

"I don't want to interrupt, but seeing you in this machine I thought you might be about to leave. And . . . and . . ."

"I suppose we are, but not without Chenille. I want to take her with me. Is she in the cenoby?"

Maytera Marble nodded. "I'll go get her in a moment, Patera. She's eating."

"But first you want to tell me something. Is it about her, or," Silk hesitated, "your granddaughter, Maytera?"

"I wanted to ask you for something, Patera, actually. I realize that you and this foreign gentleman were conferring, and that it's important. But this won't take long. I'll ask and go."

"Hossaan is from Trivigaunte," Silk told her, "like your friend General Saba. They're our allies, as you must know, and I've just learned from Hossaan that they're sending more troops to help us."

"Why, that's wonderful!" Maytera Marble smiled, her head back and inclined to the right. "But after news like that my little problem will seem terribly insignificant, I'm afraid."

"I'm certain it won't, Maytera. You're not the sort who bothers others with insignificant problems." To Hossaan, Silk added, "Now I want to say that Maytera was to me what you were to Doctor Crane, but she was far more. I came to this manteion straight from the schola, and I'd been here only a bit over a year when Patera Pike died. Maytera saved me from making a fool of myself at least once a day." He paused, remembering. "Though I wish it had been more, because I did make a fool of myself often, in spite of all that she could do."

"I intrigued against you, too," Maytera Marble confessed. "I didn't hate you, or at least I told myself I didn't. But I obstructed and embarrassed you in small ways, telling myself that it was for your own good." Her voice grew urgent. "I don't have the *right* to ask favors. I know that, but—"

"Of course you do!"

"I can't manage it myself. I wish I could. I've prayed for the means, but I can't. Do you know Marl, Patera?"

"I don't think so." Silk, who knew few chems, exhausted his mental list quickly. "She—?"

"He, Patera."

"He can't attend our sacrifices. I can't even remember the last time I saw a chem there—except you, of course."

"There aren't many left," Hossaan put in, "here or in my own city. Is he a soldier?"

Maytera Marble shook her head. "He's a valet. He works for a man called Fulmar. I don't see him often at all, but I went over yesterday, my granddaughter and I did, and . . ."

"Go on, Maytera."

"I showed him my hand. The one that my—you know . . ."

Silk nodded, he hoped encouragingly. "It's better not to dwell on that, Maytera, I'm sure. You showed him your hand."

"I brought it in a little basket, wrapped up in a towel, because there's fluid that might leak out. It's a very good hand still. It's just that I can't put it back on."

"I understand."

"Marl says there's a shop, though I'd think it would have to be a big place, really, way over past the crooked bridge, where they make taluses and fix them. Mostly it's fixing, he said, because it takes so long to make one, and so much money. We chems aren't really like taluses. We were made in the Short Sun Whorl, and we can think and see a great deal better, and we don't burn fish oil," she laughed nervously, "or anything like that. But Marl thought they might be able to do this for me—put it back—if I had the money. It wouldn't be like making a chem or even a talus, just a simple repair."

"Yes. Yes, of course. I should have thought of something like that, Maytera. Welding? Is that what they call it?"

Hossaan said, "That's what they call it when they fix a floater."

"It's not just reuniting the metal, Patera. There are little tubes in there, tiny tubes, and wires, and things like threads—fibers, they're called—that pipe light. Look." She held up her useless right arm, pushing back the sleeve so that he could see the sheared end. "Marl thought they might be able to do it. He's as old as I was, Patera, and I don't think he always reasons correctly anymore. But . . ."

Silk nodded. "It's your only chance. I understand."

"Marl would have given me the money if he'd had it, but

he's very poor. This Fulmar doesn't pay him, just clothes and a place to live. And even if I had money, they might not want to try it, Marl said, unless I had a great deal."

"Believe me, I'll help you, Maytera. We'll go as quickly as we can. You have my word on it."

She had taken a large white handkerchief from her empty sleeve. "I'm so sorry, Patera." She dabbed at her eyes. "I can't really cry, not for a long, long time. And yet I feel that way. There's so much work, with you gone and Patera Gulo gone, and Maytera Mint gone, and my granddaughter to take care of, and just one hand for everything."

Silk reached another decision. "I'm going to take you away, too, Maytera, for the time being at least. You and Mucor both. I need you both, and it's too dangerous for you—and for her, particularly—to be here alone. Will you come with me if I ask you to? Remember, I'm still the augur of this manteion."

She looked up at him with a new glow behind the scratched, dry lenses of her eyes. "Yes indeed, Patera, if you tell me to. I'll have to straighten up first and put things away. Put a notice on the door of the palaestra so the children will know."

"Good. There's a Caldé's Palace on the Palatine, as well as the Prolocutor's. I'm sure you must remember when the caldé lived there."

She nodded.

"I'm reopening it. I've slept in the Juzgado the past few nights, but that's never been more than an expedient; if Viron's to have a new caldé, he has to live in the Caldé's Palace. I'll need a place to entertain Generalissimo Siyuf when she arrives, to begin with. We'll want an official welcome for her and her troops, too, and I'll have to notify Generalissimo Oosik as soon as possible. Thousands of fresh troops are certain to change his plans."

Silk turned to Hossaan. "How long do we have? Can you give me some idea?"

"Not an accurate one, Caldé. I'm not sure when she left Trivigaunte, and Siyuf's a famous hard marcher."

"A week?"

"I doubt it." Hossaan shook his head. "Three or four days, at a guess."

"Patera." Maytera Marble touched Silk's arm. "I can't live in the same house with a man, not even an augur. I know nothing will—but the Chapter . . ."

"You can if he's ill," Silk told her firmly. "You can sleep in the same house to nurse him. I've a chest wound—I'll show it to you as soon as we get there, and you can change the dressing for me. I'm also recovering from a broken ankle. His Cognizance will grant you a dispensation, I'm sure, or the coadjutor can. Hossaan, can you take us back to the Juzgado? There will be four of us."

"Sure thing, Caldé."

"I don't have a floater at present, except for the Guard floaters, and Oosik needs those. Perhaps I could hire you and your floater—we'll talk about it.

"Maytera, do whatever you must, and tack up that note. I was hoping to sacrifice here and go to the Cock when I left, but both will have to wait. Tomorrow, perhaps.

"Hossaan, I'm going into the manse for a moment while she does all that; then we'll collect Mucor and a young woman who came here with me, and pay off my litter."

"I heard you had a pet bird," Saba said, eyeing Oreb; she was a massive woman with a marked resemblance to an angry sow.

Silk smiled. "I'm not sure pet's the correct word. I've been trying to set him free for days. The result has been that he comes and goes as he pleases, says anything he wants, and seems to enjoy himself far more than I do. Today we went back to my manteion, mostly to enlist Maytera Marble's help in airing this place out. I got some important news there, by the way, which I'll give you in a moment."

"That's right." Saba snapped her fingers. "You holy men are supposed to be able to find out the gods' will by looking at sheep guts, aren't you?"

"Yes. Some of us are better at it than others, of course, and no one's ever suggested that I'm much better than average. Don't you have augurs in Trivigaunte?"

"No cut!" Oreb required reassurance.

"Not you, silly bird. Positively not." Silk smiled again. "I got him as a victim, you see; and though I've ruled that out, he's afraid I'll change my mind. What I wanted to tell you is that I went into the manse to see if I'd left my beads there Phaesday night. I should have said earlier that he'd flown off when I got out of my litter.

"Well, I went into the kitchen because I empty my pockets on the kitchen table sometimes, and there he was on the larder. 'Bird home,' he told me, and seemed quite content; but he rode out on my shoulder when I left."

"He sounds like a good trooper," Saba leaned back in her ivory-inlaid armchair. "You have so many male troopers here. I'm still getting used to them, though most fight well enough. I have news for you, too, Caldé, when you've given me yours."

"In a moment. To tell the truth, I'm afraid you'll rush off the minute you hear it and I want to ask about augury in Trivigaunte. Besides, Chenille's making coffee, and she'll be disappointed if we don't drink it. She wants to meet you, too—you helped save her; she was one of the hostages at Blood's." Seeing that Saba did not understand him, Silk added, "The villa in the country."

"Oh, there. You were the one we came after, Caldé."

"But you saved Chenille too, and Patera Incus and Master Xiphias—you and Generalissimo Oosik, and several thousand of General Mint's people, I ought to say."

Saba nodded. "We were a little part, but we did what we could. Where's Mint, anyhow?"

"Trying to turn courageous but untrained and undisciplined volunteers into a smoothly running horde, I assume. I've tried to do that sort of thing myself on a much smaller scale—with the mothers of the children at our palaestra, for example. I don't envy her the task."

"You've got to get rough with them, sometimes," Saba told him, looking as if that were the aspect she enjoyed.

"There's times to be pals, all troopers together. And there's times when you need the *karbaj*."

Silk wisely refrained from asking what the *karbaj* was. "About augury. From what you said, I take it that it's not practiced in Trivigaunte? Is that correct?"

Saba inclined her head, the movement barely perceptible. "You try to make the gods like you by cutting up animals. We don't. I'm not trying to offend you."

"Not at all, General."

"I'm a plain-spoken old campaigner, and I don't pretend to be anything more. Or anything less. A simple old trooper. The way things are here makes me try and act like an ambassador, so I do my best." She laughed loudly. "But that's not too good, so I'll give it to you straight. Your customs seem backwards to me, and I keep waiting for them to turn around. Take her, now." Saba pointed to Chenille, who had entered with a tray. "Here's a woman and a man talking, and a woman waiting on them. I'm not saying you never see that at home, but you don't see it often."

"But to get back to—" Silk accepted a cup. "Thank you, Chenille. You didn't have to do this, and I'm not sure General Saba realizes that. Goodness and servility look alike at times, though they're very different. Won't you sit down?"

"If I won't bother you."

"Of course not. We'll be happy to have your company, and I know you were anxious to meet General Saba. She's the commander of the Rani's airship."

"I know." Chenille gave Saba an admiring smile.

"She was one of your rescuers. Generalissimo Oosik told me afterward that he'd be delighted to see the kind of efficiency her pterotroopers displayed in a brigade of our Guard."

"They're picked women, every one of them," Saba told Silk complacently. "The competition to get in is fierce. We turn away ten for each we take."

"I want to get back to augury. If I seem to be harping on it, I hope you'll excuse me; I was trained as an augur, and I doubt that I'll ever lose interest in it entirely. But first, would it be possible for me to go up in your airship sometime?"

Saba winked at Chenille, her brutal face briefly humorous.

"One of the students—his name is Horn, and he's acting as a messenger here for the present—told me not long ago that he'd dreamed of flying. So have I, though I didn't admit it to Horn, or even to myself when I spoke with him."

"Bird fly!" Oreb proclaimed.

"Exactly. We can scarcely look up without seeing a bird; and there are fliers every few days, proving it can be done. When I was a boy, I used to imagine they were shouting, 'We can fly and you can't!' up there too high to be heard. I knew it was foolish, but the feeling has never left me entirely."

"Wing good." Hopping onto Silk's head, Oreb displayed it.

"He couldn't fly for a while," Silk explained. "Before that I doubt that he took much pride in it."

"I'm going to surprise you, Caldé," Saba announced. "You are welcome to visit my airship anytime. Just let me know when you're coming so I can get things trooper-like for you."

"Of course." Silk sipped from his cup, pausing to admire the delicate porcelain, brave with gilt and holding a painted Scylla as well as coffee.

"If that were wine, I'd tell you I was going to fit you up with wings like my girls'," the teeth of Saba's underjaw showed in a savage grin, "and shove you out. But sham diplomats don't get to make that sort of a joke."

Silk sighed. "I'd thought about it. I'm not at all sure I have the courage, but perhaps I might try."

"Don't. You'd be crippled for life if you weren't killed. My girls start with a platform that would fit in this room. I—who's that!"

"Who?" Silk glanced at the doors; so did Chenille.

"There was a face in that mirror." Saba stood up, her cup still in her hand. "Somebody that isn't in here, somebody I've never seen before. I saw her!"

"I'm sure you did, General." Silk put down his coffee.

"You've only just reopened this palace, isn't that right?"

"Less than an hour ago, actually. Maytera Marble and—"

"A secret passage." Saba's tone brooked no contradiction.

"The mirror's a peephole, and somebody's spying from in there already. One passage at least, and there could be more, I've seen some at home. What's that girl doing?"

Chenille had gone to the mirror and grasped the sides of its ornate frame with both hands. "It's dusty," she told Silk. "They had dust covers over all this, but dust got in anyhow." With a grunt of effort, she lifted the mirror from its hook; behind it was featureless plaster, somewhat lighter in color than that to either side.

Silk had risen when Saba did. He limped to the wall and rapped it with his knuckles, evoking solid thuds. Saba stared, her wide mouth working.

"Want me to put this back, Patera?" Chenille inquired.

"I don't think so. Not yet, at least. I'll do it, or Master Xiphias can. Can you put it down without dropping it?"

"I think so. I'm pretty strong."

The heels of Saba's polished riding boots came together with a click. "I apologize, Caldé. I'm leaving. Again, I regret this very much."

"Don't go yet," Silk said hastily. "Your Generalissimo Siyuf is bringing us thousands of—"

Saba's cup fell to the costly carpet, splashing it and her gleaming boots with black coffee. "That's the news I was going to tell you! You—you learned that from animal guts?"

Chapter 3

THE FIRST THEOPHANY ON THELXDAY

Three busy days after Saba had dropped her coffee, Marrow the greengrocer abandoned the pleasant anticipation of the parade that was to close the market early to stare at the weary prophet nearing his stall. "Auk?" Marrow smoothed his fruit-stained apron. "Aren't you Auk?"

"That's me." The prophet stepped out of the wind to lean against a table piled with oranges.

"You're a friend of the caldé's. That's what they say."

"I guess." Auk scratched his stubbled jaw. "I like him, anyhow, and I brought a ram when Kypris came. I don't know if he likes me, though. If he don't, I don't blame him."

Marrow wiped his nose on his sleeve. "You're a friend of General Mint's, too."

"Everybody is now. That's what I hear."

"Scleroderma told me. You know her? The butcher's wife." Auk shook his head.

"She knows you, and she says you used to come to Silk's manteíon, on Sun Street."

"Yeah. I know where it is."

"She says you'd sit in a little garden they've got and talk to her. To General Mint. Would you like an orange?"

"Sure, but I don't have the money. Not that I can spend."

"Take some. Wait a minute, I'll get you a bag." Marrow hurried to the back of his stall, and Auk slipped a peach into his pocket.

"Now you're going around talking about the Plan of Pas. Would you like some bananas? Real bananas from Urbs?"

Auk looked at the price. "No," he said.

"Free. I'm not going to charge you."

Auk straightened up, filling his barrel of a chest with air. "Yeah. I know. That's why I don't want any. Listen up. I'd steal your bananas, see? That's lily. I'd steal 'em and riffle your till, 'cause that's the kind I am. I'm a dimber thief, and Tartaros needs cards for something we're planning to do. Only I won't let you give me bananas. They cost you too much, and it wouldn't be right."

"But—"

"Muzzle it." Auk had begun to peel an orange, pulling away bright cusps of rind with strong, soiled fingers. "I got a mort back in the Orilla I'm supposed to take care of. She's hungry, and she's not used to it like me. So if you want to put oranges and maybe a couple potatoes in that sack, I'll thank you for 'em and take 'em to her. No bananas, see? But nab the gelt off these that want to buy first. I'll take the sack when you're done, if you still want to give it."

"That's Auk the Prophet," Marrow whispered to the crowd around his stall. "A dozen yellow apples, madame? And two cabbages? Absolutely! Very fresh and very cheap."

A few minutes later he told Auk, "I want to take you over to Shrike's as soon as my boy gets back. Scleroderma's husband? He'll let you have a bite or two of meat, I'm sure."

There were two hundred, if not more, waiting for Auk in the Orilla, and another hundred following him. Tartaros whispered, "You are fatigued, Auk my noctolater, and cold."

"You got the lily there, Terrible Tartaros."

"Therefore you are liable to be impatient."

"Not me. I been tired and cold up on the roof, when they were looking with dogs."

"Be warned. This time the prize is greater."

Auk shouldered their way through the crowd, halted at the door of the boarded-up shop that had been his destination, and put down the bags he carried. "Listen up, all you culls."

The crowd hushed.

"I don't know what you want, but I know what I want. I want to leave this stuff with the dell inside. She's hungry, and some cullys in the market gave me this for her. If you want to see me, you've done it. If you want to hear me, you've done that, too. If it's something else, let me give her these and we'll talk about it."

A voice from the crowd called, "We want you to sacrifice!"

"You're abram. I'm no augur." Auk pounded on the warped door. "Hammerstone! Look alive in there!"

The door opened; at the sight of the towering soldier, the crowd fell silent. "This ain't one of the Ayuntamiento's," Auk shouted hastily. "He's working for the gods like I am, only when we were coming here . . ." He tried to remember when they had come; although he vividly recalled watching Hammerstone free himself from tons of shattered shiprock, he could not shut his mind upon the day. "It was when the Alambrera gave up. Anyway all these trooper culls were taking shots at him, so we figured it was better for him to pull it in."

Behind him Hammerstone hissed. "Ask if Patera's here." It was like receiving confidences from a thunderhead.

"Patera Incus!" Auk shouted. "We're looking for this real holy augur named Patera Incus. Somebody said something about a sacrifice. Is Patera Incus out there?"

Voices from the back of the crowd: *"You do it!"*

From behind Hammerstone, Hyacinth inquired urgently, "Is there food in those? I want it."

Tartaros whispered, "Tell them you will," by some miracle overcoming the clamor of the crowd.

Auk was so surprised he turned to look. "What the shaggy—I mean yeah, dimber, Terrible Tartaros. Anything."

Passing both sacks to Hammerstone, he cupped his hands around his mouth. "I'll sacrifice. You got it!"

"When?" Four men lifted a terrified brown kid over their heads; its unhappy bleats were visible, although inaudible.

"Now, Auk my noctolater."

"Now!" Auk repeated.

A thin man whose coat and hat had once been costly asked, "You say you're doing the gods' will. Will a god appear?"

Auk waited for assurance from the blind god at his side, but none was forthcoming.

Others took up the question. *"Will a god come?"*

"What do you think?" Auk challenged them, and a hundred arguments broke out at once.

From behind Hammerstone's green bulk, Hyacinth inquired, "Where're we going to do it?"

"I thought you were eating."

"She is," Hammerstone rumbled. "I can hear her."

The noise grew as fifty men and a dozen loud-voiced women shouted demands. Auk muttered, "Terrible Tartaros, you better tell me what to tell 'em or we could have a problem here."

"Have I not, Auk my noctolater? You are to sacrifice, to me or to whatever god you wish."

Auk turned to Hammerstone. "Get out of the door. I got to tell both of you, and I ain't going to talk to her through you."

The soldier emerged into the street, evoking another awed silence. Revealed, Hyacinth chewed and gulped, wiping her hands on her soiled gown. "That was a nectarine, I think, and I think I swallowed the pit. I can't remember spitting it out. Maybe I chewed it up. Thelx, was it good!"

"You take care of this stuff," Auk told her, "I got to go to Sun Street."

"I'm coming!"

Auk shook his head. "I ain't no augur—"

Tartaros whispered, "Bring the soldier and the woman."

"But I got to sacrifice. Scalding Scylla wanted me to, too. She was going to make me give her Dace, probably."

"I'll need a coat and a bath, makeup—don't you hit me! If you hit me again I'll—I'll—"

"You're coming all right," Auk told her, "and we're going now." He strode into the crowd. "Listen here! Slap a muzzle on it, you culls. Listen up!"

Hammerstone fired his slug gun into the air.

"No god's coming! You want me to sacrifice, we'll go over to Sun Street and do it right. Only no god!" Under his breath he added, "You couldn't see one anyhow, you cank cullys."

They followed him through the narrow street nonetheless, cowed by him more than by the menacing soldier beside him who never relaxed his hold on the shivering, disheveled young woman in the red silk gown.

From the highest step of Silk's manteion, Auk addressed them again. "I told you there ain't going to be a god. You jerk me around, don't you? Sacrifice right this minute! Show us a god, Auk! All your clatter. You think you could jerk me around like you do if I could jerk the gods around? I can't. Neither can you. What I'm telling you is, it's time."

He drew his brass-mounted hanger. "I can cut your goats with this. That's nothing. Can I cut myself out of the whorl? That's what matters. Think about it. Nobody but you can make you think, not even gods."

"Sacrifice!" someone shouted.

"Not even the gods!" Auk bellowed. "Only they can snuff you if you don't, see? Or just leave you to die, 'cause this whorl's finished! Tartaros told me!"

The crowd stirred.

"Ever see a dead bitch in the street? And her pups still trying to suck? That's you! And that's me!" Over his shoulder Auk added, "Open these doors, Hammerstone."

The soldier hooked a finger as thick as a crowbar through one wrought iron handle and rattled the door until it seemed it must leave its hinges. "It's locked."

"Then bust it down. We'll use the wood."

Hammerstone released the door and drew back his fist, but Hyacinth exclaimed, "Wait! Somebody's coming!"

In a moment Auk heard the rattle and squeak of the old iron

lock, and the solid *thunk* as the bolt slid back. He grasped the
handle and pulled.

"*Patera!*" Hammerstone knelt as a father does to embrace
a boy who does not like being lifted, and hugged Incus in arms
that could have splintered the ribs of a bull.

Even Auk smiled. "Hi, Patera. Where you been?"

Hyacinth, torn between the opportunity for flight and the
deliverance she sensed was almost at hand, nudged Auk. "Is
this him? The one Hammerstone talks about all the time?"

"Yeah. You want to argue with him? Me neither."

Pointing to Incus he announced, "This's the augur I asked
you about. Now we can have a regular augur, and maybe
he'll let me help. We'll need wood for the altar, you scavy?
Some of you got to go get us some. Cedar if you can find any,
any kind if you can't."

From Hammerstone's embrace, Incus protested, "*Auk,* my
son!"

"We got to, Patera. You like for lots of people to see you
sacrifice? I got you three or four hundred here. Hammerstone, loosen up or you'll chill him."

Speaking so quickly her racing words flashed past like
frightened linnets, Hyacinth gabbled, "Patera, I know what I
look like, I know how awful, but I'm not the sort that would
ever set her cap for a cully like this or even let him, you
know, talk to her even if he just wanted to talk, you know how
they do, and that's not me, and I've got money and good
clothes even if you wouldn't think it to look at me and jewelry, and I know people, I've got, you know, bucks that would
do me favors any time, commissioners and brigadiers, and I
know the caldé, I really do, he's a particular friend of mine
and this man and the soldier have been making me stay in a
dirty freezing place with rats, and you've got to help me, Patera, you've got to tell—"

Auk clapped a hand over her mouth. "She goes on like that
quite a bit, Patera, and we ain't got time for it all. Let him go,
Hammerstone. Get him inside there and up to the altar. You
can carry him, I guess, if it makes you feel better."

"I've *prayed,*" Incus managed to gasp as Hammerstone

hoisted him, "all morning, prayed upon my *knees* with tears and *bitterest groans*—don't drop me, Hammerstone my son, your shoulders are slippery—for a sign of *favor* from Surging Scylla or any other god, the smallest *morsel* of *assistance,* the most humble *crumb* of *succor* in my *divinely ordained* mission."

"I'd say maybe you got it," Auk told him. "What do you think, Terrible Tartaros?"

Briefly, the blind god's hand tightened on his. "Release the woman, Auk my noctolater. I am about to leave you. I have mended your mind, insofar as I am able."

Auk turned, although he knew he could not see the god.

"It will heal itself soon of the damage that remains. I have explained your task, and you have learned better than I could have hoped. Direct your gaze to the Sacred Window, Auk my noctolater."

"This's the Plan, Terrible Tartaros. Emptying the whole whorl. I can't do that by myself!"

"Look at the screen, Auk. At the Sacred Window. This is the last instruction I shall give you."

Auk sank to his knees. Faintly, through the open door, the silver glow shone from the far end of the manteion. "Get out of my way, Hammerstone! I got to see the Window."

"Farewell, Auk. May neither of us forget the prayers you offered nightside, while I hearkened invisible in your glass."

Auk stood up, alone.

"You're crying." Hyacinth stepped closer to peer at him. "Auk, you're *crying*."

"Yeah, I guess I am." He wiped his streaming eyes with his fingers. "I never had any father."

"I do, and he's a pig's arse." Worshippers pushed past them carrying armloads of wood; some paused to stare.

"I got to get up there and do it. You want to go, go on. I won't stop you."

"I can leave anytime I want to?"

"Yeah, Hy. Beat the hoof."

"Then I'm going to—no, that's abram. G'bye, Bruiser." Her lips brushed his.

"*Auk* my son!" Incus stood beside the altar, directing the laying of the fire. "We've more wood than we require. Tell them to *desist.*"

He did, happy to have something to do.

At Silk's ambion, Incus drew himself up beyond his full height, rising on his toes. "A holy *augur's* blessing upon each and every one of you, my children. *Silence,* back there! This is a *manteion,* a house sacred to the *immortal gods.*" It was the hour he had dreamed of since childhood.

"*Hammerstone,* my son. It is best to offer our *pious gifts* upon a fire kindled *directly* from the *beneficent* rays. This is not accorded us on this *day of darkness.* If you will look in the sacristy, behind the *Sacred Window,* you may discover a *firekeeper,* a vessel of metal or even lowly *terra cotta* safeguarding the *holy spark* against such an hour as *this.*"

"I'm on it, Patera."

Incus returned his attention to the congregation. "*At this point,* my children, I am severely tempted to *discover* to you my *own* identity, and the *multifarious vicissitudes* and *tribulations* through which I come to you *today.* I *refrain,* however. I am an *augur,* as you see. I am *that* augur whom *Surfeiting Scylla* has designated *Prolocutor-to-be,* charged with the *utter destruction* of the *Ayunta*—"

For half a minute, their cheers silenced him.

"I am *in addition*—might I say *comrade,* Auk? A *fellow sufferer* at least of Auk's."

From the manteion floor Auk shouted, "A dimber mate!"

"Thank you. Beset, as you should know, by *woe* and eager for a *situation* of *venerational tranquility,* I bethought me of this manteion, the *new caldé's own* as a place to which I might retire, pray and contemplate the *inscrutable* ways of the gods. I had not seen it and had heard much of it during the *brief days* since Auk, my dear friend *Hammerstone*—"

"I got it right here, Patera." Hammerstone displayed a pierced clay pot from which a feeble crimson glow proceeded.

"*Auk,* are you to *assist* me? Is that to be our *procedure?*"

A seemingly disembodied voice called, "He has to kill 'em!"

"Then he *shall,* and with my blessing. What of the *liturgy,* however? *Auk?*"

Auk had climbed the steps to the altar. "I don't know the words, Patera. You'll have to do it."

"I *shall.* And if *Auk* is to assist, why need my dear friend *Hammerstone* be excluded? Put the *sacred flame* to this fuel, if you will, Hammerstone.

"I obtained the *key,* journeyed *hence,* and locked myself in, counting the lock's *blessed squeakings* among the *treasures* of my *spirit.* I came, I say, in search of *quiet,* resolved upon *prayer and supplication.* I *found* it, as I had hoped, and spent hours upon my *knees,* the least supplicant of the *immortal gods.* It is a practice I recommend to you *without reservation.*"

A tongue of fire had sprung up where Hammerstone fanned the wood piled on the altar.

"I was safe from all *interruption.* Or so I thought. Then *you* arrived, a *tumultuous throng,* elevating me to this *sacred* ambion. How *clearly* the gods speak! *Surmounting Scylla* had *lifted* me to the *Prolocutorship.* Now was I *cautioned* that the *Prolocutor—I—*can be no *holy recluse,* however he may *long* for peace. *Pray* for me, my *children,* as I pray for *myself.* Let me *not* forget my *lesson!*

"*Auk,* my son. Have you the *knife* of *sacrifice?*"

Auk drew his boot knife. "This's all I got, Patera."

"Then it must *suffice.* Bring it to *me* and *I* shall *bless* it." Incus did so, tracing the sign of addition over the blade. Before he finished, Hammerstone had been forced to step back from the leaping flames.

"In a *sacred ceremony* more regular, I should now ask their presenters to which of the *Nine,* or other *immortal gods,* they wished to offer the *fair victims. Today,* however—"

Someone shouted, "To Tartaros! He's always on him!"

"They ain't black," Auk told the speaker.

Incus nodded solemnly. "In the *present instance* that must be *dispensed* with. None are *white.* Nor are any *black,* as my erstwhile comrade has *rightly* said. Therefore *each* shall be offered to *all* the *gods.*"

After glancing at the first victim, Incus faced the Sacred Window, his arms and his voice raised dramatically. *"Accept* all you gods, the sacrifice of this fine *piglet.* And speak to us, we beg, of the times that are to *come. What* are we to do? Your *lightest* word will—will—"

He got no further.

The silver radiance showed flecks of color, faded pastels that might have been shadows or phantoms, the visual illusions of disordered sight, dabs of rose and azure that blossomed and withered, shot with pearl and ebony.

Poised beside the young pig, Auk dropped his knife and fell to his knees. Momentarily it seemed that he could make out a face on the left. Then another, wholly different, on the right. A voice spoke, such a voice as Auk had never heard, filled with the roar of mighty engines. It praised him and urged him to seek something or someone. Now and again, though only now and again, he heard or at least believed he heard, a term he knew: *ghost, augur, plan.* Then silence.

Incus, too, was on his knees; his hands were clasped, his face that of a child.

The piglet had vanished, drawn perhaps into the Window, or perhaps merely fled through the dim manteion and out into the windy winter morning.

Hammerstone stood at rigid attention, his right hand raised in a salute.

For a time that might have been long or short, after the voice spoke no more and the half-formed colors had gone, all was silence; the congregation might have been so many statues, there in the old manteion on Sun Street, statues with starting eyes and gaping mouths.

Then the noise began. Men who had been sitting sprang to their feet; men who had been kneeling jumped up to dance upon the pews. Some howled as though in agony. Some shrieked as if in ecstasy. A woman fell in a fit, thrashing, contorted as a swatted fly, belching bloody foam as her teeth tore her tongue and lips; no one noticed her, or cared.

"He's gone." Auk rose slowly, still staring at the now-empty Window. More loudly, loudly enough to make himself heard by Hammerstone, he said, "He ain't here, not any more. That was him, wasn't it? That was Pas."

Hammerstone's steel arm crashed to his steel side, a sound like the clash of swords.

"Did anybody . . . You understand him, Patera? It sounded like he was talking about—about—" A man Auk did not know reached out and touched Auk's coat as he might have touched the Sacred Window.

"He liked me," Auk concluded weakly. "Kind of like he liked me, that was what it sounded like." No one heard him.

Incus was on his feet. He tottered to the ambion; although his mouth opened and shut and his lips appeared to shape words, no words could be heard above the din. At last he motioned to Hammerstone, and Hammerstone thundered for silence.

"It is my task—" Incus's voice had risen to a squeak; he cleared his throat. "My task to *explicate* for you the *utterance* of the god." The recurrence of something near his accustomed singsong restored his confidence. "To *gloss* upon his *message* and *relay* his *commands.*"

A man in the second row shouted, "It was Pas, wasn't it?"

Incus nodded, his cheeks trembling. "It *was*. Lord *Pas,* the *Father* of the *Whorl* and the *Builder* of the *Gods.*" Neither he nor his hearers noticed his mistake.

"He talked to me," Hammerstone told Auk. His voice held a dawning joy. "I seen him once, way off, reviewing the parade. This time he talked to me. Like I'm talking to you, and he gave me a order."

Auk nodded numbly.

"Patera will have heard, won't he? Sure he will. We'll talk about this years from now, how Pas talked to us and gave me the order. Me and Patera."

"Ere I *commence* my *exegesis,*" his voice was stronger, and carried an authority that stilled the congregation, "I shall *confide* to you something not generally known, which I *myself* learned only *today*. There has been no *announcement,* but I was not sworn to *secrecy*. On *Molpsday* Great *Pas* granted a *theophany* to the—the *aged worthy augur* who has for *innu-*

merable decades served us as *Prolocutor.* His office has been *attorned* to me by *Saving Scylla,* who would doubtless see his *protracted devotion* rewarded with that *freedom* from *concerns* which is the *perfumed ointment* of *superannuity.* It was that, I *confess,* which sent me in search of *tranquility,* as I have *related.* The *disquieting intelligence* that the *Father* of the *Seven* had *manifested* himself to one whom I have been *only too ready* to reckon a *rival."*

"Did he say something about me?" Half pleading and half threatening, Auk closed upon the ambion. "He said something, didn't he? What was it?" Hammerstone interposed himself.

"I *prayed* to *Pas,"* Incus continued, wondering. "I urged the *justice* of my *cause* with *tears.* Now how *clearly* do I see this lesser *plan,* the *plan* that is to set in motion his *greater Plan!* First he *bestowed* his *benefaction* upon the *Prolocutor* that was, then upon the *new."* Incus indicated his own stomach. "It is the *hallmark* of the *actions* of the *gods* that, however *unanticipated* they may be, once done they are seen to be both *perfect* and *inevitable.*

"And *now* I confide the *divine utterance* that *Great Pas* has *vouchsafed* to us."

High above the mummy-colored bead that was General Saba's airship, but five hundred cubits below the low winter clouds, Fliers whom Caldé Silk was just then likening to a flight of storks rode the blustering north wind.

From their center, Sciathan studied his companions. Their eyes were on the clouds, as he had expected, or else the sere brown fields, the silver threads of streams, or the shrinking lake; no mere emergency could overcome the habits of years, no urging—not even a god's—bring them to consider the teeming Cargo below relevant.

Sciathan himself glanced up at the clouds and scanned his instruments before abandoning both. A long yellow-brown column of marchers was approaching the city from the south. He had glimpsed similar parades often, giving little thought to them and what they might portend; soldiers and troopers could be halted by avalanches, turned aside by floods and forest fires, and dispersed by storms not much less readily than flotillas. No host had ever succeeded in crossing the Mountains That Look At Mountains; and in all likelihood, none ever would. Here in the hold, hordes like the one below would be a different matter.

Chapter 4

SWORDS OF SPHIGX

Standing stiffly in his official cloak of tea-colored velvet, Caldé Silk cursed himself mentally for not providing chairs—or rather, for not seeing to it that chairs were provided. He had supposed (such, he told himself, had been his lamentable innocence, his utter unfitness for the position thrust upon him) that he, with Quetzal, Oosik, and Saba—and Maytera Mint, if she could be found—would take their places on this platform, at which the force dispatched by Trivigaunte to the aid of Viron would appear.

The fact, of course, was otherwise. The fact was that even Generalissimo Siyuf's highly disciplined horde of seventy-five thousands remained a mass of seventy-five thousand women and men—to say nothing of thousands of horses and none but the Nine knew how many camels.

Camels!

As a precociously pious boy, he had considered Sphigx the least attractive goddess, a tawny-maned virago, more lioness than woman. Now it appeared that real lions had nothing to do with real warfare; horses, mules, and camels were the pets of Stabbing Sphigx, and he would have accepted them happily (or even gerbils, guinea pigs, and geese) if only they would appear in reality.

A freezing gust shook the triumphal arch. It had been hastily erected, and would almost certainly collapse if this winter wind blew even a trifle harder; indeed, it was liable to collapse in any event if Siyuf's troopers did not put in an appearance soon.

Surely there ought to be somebody in the crowd around the platform who could and would fetch chairs. First, he decided, he would ask that a chair be provided for Quetzal, who was of advanced years and had been standing for the better part of an hour; then, as if it were an afterthought, he could order chairs for Oosik and Saba, and himself as well. Five minutes more and he would leave the platform, collar a commissioner, and demand chairs. He must and he would—that was all there was to it.

The wind rose again, and he clenched his teeth. Yellow dust gave it a score of visible bodies, whirling devils that skated over the Alameda. A streamer of green paper tore free of the arch to mount the wind in sinuous curves, vanishing in a few seconds against the heaving bulk of the tethered airship.

From that airship, he reflected, it should be simple to gauge the advance of Siyuf's troops. Given just one more day, he might have arranged for signals: a flag hung out from the foremost gondola when her advance guard entered the city, or a smoke-pot lit for an unanticipated delay. To his own surprise, he found that he had lost none of his eagerness to board that airship, in spite of multiplying duties and the winter wind. Like Horn (just the person to find chairs, or boxes at least) he longed to fly as the Fliers did.

There were a lot of them today. More, he decided, than he had ever seen before. An entire flock, like a flight of storks, was just now appearing from behind the airship. What city sent them to patrol the sun, and what good could such patrols do?

A fresh gust roared along the Alameda, shaking its raddled poplars. To his right Saba stiffened, while he himself shivered shamelessly. The Cloak of Lawful Governance tossed like Lake Limna about his shins, and would have streamed behind him like a banner if he had not been holding it with both hands. Hours ago, when he had put it on in the Juzgado, it had carried in its long train a sensation of oppressive and almost suffocating warmth; he had been sorely tempted to substitute a cheap (and therefore thin) augur's robe for the luxuriously thick one he was wearing under it, although Master Xiphias and Commissioner Trematode had dissuaded him. By this time it should have been soaked with his perspiration; instead he found himself wishing fervently for a head covering of some kind. Saba had her dust-colored military cap, and Oosik a tall helmet of green leather. He had nothing.

The old broad-brimmed straw hat he had worn while repairing the roof was gone—lost at Blood's, like Maytera Mint. The new broad-brimmed straw he had bought at the lake was gone too, left in the room from which the talus had snatched him. Patera Pike's cap, the black calotte that Patera had worn in winter, was back at the manse—he had scarcely dared to touch it after Patera's ghost had dropped it on the landing.

All were dead now, Pike, Blood, and the talus. The second and third by his own hand.

Would this Siyuf and her troopers never come? He searched the clouds beyond the airship for a glimpse of the sun. The dying Flier had said they were losing control. With what chains did one control the sun? With what tiller was it steered?

But no doubt the sun was merely masked by the threatening clouds; it would be childish to complain because winter had come at last when the calendar declared it half over.

Spring soon, unless this winter proved to be as protracted as the summer that had preceded it. If the rains failed then, so would he; if the new corn sprouted and died, Viron's new god-appointed caldé would surely die with it. He pictured himself and Hyacinth fleeing the city on fast horses, but Hyacinth was as lost as Maytera Mint, and he knew nothing about horses save that they might be offered to Pas without impropriety. This though Pas was dead.

Was Hyacinth dead as well? Silk shivered again.

A band struck up in the distance, and ever so faintly his ears caught the clear, brave voices of trumpets and the clatter of cavalry.

Someone, it might have been Oosik, said *"Ah!"* Silk felt himself smile, happy in the knowledge that he had not been alone in his misery and impatience. On his right Saba murmured, "I can identify the units as they approach, if you want, and tell you a little about their history."

He nodded. "Please do, General. I'd appreciate it very much." He was tempted to ask her about the Fliers, as commander of the airship, she might know something of interest—possibly even of value. But it would be the height of bad manners for him to display curiosity about anything other than the military might of Trivigaunte at this moment.

A young woman's dark face (after a brief uncertainty he recognized Horn's sweetheart, Nettle) appeared at the left side of the platform. Loudly enough for him to overhear, she asked, "Wouldn't you like to sit down, Your Cognizance? There's a man renting folding stools."

Quetzal beamed. "How kind you are, my daughter! No, I've got my baculus, so I'm better off than the others." (It was not entirely true; Oosik had his heavy sword in front of him and was leaning upon it as if it were a walking stick.) "Patera Caldé isn't as lucky," Quetzal continued. "Would you like this kind girl to rent you a stool, Patera Caldé?"

It would be unthinkable, of course, for him to sit while the Prolocutor stood. Silk said, "Thank you very much, Nettle. But no. It's not necessary."

"I've just decided," Quetzal told Nettle, "That though I wouldn't like *one* stool, I'd like *two*. One for me and one for Patera Caldé. Have you enough money for two?"

Nettle assured him she had, and disappeared in the crowd.

On Silk's right Saba muttered, "You men lack the stamina of women. It's biology and nothing to be ashamed of, but it shows why we make the best troopers." His cheeks burned; a subtle alteration in Quetzal's posture hinted that he too had heard, and was awaiting Silk's reply.

What would Quetzal himself have replied? Saba's remark

bordered on inexcusable arrogance, surely, and such arrogance was punished by the just gods—or so he had been taught in the schola. Reflecting, he decided it was one of the few things he had been taught that seemed undeniably true.

He smiled. "You're entirely correct, General, as always. No observer can help noticing that women endure far more than men, and with greater fortitude."

On Saba's right, Oosik muttered, "Our caldé has a broken ankle. Haven't you seen how he limps?"

"It had slipped my mind, Caldé." Saba sounded honestly contrite. "Please accept my apologies."

"You have nothing to apologize for, General. You stated an inarguable fact. Sphigx and Scylla might apologize for facts, I suppose—but a mortal?"

"Just the same, I—here they come."

The first riders, tall women on spirited horses, could be seen through the arch. Each bore a slender lance, and a yellow pennant stood out below the head of each lance. "The Companion Cavalry," Saba told Silk in a low voice. "All are wellborn, and in addition to their regular duties, they supply bodyguards to the Rani."

"I know nothing about these matters," Silk leaned toward her, "but wouldn't slug guns be more effective than lances?"

"You'll be able to see them better in a moment. They have slug guns in scabbards, left of their saddles. Their lances are used in a charge. You can't fire a slug gun with its muzzle at the horse's ears without panicking the horse."

Silk nodded, but could not help thinking that from the accounts he had been given, Maytera Mint and her volunteers had fired needlers when they charged the floaters in Cage Street. Presumably, the moderate crack of a needler did not disturb a horse like the boom of a slug gun. To him at least, it seemed that even a small needler like Hyacinth's, with a capacity of fifty or a hundred needles, would be a superior weapon.

Nettle reappeared, holding up folding stools with canvas seats. Quetzal accepted one, and Nettle went to the front of the platform to pass the other to Silk.

He took it and exhibited it to Saba. "Wouldn't you like this, General? You're welcome to it."

"Absolutely not!"

"We could sit alternately, if you like," Silk persevered. "You could rest a while, then return it to me."

She shook her head, her lips tight; and Silk put down the stool, empty, between them.

The Companions had ridden in threes and had appeared to be scanning the crowd; having kept a rough count, Silk felt sure there had been no more than two hundred. The troopers behind them bore no lances and were neither so regular in size nor so well mounted; but they rode ten abreast, led by an officer in a dusty old cloak on the finest horse that he had ever seen.

"Generalissimo Siyuf," Saba muttered. "She's related to the Rani on her father's side, as well as her mother's."

"Your supreme military commander."

Saba nodded. "A military genius."

Surveying that hawk-like profile, he decided it might well be true, and was certainly true enough to make Siyuf a valuable ally; genius or not, she radiated resolution and intelligence. He could not help wondering what she had been told about him, and what she thought of him now, the insecure young ruler of a foreign city; the urge to comb his untidy hair with his fingers, as he would have in a conversation with Quetzal, was practically irresistible. For half a second, his eyes locked with hers.

Then Saba saluted, and her salute was returned negligently by Siyuf; at once Oosik saluted her, in accord with the protocol agreed to Tarsday. Behind her, rank after rank of disciplined young women drew sabers and faced right, seemingly oblivious to the swirling dust and biting wind.

"Generalissimo Siyuf rides at the head of her own regiment. She joined eighteen years ago as a brevet lieutenant, and it's known now as the Generalissimo's Auxiliary Light Horse. . . ."

Saba fell silent; shivering, Silk murmured, "Yes?"

"Your people aren't cheering, Caldé. Not nearly enough. The Generalissimo won't be pleased."

He seized the opportunity. "Perhaps they're afraid they may panic your horses." It had been juvenile, but for a minute or more he enjoyed it.

A wide break in what had threatened to become an infinite succession of mounted troopers apparently marked the end of the Generalissimo's Auxiliary Light Horse. It was followed by the yellow, brown, and red flag of Trivigaunte, borne by an officer on horseback and escorted by an honor guard clearly drawn from the Companion Cavalry, and the banner by the band whose martial music had been the first indication that the Rani's troops were near. The musicians, marching with the precision of a picture in a drill book, were all men and all bearded; the onlookers' cheers increased noticeably as they passed.

"They're really very good," Silk told Saba, hoping to restore friendly relations. "Very skillful indeed, and our people seem to love their music."

"I'm an old campaigner, Caldé."

Privately wondering what the campaigns had been, and how Generalissimo Siyuf had revealed her military genius in them, Silk ventured, "So I understand."

"Your people are cheering because they're men. You think we keep our men chained in the cellar, but most of our support troops are men."

"With beards," Silk commented; it seemed safe.

"Exactly. You shave yours off to make yourself look more like a woman. I'm not criticizing you for it, in your position I'd do the same thing. But we don't let our men do it at home. They can trim their beards with scissors if they want to, and these support troops are required to. But they can't shave, or pull the hairs out."

Silk felt himself wince and hoped she had not noticed it.

"We've only let them use scissors for about twenty years," she continued. "When I was a lieutenant they couldn't, and you saw a good many with beards below their waists. We let them tuck them into their belts, and some people felt that was going too far. The idea is that a beard makes it easy to cut a man's throat. You grab it and jerk his head up."

"I see," Silk said. Mentally, he cancelled the beard he had only just resolved to grow.

"These are Princess Silah's Own Dragoons. You'll notice—"

Oosik interrupted. "I do not mean to begin an argument, General, but I question that it is actually done. If it is, it cannot be done often. Men are much stronger than women."

Saba indicated the mounted troopers passing before them. "Horses are stronger than women, Generalissimo."

Silk chuckled.

"Don't you believe me, Caldé?" Saba was holding back a smile. "It's true, I swear, in our city. We've been breeding chargers since Pas laid his first brick, and our horses are stronger than women and—"

"Wiser than men," Silk finished for her. "I don't doubt it for a moment."

"Who is?" inquired a new voice. "Everyone, I think."

Silk turned to look as Generalissimo Siyuf stepped onto the reviewing platform. "Here you are." He offered his hand. "I was afraid you'd be delayed. It's an honor to greet you at last, and a great pleasure. Welcome to Viron. I'm Caldé Silk."

She shook his hand awkwardly, unsmiling; her own was hard and dry, not quite as strong as he had anticipated. "It is my joy to see your lively city, Caldé Silk. Most of my life I have spend in the south. Your Viron is not more than a name on my maps, one week ago. My parade is bad, I know. When they must march they cannot be drilled. When they fight it is the same."

Silk assured her that he had been enormously impressed by what he had seen, and introduced her to Quetzal and Oosik.

"We will see your troops after mine," she told Oosik. "We pass them waiting. Ah, you have a stool for me, Caldé. Thank you." She seated herself between Silk and Saba. "This is most welcome. I have been up since three, in the saddle since five. I have tired two horses. I must have a fresh one for this."

"It was very good of you to join us after you'd marched,"

Silk told her sincerely. "We've all heard great things about you. We were anxious to meet you."

Siyuf's eyes were on her troops. "I do not come for you, Caldé Silk. I come for me. Soon we fight together. Is this right? Or does this mean you will fight me and I you?"

"No. That's perfectly correct. Together, we'll fight the Ayuntamiento, if we must. I'd much rather we didn't have to."

"And I. Both." Siyuf pulled her cap down and drew her streaked old cloak over her knees.

For a time, no one spoke. Silk pretended to watch the parade as cavalry gave way to infantry, attractive young women who saluted the reviewing platform by holding their slug guns vertically at their left shoulders and marching with a stiff stride that reminded him of sibyls dancing at a sacrifice.

Mostly, he studied Siyuf and reexamined her remarks, and his own. Her cap was clean and well-shaped, but by no means new, her cloak frankly soiled; no doubt she had changed horses as she had said, but she had not changed clothes. Her boots were slightly scuffed, her spurs (he risked a surreptitious glance at Saba's feet) markedly larger than her subordinate's.

She had not hesitated to claim the empty stool. Silk tried to put himself in the place of one of the expressionless women marching past. Would they feel ashamed of their Generalissimo? Would they think her weak?

Would he, if he were somehow a member of Siyuf's horde? After arguing the point with himself, he decided that he would not. Sitting when others had to stand was one of the surest signs of rank, and her clothes proclaimed that she need answer to no one, that no bullying sergeant or trumpeting colonel dared rebuke her. In imagination, Silk soared from the platform to a gondola of the airship, and from it scanned the parade. There was the reviewing platform, on it various dignitaries of Viron and Trivigaunte. Who was in charge? Who commanded the rest?

It was unquestionably Siyuf, who was seated with Quetzal and himself to her left and Saba and Oosik to her right—the civil authorities, religious and civic, on one side in other words; and the military, Trivigaunti and Vironese, on the other. When Viron's own troopers marched past, they would receive the same impression.

"Is it always so cold here in the north?" Siyuf pulled her cloak more tightly about her.

"No," Silk told her. "We had a very long summer this year, and a very warm one."

"I wish we have come to your city then, Caldé. When I was small my teachers told me this north was cold. I learn to write it on examinations, but I do not believe. Why should it be so?"

"I have no idea." Silk considered. "I learned it just as you did, and I don't believe I ever thought of questioning it. To tell you the truth, I accepted just about everything I was taught, including many things I ought to have questioned."

"The sun," Siyuf pointed up without looking upward. "This begin at the east and end at the west. That is only because we say it so, I know. Here you may speak different. But from East Pole to West Pole or West Pole to East. Your day in Viron is soon our day in Trivigaunte. Is that true?"

"Yes," Silk said. "Of course."

"Then what do you do to make your day so cold?"

Saba laughed, and Silk and Oosik joined her.

Quetzal seemed not to have heard, contemplating the ranked women passing before him through half-closed eyes. Studying him sidelong, Silk sensed a need, a longing, that he himself did not feel, and puzzled over it until he recalled that Saba had said that sacrifices were not offered in her city. The Chapter would be different there, quite possibly known by another name; each of the marching women was, in that case, a potential convert to Viron's more dignified mode of worship. No wonder then that Quetzal eyed them so hungrily. To amend the religious thinking of even a few would be a signal accomplishment and a glorious conclusion to his long, meritorious career. Furthermore, there were thousands and thousands of them, the vast majority still young, still malleable, as Saba for example was not.

As if the comparison had stirred her to speech, Saba asked, "What do you think, Generalissimo? A fine body of women?"

Oosik declared that he had been favorably impressed.

"How old are they?" Silk inquired suddenly; he had not intended to speak.

"We take them at seventeen," Saba told him. "There's a year of training before they're assigned to permanent units. After that we keep them four years."

"Do you mean that they have to become troopers? What if one doesn't want to?"

Saba pointed. "See that one with the big feet? And her over there, the tall one with a stripe?"

"At the end of the line? Yes, I see her."

Saba pointed again. "There, that little fat one. None of them wanted to."

"I see. I'm surprised you know these troopers so well, General. Is this group a part of your airship's crew?"

"No, Caldé." Saba glanced across Siyuf's head with the suppressed smile he had noticed earlier. "In weather like this we need everybody on board. I picked them by chance, but that's the truth about them. Who'd want to be a trooper?"

Silk glanced at Oosik, who was looking at him; troopers in Viron served voluntarily.

Another band, then hundreds of saddleless horses herded by mounted men. Seeing Silk's puzzled expression, Saba explained, "They're remounts. When a trooper's horse is shot, she has to fight on foot unless there's a remount for her."

Siyuf looked up at him. "Do you not have remounts for your own cavalry?" He found her steady eyes disconcerting.

Oosik said quickly, "Our practice is to issue two horses to each mounted trooper. He is responsible for their care, and is to ride them alternately unless one goes lame. In peacetime he rides one on one day and the other on the next."

"You, Generalissimo. Were you a horse officer? We say cavalrywoman, but I do not think you will say that here. A cavalryman, I think?"

Oosik made her a small bow. "Correct, Generalissimo. No, I was not, nor are most of our officers. We have only one mounted company per brigade, though the second has two at present. My son is a cavalryman, however."

For the first time, Siyuf smiled; seeing it, Silk could readily imagine her subordinates risking their lives to earn that smile. She said, "I hope to meet him. Tomorrow or the day after. We shall speak of horses."

"He will be honored, Generalissimo. Unfortunately he is unwell at present."

"I see." She turned back to the parade, and her voice became indifferent. "It is sad that boys must fight here."

Mules hauling cannon followed the horse herd. "I expected camels," Silk told her.

"Horses and camels do not make friends," she said absently. "It is best we hold them apart. Mules are more . . ." She snapped her fingers.

"Easygoing," Saba supplied. "They don't mind camels as much as most horses do."

"Does it really take eight to pull one of these big guns?"

"On your street of fine stones? No. But over our desert where is no road, many more sometimes. Then one must lend to another its mules and wait. I have seen sixteen unable to pull a single howitzer from the mud. That was not on this march, or we would not be here."

Saba asked, "Didn't you notice the mixed gun crews, Caldé? I expected you to ask about them."

Already the last cannon was rumbling past. After it came a long triple line of small carts with male drivers; each cart was drawn by a pair of mules.

Silk said, "I'm accustomed to working with women, General. With Maytera Marble and Maytera Mint at my manteion, before I became caldé—with Maytera Rose as well until she left us. Your mixed crews seem more normal to me than," he groped for an inoffensive phrase, ending lamely, "than the other thing, just women or just men."

"Men drive the mules and hump shells. They do those almost as well as women could. Women lay the guns and fire them."

Siyuf asked, "Where is General Mint? Did you not call her Mother Mint just now? Or are there two of this name?"

"No, they're the same person. She's a sibyl as well as a general, just as I'm an augur as well as caldé." Silk was tempted to add that he hoped to drop the first soon.

"She marches with her troops today?"

"I'm afraid not." A bare-faced lie would serve best, but he was unwilling to provide one. "We're still engaged with the enemy, Generalissimo."

If Siyuf suspected, nothing in her face revealed it. "I am sorry I do not meet her. Next you see camels."

Silk, who had seen camels singly or in small caravans of a dozen or a score, had scarcely imagined that there were so many in the whorl—not hundreds but thousands, innumerable camels tied one behind another in strings of thirty or more, each such string led by a single camel-driver riding its big lead camel. They grunted continually as they walked, peering at everything with haughty eyes in faces that recalled Remora's.

"They carried food, mostly," Saba explained, "and oats and barley for the horses and mules. They're lightly loaded now."

Here was one of the most sensitive points. "You have to realize there's very little food in Viron." Silk picked his way among snares. "We're delighted to have you, and we'll do our best to feed you and your troops; but the harvest was bad, and our farmers have been hoarding food because of the fighting."

"We know your difficulties." Siyuf's dust-colored cap and hunched shoulders spoke. "We will send out foraging parties."

"Thank you," Silk said. "That's extremely kind of you."

Oosik stared.

"Which reminds me," Silk hurried on, "I've planned a small, informal dinner tonight at the Caldé's Palace." (He found he could not bring himself to say, *"At my palace."*) "You're all invited, and I hope that all of you can attend. We haven't got a real kitchen yet, but I've arranged to have Ermine's cater our dinner; Ermine's serves the best food in our city, or at least it has that reputation."

"I must bring with me a staff officer." Siyuf turned to face him. "This our custom demands. May I do this?"

"Of course. She will be very welcome."

"Then I come. Saba also, if you wish it."

"I certainly do," Silk assured Siyuf.

Saba nodded reluctantly.

Oosik said, "You may rely upon me, Caldé."

"Thank you. And you, Your Cognizance?"

With the help of the baculus, Quetzal rose. "I've no food, Patera Caldé. That's what you'll talk about, isn't it?"

"I'm sure we will; we have that to discuss, along with many other things. You have wisdom, Your Cognizance, and we may need it more than food."

"Then I'll be there. I may even have suggestions."

Chapter 5

THE MAN FROM MAINFRAME

A hand signal held the group parallel to the human stream below; Sciathan reinforced it with helmet notification: "Two east." As each agreed, he checked them off mentally: Grian, Sumaire, Mear, and Aer were still willing to accept his leadership. His right arm stiff, he slapped toward Viron's thatch and shingles, palm down. "Going lower." Fingertips to forehead. "You may follow if you choose."

Aer almost certainly would.

Was this man Auk among the marchers' creeping rectangles? One of the spectators whose cheers had dwindled to chirps in the vastness of the sky? Either way this Auk was a lone individual, his fellow citizens a myriad of myriads. As he had from the beginning, Sciathan told himself that he should be bursting with pride; for this daunting, almost impossible mission, Mainframe had chosen them.

The possibility that Mainframe wished to destroy them had to be dismissed unheard, like the equal possibility that he, Aer, and the rest had been chosen because they were expendable.

Right arm pointing, hand cupped. "I fly east."

Four acknowledgments. They were all coming.

He had begun a circuit of the city. They would have to land soon, have to remove and secure their wings, question and persuade its inhabitants in the Common Tongue. Whether he was a miracle worker or a malcontent, his fluency had no doubt been a factor.

Where was there a good, big field, with people near but not too near, close to the city? Below him, a house with a desert-colored peaked roof sprang up like a mushroom.

Right arm extended, palm flat, motioning down. "Lower."

It seemed that he could read the character of each of his companions in their acknowledgments: Grian weighing the odds; Sumaire narrow-eyed, her hands deadly still; Mear frantic for adventure; Aer concerned for everybody except herself.

At this altitude they were within the reach of small-arms fire, and small arms were evident; all the overseers of the bearded men erecting tents seemed to have them. He reminded himself that once they had landed the presence or absence of weapons would make no difference, that any mob of Cargos could kill them with stones or sticks. In fact the weapons that these Cargos had should be an advantage; armed, they would be less apt to feel threatened.

Pointing arm, hand a fist. "North." Two fingers down, separated. "Terminate flight."

"Aye, Sumaire." Taut face, dry lips, hooded eyes.

"Aye, Mear!" Descending too fast and glorying in it.

"Aye, Grian." Picking his spot.

"Aye, Aer." Worrying about him, worried not that he would crash but that he would bungle his approach.

Grassy land, a little uneven. No more time for character or planning. Reverse thrust, legs down and feet together, hands braced for a fall that must be straight forward.

Mear was already down, having pulled up at the precise moment and landed striding; reckless though Mear was, no more skilled Flier ever tuned the sun. Now he, too, would have to land without a fall or lose what authority he had. Four cubits, stall, drop into the wind. Did it!

At once a gust nearly blew him off his feet.

Grian, Sumaire and Aer came down as he was taking off his wings and PM, Aer too close, perhaps; Sumaire four-pointing; Grian dropping a full eight, wings bow-bent when he hit.

Big women were running toward them from the tent ground, pursued, overtaken, and surpassed by a lone woman on horseback.

"Peace!" He raised both hands, palms out. "We who serve the gods mean no harm."

The rider reined up, a handweapon drawn. "There are no gods but the goddess!"

Could the database be wrong? "We are her supporters and servitors!"

A dozen towering women surrounded them, some staring, some leveling short, gap-mouthed guns, some clearly waiting for the mounted woman's instructions.

"We come from Mainframe," Sciathan explained. "Mainframe, the home of the goddess. At her order we come to find Auk." Privately he wondered which goddess it was.

"We'll help you, but first you must give your weapons to us." There was calculation in the mounted woman's eyes.

Aer said, "No gun, no knife."

The mounted woman's attention went to her at once. "You're in charge?"

Aer shook her head. "Fliers." She touched her chin. "Aer I am. All fly."

Mear joined them carrying his wings and PM, and accompanied by a gaggle of big women. "Each is one. Five ones."

"Surrender your weapons," the woman on horseback told him.

Coming up behind Mear, Sumaire held out her hands. "Mine. With these I kill."

Calculation again. "You're the leader."

"Yes. My own."

Mear said, "I am mine. No weapon. No gun. You give?" One of the big women laughed loudly and the horse shied, neck bent and hooves dancing.

"Quiet, you!" Pulling up the reins, the mounted woman scrutinized them. *"Marhaba! Betifham 'arabi?"*

Aer and Mear looked to Sciathan; he could only shrug.

She holstered her weapon and dismounted; her smile could not vanquish something vindictive that had made her face its own. "We started badly," she told Aer. "Let's start over and be friends. I'm Major Sirka, Flier Aer. I command the advance party of the Horde of Trivigaunte. I can't welcome you to this city, because this city's not mine. Mine's to the south. You have flown over it many times. You must know it."

Aer nodded and smiled. "Beautiful!"

"This man," Major Sirka nodded at Sciathan, "came looking for a Vironese, another man. Are you looking for a woman?"

Sumaire said, "The man. Where will we find Auk?"

Grian, who arrived still wearing his PM, said slowly, "We are not like you are, Woman."

"I wouldn't expect you to be, little man. Now listen to me. You're . . ."

Her voice faded; she had become a painted figure, an image of gray on a featureless plain. Sciathan felt his lips drawn back and lifted in a grin by someone else.

Aer gaped at him, eyes wide as her mouth. Now, when all other color had fled, the blue of her eyes was still bright. Someone else reached out to her with Sciathan's arms, and in a distant place she screamed.

The flash and boom of the shot so startled him that almost he woke; colors were briefly real, the scarlet-daubed thing at his feet Aer. He felt himself thrust violently down and back into a helpless dark at the edge of oblivion.

Sumaire slew with a touch and Mear fought with desperate valor until more shots threw both to the ground in their first embrace. Still carrying his wings, Grian shot straight up. He, Sciathan, should fly too; but his PM was gone, his hands bound. Turning, he saw his wings and kicked and stamped them.

"Let me think, Patera." Maytera Marble cocked her head to one side. "The generalissimo from Trivigaunte and another one, but we don't know her name. I'm assuming it will be a woman."

Silk nodded. "I believe we can rely on it."

"We don't know how much either one eats. Probably a lot. Then there's General Saba and Generalissimo Oosik. I've seen them, and they'll want a whorl of food. Are each of them going to bring somebody, too?"

"That's a good point." Silk considered. "Oosik's almost certain to, because Siyuf said she'd bring one of her staff. Let's assume that they both do. That's six so far."

"All big eaters."

"I'm sure you're right, but His Cognizance and I won't eat much and you'll eat nothing."

"Am I invited?" It was difficult to read Maytera Marble's expression.

"Of course you are. You're the hostess, the mistress of the house—of this palace, I should have said."

"I thought Chenille might do it, Patera."

"She's a guest." Silk settled himself more comfortably in the big wingback chair, conscious that he would have to leave it soon. "She's here only because she may be in danger."

"She's a real help, that girl. She does everything I tell her to and looks for more. There are times when I have to hold her back, Patera."

"Now I understand. You were afraid I wouldn't invite her, that I'd ask her to wait on table or something. She's invited— or she will be as soon as I see her. I want her, and your grand-daughter and Master Xiphias; I sent Horn to tell him."

"I teach arithmetic." Maytera Marble sighed. "And now I want to count on my fingers. What's worse, I can't. Only up to five, and we had six with Generalissimo Oosik and all those foreign officers. You and His Cognizance make eight. The old fencing master nine. Chenille, ten. Mucor and me, twelve. If you're going to invite anybody else, you'd better make it two, Patera. Thirteen at table's not lucky. I don't know why, but you're supposed to bring somebody in off the street if you have to, to make fourteen."

Silk stood up. "No, that should be all. Now come with me.

I asked Hossaan to bring the floater, and I think I heard it a moment ago."

"Where . . . ? I can't go away, Patera. Not with company for dinner tonight."

Silk had anticipated that; he imagined himself arguing with Siyuf and was firm. "Of course you can. You're going to. Go get your hand."

"No. No." Maytera Marble's one functioning hand gripped the arm of her chair so tightly that the upholstery rose like dough between its metal fingers. "You don't understand. You're a good man. Too good, to tell the truth. Too good to me, as you always have been. But I've a thousand things to do between now and dinner. What time will it be? Six?"

"Eight. I do understand, Maytera, and that's why we're going to that shop the valet—what was his name?"

"Marl. Patera, I can't."

"Exactly. You can't because you have only one hand. You have to tell Chenille, for the most part, and get her to do it. So we're going to get your right hand reattached. As you say, there's a lot to be done, and with two hands you'll be able to do twice as much as Chenille, instead of half as much."

Without waiting for her to reply, he strode to the door. "I'll be outside; I want to ask Hossaan why their generalissimo speaks the way she does. We'll expect you in five minutes, with your hand." As he stepped into the reception hall, he added, "You and Chenille, and your granddaughter. Bring her, too."

Maytera Marble's last wailing *"Patera . . ."* was cut off by the closing of the door. Grinning, Silk limped the length of the reception hall and got an overrobe of plain black fleece from the cloakroom off the foyer.

The outer door swung toward him before he could open it, and Hossaan stepped inside with Oreb perched on his shoulder. "Your bird was out there, Caldé. I guess he couldn't find a window open, so I brought him in."

"Girls fly," Oreb croaked, fluttering. "Bird see."

"Yes, and just in time, silly bird. Come here."

Oreb hopped to Silk's wrist. "Men perch!"

"He's been flying up to the airship," Silk explained. "By now he probably understands it a great deal better than I do. They lower people from it in a thing like an oversized bird-cage, and bring people and supplies up; that seems to interest him." He hesitated, then waved toward a long divan. "Let's sit down for a moment. There's something I want to ask you."

"Sure thing, Caldé."

"We could do this in your floater, but I have the feeling there'd be somebody wanting to talk to me, and I don't want to be interrupted. Did you see the parade?"

Hossaan nodded. "I was keeping an eye on you up on that stand, Caldé, in case you wanted me."

"Good. Then you saw me talking to Generalissimo Siyuf and General Saba. Do you know either of them, by the way?"

"Personally, you mean, Caldé? No, I don't. I know what they look like."

"You haven't spoken to them."

Hossaan shook his head.

"But you've traveled. You're from Trivigaunte originally?"

"Yes, Caldé. I was born there. You'd be a fool to take anything I tell you at face value. You realize that, I'm sure."

"Good man!" Oreb defended him. "Men fly. Perch!"

"Of course. I understand that your primary loyalty must be to your native city."

"It is. And you're right, I've traveled more than most men ever do. I can tell you about some of the places I've been, if you like, but I can't always tell you what I was doing there."

Silk nodded thoughtfully. "Here in Viron, we sometimes say that someone speaks Vironese, as if it were a separate language. It isn't, of course. It's just that we have certain idiomatic expressions that aren't used, as far as I know, in other cities. There are words we pronounce differently as well. I know very little about other cities, but I wouldn't be surprised to learn that they have peculiarities of their own."

"That's right. I think I know what you're going to ask me, but go on."

"Is there any reason you shouldn't tell me about it?"

"Not a one."

"All right. I was going to say that there actually are other languages, languages quite different from ours. Latin, for example, and French. We have French and Latin books, and there are passages in the Writings in those languages, which makes them of interest to scholars and even to ordinary augurs like me. Presumably there are cities in which those languages are spoken just as we speak Vironese here."

"The Common Tongue," Hossaan said. "That's what travelers generally call it, and it's what we call it in Trivigaunte."

"I see." Silk's forefinger traced small circles on his cheek. "In that case you, from your foreign perspective, would say that both Viron and Palustria, for instance, speak the Common Tongue? Palustrian is similar enough to Vironese that one might have to listen to a speaker for several minutes to determine his native city. Or so I was taught at the schola."

"You've got it, Caldé."

"Very well then. I can imagine a foreign city in which another language is spoken, Latin let us say. And I can easily imagine one like Palustria, where the Common Tongue is spoken; I can't prove it, but I suspect that there may be more differences between the speech of a Vironese of the upper class and a beggar or a bricklayer than there are between an ordinary merchant from Viron and a like merchant from Palustria. What I cannot imagine is a city in which some citizens speak the Common Tongue, as you call it, and others Latin or another language."

Hossaan nodded, but said nothing.

"Men fly!" Oreb announced, having lost patience with his owner. He launched himself from Silk's shoulder and flapped around the room spiraling higher. "Fly! Fly! Girls! Men!" He extended his wings in a long glide. "Perch!"

"Great Pas guide us!" Maytera Marble was coming down the staircase with Chenille and Mucor. "What's gotten into your bird, Patera?"

"I don't know," said Silk—who thought, however, that he did. "Hossaan, he came to you while you were waiting in the floater, is that right?"

"He landed on the back of the seat, Caldé, and started talking. I couldn't understand him at first."

"Yet another language, or at least another way of speaking the Common Tongue." Silk smiled wryly. "What did he say?"

" 'Bird out, bird out, Silk in.' Like that, Caldé."

Silk nodded. "Go out and wait for us. Put the canopy up. I don't know how long the wait will be, and there's no point in your freezing."

As Hossaan left, Chenille asked, "Aren't we going, Patera?"

"In a moment. Step into the library, please, everybody. Oreb, where are the flying men and flying girls who perched?"

Oreb hopped to a corner occupied by a fat-bellied vase and rapped it sharply with his beak.

"Northeast, Mucor," Silk muttered. "Did you see that?"

Her skull-like face turned toward him as a pale funeral lily lifts its blossom to the sun. "Flying, Silk?"

"Fliers, I believe. The people who fly on wings made of something that looks like gauze."

Chenille added, "Like the Trivigaunti pterotroopers, only their wings are longer and look like they'd be lighter."

The night chough flew to Silk's shoulder.

"One more question, Oreb. Were there houses where the flying people landed?"

"House now! Quick house!"

Silk took a handkerchief from his pocket, shook it out, and draped it over his spread fingers. "Like this?"

"Yes, yes!"

"Sit down, please," Silk told the three women. "Mucor, as a great favor to me, and your grandmother, too, do you think you could find out what these Fliers are doing?"

When she did not answer, he said, "Search the grazing land north and east of the city, where the Rani's men are putting up their tents. I believe that may be what he means when he says quick houses. The Fliers will have taken off their wings when they landed, I imagine, and they'll probably leave at least one of their number to guard them."

"As Patera says, this is for both of us, Mucor." Maytera Marble patted her knee. "I don't know why it's important, but I'm sure it must be."

Chenille remarked, "You know, I've been wanting to have a look at this ever since that Trivigaunti saw her in the mirror, only now I can't even tell if she's doing it. You ought to be chanting and sprinkling perfume on Thelxiepeia's picture."

"The miracle—or magic, if that's what you wish to call it—is in Mucor," Silk told her.

"Auk believes in the gods, Patera. He's really religious in his way, and he knows I had Scylla inside running things. But what I'm seeing wouldn't make him believe in this."

"Auk," Mucor repeated suddenly.

Oreb cocked his head like Maytera Marble. "Where Auk?"

Mucor's toneless voice seemed to emanate from a forsaken place beyond the universe. "Where Auk is . . . Silk? Chain my hands. Feet smash strong wings."

Chapter 6

IN SPIDER'S WEB

"Are we truly, um, abandoned, Maytera? Solitary? Or are there other ears, eh? In this dark and—er—noisome. That's the question, hum?"

"I don't know. I have no way of telling. Do you?" The question Maytera Mint herself was debating was whether it would be disrespectful to lie down before Remora did.

"I—ah—no. I have none, I confess."

"Do you have a secret that would let Potto and the other councillors return to power in defiance of the gods?"

"I would—um—General. Be safer not, eh? Not to speak upon such, er, topics."

"It certainly would if you had one, Your Eminence. Do you?" She was trying to forget how thirsty she was.

"Positively not. Not privy to military matters, eh?"

"Neither do I, Your Eminence, so let them listen all they want." It was ecstasy to take her shoes off; for half a minute she debated taking off her long black stockings, too, but self-control prevailed. "By now Bison's taken charge. Or someone else has, but probably it's Bison. He was my best officer, absolutely steady in a crisis but not very imaginative. If he can find somebody a little more creative to advise him, Bison should give the Ayuntamiento a very difficult time."

"I am, er, suffused with pleasure at the prospect."

"So am I, Your Eminence. I just hope it's true." She leaned back against the wall.

"You will, um, reproach me."

"Never, Your Eminence."

"You, or others. One never lacks for, um, critics? Patera Feelers. Faultfinders. You will—um—er—vociferate that as a, um, intermediary I must restrain my partisanship."

She laid her arms on her knees, and her head upon her arms.

"I rejoin, General, by, er, asseverating that I have done so. And do so, eh? In our, um, current instance and beyond, hey? It is not partisanship but reason, hey? I am a man of peace. I have so, um, declared myself. Under flag of truce, eh? Having consulted Brigadier Erne. Having likewise consulted Caldé Silk. Brought the, um, exceedingly significant—hum. You, General. I brought you to discuss, er, armistice. An—ah—feat of diplomacy? Triumph. Is my, er, our persons. Are they respected? They are not!"

"I'm going to stretch out, if that won't upset you, Your Eminence. I'll tuck my skirt around my legs."

"No, no, Mayt—General. I can scarcely make out your, ah, self in this—er—stygian. There is one quarrel that cannot be mediated, hey?"

"We certainly haven't succeeded in mediating this one."

"I refer to the quarrel between good and, um, evil. Yes, evil. As a man of the cloth, an augur erstwhile destined, eh? Destined for—ah—greatness. As that, um, augur, fallible, eh? At whiles foolish, eh? Yet sensible of the ultimate, hey? I cannot mediate all quarrels, for I cannot mediate that one. I have set down my name in the lists, eh? Long since. I am for good. I cannot close my eyes to evil. Will not. Both."

"That's good." Maytera Mint closed hers. The only light in the dark, bare room was a long streak of watery green under the door; closing her eyes should have made little difference, yet she found it deeply restful.

"If—er—ah—um—hum," Remora said; or at least, so she heard him. The façade of the Corn Exchange was falling very slowly, while she waited powerless to move.

She woke with a start. "Your Eminence?"

"Yes, General?"

"Some dreams are sent by the gods."

"Ah—indubitably."

"Has anyone ever proposed that all dreams are? That every dream is a message from the gods?"

"I—um. Cannot recollect, eh? I shall devote thought to the, er, query. Possibly. Quite possibly."

"Because I just had a very commonplace sort of dream, Your Eminence, but I feel that it may have been sent by a god."

"Unusual? Extraordinary. If I do not presume, hey? No wish to, er, intrude. But I offer my, um, if desired."

"I dreamed I was standing on the street in front of the Corn Exchange. It was falling on me, but I couldn't run."

"I—ah—see."

"It actually happened a few days ago. We pulled it down with oxen. I could've run then, but I didn't want to. I wanted to die, so I stood there and watched it fall until Rook carried me out of danger. He was nearly killed, as well as I."

"The—ah—import? I fail to see it, General."

"A god, I think, was telling me that since I'd chosen to die then, I shouldn't be afraid of dying now, that nothing they can do to me could be worse than being crushed by that building, which was the way I'd chosen to die not long ago."

"What god, hey? What god, General? Have you any notion?"

She knew from an alteration in Remora's voice that he had straightened up. She had, temporarily at least, ransomed him from self-pity; she wished fervently that someone would ransom her. "I haven't the least idea which god may have favored me, Your Eminence, assuming one did. I don't recall anything that would furnish a clue."

"No animals, eh?"

"None, Your Eminence. Just the street, and the falling stones. It was after shadelow, and all I remember is how dark they looked against the skylands."

"Not, um, Day-Ruling Pas. Sun god, eh? Master of the Long Sun and all that. Tartaros, hum? Night god. Dark stones, dark god. Bats—ah—flittering?"

Maytera Mint rolled her head so that the tip of her sharp little nose made a small arc of negation. "No animals, Your Eminence, as I said. None whatsoever."

"I shall—ah—prefer. I prefer to, um, suspend? No, table. Table the question, eh? If only for the nonce. In my, er, not inconsiderable experience an, um, signature may be—ah—described by one who, eh? Shall peer about. Let us peer about, Maytera. What day is this, would you say?"

"Now?"

"Ah—yes. And then, eh? What day did you feel it to be in your, um, envisagement?"

"If you mean the night it happened . . . ?"

"No. Did it, ah, seem to you a particular day, eh? Were you, um, conscious of a—ah—the calendar?"

"No, Your Eminence."

"What day is it now? As we, ah, converse."

How many times had their captors halted to eat and sleep? Three? Four? "I can't be sure." Maytera Mint was beginning to regret mentioning her dream; she let her eyelids fall.

"Guess, General. What day?"

"Hieraxday or Thelxday, I suppose."

"Bodies, eh? Vultures?"

"No. Just the skylands, the building and the stones."

"Mirrors, monkeys, deer? Cards, teacups—ah—string? Any colored string? Poultry, nothing of the sort?"

"No, Your Eminence. Nothing of the sort."

"Space—um—largeness? Skylands, eh? You were—ah—not insensible of them?"

"I knew that they were there, Your Eminence. In fact they seemed significant, though I can't say how."

"We, er, progress? Yes, progress. Actually happened, you said? Building fell, eh? You rescued."

"Yes, it was at the beginning of the fighting. I mean to say, Your Eminence, that it was at what we call the beginning now. At the time we felt we'd been fighting a long while, that those of us who'd been fighting from the start had done a great deal of it." Maytera Mint paused, reflecting.

"We were like children who have gone to palaestra for the first time the year before. When the next year starts, children like that feel themselves old hands, veterans. They give advice to the new children and patronize them, when the truth is that their own education has scarcely begun."

Remora grunted assent. "I have observed, um, similar."

"And now—I mean before we went out to that house where the caldé was rescued. Things had quieted down. We had the Fourth penned up, and nobody wanted to go after it right away. We sensed that Erne was wavering, and you confirmed it. The Ayuntamiento was down in these tunnels, and those of us who thought about it saw how difficult it would be to root them out. We dared hope that some other way could be found. That was why I went out there with you."

She waited for Remora to speak, but he did not.

"People came forward. They would appear, so to speak, to tell us how bravely they'd fought and all they'd done. And I'd think, who are you? Why didn't I ever notice you before, if you were such a famous fighter? Bison had done everything, taken part in almost every fight.

"And Wool, I'd think. Wool has done a great deal, never shirked, not always saying I'll do it, General, like Bison, but when we were repulsed and I'd look back and see one person still there, still shooting when the rest had fallen back and there were hoppies—Guardsmen, Your Eminence, troopers of the Civil Guard—close enough to touch, it would be Wool.

"Then I'd remember that Wool was dead, and think where were the ones who rode with me, where was Kingcup who brought us her horses when her horses were all she had? I hope she's alive, Your Eminence, but I couldn't locate her, couldn't find her, and all these new people telling about the wonderful things they'd done, when I didn't remember them at all. Skink led an attack on the Palatine and had both his legs blown off. Where was he? Where was the giant with the gaps in his teeth? I don't even remember his name, but I remember looking up at them, he must have been twice my height, and wondering who had been big enough to hit him way up there, and what he'd hit him with, and what had happened after he did it."

"What was his name?"

"The giant, Your Eminence? I can't recall it. Cat? Or Tomcat, something like that. No, Gib. That was it. Gib. It means a male cat, Your Eminence, so that would make it Snarling Sphigx, the Patroness of Trivigaunte. Cats are hers, cats and lions. But Gib wasn't in my dream."

"The man who saved you."

"Oh, him. It was Rook, but rooks aren't sacred to any god, are they, Your Eminence? Eagles for Pas. Hawks, too, because hawks are little eagles, or something like them. Thrushes and larks for Molpe, but rooks can't sing. Poultry for Thelxiepeia, as Your Eminence said a moment ago, but rooks—wait.

"I've got it, Your Eminence. I was thinking lists, wasn't I? Thinking about lists instead of animals and what they look like. And a rook looks like a night chough, like the caldé's pet. The caldé got him to give to the god who enlightened him. People think it was Pas, almost everyone seems to think that, but I asked the caldé about it and he said it wasn't, that it was one of the minor gods, the Outsider. I don't know much about him, Your Eminence. I'm sure you must know much more than I, but night choughs must be sacred to him. Or if they aren't, they're associated with him now, because that was the sacrifice the caldé chose. Isn't that correct, Your Eminence?"

Remora did not reply.

Maytera Mint thought of getting up to see whether he had gone. It seemed to her that she had slept even as she spoke aloud; but it was too delicious, far too delicious to lie where she was, with Bison in the other bed snoring softly and Auk to watch over them. "Auk?" she called softly. "Auk?"

Auk would bring them water, would surely bring water if

she asked for it, a carafe of cold clear water, fresh from the well, and glasses. More loudly this time: "Auk!"

Yeah, Mother. Right here.

"Auk, my son?"

"Sorry Patera." Shivering in the afternoon sunlight, Auk returned his attention to Incus. "Thought I heard something."

"You desired to speak with me?"

"Right. Back in the manteion you explained what he said." Auk felt uneasy among the Palatine's gracious mansions of gray stone; until now he had visited them only to steal.

"I *endeavored* to explain, certainly. It was my *sacred duty* to do so, thus I *strove* to make clear the *divine utterances.* "

"You were clear as polymer, Patera," Hammerstone declared loyally. "I felt like I could understand every word Pas ever said before you finished."

Voices called for them to halt, and they did.

"Bios with slug guns, Patera. I heard them behind us, but I was hoping they wouldn't mess around."

Afraid he was about to be arrested, Auk grumbled, "Can't a man walk uphill any more?"

By then the patrol leader had noted Incus's black robe. "Sorry, Patera. It's the soldier. They say some are on our side. Is he one?"

Hammerstone nodded. "You got it."

"Indeed, my son." Incus favored the patrol with a toothy smile. "You have my *sacred word* as an augur and your— well, let us not go into *that.* You have my *sacred word* that Corporal *Hammerstone* longs for the overthrow of the Ayuntamiento, even as I do myself."

"I'm Sergeant Linsang," the patrol leader said. "Are you going to the Grand Manteion, Patera?"

Incus shook his head. "To the *Prolocutor's Palace,* my son. I am a resident *thereof.* " His voice grew confidential. "I have been favored with a *theophany. Great Pas himself* so favored *me.* It is not the first, but the *second* time that I have been thus *favored* by the gods. You will *scarcely* credit it, I know, for I scarcely credit it *myself.* But *both* my companions were present upon the *latter* occasion. They will *attest* to the *theophany,* I feel quite *certain."*

One of Linsang's troopers raised his slug gun so that it no longer pointed at Auk. "Aren't you Auk? Auk the prophet?"

"That's me."

"He's been going all over the city," the trooper explained to Linsang, "Telling everybody to get ready for Pas's Plan. He says Tartaros told him to."

"He did," Auk declared stoutly. "Pas wants me to keep on doing it, too. What about you, trooper? Are you set to go? Set to give up on the whole whorl?"

Linsang asked, "What did Pas say? That is if I'm not—"

"It is *irregular,"* Incus conceded, "but not *contrary* to the *canon.* Do all of you *desire* to hear the words of the *Father of the Gods?"*

Several assured him that they did.

"And *will* you," Incus pursued his advantage, "permit us to *proceed* upon our *sacred errand* once you have *heard them?"*

Linsang's troopers nodded. They were in their teens, and identifiable as troopers only by their slug guns and bandoliers.

Linsang objected. "I need to get it from this soldier, first. Hammerstone? Is that your name, Corporal?"

"Present and accounted for." Hammerstone's own slug gun was pointed at the skylands, its butt on his hip.

"Are you for the Ayuntamiento or the caldé?"

"The caldé, Sergeant."

"How do you feel about the Ayuntamiento?"

"If the caldé or Patera here said not to shoot them, I wouldn't do it. If it's up to me, they're dead meat."

One of the troopers ventured, "A soldier killed Councillor Potto. That's what we heard."

Hammerstone grinned, his head back and his chin out. "It wasn't me, but I'll shake his hand first chance I get."

"All right." Linsang grounded his slug gun. "You can go on to the Prolocutor's Palace, Patera. Them, too. Only tell us what Pas had to say."

"I fear *not."* Incus shook his head. "You would not *accept* my *sacred word,* my son, but *insisted* that Hammerstone speak for *himself.* As it chanced, though nothing is mere *chance* to the *immortal gods,* but a moment previously he had *declared* that he *comprehends* the god's entire *message,* while my other companion, *Auk,* wished a fuller *exposition."*

Incus turned to the prophet in question. "Is that not *so,* Auk? Am I not *correct?"*

"You got it, Patera. Maybe I'm dumb. There's not many that said so where I could hear 'em, but maybe I am. Only this is important, and some was about me. I got to be sure I got it straight, so I can do what he wants me to."

"Would that such *stupidity* as yours were more *widespread.* The *Chrasmologic Writings* assert that the *wisdom* of the *immortal gods* is but *folly* in the ears of *mortal men. Persevere* in your *stupidity,* and you will be welcomed to *Mainframe."* Incus nodded to the big soldier. "Tell us, *Hammerstone,* my son, and do not fear that you may *blunder* or omit a *sacred* injunction. I shall *amend* any such *innocent errors,* though I *anticipate* none."

"I can't do it as good as you, Patera, but I'll give it my best shot. Let me get my thinking works going." For eight or ten seconds, Hammerstone was as immobile as a statue.

"All right, I got it. It was when that bio was bringing up the pig. First the colors came on, right? Then his face. He started off by blessing everybody and said that everybody that was there 'cause they came with Auk—that was everybody but you, Patera—he blessed twice, once for coming and once for following Auk. Have I got that right?"

Incus nodded. *"Admirable,* Hammerstone, my son."

"Then he said he was giving us this theophany 'cause his son told him what was coming down in the manteion we were at, only he didn't say which son it was."

"Terrible Tartaros," Auk assured him.

Incus raised an admonitory finger. "He did not *so state."*

"Maybe not, but I'd just been talking to him. That's who it had to be."

"He said his son'd given Auk his orders, and they were the right ones. He and his son were going to see to it everybody got the word. We'd been thinking about his Plan like it was way off, when it was already time to move out. . . ."

"*Continue,* my son."

"I'm sorry, Patera. That's when he started talking about me, and I get kind of choked up. It was the greatest moment of my life, right? I mean, if I was to make sergeant or anything like that I'd feel pretty good. But this was Pas. I got his drift and later you explained, and it was like I'd been feeling it was, just exactly. Hearing you say it was just about like I was hearing it all over again from him. I'm thinking there's a war, and all the good people's on his side. That's this son—"

"Terrible Tartaros," Auk put in.

"And the caldé and Auk and naturally you are, Patera. And it's the side I'm on, too. He said how Auk got hurt when he was underground with us and how hard he'd been working for his Plan, and he was sending somebody from Mainframe to help him out."

"From the *Pole,* Corporal. That is the term which the god *himself* preferred to employ. That *Mainframe* is at the *Pole,* I freely concede."

Auk edged nearer. "To help *me* out? I'm the cull?"

"Yeah, you're the one, only I'm supposed to help too. He said he was going to decorate you for what you've done soon as you do what he wants you to next. Only here's where Patera said something I got to say too, so it'll make sense to these other bios. Pas is us chems' god. He's the god of all the digital, nuclear-chemical stuff. You got to buy that if you want to see where Pas's coming from. Isn't that right, Patera?"

Incus nodded solemnly.

" 'Cause Pas told us what Auk's decoration's going to be. Anytime he sees anything like me, he's going to understand it straight off. How it goes together and what it's supposed to do, and how. Pas means to stick all the data into Auk, 'cause he'll need it to carry out the Plan."

Linsang and his troopers stared at Auk openmouthed. Auk endeavored to appear humble.

"That was when he gave me my direct order, and it wasn't just 'cause I happened to be around. I never thought anything

like this would happen to me. I asked Patera about it back at
the manteion, and he says if I hadn't been the one Pas wanted,
I wouldn't have been there, it would've been some other tin-
pot. But it wasn't. I'm the one. Patera says it was probably
'cause him and me are, you know, like brothers only closer,
and he's a holy augur, and as soon as he said it I knew it was
right.

"Pas needs a soldier, so which one? There's thousands.
Why, the augur's friend, doesn't that make sense? The friend
of the augur Scylla picked to be the new Prolocutor, that's the
one you need. A god don't have to think about stuff like that,
he just knows. He said, talking to me, Auk might have a little trouble at first. You stick with him and help him over the
tough spots. You're a mechanism, help him out and he'll help
you. So here we are, Patera and me both, and we're trying to
help."

Linsang asked Incus, "Was that all, Patera?"

"*All?* I should say it was more than *enough,* my son. But
no. It was *not.* Let us have the *remainder,* Hammerstone."

"He said that a while back, forty years, he said, he knew
he was going to die—"

"To die?" Linsang was incredulous.

"That's what he said. He saw it coming, so he sort of took
off little pieces of himself and hid them in various bios where
they wouldn't be found. Then he died, and he's been dead for
quite a while."

Incus cleared his throat. "All of *you,* and I, *similarly,* must
comprehend the *difficulties* under which a god seeking to
communicate with *human kind* labors. He can but speak to us
in words mere *mortals* apprehend. Thus by *die,* the *Father* of
the *Gods* indicated his own *renewal.* That *noblest* of *trees,* the
goldenshower, is sacred to *Great Pas.* You cannot be ignorant
of so *elementary* a fact."

Linsang and several of his troopers nodded.

"*Suppose* that a *forest* of goldenshowers could *speak* to
us. Would it not say, 'That *I,* the *sacred forest,* may remain
young and *strong,* my *aged* trees must *fall,* though they have

endured for *centuries*. Let *young* trees spring up in their *places*. I, the *forest, endure.*' Hammerstone?"

"I'm on it, Patera. He said now when his Plan's starting to move, he's putting himself back together. He said right now he was his own ghost, Pas's ghost, but with more of his pieces getting found, he'll be Pas again. He wants us to help. Auk in particular, but everybody's supposed to pitch in. We got to find this one particular bio, Patera Jerboa, 'cause he's got the piece for Viron. There was maybe five or six hundred bios in the manteion, but after Patera'd explained the whole thing to them, there wasn't one that knew who this Patera Jerboa was or where we could maybe find him.

"So Patera told them not to bunch up, but scatter and start asking people all over, and bring him to Auk when they got him. Then he told Auk the Chapter's got records about all this stuff, where every augur's at and what he's doing there, and they're in the Palace, and Patera knows where and how to read them. He's worked with them for years, right Patera? So him and Auk and me started off to take a look, and here we are."

"The *majesty* of diction was lacking, *Hammerstone,* my son, yet the *matter* was in *attendance.*" Incus regarded Linsang and his troopers. "What of *you?* We seek to obey the dictates of the *Father* of the *Seven.* Can you *assist* us? No *holy augur* can know every other. We are *far* too *numerous.* Do you know of a *Patera Jerboa?* Any of you? *Speak.*"

No one did.

Shots woke Maytera Mint. At first, as she lay blinking in the darkness, she did not know what the sounds had been; she was hungry and thirsty, vaguely conscious of the cold, and conscious that she had been cold for a long time, shivering as she slept. Her buttocks and shoulder blades, pressed by her slight weight to unyielding shiprock, were numb, her feet freezing.

She sat up. Her room had been the smallest and meanest in the old cenoby on Silver Street, with a ceiling that dripped at every shower; yet it had not been too small or too mean for a window past whose threadbare drape wisps of light crept on even the darkest nights.

Three sharp bangs, unevenly spaced. Pictures falling? She recalled an incident from her childhood: an old watercolor had fallen when its yellowed string rotted through at last, and had taken another picture and a small vase down with it. Once she had heard a horse trying to kick its way out of its stall. The shots had sounded like that.

"Ah, General?"

The voice had been Remora's; his nasal tones brought it all back to her. "Yes, Your Eminence."

"You have, um, familiar with the sound of gunfire, hey? During the past—ah—fighting."

"Yes, Your Eminence. Tolerably so." Against her will, she found herself wondering how many Remoras there had been, how many augurs and sibyls who had responded to Echidna's theophany by going to the safest place they could find and staying there. Patera Silk had not. (But then, he wouldn't.) Patera Silk had been shot in the chest, had been captured, and had contrived, somehow, to turn Oosik and the whole Third Brigade, the act that had done more than any other to determine the course of their insurrection. But how many more—

"Er, General?"

"Yes, Your Eminence. I was considering the matter. The door is thick and rather tightly fitted, and these walls are shiprock. Those factors must have affected the quality of the shots as we heard them."

"You—ah—believe them shots, eh?"

"I'm putting on my shoes, Your Eminence." She groped for them in the dark. "If we're to be taken somewhere—"

"Quite right." Remora sounded cheerful. "Quetzal, eh? Old Quetzal. His Cognizance, I ought to say."

More thirsty than ever, Maytera Mint licked her dry lips. "His Cognizance, Your Eminence?"

"Rescue, eh? He's come for me, er, we. Or—ah—sent somebody. Shrewd, eh? Plays a deep game, old Quetzal. Card sense in both—um—the applicable senses."

She tried to imagine the elderly Prolocutor fighting, slug gun in hand, against Spider and his spy-catchers, and failed utterly. "I would think Bison's sent scouts into the tunnels by this time, Your Eminence. If we're lucky, it may be some of them we heard. But even if they notice this door, they may not be able to get it open."

Another shot, and it was definitely a shot.

"They will notice it, General. I—um—my word on it. My gammadion, eh?"

"Your gammadion, Your Eminence?"

"Not you, ah, sibyls. But we augurs. Holy augurs, eh? Wear Pas's voided cross. Comes apart. Use to test a Window, hey? Tighten connections, make adjustments, all that sort of, er, operations. Gold, hey? Mine is. Coadjutor, eh? Stones. Not like old Quetzal's, I, um, but gems. Amethysts, largely. Gold chain. Under my tunic, generally. Out at sacrifice, hey?"

"I'm familiar with them, Your Eminence."

"I've—ah—slipped it beneath the door, Maytera. Push it out, eh? Pull it back in. Moving object, hum? Catches the light, ah, attracts the eye."

She went to the door (almost tripping over Remora) and rapped it sharply with the heel of one shoe.

"Admirable—ah—admirable. Crude, eh? Yet it—ah!"

The latch outside rattled and the door swung in, impeded by Remora. The burly Spider growled, "What's that noise?"

The lights in the tunnel were so dim that Maytera Mint did not blink. "I was pounding on the door with my shoe. We heard shots and hoped we'd be freed."

"Come on." Spider gestured with the barrel of his needler.

"We, um, require food," Remora ventured. "Water or—ah—similar, er, potable."

"You won't if you don't get movin'."

"You don't dare shoot us," Maytera Mint declared. "We're valuable hostages. What would you tell—"

He caught her arm and jerked her through the doorway. "I'm strong, see?"

"I never doubted it." She tested her shoulder, fearing he had dislocated it.

"Strong as a chem. Not one of them soldiers, maybe, but a regular chem. You with me, sib? So I don't have to shoot you. There's twenty, thirty things I could do." One of Spider's men was lounging in the tunnel; he held a gleaming slug gun. "I'm ready to try a couple," Spider continued. "You scavy Councillor Potto's kettle? Wasn't anythin'. He was just playin', he's like that. I don't fool. We get lots of spies."

"I'm delighted to hear it." Maytera Mint had feared that she would not be allowed to resume her shoe; she tightened the bow and straightened up with an odd little thrill of triumph.

"I learned a lot, workin' on them. I never seen one so tough I couldn't get him to tell me anythin' I wanted to know. That way, and keep movin'."

"I, er, weak. Thirsty, eh? What one physically—ow!"

Remora had been prodded from behind by the man with the slug gun, who said, "I kicked a dead cull once till he got up and ran."

"The gods—ah—Pas. Tartaros, eh?" Remora progressed with rapid, unsteady strides, outdistancing Maytera Mint.

"Slow up!"

"I—ah—prayed. Beads eh? The, um, general slept."

"You should have awakened me," she protested, and got a shove from Spider.

"Never! Wouldn't, um, consider—" Remora froze until he was prodded from behind. Somewhat nearsighted, Maytera Mint blinked as she tried to peer ahead through the watery light.

"Dead cull," Spider told her. "One of mine."

"Was that the shooting we heard?"

Spider pushed her forward. "Yeah." Another push. "He was watchin' your door. Sib, you better shaggy learn to drive your shaggy ass or you're going to learn a shaggy bunch you don't want to know."

She whirled, facing him. "I've already learned something, but it was something I wanted to know. That I wanted very much to know, in fact."

He struck her face with the flat of his hand, spinning her around and knocking her down, the blow as loud as the boom of a slug gun. "Pick her up," he told Remora.

Remora did, carrying her like a child as he staggered down the tunnel. When they reached the corpse, the man with the slug gun caught his arm and ordered him to stop, and he set her on her feet. "You're cryin'," Spider told her.

"I am. I shouldn't," she wiped her eyes, "because I know our hour will come. Perhaps I should cry for you instead, but that will come later if it comes at all."

Remora had knelt beside the corpse; he rose shaking his head. "The spirit has, ah, dispensed with its house of flesh."

The man with the slug gun asked, "You were going to say the words over him?"

"I—ah—so intended. It is too late."

"He never believed in it."

Maytera Mint said, "Then I should weep for him. A short life and a violent death in this wretched place. You can write on his stone, here lies one who sought no succor from the gods, and hence received none."

The man with the slug gun chuckled. "Maybe you can. How about it, Spider?"

"Sure, why not? She can do it while we're waitin'."

Remora ventured, "May we be seated? My legs, er, flaccid."

"Go ahead. They'll be along in a minute."

"If you mean Bison's scouts, I feel certain you're right," Maytera Mint told him.

He took off his cap and ran a dirty comb through greasy, graying hair. "You figure Bison's boys chilled him? You're abram."

"I doubt that you even know who Bison is."

"The shag I don't. I got people all through your knot. You think I don't?"

"Thank you very much." She wiped away the last tears with her sleeve. "We appreciate all who come to us."

He laughed. "You appreciate them? They're tellin' us what you do, every move you make."

"Meanwhile they must work and fight for us, if they're not to be detected." She sat down next to Remora. "They would like to rise in our councils, I suppose. To do it, they'll have to work and fight well."

"S'pose all you want to," Spider grunted.

"You are, um, confident it was not one of Colonel Bison's men—er—persons. Troopers. Who shot this, um?"

"Sure. Sib, how come my culls don't faze you?"

"Isn't it obvious? Because we're hiding nothing. You want to learn our secrets, but they're only virtue and prudence. His Eminence and I had hoped to arrange a peace in which your spies and you might live. Now there will be none. We—"

"All right! Muzzle it!"

"Will root you out. We'll go down into this wretched hole and fight, find the underwater boat on which—"

He kicked her.

"You held the caldé—"

He kicked her again, and she screamed.

Remora lurched to his feet. "Really, I cannot—simply, ah, will not tolerate this. Kick me, if you like." Spider pushed him; he staggered, tripped over the corpse, and fell.

"And drop stones on it from the surface or catch it in a net," Maytera Mint finished. "If you want our plans, there you have them. Your spies can tell you nothing more."

"You're one tough little girl."

"I'm a gross coward," she told him. "I realized it about an hour after Echidna declared me her sword. We were storming the Alambrera. It might be more accurate to say we were trying to. I—shall I tell you?"

Spider put away his comb. "I'll break you."

"You have already. I screamed, didn't I? What more do you need to complete your triumph? My death?" She threw her arms wide. "Shoot!"

"Another time, maybe." Spider turned his attention to Remora, who was sitting up and rubbing the back of his head. "You, Patera. Your Eminence. Is that what they call you?"

"You may call me either. Or neither, eh? I should, um, opt for neither, given the choice. I—ah—covet no honors from you."

"You can die, too, Patera."

"I, um, well aware. Thinking, hey? Thinking while I, um, bore the general. Not valiant, eh? Not like, er, she."

"Your Eminence, I am *not* brave!"

"You are, Maytera—ah—General. Yes, you are. Not, um, sensible of it, conceivably. I—ah—am not. Was a, um, prisoner of Erne's. I told you, eh?"

"You told me you'd conferred with him, not that you were his prisoner."

Remora looked toward Spider, seeking his permission; Spider said, "Sure, I'd say we got time."

"In the, um, Palace, eh? Eating dinner. Warned, eh? By a page. Guardsmen coming. Thought they wanted—ah—consult me. Waited for my sweet. In they tramped, these, er, troopers. Where's the Prolocutor? That was the, um, term they employed. I endeavored to explain. His Cognizance comes and, ah, departs at his, er, pleasure. Arrested me, hey? Hands bound, all that. Under my robe, eh? I, um, petitioned that favor, and they, er, condescended. Marched me out."

Remora paused to swallow. "Frightened, General. Badly frightened. Horribly, er, affrighted. Coward. Questions, eh? Questions, questions. Read, um, statements I never made, eh? Spoke in my own defense. Struck. Said I'd lied. Struck, eh? On and—ah—more of the, er, like treatment."

Maytera Mint nodded. Her right cheek was beginning to swell, but her eyes were full of sympathy. "I'm sorry, Your Eminence. Truly sorry."

"Said they'd kill me, eh? Needler at my head. All that. Coward, lost control. Bowels, er, voided. Soiled my clothes. Had to speak to the Brigadier. Said that over and over. I—ah—know him. Knew him, eh? In better days. Yes, in better days. Saw him at last. Truce, eh? Truce, cease-fire. I can, er, bring one about, hey? Caldé's an augur. Let me go. Spoke through glass to—ah—Councillor. Loris. Councillor Loris. He said—um—let him go. And they—ah—did. Brigadier Erne did. Fellow I'd—ah—chatted with, hey? Ten, twenty, er, occasions. Parties, dinners, receptions. Gossip, prattle over wine. Beaten, wet—um—stinking. But free. Free."

Spider laughed.

"Back to the Palace, hey? Frightened—ah—terrified. Shooting augurs, eh? Sibyls, too. I, um, didn't see it. For that thank—ah—Tartaros. Thanked Tenebrous Tartaros for it, for, er, shielding my eyes. But I knew, eh? They told me. Felt the—ah—slug. Needle strike my back a score of times in—er—three streets. Roughly, eh? Roughly three. Dead twenty times. Back to the Palace, washed. Listening all the while. Listening for them. Why, eh? Why listen?" Remora's bony fingers laced and loosed, knotting and writhing free to form new knots.

"My—ah—rise. Page as a lad. Schola. Augur. My mother, eh? Be Prolocutor someday, eh? Mother, couple aunts. Father, too, hum? Acolyte, desk in the Palace, higher every year or so, hey? Father died. Careful, hey? Careful, worked hard, hey? Always careful, no enemies, hey? Long hours. Aunt died. Work and wait, eh? Coadjutor died. Younger than old Quetzal, hey? Dead at his table, eh? Lying on his—um—documents. Coadjutor, Mother. Old then, eh? Very. But her eyes shone, Maytera. Er, General. Her eyes shone." Remora's own were full of tears.

"There is no need for you to torment yourself like this, Your Eminence."

Spider told the man with the slug gun, "See what's keepin' them." He rose, nodded to Maytera Mint, and walked away, down the tunnel.

"Mother . . ." Remora coughed, a racking cough deep in his chest. "Sorry. My, um, couldn't prevent it. Mother dead, hey? Mother dead, General. All dead, then. Mother, father, both, er, sisters. Not Mother's—ah—her vision. Vision for me. Prolocutor. Why afraid? Beatings. Blows, eh? 'Fraid of them, too. Most of all—ah—her vision." He fell silent.

Wanting desperately to change the subject, Maytera Mint asked Spider, "Where is that man going? What are we waiting here for?"

"A stretcher." Spider shifted his weight from one foot to the other. "For him." He gestured toward the corpse.

"You're going to carry it away for burial?"

"Cleaned up, hey?" Remora had not been listening. "Lay clothes. Left the Palace. Soon as I could. Went to Ermine's. Caldé might come. I knew. I knew. In the, um, his letter."

Maytera Mint nodded, supposing that the letter had been addressed to Remora.

"Went to Ermine's. Drinking den there. Lay clothing so they wouldn't—ah—shoot. Waited. Porter dropped something in the street. Up like a rabbit. Die, never Prolocutor. Her spirit, eh? Her ghost. Her vision for me."

"It never occurred to me that you were waiting for a means carry the body," Maytera Mint told Spider. "It should have, but I've seen so many left lying where they fell."

He cleared his throat. "We got a place. You'll see it."

"Down here?"

"Yeah. Eight, ten chains from here."

Maytera Mint indicated the corpse. "Did you like him, Spider? You must have."

"He was all right, and I worked with him ten years."

"Then you would not object if I covered his face?"

"Nah. Go ahead."

She did, standing and smoothing the black skirt of her habit, taking short steps to the side of the corpse, kneeling, and spreading a dirty handkerchief she took from her sleeve over its face. "May Great Pas pardon your spirit."

"No more—ah—the vision." Remora was addressing no one. "An, er, administrative post, eh? Finance. Most, er, plausibly. Finance. No."

"Muzzle it," Spider told him. "See, sib, there's this place where they was diggin' one of these tunnels. They put a big door in it like they did. You seen some."

Maytera Mint nodded.

"Martyr, hey? No martyrs since, ah—"

"They went fifty, sixty steps in and quit. I don't know why. Quit in dirt. We're under the city, and it's mostly dirt up here."

"Are we? I thought you were taking us to the lake."

"Maybe we will, but we're takin' you here for now. We meet down here sometimes. Meet with Councillor Potto, and when we get somebody, we generally leave him where you two were. It's an old storeroom, I guess, but I don't—" They heard the thunderous boom of a slug gun, attenuated by distance but unmistakable.

"Guan must of shot somethin'," Spider told Maytera Mint.

"Or he was shot himself."

"He's a rough boy. He can take care of himself. What was I talkin' about?"

"How you bury the other rough boys." She sighed. "It was interesting. I'd like to hear more about it."

"Sure." Spider sat down facing her, his needler still in his right hand. Settled in his place, he held it up. "I could put this away. You aren't goin' to jump me, either of you."

"I—ah—intend it," Remora muttered.

"Huh! I don't think so." Spider thrust the needler into his coat. "Like I said, sib, there's a big door, and I got the word for it. Councillor Potto told it to me a long time back. So you go in and where it ends there's dirt. Down towards the lake, where they run deeper, it's all rock or shiprock, but up this high there's a lot of dirt."

"I understand."

He touched the shiprock wall. "Behind here's dirt. I can tell from how it's made. What we do, when somebody's chilled up in the city and there's nobody for them, we bring them down. Or if somebody dies down here. That happened one time."

Seated again, Maytera Mint nodded toward the corpse.

"Lily. Twice, now. But before, one of my knot got hurt up there and we brought him down, but he died. We dig straight in, like, into the dirt till the hole's long enough. We got rolls of poly. We lay some poly in the hole and wrap them up in some more, and slide them right in." He looked at her quizzically, and she nodded.

"Then we put some dirt back to fill the hole, right? And everybody's got a shiv." He took a big stag-handled clasp knife from his pocket. "We write the name and some stuff about him on a piece of paper, and we stick it up with his shiv so we don't dig there again for anybody else."

"As a memorial, too," Maytera Mint suggested, "Though I doubt that you would admit it."

"That's lily, sib, I wouldn't. It's just somethin' for the older bucks like me. When we go in there again we look at them, and then maybe we tell the new culls. Like we used to have cull name of Titi that would put on a gown and pay his face like they do. Not you, sib. You know what I mean, powder and rouge, and all that. Perfume."

She nodded. "Indeed I do, and I'm not offended in the least. Go on."

"Give Titi a half hour, and he's the best lookin' mort in the city. He kept his hair kind of long, and he could fix it just a little different and it was a mort's hair cut short. Not as short as yours, but short, and soon as you saw it you knew it was a mort's hair. If Titi hadn't paid his dial, that shaggy hair'd make you abram. You'd be talkin' to yourself."

"A person like that must have been of great value to you."

"Lily, he was. He was a bob cull, too. There was this time when we were workin' on a knot from Urbs. We knew who they was and what they was after, and was peery a while to see what they done and who they talked to. We do it in our trade all the time. We'd see they found out things Councillor Potto wanted Urbs to know, and we'd foyst in queer, too, fixed so they'd like it. One came fly. Know what I mean, sib?"

"I believe so."

"We could've done for him. Chilled him, you know. But we don't unless we got to."

Remora looked up. "Um—irrevocable. No—ah—going back after, eh?"

"Slap on, Patera. That's her in a egg cup. You know this one, see? He's a hog grubber, won't spend. Or he's one of them that lushes till shadeup and don't forget a thing. Whatever. Soon as he's cold, it's all down the chute, and Urbs'll send a new cull.

"So what I laid to was to get him nabbed. I got Titi to hook him and go 'round to two, three places so's to get some to say they seen them. Then Titi went to Hoppy and capped I been ramped. The Urber done it. They got him to go along to finger.

"I knew the ken, so'd Titi, and I was keepin' him there. I'd planted books goin', to keep him on top. Not lumb, but lowre enough, you know, to have him sure he'd draw my deck."

"I—ah—dishonest game? You, er, cheated?"

"Yes, Spider. Did you?"

"Sure thing. But not skinnin' him. I'd take his gelt and let him win back and more to the bargain. He had to lose swop, or I'd been shy more'n I had. Larger, he'd got to win so he wouldn't stamp. I'd say haven't you nicked me proper and push my chair, you know the lay, and he'd say one more hand. I knew Titi was goin' to have to let the hoppies carry him two or three places 'fore he steered 'em right.

"In they prance, and Titi fingered the Urber and blubbed like two morts, and the hoppies grabbled him and what's your name, you're for iron."

"Rape is a very serious charge," Maytera Mint protested. "He could have been sent to the pits."

"Sure thing, but Titi wasn't goin' to dock. I wanted him shy of his knot to Pasday, that's all. Well, he broke and run at Titi. Petal, what're you doing to me, and the rest, and he's nabbed a flicker and bashes it on the cat ladder."

"A wine bottle as a weapon, you mean?" This was a foreign whorl to Maytera Mint.

"A glass tumbler, sib, but it's the same notion." Spider chuckled. "Titi fans him so hard he's back across and on my knee if I hadn't hopped. Knocked over my perch and both down together.

"Now right here's where my jabber pays. Titi run to him bawlin' like a calf with the cow in the kitchen, and Hoppy? Never twigged. I was on velvet. Showed me the door. Titi had to stay and cap, which he did, and Hoppy never twigged. I'd like to turn up another, but I've never seen any half so fine, not even on boards."

"Yet he's dead," Maytera Mint said pensively. "He's dead and buried in that place you told us about, because there was no one else who cared enough to bury him. Otherwise we would not be talking about him. How did he die?"

"I was hopin' you wouldn't quiz me, sib."

She smiled. "I'll withdraw the question if you'll call me Maytera. Will you do that for me?"

"Sure thing." Spider's hand massaged his stubbled jowls.

"I'm goin' to tell you anyhow. Thing is, some culls nicker. All right, it's abram. But, well . . ."

"But he was your friend."

"Nah. I miss him, though. I brought him in. I found him, and I got him in, helped him out of a queer lay he was standin' and all that, and pretty quick he's a dimber hand. Everybody knew, all my knot. They stood him wide. You wouldn't think, and they didn't to start, but after a while. I told about how he said the Urber ramped him."

"Yes, you did."

"A buck tried it, see, Maytera? He got down to shag and twigged Titi's yard, and did for him on account. Squeezed his pipe for him."

"That's sad. I understand perfectly why you dislike it when people laugh. May I ask about him, too? She gestured toward the corpse. "What was his name?"

"Paca." While seconds crawled by, Spider stared at the handkerchief-shrouded face. "He was a pretty good all-round cull, know what I say? For jabber or a breakin' lay or rags-and-tags, any of the jobs we do, smokin' or liftin' seals—"

Remora looked up.

"Any game you name, I could name you better. You don't always know, though, and sometimes that cull's got his plate full or he's crank, and Paca could take it. Once in a while he'd big my glimms."

Spider spoke to Remora. "I was goin' to ask, Patera, if you'd cap for him. Think you could?"

"Pray for, um, Peccary? Paca. I, er, have. Privately, eh? While we, er, now."

"When I slide him in," Spider explained impatiently. "Cut bene whiddes for everybody."

"I—ah—indeed. Honored."

"What about Guan?" Maytera Mint inquired. "Aren't we going to bury him, too? Wouldn't you like His Eminence to pray for him as well? Perhaps we could make it a group ceremony."

"Guan's not for ice."

"Certainly he is." She sighed. "Where is your stretcher?"

"He'll be along in a minute."

"Thirsty, eh? Might we, um, hungry, likewise."

"So am I," Maytera Mint declared. "You have a stretcher somewhere, or so you say, Spider. If there's food and water there, too, may we not go to it?"

"I, ah—"

"You ate and drank last night, I assume, and this morning. You, Guan, Paca, and the others. We didn't."

Spider clambered to his feet. "All right, you two, you got it. Come on. I want to see what's keepin' those putts."

"Ah—water? And, um, something to eat?"

"Sure thing. We got prog and plonk. There's a well, too. I ought to of let you have some last night. You need a hand up, Patera? How 'bout you, Maytera?"

"I'm fine, thank you, Spider."

"I—ah—give warning," Remora said as Spider helped him to stand. "The next, um, instance. Strike the General. Or me. I shall attack, eh? Will. Martyr, hey? Gone but—um, er—commemorated. Unforgotten."

"He isn't going to," Maytera Mint told Remora briskly. "We are past all that hitting and hating with Spider. Don't you understand, Your Eminence?"

"Come on," Spider repeated, and started down the tunnel. "You want to eat? I'll bet you anythin' they aren't cold."

"Um, forbidden."

"Wagering is contrary to the regulations of the Chapter," Maytera Mint explained, "but I am prepared to violate them and accept whatever punishment may be meted out to me. I say that they are dead, all of them. The men you sent for the stretcher, and Guan, too. As dead as Paca. Will you take my bet?"

"Sure thing." Spider had drawn his needler again. "I got a card says I'm right."

"I don't want your card. What I want are answers to three questions. You must promise to answer in full. No lies and no evasions. No half truths. What will you have from us if we lose? We haven't any money, or at least I have none."

Spider halted, waiting for her. "I donno, sib. Maytera, I mean. That's better, huh? You call each other sib, though."

She nodded. "We call one another sib, which is short for *sibyl*, because *maytera* is reserved for the sibyl in charge of the cenoby in which we live. There's only one other sibyl in my cenoby since Maytera Rose passed on, Maytera Marble. She is senior to me, so she is in charge. I will call her Maytera when next we meet, assuming that Maytera Rose has been buried."

"You, too, huh? Well, I'm sorry, Maytera. Come on, Your Eminence, shake it up."

"His Eminence has a gold gammadion set with gems," Maytera Mint confided. "He might be willing to make it my stake in our bet. I'll try to persuade him."

Spider shook his head. "I could nab it anytime."

"Certainly you could, but you would have stolen it. Though Tenebrous Tartaros, whose realm this surely is, is the patron of thieves, I doubt very much that he approves of stealing from augurs, and all the other gods surely condemn it. If you won His Eminence's gammadion you would have acquired it honestly, and would have no reason to fear divine retribution."

"Yeah. But you don't think I'll win."

Maytera Mint shook her head. "No, I don't. I will not deceive you, Spider. I am as sure as I can be without having seen them that all those men are dead. If you accept my bet, you'll have to answer my questions, one for each dead man."

"All right, I'll tell you what I want, Maytera. But I'm goin' to call you General. That's who I want to bet with, the rebel general. Can I do that? Patera does."

"Certainly. I'd prefer it, in fact."

"You figure I'm a thief. I can tell by the way you were talkin' a minute ago. That's the lily, isn't it, General?"

"You employ a great deal of cant, Spider, and cant is used principally by thieves. Also by prostitutes, with whom I've spoken now and then, but most of them steal when it seems safe."

"Most everybody will," Spider told her positively.

"Perhaps. If so, it is small wonder that the gods show us no more affection than they do."

"Well, I ain't a thief. I talk like I do 'cause we're with them a lot. Spies don't ken with people like you, General, or this other sibyl you call Maytera. She don't know anythin' they need, see? You do, but if they were to ken with you, they'd need a shaggy good reason or you'd start thinkin', why's he around all the time?" Spider paused for breath.

"You go to some city to look into things, you know, and you want somebody local to help out, what you want's a thief six to one. When we got to have new blood, that's where we look, too. Not always, but mostly."

"I understand, Spider. . . ."

"Out with it."

"Very well." Maytera Mint took a deep breath. "Were you a thief previously? Is that how you came to be a spy-catcher?"

He grinned at her, displaying crooked and discolored teeth. "What makes you think you can believe me, General?"

"I'm a good judge of character."

"I'd lie to you."

"Indeed you would, and you might do it so skillfully, that I would think you were telling the truth. But you won't lie to me about this, not here and not now. Were you? It's none of my affair, and to confess the truth there is a thief I taught when he was a child of whom I'm very fond. His name is Auk."

"I know him," Spider said.

"You do? That hadn't occurred to me, but now that you've mentioned it, no doubt you must. Does he—is he one of your knot, as you call it?"

"That'd feague you, huh? He's not. Auk won't work for anybody else, and he's too peppery for my trade anyhow. I wasn't a thief, either. I was a hoppy. You believe that?"

"If you say it's true, absolutely. May I ask why you left the Caldé's Guard?"

"They callin' it that again? That's what it was when I went in, then they changed it. They kicked me out. Let's not talk about why."

Remora, who had caught up with them and overheard much of their conversation, muttered, "No, ah, never. Only shriving, hey? There—um—solely."

"I won't ask," Maytera Mint promised.

"Pulled off my stripes and put them on my back. I could show you the scars. Cull called Desmid brought me in. He's cold. I been catchin' spies for Viron twenty-two years now. I don't know how many I've nabbed or helped nab, thirty or forty. Could be more, and there's a lot we don't want to nab but could anytime we wanted to. I'm telling' you 'cause of what I want my end of our bet to be. I'm stickin' with Councillor Potto, see? Twenty-two years I been workin' for him, and he took me when I didn't have two bits or a padken. I'm his man, always will be."

"In that case, let us hope a peace can be arranged that will permit Councillor Potto to retain his seat."

Spider nodded. "Sure thing. All right, let's talk about this bet. First off, these three questions. Suppose you were to ask me who my boys are, the ones you think's yours. I can't tell you names. You see that? I won't lie to you, General, but I won't tell, either."

"I understand. I won't ask you to betray your friends."

"All right, here's what I want. If your side wins and you get loose, you don't nab me and my knot for spyin' on you, or for holdin' you like we're doin'."

Maytera Mint started to speak, but Spider raised his hand. "That's not all. You let us keep doin' what we been doin' for Viron. You're goin' to need us worse than you think. If you do that, I'll tell what's gone on before, and give you the files."

"I can't. I would accept that bet if I could, cheerfully and without hesitation. But those are matters for the caldé and the new Ayuntamiento, not for me."

"The, um, terms. He, er, designated? Specified yourself, General. Not the—ah—reconstituted Ayuntamiento or the caldé, hey?"

"But he means our side. The caldé, Generalissimo Oosik, and even the Trivigauntis. Don't you, Spider? For myself, I would give you my word, as I said. In fact, I do, whether I win or lose. But I cannot bind the caldé and an Ayuntamiento that does not yet exist."

"But you'll promise, General? Personally?"

"Absolutely. I have and I do."

Spider indicated Remora with a jerk of his thumb. "Have him flash that gaud. Pas's cross. You can swear on that."

"If you wish. Will you allow me my three questions, when I win? Full, honest answers?"

"Sure thing. I'll swear too, if you want."

"Then it won't be necessary."

Remora had produced his gammadion; Maytera Mint laid her hand upon it. "I, General Mint of the Horde of Viron, called by some the rebel or insurgent forces, I who am also Maytera Mint of the Sun Street manteion, do hereby swear that should we prevail I will not punish nor attempt to punish this man Spider and his subordinates for their activities in collecting intelligence for the Ayuntamiento as presently constituted. I further swear that I will do everything I can to prevent others from so punishing them, short of force. In addition, I will actively support their being retained in their function, that is to say the counterintelligence function, in which they have served our city faithfully. I will do these things whether I win my wager with Spider or lose it."

She drew breath. "Is that satisfactory?"

"Ought to cover it."

"Great Pas, bear witness! Ophidian Echidna, whose sword I am, bear witness! Scintillating Scylla, Patroness of Our Holy City of Viron, bear witness!"

"Good enough." Spider held out his hand. "Have we got a bet? Shake on it." Solemnly they shook hands, her own small hand enveloped in a thickly muscled one twice its size.

"All right, I'll tell you right now I got a lock. We're almost there." He gestured. "See that side tunnel up ahead? We go in there, and the old guardroom's only four, five steps. If they were cold, we've have made them before this."

She shook her head. "To the contrary, though I wish you were correct. They would have heard our voices and called out."

A hundred steps brought them to the side tunnel's entrance. As soon as they turned into it, she caught sight of a man's feet protruding from a doorway. "That will be Guan," she murmured.

Spider stopped her, spreading his arms to hold Remora back as well. "That's Hyrax. I always twig a cully's shoes, or a mort's either. Shoes tell more than any kind of kick. A lot know it, but that don't stop it from bein' true."

"Wasn't the other man with Hyrax, Spider? Where is he?"

"In there." Spider's breath rasped in this throat. "Just out of sight, most likely. You don't shoot a cull soon as you see him through the door, not if he's comin' in. You let him get inside. That way you got two tries if he beats hoof."

He turned to Remora. "You first, Patera. Pull out Pas's cross and have it where they can see, and hold your hands up. You're a augur in a robe, not holdin' a slug gun or anything. They won't shoot you, or I don't think they will. Tell them I got the general. Leave us be, or she's cold."

Remora looked stricken.

"You wanted to die down here, didn't you? This's your chance. Go on before I shoot you myself. They won't."

"They must know we're out here," Maytera Mint said. "They will have heard us. If not before, they will certainly have heard that." Spider did not reply; his eyes were on Remora.

"I, er, shall." Remora backed away, raised his hands, and turned toward the doorway.

"Pas's gammadion," Maytera Mint prompted him. "Take it out so they can see it."

If Remora heard her advice, he ignored it. She watched him pause at the threshold, then step through. There was no shot.

"They used to have soldiers down here awake and ready to go if there was trouble," Spider told her. His hoarse voice was close to a whisper. "That was before the Guard. That's what Councillor Potto told me one time, and he ought to know."

They stood side-by-side in silence after that. There was no sound from the guardroom, no sound from any source save the almost inaudible sigh of the cool wind that filled the tunnel.

At length Spider said, "I should of told him to take a look around in there. I guess he's doin' it anyhow."

"I'm going too." Maytera Mint started toward the doorway.

"Hornbuss!" Spider caught her arm. "You're goin' to do what I say, and I say you can't."

"Your Eminence!" she called. "Are you all right?"

For a few seconds her words echoed hollowly from the gray walls, and she felt certain that she and Spider were the only living people within earshot. Then Remora stepped out of the doorway, avoiding the dead man. He held out a bottle of thick, mottled glass. "Water, Maytera! General. Ah—potable. Um, pure, in so far as I can, um, gauge its qualities."

Spider snapped, "Nobody in there?"

"Not—ah—dead men. Two, in addition to the one you, üm, observe in the entrance. Shot with slug guns, I—ah— or, um, both with a single such gun. Quite possibly. Our, ah, companions, eh? Yesterday, likewise earlier. One the, um—"

"Guan."

"Er, yes. Ah—the name you gave. Furnished? Supplied." Having come near enough, Remora handed the bottle to Maytera Mint. "He dropped this, I fancy, General. So it appeared, eh? When he—um—attained life's culmination. Some spilt, eh?"

She was drinking and did not trouble to reply. The water was cool and clean and tasted fresh and unspeakably delicious. All her life she had been taught that Surging Scylla, the water goddess, was first among the Seven; she had not realized either how true or how important that insight was until this moment.

Chapter 7

THE BROWN MECHANICS

Silk looked around curiously, finding it hard to believe that this enclosure, this collection of sheds surrounded by a fence, produced taluses. On his shoulder, Oreb croaked in dismay.

"It's starting to rain," Chenille announced; she pushed back raspberry curls to squint at the sky.

"I've been trying to remember where I came from," Maytera Marble ventured. "I don't think it was like this at all." She edged Mucor toward the shelter of the sentry box as she spoke.

If Fliers were a rain sign, what might Fliers who landed presage? The final days of the whorl? Silk decided to keep the speculation to himself. "I should have asked you about that long ago, Maytera. Tell me about it."

"I couldn't remember a thing then, I'm sure. Not till poor Maytera Rose bequeathed me my new parts. I'm sure I must have told you about them."

Silk nodded.

"A week last Tarsday, that was. They're much better than my old ones, but after I'd put them in, it was hard for me to keep straight which memories were Marble's and which were mine."

Chenille corrected her. "The other way, Maytera."

"You're quite right, dear. Anyway, I recollect a big room with green walls. There were pallets, or perhaps metal tables, little ones about as high as a bed."

"Here comes one of the guards." Chenille pointed.

"I was lying on one, and I didn't have any clothes on. Perhaps I shouldn't talk about this, Patera."

"Go ahead. It's not immoral, and it could be important."

"I was trying to boot, and I remember that the girl next to me sat up and said she was naked, which she certainly was. When she did, somebody brought her a dress."

The guard halted with a clash of armored heels, one hand leveled across his slug gun. "Follow me, Caldé."

"No wet," Oreb muttered.

"He has a point," Silk remarked as they set out. "Could we borrow umbrellas? If we're going to have to walk between these buildings, as I expect we will."

"I'll get some while you're talking to the director," the guard promised; he trotted ahead to open the door of a brick structure not much different from a modest house.

"We can wait outside," Chenille told Silk. "I mean, in the hall or whatever, just as long as it's out of the rain."

He shook his head, entering a reception room presided over by a woman rather too large for it. She smiled. "Go right on in, please, Caldé."

"Will there be enough chairs? There are four of us."

From the room beyond, a short man beginning to go bald told him, "Three chairs and a settle. Come in!" He offered his hand. "Swallow's my name, Caldé." Silk shook it and introduced Maytera Marble, Mucor, and Chenille.

Swallow nodded, still smiling. "Sit down, please, ladies, Caldé. You're lame, I hear, and I see you're limping." He shut the door. "Everybody's got some tidbit about you. You're lame, you've got that tame bird, and you predicted the downfall of the Ayuntamiento. I'm sure you've heard it all."

Silk took a leather armchair near Swallow's table. "And

now you're surprised to see how young I am, and would like to ask my age."

"Why, that's none of my affair, Caldé."

"I'm twenty-three. You must be," he glanced at Swallow's hands, "in your forties. Forty-five or forty-six. Am I right?"

"I'm glad you're not, Caldé. I'm forty-three."

"Twenty years older than I am, precisely. You must think I'm very young and inexperienced to head the city government. I am, and I realize it. I have to depend on the judgement of more experienced men and women. That's one reason Maytera Marble's with me today; it's also the reason I'm here talking to you, an older man with experience I haven't got but need to draw upon."

"I'll be happy to help you any way I can, Caldé. Would you like something before we get started? Coffee, wine, tea? Would the young ladies? Chamomile can fetch us some."

Chenille shook her head; Silk said, "No thank you. You build taluses here?"

"We do. That's our business and our only business."

Oreb offered his judgement on taluses. "Bad things!"

"Be quiet, silly bird." Silk leaned back, the tips of his fingers together. "I know nothing about business, and this must be a remarkable one."

"Not to me." Swallow smiled. "I grew up in it, working in our shops. But you're right, it's unique. That's the word we like to use. Call it self-promotion if you want, but it fits."

"Because a talus is a person," Silk continued, "both in law and in fact. There are boatyards along the shore of the lake, where I was a few days ago. The boatwrights build a boat there; and when they're through, the fishermen paint eyes on it and call it 'she.' They give it a name, as well."

Swallow nodded.

"A boat has a certain character, just as this chair does. This is comfortable and solid, brown, and so forth. A boat may be a willing or a reluctant sailer, it may be stable or prone to rock. But a boat isn't a person."

Maytera Marble cleared her throat, a rasp like the scraping of a crusted pan. "Are you going to ask how they can build a talus with a certain character, Patera? I don't think they can, really. I've never . . ."

"Go on, Maytera."

"Never built a child. With a man, you know. But—but from what I understand, we can't either. We do our best, give the child all the advantages we can. But after that, it's up to the gods. To Molding Molpe and Lord Pas, principally."

Swallow nodded again. "It's no different here, Maytera. The layman thinks taluses are all alike. That's because they all sound the same to him. When you've spent a while talking to them, you find out they don't really talk alike even if they all sound like taluses. When it comes to ingenuity or honesty, that kind of thing, they can differ pretty widely. As you say, it depends on the spirit they get from the gods."

"They're all boring," Mucor told him; he seemed about to reply, but meeting her corpse-like gaze quickly looked away.

"There is another difference I wanted to inquire about," Silk interposed. "I mean between taluses and boats, or any other man-made object. If I were to go to Limna with a case full of cards, I could buy a boat; and once I had paid for it, it would be mine. I could sail it or leave it tied to a pier. I could burn or sink it if I wanted to, or give it to Maytera here, or to Chenille or anyone I chose. A talus is a person, and I would assume that in cities in which slavery is legal, anyone with sufficient funds could go to a facility such as yours and order a talus built—"

"You can do that here, Caldé," Swallow put in.

"Ah. That's interesting."

"Good thing?" Oreb inquired.

Maytera Marble said, "It seems to me that all this applied to me once as well, Patera. No one owned me. I've always been free, I'm sure, and yet I did what I was told. I still do, for the most part. I respect authority, and when I was younger, I don't think it even occurred to me to question it." She looked thoughtful, her head down and inclined to the left.

To encourage her Oreb croaked, "Talk now."

"Most bio—do you really want to hear this, Patera? I could tell you later, if you like."

"Of course I do. Tell us."

"I was just going to say that most bio children are like that, too. I don't mean that there are no bad children, though foolish people say that because it makes them feel virtuous. But there are really very few. I've taught children for a long time, and most can be controlled quite easily with a few little scoldings and a few words of praise." She paused, lifting her head and squaring her shoulders. "So can most grownups. Not quite so easily, but it isn't a lot more difficult."

Swallow chuckled. "She's right, Caldé. I boss almost two hundred employees here, and as a general thing a good chewing out now and then and a pat on the back for good work are all it takes. Once in a rare while we take on somebody that doesn't work out, stealing tools or whatever, and we've got to get rid of him. But it doesn't happen often."

"I've been thinking about Marl, Patera."

Silk nodded, noting as he did the first large drops of the rain that had been threatening; they were tapping on the window panes tentatively, but with growing urgency.

"Marl doesn't receive any wages at all. I told you."

Swallow raised an eyebrow. "Black mechanics, Maytera? It sounds like it."

"I don't know. I really hadn't considered it. I was just going to say that Marl seems like an extreme instance of—of pliability. I suppose you could call it that. . . ."

Maytera Marble's remaining hand tightened its grip on the handle of the small basket in her lap. "And if you can make use of that pliability to control others as you do, Director, with a little money and scoldings and praise, then it seems to me people like you don't really need slaves, except as sops to their egos. I'm expressing this offensively, I know, but I think you see what I mean. As for black mechanics, aren't they legendary? Largely legendary, I should have said. I know that some people practiced the black art in the past."

"There's still a bit around in my opinion, Maytera. In my business we hear things, and that's one of the things we hear." Swallow turned to Silk. "I'm a blunt man, Caldé, and I'm going to ask you straight out. Are you interested in getting a new talus for the Guard? Is that why you're here?"

"I've been considering it," Silk admitted. "Several, perhaps."

Swallow smiled. "Good. Very good! I'm delighted to hear it. I've been telling our people that this unrest was sure to bring in some fresh business, and I'm glad to see I was right. You're wondering why you should have to pay for something that the city can't own, aren't you?"

"I am. Also how I can be assured that the taluses Viron pays for will be loyal and obedient."

"It's a good question." Swallow hitched his chair nearer his office table, resting his elbows on it. "First of all, if you want absolute assurance, I can't give it to you. Nobody can. I'm told there's an outfit in Wick now that tells people that, but they're lying. Suppose you went to that boatyard in Limna. Could the people building boats there give you an iron-clad guarantee that any boat they sold you would never sink or turn over? Under any circumstances?"

"I doubt it."

"So do I. If they did, they'd be lying exactly like those fellows in Wick. Here's the guarantee we offer. If one of our taluses betrays your interests or won't carry out a legitimate order, within the first two years you employ it, we will refund the entire amount you paid. When I say 'you' now, I mean the city. For the third year, the amount is cut by a quarter. You get three quarters of what you paid us back. During the fourth you get half, then a quarter."

"Nothing after the fifth year?" Maytera Marble asked.

"That's right. But you will have had five years service from your talus by that time, don't forget."

Silk nodded thoughtfully.

"I'd like to have your business," Swallow continued. "I don't deny that. We rarely receive an order for more than a single talus. And it would be a feather in our cap to be able to say we already had a large order from the new government. So here's what I'll do. I said a full refund if there's any serious trouble during the first two years. All right, for each talus you get over one, I'll increase the guarantee by one year. Say you were to order three. Is that about what you're thinking of, Caldé?"

"Perhaps."

"Then let's say three. That's two over one, so you'd get a full cash refund—we're talking here about the price of the individual talus, not the price of all three."

"I understand," Silk said.

"A full refund on that talus for serious trouble during the first four years. After that, three quarters, then half and a quarter, as I've already outlined it to you. You'll be entirely covered or partly covered for . . . How long, Maytera?"

"Twenty-five percent in the seventh year, Patera," she told Silk. "Nothing after that."

"Good deal?" Oreb tugged a lock of Silk's hair.

"A safe one, at least, I believe. You don't have to pay often, do you, Director Swallow?"

Swallow smiled and relaxed. "No, we don't. If we did, we'd be bankrupt. We paid a quarter-price refund fifteen years ago—no, make that sixteen. I was foundry supervisor then, and I felt it was a pretty dubious case. All of us knew it was, really, and if we'd fought it in court, we'd probably have won. But it was only a quarter, the customer was making a lot of noise, and the director we had then wanted to establish that we keep our promises. I'm not saying he was wrong, just that the talus in question had been abused. The customer'd had it piling bricks, which isn't natural."

"What is?" Silk inquired.

"Fighting and protection, the same things you'd expect from a watchdog." Swallow cleared his throat. "Can I get a little bit personal, Maytera? No disrespect intended, but you brought up an important principle, obedience to authority. What you said made a lot of sense, and I'd like to use you for an example."

Chenille said, "I don't think you ought to. Tell him no, Maytera. I don't think this is a good idea at all."

"Because it will make me more aware of my nature, dear? I don't believe it will, since I'm very much aware of it already.

I've spent many, many hours thinking about who I am and what the gods require of me. But if it does, even a little, I'll thank the director very sincerely for the insight."

"No talk," Oreb advised Swallow.

He chuckled. "I won't say what I was going to, I promise. But I will say this. What I was going to say, I could have said about myself or anybody else in this room. I just thought the clothes might make it clearer."

"The clothes that were given to me when I woke? I didn't get to them, but you're right. After a while I sat up too, and another girl gave me my first clothes. Were you going to ask me what kind of clothes they were?"

Swallow nodded. "That's right, I was."

"A little black dress, very simple, with rather a short skirt. Underclothes." Maytera Marble paused to smile. "I was about to say I'd prefer not to describe them, but they were so plain that there's hardly anything to describe. Black shoes with low heels, but I don't think there were any stockings. A pretty little lace apron and a matching cap. It's easy for me to describe those clothes, because people from Ermine's came to Patera's palace just before we left, and there were young women dressed exactly as I was then, except that they had stockings."

"Did they come to clean?" Swallow asked. "Sweep and dust?"

"Dear Chenille and I have done that already. To wash the dishes they'll need tonight and set the table, and wash walls we haven't gotten to. At least I hope they'll wash those walls and the downstairs windows. I asked them to."

Swallow nodded again. "You see, Caldé, each of us is born to do certain things. Maytera was born to sweep and dust, and wash walls and floors, and she's still doing it. Did you have to urge her to?"

Silk shook his head.

"I would have been surprised if you'd said you did, and it shows the important principle I want to explain. When you're born to do a thing, and somebody gives you a chance to do it, that's all it takes. Everybody else is afraid I'll embarrass her, so let's talk about your bird."

"Oreb," Oreb elucidated.

"Nobody's got to make him fly. He flies because it's his nature. Nobody has to make him talk either. He was born to."

"Talk good!"

"There you have it. All right, it's a talus's nature to fight and protect property. Give your talus a chance to do those things, and it will do them. You're afraid the ones we build for you will give you a hard time, but you're caldé, and if they did, you'd give them a hard time, too, wouldn't you? Have them arrested and disarmed? And tried, too, eventually?"

"I suppose so."

"Naturally you would. So why should they make trouble, when what you want them to do is what they want to do? The things they were born to do?"

"I was at a country house guarded by a talus not long ago, and Mucor told me it could be bribed, though it took a great deal of money." Silk looked at her for confirmation.

"Musk said so."

Chenille asked, "What would a talus do with money?" and Maytera Marble ventured, "The same things that you or I would, I suppose, dear."

"You were asking how you could buy something you couldn't own, Caldé." Swallow picked up a pencil, apparently to rap the tablet before him. "Let me tell you about that now, about the financial arrangements. When a talus is finished, it owes us, by law, the cost of its manufacture plus fifteen percent."

"Even though the city has paid for it?"

"Exactly. What the city's doing, you see, is advancing us the money we'd eventually get from the talus. We make no more than we would if we'd built without an order. Which we seldom do, by the way, since by building to order we get our money a lot sooner. What's even more important, we don't have to worry about the talus getting killed before it can pay us."

Silk nodded while his right forefinger drew small circles on his cheek. "I see."

"We require payment in full before the talus is finished.

When it's finished, we explain that it has been built because there's an employer anxious to hire it. That's you, Caldé. We also explain the nature of wages, what wages it can reasonably expect, and what bonuses."

"But I don't actually pay it. Isn't that correct?"

"I can see you grasp the idea already. That's right, you don't. Let's say that you and your talus agree on five cards a month, a fair wage. From that, you deduct your expenses for fuel, maintenance, and repairs, if any. Most employers furnish ammo free of charge. It's customary."

Silk nodded again.

"You report the net to us, or you can have the talus do it. We deduct it from the talus's debt. Eventually its indebtedness will be wiped out and it can keep the wages it earns."

"Provided it survives that long."

"You've got it." Swallow glanced over his shoulder at the windows behind him, where the tapping of raindrops had mounted to a steady, insistent pounding. "If you'd rather have a look at our shops another time . . . ?"

"Patera," Maytera Marble began, "I don't—"

She was interrupted by Silk, who stood as he spoke. "I'm eager to see them, and I'm sure a little rain won't hurt me. I was caught in that downpour a week from yesterday, but here I am. I don't want you to feel that you have to take us around in person, however, Director. Someone else can do it."

"Not take the caldé around?" Grinning broadly, Swallow rose too. "I wouldn't miss it for any money. The ladies can wait in here if they like."

"I'm coming," Maytera Marble declared. "My granddaughter can stay here with Chenille."

"Me too," Chenille announced. "I want to see this."

"In that case Mucor will have to come with us, Patera."

"I can fly," she informed Swallow gravely. "Even in the rain. But they can't."

The promised umbrellas had been left on a chair in the outer room. Chenille picked one up. "Here's a black one for you, Patera, if you want it."

Silk shook his head. "Let Maytera have it."

Hanging her basket on her right forearm, she accepted the black umbrella and shook it out. "It's bad luck to open them indoors, they say, but I've already had mine. I can't thank that nice young man for getting these for us."

"One of your guards," Silk explained. "Now that I come to think of it, it seems strange that you've hired bios to protect this place instead of a talus."

"We do have a talus." Swallow accepted a yellow umbrella from Chenille. "As a matter of fact we have two now, because of the unrest. They're in the guard shack."

He went to the door, opening his umbrella. "You went by it on your way here. They have windows so they can keep an eye on the gate, but mostly they listen for shooting or shouting. A lot of the little matters that our guards handle, a good bio can take care of better than any talus. Suppose you had taluses patrolling the streets instead of troopers, Caldé. You'd have a dozen people shot every night, instead of one or two a week."

Opening the green umbrella that Chenille handed him, Silk followed Swallow out into the rain. "I've dealt with taluses once or twice, and I'm sure you're right."

"They protect the plant at night, and we have them there ready to roll in case of serious fighting. So far it's been around the Palatine and the Alambrera. I'm sure you know."

Silk nodded.

"Would you like to look at them? There's the guard shack." Swallow pointed at a weathered wooden shed.

"Not now, thank you." Silk had to raise his voice to make himself heard above the rattle of rain on his umbrella. "Later, perhaps. Right now I'd like to see how they're made."

"Good. That's where I'm taking you. Excuse me a minute, and I'll get the door."

Swallow strode off through the rain; Silk limped after him as rapidly as he could, splashing through deepening puddles in shoes that were already sodden.

The wide wooden door Swallow had opened let them into a cavernous structure whose floor was covered with coarse sand; three men were working in a pit a few steps from the doorway, illuminated by a single bleary light high overhead. "This is the foundry," Swallow announced as Maytera Marble and Mucor entered under a single black umbrella. "I always start visitors here, because it's where I started myself. I sifted, shoveled, ran errands, and the rest of it. It's hard, dirty work, but I was bringing home a little money to help my folks, and I've never felt so good about anything I've done in my life."

Chenille exclaimed, "You make those great big things out of sand? I don't believe it!" Oreb flew off into the darkness at the other end of the building to explore.

"There are some glass parts, and they really are made out of sand, but not by us." Swallow shut his umbrella and thumped its tip on the sand-strewn floor. "This is foundry sand and wouldn't make good glass. But we cast some big parts in sand, which is what these men are getting ready to do."

He pointed with his umbrella. "You see the hollow left by the form when it was lifted out? Those round pieces are called cores. They're made of compressed sand with a starch binder, and if they aren't positioned exactly right, and firmly enough that they stay in place when the iron's poured, the whole piece will be ruined. What they're doing here is preparing to cast an engine block, Caldé." At the last word, the workers looked up.

Silk had been trying to locate Oreb in the darkness. "This seems a very large place for three men."

"When we're going full tilt, which we will be tomorrow if we get your order today, there will be eighteen men and six boys working in here, Caldé. I've had to lay off everybody except my best men, which I don't like to do."

Taking Silk unobtrusively by the elbow, Swallow led him deeper into the building, his voice kindling a second light. "They're all good men to tell the truth, and the boys are smart lads who'll be good men too before long. We can't use anything else. I hate layoffs because I know the people I let go won't be able to find another job, generally. But if they could, I'd hate them worse because I'd lose them, and you can't just bring in an untrained man and have him go to work. It takes years."

Maytera Marble inquired, "How old are the boys?"

"We start them at fourteen nowadays. I was twelve when I started." Silk heard the soft exhalation of Swallow's breath. "We had layoffs then, too, though it wasn't as hard as now. Not usually. I never got to go to palaestra, but there was a woman on our street who had, and she taught me to read and write and figure during layoffs. I'm pretty good with figures, if I do say it. She was a friend of Mother's and wouldn't take anything for it, but I always thought that someday I'd get to where I could pay her. I was just about there, just made lead-man here, when she died."

Silk asked, "May I speak as an augur instead of calidé?"

"Go ahead. I'm not religious, but maybe I should be."

"Then I'll explain to you that the woman who helped you out of friendship for your mother had been helped herself, when she was younger, by some earlier person you never met."

Swallow nodded. "I suppose it's likely enough."

"She couldn't repay that person any more than you could repay her, but when she helped you she wiped out her debt. When you help someone, you'll wipe out yours. Possibly you already have—I have no way of knowing."

"I've tried once or twice, Calidé."

"You say you're not religious. Nor am I, though I was very religious not long ago. Because I'm not, I'm not going to say that this passing forward from one generation to the next is the method the gods have ordained for the settlement of such debts, though perhaps it is. In any event, it's a good one, one that lets people die, as everyone must, feeling that they've squared accounts with the whorl."

Maytera Marble said, "Perhaps he already has, Patera, by employing those boys."

Swallow shrugged. "They don't pay, and that's the truth. We pay a card a month, and they're not worth it to us. But we're not doing it from charity. We have to have them so they can learn the work. If we didn't, someday we'd need foundrymen and there wouldn't be any, no matter how much we offered."

"Then it was good of you to . . . Lay them off? Is that what you call it? So they could attend a palaestra. Because I'd think that if you were teaching them, they'd be the last ones you'd want to send home."

"They were," Swallow told her shortly.

Chenille had been looking at the largest ladle Silk had ever seen, a great cup of scaly pottery large enough to hold a man. "Is this what you melt the iron in?"

"That's right." Swallow was himself again at once, brisk and all business. "It's heated in this brick furnace here." He went to it. "It burns charcoal with a forced draft, and it takes a lot. Those bunkers you saw against the wall where we came in were for sand. Every casting we make uses up a little, and they're our reserve. These bunkers hold charcoal and steel scrap. We fill up that crucible with scrap, lower it into the furnace, and put the lid on. When it's been in long enough, depending on how much scrap was in it, we lift it out the same way and pour."

A slightly smaller crucible stood on the other side of the brick furnace; reaching into it, Chenille displayed an irregular scab of shining yellow metal. "This looks almost like gold."

Oreb flew over for a closer inspection.

"It's brass," Swallow told her. "A talus's head requires some pretty complicated castings, and brass is easier to cast than iron, so we use that for the head."

Silk said, "Some taluses wear helmets, I've noticed, while others don't."

"The helmet's actually a part of the head," Swallow told him. "Or you could say it takes the place of the skullplate. Would you like helmets on the taluses we're going to build for the city? I can specify them in the contract."

"I don't know. I was wondering whether a helmet furnished better protection for the head." In his mind's eye, Silk saw the talus he had killed; the shimmering discontinuity that was the blade of the azoth he had thought Hyacinth's had struck it below the eye, vaporizing metal and inflicting a mortal wound.

"Not really." Swallow clapped his hands to brighten the lights. "Over here we have the forms for various head designs. They're made so the parts can be switched. Say you like the nose on one head, but you'd rather have the mouth on another. We can give you both without any additional charge. We cast the nose you want and the mouth you want, and after the castings have been cleaned up, they'll fit together."

"How thick is the metal?" Silk inquired.

"Two to four fingers, depending on where you measure. It has to be at least two, to get enough melt through the space." Proudly, Swallow gestured toward a row of somewhat worn-looking wooden heads, each nearly as tall as he was. "There they are, Caldé, twenty-nine of them. Since all of them trade parts, there's almost no limit to the number of faces we can provide."

"I see. Is two fingers of brass enough to stop a slug?"

"No shoot," Oreb advised from Chenille's shoulder.

"It depends, Caldé. How far away was the trooper when he fired? That can make a big difference. So can the angle it strikes at. If it hits square on, it might go through if the trooper was standing close. I've known that to happen. The talus has its own guns, though, and unless it's out of ammo, an enemy trooper that close isn't likely to be alive."

Chenille grinned. "I'll say!"

"What we've found," Swallow continued, "is it's pretty rare for a trooper to shoot at the head at all. The thorax plate and the front of the abdomen are bigger targets, but they're steel. I'll show you some in the welding shop."

"Will a slug penetrate them?"

Swallow shook his head. "I've never known it to happen. I won't say it can't, I'd want to run some tests. But it's very unusual, if it happens at all."

Silk turned to Chenille. "You and Auk were riding on the back of a talus when it encountered some of the Ayuntamiento's soldiers in the tunnel. You told me about that."

She nodded. "Patera Incus was with us, too, Patera. So was Oreb here."

"Later on, one of the wounded soldiers?"

Chenille nodded again. "The talus stopped to shoot, I guess that's why it stopped anyhow, and Auk got on Patera about not bringing the dead ones Pas's Pardon. We could see a bunch of dead ones in back of us. There were lights in that tunnel, and some of the dead ones were on fire."

"I understand."

"So Patera did. He got off the talus. Auk was just—he couldn't believe it. Then the talus saw what had happened and said for Patera to get back on, and he said only if you'll take this soldier too. That was Stony, we found out his name later."

Maytera Marble asked, "Wasn't this nice talus that let you ride on it killed, dear? I think you told me about its death, and how the holy augur who was with you brought it the Pardon."

Silk nodded. "That's the point I particularly want to hear about, Chenille. How was that talus killed? Where did the slug strike it?"

"I don't think it was a slug at all, Patera. Stony said it was a missile. Some of the soldiers had launchers—I got one myself, after—and they were shooting them."

"You'll have to excuse my ignorance," to relieve the pain in his ankle, Silk backed to the crucible and sat down on its rim, "but I'm not familiar with those. What's the difference between a missile and a launcher?"

"The launcher fires the missile, Caldé."

"That's right. Just almost exactly like a slug gun shoots a slug. Maybe they ought to call a launcher a missile gun, but they don't."

"You had one of these weapons, Chenille? Where is it now?"

"I don't know. Stony took it to shoot at the Trivigaunti pterotroopers. That was while me and Auk were in the pit with Trivigauntis flying all around and you talking at us from that floater up in the air. Somebody yelled for us to get back in the tunnel, and it sounded like a real good idea to me."

Swallow said, "A missile's a very different proposition

from a slug, Caldé. A slug's just a heavy metal cylinder. It hits the target a lot harder than a needle or a stone from a sling, but that's only because it's heavier than a needle and going faster than a stone. Missiles carry an explosive charge, and that lets them do a lot more damage."

"Missiles are heavier, I think, too," Chenille told Silk. "I've seen troopers carrying forty or fifty slugs—"

"Cartridges," Swallow corrected her.

"Whatever. They had them on a special canvas strap, and they were walking around fine. I think if you loaded a trooper down with forty or fifty missiles, he couldn't hardly stand up. My launcher was nice and light when I found it, but Stony helped me load it, and it was really heavy after that."

"Director Swallow."

"Yes, Caldé?"

"You mentioned a part called the thorax plate. I take it that's the part covering what I would call the talus's chest."

"Exactly right, Caldé."

"Chenille says the soldier Patera Incus befriended felt that their talus had been killed by one of those things—by a missile fired from a launcher. Are those the terms?"

Swallow nodded; Chenille said, "That's it, Patera."

"But if I understood her, he was on the talus's back at the time that it was shot. How could he have known?"

Swallow fingered his chin. "He lived through this, didn't he? He must of, since the young lady said he took her launcher later. If he had a chance to see the talus afterward—"

"Man see," Oreb announced confidently. "Iron man."

"In that case, Caldé, it wouldn't have been hard for him to tell the difference between a wound from a slug gun and one from a missile."

Silk nodded again, largely to himself. "Was this a facial wound, Chenille? Do you recall?"

She shook her head. "He talked to us after. I'm not sure where he was hit, but lower down."

Silk stood up. "You mentioned your welding shop, Director. I want to see it—and ask a favor. May we go now?"

As they left, Silk lagged to question Mucor. "You told us

you could fly in the rain," belatedly he opened his umbrella, "But they couldn't. By 'they' did you intend the Fliers?"

She only stared.

"Is that why it rains after they've flown over? Because they somehow prevent it when they're present?"

"Answer him, dear," Maytera Marble prompted, but Mucor did not speak.

As they splashed along a rutted path between sodden wooden structures that could easily have been barns, Swallow remarked, "I wish you had better weather for this, Caldé, but I hear the farmers need rain pretty badly."

Silk could not help smiling. "They need it so badly that the sight and sound of it fill my heart with joy. All the time we were in your foundry I was listening to it, and the finest music in the whorl couldn't have moved me half so much. I don't suppose Chenille or Maytera like it—I know Oreb here doesn't, and I'm a bit worried about Mucor, whose health is frail; but I'd rather walk through this than the clearest sunshine."

Swallow opened the door of another ramshackle building, releasing a puff of acrid smoke and revealing a large and dirty canvas screen. "Foundry work's pretty crude, Caldé. In the old times they knew a lot we don't, though I've spent a good part of my life trying to learn their secrets. What I'm going to show you now's closer to what you might have seen on the Short Sun Whorl. But before I do, I've got to warn you. You mustn't look at the process. At the blue welding fire, in other words. The light's too bright. It can make you blind."

Silk shook his umbrella. "Smiths join iron by heating and pounding it. I used to watch them as a boy. I wasn't blinded, so what you're doing here must be a different process."

Chenille tossed back wet raspberry curls. "Better make sure Oreb doesn't watch either, Patera."

"I certainly will." For Swallow's benefit, Silk added significantly, "At times we all look at things we shouldn't. Even birds do it."

Swallow blinked and abandoned his study of Chenille's damp gown. "Sometimes people think we do it different be-

cause we're working with steel instead of iron, but that's not
true. We use this method because it works on pieces your
smith couldn't have welded, because they're too big to be
hammered." Light showed above the canvas screen, brilliant
enough to make the rafters cast sharp shadows on the under-
side of the roof.

"One of our men's making a weld now. We'll wait here till
he's through, if it's all right with you, Caldé. Then we can go
in, and I'll show you what he's doing and how he does it. He'll
be welding up a thorax plate, I think."

While her remaining hand closed the black umbrella she
had shared with Mucor, Maytera Marble gave Silk a significant look.

He nodded. "I want to see it. In fact, I'm very eager to, Director. You spoke of thick pieces in connection with these thorax plates and so on? How thick are they?"

"Three fingers." Swallow held them up.

"I want mine thicker. Six at least. Can you do that?"

Swallow looked startled. "Why . . . ? Could we weld them,
do you mean? We could, but it would take longer. It would
be a lot more work."

"Then do it," Silk told him.

Oreb whistled.

"Put it in our contract, six-finger thorax plates. What was
the other piece? Below the thorax plate?"

"The abdomen front plate?" Swallow suggested.

"That's it. How thick is it?"

"Three fingers, too, Caldé." Swallow hesitated, his eyes
thoughtful. "Do you want them thicker? I suppose it could be
done, but it may take us a while to find steel that thick and
work out a way to bend it."

Oreb exclaimed, "No, no!"

"We cannot afford delay, Director. Viron requires these
taluses immediately. I realize you can't supply them today, but
if you could, I'd accept them and pay you for them, and thank
you. You join steel here—that's what the workman on the
other side of this screen is doing?"

Swallow nodded.

"Then make my thorax plates and abdomen front plates out of two pieces of the steel you have, each three fingers thick. Maytera here could make me a robe from doubled cloth, if I had need of such a thing. Why couldn't you do this?"

"We can, I think." Swallow cleared his throat. "There'll be problems. With all respect, Caldé, welding steel isn't as simple as sewing, but I think it could be done. Can I ask . . . ?"

"Why they need it? So they can fight the Ayuntamiento's soldiers in the tunnels, of course. I've been down in those tunnels, Director—I even fought a talus there. There was only a step of clearance between the sides of that talus and the sides of the tunnel. A soldier who got that close would be very close indeed; and the taluses I want you to build will have troopers protecting their backs. The danger will be in front, where it will come from soldiers armed with weapons like the one Chenille had."

"Launchers," she supplied.

"Exactly. Launchers shooting missiles." Silk collected his thoughts. "The heads still trouble me. You say you can't cast them from iron?"

"No, Caldé. We usually paint them black. Nearly always, because it makes the eyes and teeth show up better. If we could cast them from iron we wouldn't have to paint them or touch up scratches, so we've tried it. Iron won't make castings that detailed, not till we learn more about casting it, at any rate."

"Too bad!" The light above the screen had vanished; Oreb flew up to peer over.

"Yes, it is," Silk confirmed.

"But you're worried about strength, Caldé. Resistance to slugs and that sort of thing. And to tell you the truth, iron wouldn't be a lot better. It might even be worse. Cast iron's a wonderful material in a lot of ways, but it's pretty brittle. That's why we use steel plate for the abdomen and so forth."

"Patera? Director?" Maytera Marble looked from Silk to Swallow and back. "Couldn't the talus hold something in front of its face? A piece of steel with a handle like an umbrella?"

Silk nodded. "And look over the top. Yes, that could be done, I'm sure, Maytera."

"There's one other possibility, Caldé," Swallow offered hesitantly. "This is from the old days too. But it was done right here, I understand, though it was before my time. We might try bronze."

Silk looked around at him sharply. "Isn't that what they are now?"

Chenille shook her head. "It's brass, Patera. Remember when I held that piece up? He said brass."

"Bronze would be a lot stronger, Caldé." Swallow cleared his throat again. "Tougher, too. I mean real bronze. This is kind of hard to explain."

"Go ahead," Silk told him. "I'll make every effort to understand you, and it's important."

"Let me start with iron, maybe that will make it clearer. You and I talked about iron. Casting it and so forth."

Silk nodded.

"What people call iron's really three different materials, Caldé. The commonest is just soft steel, any steel that doesn't have a lot of carbon in it. People call that tin when it's rolled out as sheet metal, and sometimes it's plated with tin. Most people have never seen a real chunk of solid tin."

"Go on."

"When you watched that blacksmith making horseshoes, that was what he was using. He probably called it iron, but it was really soft steel, iron with just a little touch of carbon. If there's gobs of carbon in it, it's cast iron, the melt we pour in the foundry. You can't pound cast iron the way a smith does. It'll break."

"I remember that you said it was brittle."

"That's right, it is. It has lots of uses, but you can't use it for armor or a hammer head, or anything like that."

Swallow took a deep breath. "Number three's wrought iron, and that really is iron, though there's generally some slag in it, too. We start with cast iron and burn all the carbon out, when we want some. It's pretty soft, and it'll take almost any amount of bending. Mostly it's used for fancy window grills and that kind of a thing."

"You still haven't told me anything about bronze."

"I thought this might help make it clearer, Caldé. You see, there's a couple dozen alloys people call bronze, because they look like bronze. Most have quite a bit of pot metal in them and no tin at all. Tin costs too much. Real tin."

Silk stirred impatiently.

"That makes real bronze cost a lot, too. Real bronze, not the stuff you'd get if you bought a bronze figure of some god, is half tin and half copper."

"Is that all?"

Swallow nodded. "It's a pretty simple alloy, but it's got marvelous properties. It's tougher than steel and almost as strong, and you can hammer and weld it, and machine it easier than anything except cast iron. I know that because we still make some little parts out of it, sleeve bearings mostly, and the worms for the big worm gears. But when I was a boy, the older men said they used to cast heads out of it, and there were still some old taluses around with those bronze heads."

Silk leaned against the doorframe; he was already tired, had been tired before the parade had ended, and there was still the dinner tonight; he resolved to get an hour's sleep before eight, no matter what happened. Aloud he asked, "Can you cast bronze—this real bronze—as well as brass?"

"Better, Caldé. We cast those worms I mentioned, and then machine the bearing surfaces, so I know. It would speed things up too, because the parts wouldn't need so much cleanup. But it would be expensive, because of the cost of the tin."

"Have you got the tin? Here right now?"

Swallow nodded. "Because we still use bronze for the worms and so forth."

"Then do it. Use it."

"I'll have to up the price, Caldé. I'm sorry, but I will. Even if you order two or three."

"Then up it." Longing for the brown leather chair he had occupied earlier, Silk added, "We'll talk about how much when we get back to your office. And don't forget the double-thick thorax and front plates. Obviously you'll need a little more for those, and the steel umbrellas—shields, I suppose you'd call them—that Maytera suggested."

Mucor said, "The storm will pass over soon," surprising everyone; then, "I'm tired."

"She ought to sit down," Silk told Swallow, "and so should I, but first I must ask you about Maytera's hand. She's got it in her basket. Maytera, will you show it to him, please?"

"Man cut," Oreb remarked from his perch on the top of the screen. Silk was not certain whether he meant that Blood had severed it or that Blood himself had been killed—by him—as animals were as sacrifice.

Maytera Marble had passed her basket to Swallow; he took off the white towel that had covered her now-lifeless right hand and held it up, in appearance the hand of an elderly woman. A short cylinder of silvery metal extended from its wrist. "I lost some fluid," she told him, "but not very much. There are valves and things to control that. I'm sure you know."

He nodded absently.

"But the tubes would have to be mended some way. The one that brings the fluid to move my fingers, and the one that takes it back."

Silk said, "We'd appreciate it very much, Director, if you would do everything you can for Maytera. She can't pay you; but I may be able to, if it isn't too much. If it is, I feel sure I can arrange for you to be paid."

"Don't worry about that, Caldé." Swallow returned the severed hand to its basket. "We'd be happy to do what we can for Maytera here as a courtesy to you. We could rejoin those pressure and return tubes, though it'll take delicate work."

Maytera Marble smiled, her face shining.

"The load-bearing part's no problem at all. Or I don't think it should be. It won't look quite as pretty as it did, though. Repairs never do."

"I won't mind a bit," Maytera Marble assured him.

"The difficulty—pardon me, Caldé." Swallow closed the door, the only source of daylight on their side of the canvas screen. "Maytera, will you hold up your arm a minute? I need to show the caldé something."

She did, and Swallow pointed. "Look down in here, Caldé. Maytera, I want you to try to move your fingers. Pretend that you're going to grab hold of my nose."

Minute glimmerings appeared in the shadowy interior of the stump of arm, pin-point gleams that reminded Silk oddly of the scattered diamonds he had seen beneath the belly of the whorl.

"There! See that, Caldé? Those are glass threads, like very fine wires, with light running through them. It's fluid that powers her fingers, like she said, but it's those twinkles that steer them. The twinkles are messages. They're supposed to tell every joint in her hand how to move."

Hesitantly, Silk nodded.

"Suppose you were to put a man on a hilltop twenty miles away, and tell him to ride as soon as he saw a lantern run up the flagpole of the Juzgado. It's the same principle."

"I believe I understand."

"When ordinary wire like we use gets cut, you can fix it by wrapping the ends together. With glass threads like you find in chems, that won't work. You've got to have a special tool they call an opticsynapter. We don't have one here because we don't use glass thread. We haven't any way to make it."

Silk endeavored to ignore Maytera Marble's disappointment. "Then we must locate one of these tools—and someone who knows how to use it, I assume—and tie the glass threads? Is that correct? Then you can complete the repair?"

Swallow shook his head. "If she went around with her hand hanging from the glass string, it would probably break. We can do the welding right now, and we'd better. When you find an opticsynapter she can take off her hand in the usual way. The operator shouldn't have any trouble fishing out the other end of the string."

"Where would we find one?"

"There you have me, Caldé. A doctor who specializes in chems should have one, but I don't know of one here in Viron."

Chenille snapped her fingers. "I know somebody!"

"Do you, dear? Do you really?" Maytera Marble's voice, usually so calm, trembled noticeably.

"You bet. Stony had one of those strings cut where our talus had shot him, and Patera Incus fixed it for him so he could move again. He had a gadget to do it with, and that's what he said it was, an opticsynapter. I was watching him."

Silk turned to Blood's emaciated daughter. "You were gone a few minutes ago, Mucor. Are you back with us? Please answer, if you can."

She nodded. "With the Flier, Silk. Women have him. They want to know about the thing that lets him fly."

"I see. Perhaps it would be wiser for us not to speak of that at present. I want you to search for Patera Incus for me, as well as Hyacinth and Auk. Do you know him?"

After a silence that seemed long, Mucor said, "No, Silk."

"He was a prisoner in your father's house for a while, at the same time I was. He's an augur too, short, with a round face and prominent teeth. A few years older than I. I realize you don't see things as we do, but that is how we see him."

Mucor did not reply, and Maytera Marble passed her working hand before Mucor's eyes without result. "She's gone, Patera. She's looking for him, I think."

"Let's hope she finds all three soon." Silk glanced up at Oreb. "Has the man finished working over there? Joining the iron, or whatever you'd call it?"

"No fire! No more!"

"Thank you. Come along, Director. As interesting as all this is, and potentially valuable, I can't spare more time for it. Your workman must begin Maytera's repair. You and I can discuss our contract while he works. How many taluses could you build at the same time if you called back all of the employees you've sent home? Don't exaggerate."

"I won't. I just wish I had my charts here. The movement of parts, you know, Caldé, and the time required to make them."

"How many?" Silk stepped around the screen into a clutter of metal tables, remembering at the final moment to smile at the leather-aproned craftsman at work there. "Good afternoon, my son. Thelxiepeia bless you."

"Four, Caldé." Behind him, Silk heard Swallow's relieved exhalation. "I want to say five, but I can't guarantee it. We could start a fifth, once the first four are moving along."

"Then the city will order four," Silk decided, "with the double front plates I described, heads of real bronze, and the shields. We must consider armament, too, I suppose, and price. How long will four require?"

Swallow gnawed his lip. "I'm going to say two and a half months. That's the best I can promise, Caldé."

"Six weeks. Hire new people and train them—there are thousands of unemployed men and women in this city. Work day and night." Silk paused, considering. "The city agrees to pay a premium of six cards for each day less than forty-five. You have my word on that."

Swallow licked his lips.

From his perch on the screen, Oreb crowed, "Silk win!"

Chapter 8

TO SAVE YOUR LIFE

Repressing a shudder, Maytera Mint stepped over the dead man's leg, the last to go into the guardroom. Over Hyrax's leg, she told herself firmly. It was only Hyrax's leg, and not a thing of horror; *Hyrax,* a near-homophone of *Hierax,* was a name often given boys whose mothers had died in childbirth.

Now, Maytera Mint reflected, Hierax had come for Hyrax.

"They, the—ah . . ." Remora began, and fell silent.

"Soldiers." Spider seated himself on a stool. "Soldiers got them." He pulled up his tunic and thrust his needler into his waistband, let the tunic fall into place again, and wiped his hands on his thighs. "See how good they got shot, Patera? Dead center, all three. That's soldiers' shootin'."

"I would have thought that Hyrax's body would warn Guan," Maytera Mint ventured. She was looking down at Guan's body as she spoke. "He must have seen it, exactly as we did."

Spider nodded. "That's why he figured there wasn't no-body layin' for him. He figured they'd of moved it if they were, and he had a slug gun, didn't he? I'd want to know more than feet in the door, wouldn't I? So he went in careful and had a look around, see? That's how I would of done, and that's how Guan did. Then he set his gun down, probably stood it in the corner, and got that water. That's when they got him, shot him from in back. See where he's lyin'? He was watchin' the door while he drank. He couldn't shut it without movin' Hyrax, and he hadn't done that yet, but he was watchin', only a soldier was in here with him that he didn't know about, and that's when he shot him."

"May I sit, too?" Maytera Mint had found another stool. "May His Eminence?"

"Sure."

"We—er—arms? Should be armed." Remora was poking about the guardroom. "Slug guns, hey? Slug guns for soldiers, um, chems. Chemical persons, eh? All of them. The slug guns of the, um, departed."

"They're gone," Spider informed him. "They all had slug guns. That's Guan, Hyrax, and Sewellel. A slug gun'll do for a soldier, and soldiers don't like them lyin' around."

"I am sorry," Maytera Mint told him. "Genuinely sorry. You must understand that. I sympathize with your grief, not just conventionally but actually."

"All right. Sure."

"Nevertheless, I have won our bet. You pledged your word to give me honest answers to three questions. If you would prefer to wait, I understand. We may not have long, however."

"I might not," Spider told her. "That's what you're thinkin', isn't it? Say it."

She shook her head. "I'm not, because I don't understand the situation sufficiently. When you've answered my questions, I may. Here is the first. The Army is by no means alone in its possession of slug guns. All Bison's troopers have them, as do many others. Yet you were entirely certain it was not one of Bison's troopers who had killed Paca. Why was that?"

Remora put in, "He's answered already, hey? The—um—um—accuracy. Precision."

"Yeah, that. But we saw them, and the other boys shot at them. You said you heard shootin' when we had you locked up. Well, that was what you heard. It was soldiers, two or three, maybe. If they'd known there wasn't but five of us and me with no slug gun, they'd have shot it out, but they couldn't be sure we didn't have a couple dozen, that's what I think. So they beat hoof figurin' to chill us one at a time." He sighed. "We ought to of stuck together, but I didn't see it like that then."

"Thank you." Maytera Mint laced her fingers in her lap as she considered. "If they have come to rescue His Eminence and me, there would be no reason for us to shoot them if we had slug guns to do it. That's not a question, Spider. It's a comment."

"It's right enough, whichever it is. But if you're tryin' to find out who sent them or why, you're not goin' to get it out of me. I don't know. The Army's ours, the Ayuntamiento's. All the soldiers are supposed to know about us."

"Possibly, um, councillor, eh?" Remora had carried over a stool. "Might not he have come to—ah—dubiety? You have, um, informers? Against the general's forces, eh? Might not the councillor have come to fear that the Caldé, er, likewise? You?"

"Maybe." Spider rose, went to the door, and taking Hyrax's wrists pulled him into the room. "But I don't believe it."

"Nor do I," Maytera Mint murmured as Spider shut the door and bolted it.

"You gamble, eh? Put yourself at hazard. And us. If the soldiers you apprehend are concealed, hey? There are other, um, chambers? In addition to this in which we, er, presently?"

"That's the latrine," Spider told him, nodding toward an interior door. "We got one of those portable jakes in there. The other's the storeroom. Yeah, they could be in either one. Or locked out. I'll take that for now."

He turned to Maytera Mint. "You got two more questions, General. You goin' to ask them? Or you want more water and somethin' to eat? You can eat first if you want to."

Observing Remora's expression, she said, "Why can't we eat while I ask? We're adults."

"Swell. Patera, you're the hungriest, right?"

"I, er, possibly."

"Then you go in and get it. The door's not locked. Go in there, have a look at the prog, and bring out whatever you and the general want. Fetch along some wine, too, and more water if you want it."

Remora gulped. "If they are, hey? Inside?"

"They most likely won't shoot you. Tell them they won't have to shoot me, neither. Tell them all I got's a needler. When we went up to that house, I figured a needler'd be plenty and leave a hand free. Besides, it's what I usually pack."

"I shall emphasize the point, um, assuming." Remora faced about and bowed his head.

"Well, get to it. Open the shaggy door."

"He's praying," Maytera Mint explained. "He knows that he may be shot as soon as he does. He's commending himself to High Hierax and offering the other gods what may be his final prayers as a living person."

"Well, make it quick!"

"Thank you for answering my first question," Maytera Mint said to distract Spider. "I agree that you've answered fully and fairly, as specified. My second may be a bit touchier. I want to point out in advance that it concerns no confidential matters of our city's. Or of the Ayuntamiento's, in so far as the two can be distinguished.

"Before I ask, would you like to pray too? If there are soldiers in there, which you seem to think possible, they are more likely to shoot you than His Eminence. And if they shoot His Eminence, they will certainly shoot us as well."

Spider gave her a twisted grin. "How about you, General? You're a sibyl. Why aren't you prayin'?"

She took out her beads and fingered them while she framed her answer. "Because I have prayed a great deal already during the past few days. I have been in danger almost constantly, and I've sent others into dangers far worse and prayed for them. I would only be repeating the petitions I've made so often. Also because I've told the gods again and again that I'm very willing to die if that is their will for me. If I were to pray, I would pray only that His Eminence, and you, be spared. I do so pray. Great Pas, hear my plea!"

Spider grunted.

"Furthermore, I don't believe there are soldiers hiding in here. I think that what must have happened was that one of them was in here looking for something. He heard Guan come in and hid, then came out and shot Guan after Guan's first and perhaps rather cursory examination failed to find him. Would the water have come from the storeroom?"

Spider nodded. "Right."

"Then I should think that the soldier was in the latrine. Since chems don't use them, he might have thought Guan wouldn't expect him there."

Spider said nothing, sitting with eyes half shut, his back against the shiprock wall.

"Here is my second question. You'll recall that Councillor Potto described the situation on the surface to His Eminence and me, then asked who was master of the city. His description made it clear that he was implying the Rani was. I take it you will concede that. You were present."

"Sure. When her troopers come out of her airship, some of yours took shots at them. You know that?"

"I do. Many died as a result of that tragic error."

"Those troopers thought Viron was bein' invaded, and they were right. Sure, the Trivigauntis are goin' to help you fight us. Sure, they're goin' to make this Silk caldé. But he'll lose his job the first time he balks. What's the question?"

"You've answered it already, at least in part. I planned to ask what you know of the plans of the Trivigauntis."

Remora cleared his throat. "I am—ah—readied. Also resolved. You yourselves, eh? Are you, um . . . ?"

"Go ahead," Spider told him.

Remora took two determined steps to his right and threw wide the door.

"That's the latrine, you putt!"

Calmly, Remora turned. "I am, ah, was aware of it. I, um, eavesdropped, eh? Couldn't help it. The General, um, indicated that this, ah, necessary room would be the point of greatest, er, greater hazard. I revere her intellect. More than your own, if I may be thus—ah—incivil."

"Usually I do better than this," Spider told him. "Now get in there where you're s'posed to, and don't forget to bring me out a bottle."

"You would—ah—indubitably have had me, um, risk the necessary room as well." Remora opened the storeroom door as he spoke. "I therefore, eh? Advised by the immortal gods. Or so I would like to, um, have it. The greater risk first."

He stepped into the storeroom. "As for, ah, this . . ." He clapped to brighten the single dull light on the ceiling. "It is equally, um, innocent? Unpeopled."

"In that case, I would like another bottle of water, Your Eminence," Maytera Mint declared firmly, "if it's not too much trouble. And some bread, if there is any. Meat, too. I would be very grateful." To Spider she continued, "I inquired about what you knew, you'll notice, not what you guessed. Do you know this? Or is it speculation?"

"I know it. Now you'll want to know how I know."

She shook her head, marveling to find herself—little Maytera Mint from Sun Street!—haggling with such a man over such a matter. "I won't require you to reveal your sources."

"I'll tell you anyhow. Councillor Potto told me before we went up there. He wasn't just guessin', neither."

Remora emerged from the storeroom with a dusty wine bottle, two even dustier bottles of water, and several small packages wrapped in tinted synthetic.

Spider accepted the wine. "Brown's bread and red's meat. I ought to of told you, but I guess you worked it out yourself."

"It was not—ah—cryptic." Remora sat down. "This, er, packet is unopened, Maytera. I, hum, sampled the other. Somewhat saline, but tasty."

She accepted a red package and unwrapped it eagerly; it held flat strips of what seemed to be dried beef. "We thank all gods for this good food," she murmured. "Thanks to Fair Phaea, especially. Praise Pasturing Pas for fat cattle." She tore the leathery meat with her teeth and thought it sweet as sugarcane.

"Councillor Potto can lie birds out of a tree," Spider drew the cork of the wine bottle with a pop. "I've heard him to where I just about believed him myself. You said while we were talkin' in the tunnel that you figured I could fool you if I wanted to. I'm not so sure, but Councillor Potto could put it over on me, and I know it. Only this wasn't that. He just said it, listenin' to himself. I don't think he cared a sham shaggy bit whether I believed it. But I do, and I've known him twenty years, like I said."

Maytera Mint nodded and swallowed. "Thank you. And thank you, Your Eminence, for this food. I thanked the gods, I fear, but not their proximal agent."

"Quite all right, eh? Um—delighted. Have some bread." Remora handed her a brown-wrapped package. "Strengthening. Ah—fortifying."

"Thank you again. Thank you very much. All praise to Fruiting Echidna, whose sword I am."

She paused as she tore the loaf. "Spider, I'll ask my final question, if I may. I won't be able to, with my mouth full of this good bread. You may not know the answer."

"If I don't know, I don't." He wiped the top of the wine bottle on his cuff and held it out to her. "You want to bless this, too, while you're doin' everythin' else?"

"Certainly." Maytera Mint laid the bread in her lap with the remainder of the dried beef and traced the sign of addition over the bottle. "Praise be to you, Exhilarating Thelxiepeia, and praise to you, likewise, dark son of Thyone."

"Want a drink? Help yourself."

She sipped cautiously, then more boldly.

"I bet that was the first wine you ever had in your life. Am I right?"

She shook her head. "Laymen—they are men in fact, very largely—give us a bottle now and then. When it happens, we have a glass at dinner until it's gone." She hesitated. "We did, I should have said. Maytera Rose and I did, but we won't any more. She passed away last Tarsday, and I've scarcely had a moment to mourn her. She was . . ."

"A, umph, excellent sibyl," Remora put in. He chewed and

swallowed. "Doubtless. I did not have the—ah—happiness of her acquaintance. But doubtless, eh? No doubt of it."

"A good woman whom life had treated sufficiently roughly that she struck out, at times, before she was struck." Maytera Mint finished pensively. "Toward the end she struck at others habitually, I would say. It could be unpleasant, and yet her asperity was fundamentally defensive. That's good wine. Might I have a little more, Spider?"

"Sure thing."

"Thank you." She sipped again. "Perhaps His Eminence would like some too."

"Dimber with me."

Maytera Mint wiped the mouth of the bottle and passed it to Remora. "My third question now. As I said, you may not know the answer. But what was the original purpose of these tunnels? I've been wondering ever since our caldé described them to me, and it may be important."

Spider leaned back, his homely heavy-featured face tilted upward and his eyes closed. "That's somethin' I can tell you all right, but I got to think."

"As I say—"

He leaned forward once more, his eyes open and one large hand tugging at his stubbled jaw. "I didn't say I don't know. Councillor Potto told me about them. One thing he said was it wasn't just one thing. There's three or maybe four, and they go under the whole whorl. You know that?"

Her mouth full, Maytera Mint shook her head.

"If you went along the big one we turned off of," Spider jerked his thumb at the door, "far enough, you could get clean to the skylands, maybe. I don't know anybody that ever tried it, but that's what Councillor Potto said one time. You can be way out in the sticks where there isn't any houses or anythin', nothin' but trees and bushes, and maybe there's one right under you. Could be a hundred cubits down or so close you'd hit it puttin' in a fence post."

Hoping her face did not betray the skepticism she felt, she said, "The labor involved must have been incredible."

"Pas built them. It's queer, tellin' you two that. You ought to tell me. But he did. He did it when he was buildin' the whorl, so it wasn't as bad as you'd figure."

The wine returned to Spider, who drank and wiped his mouth on the back of his hand. "His boys did the real work, accordin' to the councillor. When we say Pas made it, it just means he had the idea and ran the job."

"His divine—ah—puissance animated his servants."

"If you say so. But there was a lot, see? He wanted the job done fast. Mind if I have a little of that?"

Spider took two strips of dried meat from Maytera Mint's lap. "I'm with him there, I'm the same way. You got a job to do, you do it. Wrap it up and tie the string. Let one drag, and somethin' always goes queer." He bit through both strips.

"If they were indeed constructed by Pas, it must have been for some good reason. It's one of the paradoxes of isagogics—" Maytera Mint looked to Remora for permission to speak on learned and holy topics, and received it. "That Pas, with all power at his disposal, squanders none. He never acts without a purpose, and educes a multitude of benefits from a single action."

She paused, inviting contradiction. "We sibyls don't go to the schola, but we receive some education as postulants, and we read, of course. We can also question our augurs if we wish, though I confess I've seldom done so."

"All—ah—admirably correct, Maytera. General."

Spider nodded. "Councillor Potto said somethin' like that about the tunnels. We were talkin' about when they got built."

"I'd like to hear it."

"It was while they were buildin' the whorl, like I said. To start it was just a big hunk of rock. You know that?"

"Certainly. The Chrasmologic Writings emphasize it."

"So how could they get in and get the rock out? They dug a bunch of tunnels. Then they had to haul in dirt and trees, and pretty soon a big cart would come out and it'd be tearin' up stuff they just planted. These tunnels are shiprock in lots of places, especially high up. You twig that?"

"Most have been, I believe. Nearly all."

"All right. They made those before they brought in dirt,

see? Up on the surface, only it was bare rock then, and now that's maybe ten, twenty cubits down. They set those stretches up and shoveled dirt around them. Then they could cart in more, and the trees, without tearin' up what they'd already finished."

Maytera Mint swallowed bread. "But the deeper tunnels are bored through stone? That's how our caldé described them."

"Sure, that's how they got the rock out. Look up at the skylands next time you're out in the open. Look at how much room there is, just clouds and air, and the sun and the shade, all right? What's a few tunnels compared to that?"

Remora nodded vigorously. " 'How mighty are the works of Pas!' The, er, initial line of the Chrasmologic Writings, eh? Therefore known to—ah—all. Even laymen. We clergy, um, prone to forget."

"He pumped water through them too," Spider continued. "You take the lake. That's a shaggy lot of water. Think if old Pas had to bring it in barrels. So for the little stuff, he just run pipes down the tunnels, but for big ones like the lake, he put in doors to keep the water out of the ones he wanted to stay dry, and pumped. I could show you a cave by the lake with one of those doors in the back. That's where Pas pumped in water to fill the lake, and he put in that door 'cause he didn't want the water to wash back into his tunnels when he was done. That cave used to be under the water when the lake was bigger."

Spider fell silent, and Maytera Mint remarked, "Something's troubling you."

"I was just thinkin' about a couple things. I told you this side one ends in dirt, and that's where we bury them?"

She nodded.

"There's one of those doors in front of the dirt. I guess the big tunnel was one of them they pumped in, and they didn't want water in it. What we're in now was probably put in after. Anyway, talkin' about doors reminded me we're goin' to have to bury these culls. It'll take a lot of diggin'."

"I had assumed we would," she said. "You indicated there

were two points troubling you. May I ask what the second was? And what the other uses of these tunnels are?"

"That's the same question two times." Spider shrugged. "You never asked me why the lake keeps gettin' smaller."

"I didn't suppose you knew, and to tell the truth, I've never thought much about it. The water has gone elsewhere, I suppose. Down into these tunnels, perhaps."

"You couldn't be any wronger about that, General."

Remora put his water bottle on the floor between his feet. "You know, eh? Privy to the, um, information?"

"Yes, I'd like to know, too," Maytera Mint said, "if you don't mind. And I've by no means finished eating yet."

"It's all the same. You wanted to know what else they're good for and something else. I forget."

"The second consideration that troubled you."

"Same thing. The sun shines all the time, don't it?"

"Certainly."

"But we get night half the time 'cause the shade's there. It cools things off, right? When it's hot, you're happy to see the shade come down, 'cause you know it's goin' to get cooler. Wintertime, you don't like it so much."

"Primary. Um, puerile. What—ah—the significance?"

"See this room, Patera? Three doors. Let's say they're all shut. No windows, all right? Now s'pose the sun started at that corner there and run over to that one, about as big as a rope. That's the whorl. That's what it's like, see? Goin' to get pretty hot in here, right?"

"I take your point," Maytera Mint told Spider, "but I do not understand it. The whorl is very large."

"Not that big. It's been goin' for three hundred years and over. That's what they say."

"The, um, fact. Provable in a—ah—many ways."

"Good here, Patera. It had to be hot enough for people to live in when Pas started it, see?"

Neither Remora nor Maytera Mint spoke.

"But it couldn't get much hotter or we'd fry. Couldn't get much hotter with the sun goin' all the time. So there had to be some way to get shut of the heat."

"The—ah—outside, eh? Beyond the whorl. The, um, Writings state, hey? A—uh, um—frigid night."

"You got it. Notice how the wind blows all the time down here? It's cold, too, colder than up top, anyhow."

"I, um, fail—"

Maytera Mint interrupted. "I see! Air circulates through these tunnels, doesn't it, Spider? Some of them must be filled with warm air bound for the night outside. The ones we've been in are carrying cold air back to the surface."

"Bull's-eye, General. Well, it's not workin' as good as it did. You said about lake water goin' in the tunnels."

She nodded.

"Suppose it fills a tunnel half up. The wind can't blow as much, see? If it fills the whole tunnel in just one spot, the wind can't blow at all. There's places where the shiprock gave way, too, and wind can't blow there either. So it's gettin' hotter. We don't notice, 'cause it's too slow. But talk to old people and they'll say winters used to be colder, and longer, too." Spider stood. "I'm goin' to start diggin'. You want to eat more, bring it along."

"I do and I will," Maytera Mint gathered up what remained of her bread and meat, picked up her bottle of water, and rose. The bolt of the outer door clanked back; the shadowy side tunnel beyond was deserted.

"They've gone off," Spider told her over his shoulder. "I'd like to know why they started shootin' at my boys."

She sighed. "Because they were Ayuntamientados, I should imagine. Four brave men who had kept Viron secure for years, slain by others who've guarded it for centuries. That's what we've come to."

"Not all, eh?" Remora closed the door behind him. "All the, um. Not, ah, er, fah . . ." His mouth worked soundlessly.

Maytera Mint looked around at him in some surprise. His eyes seemed to have sunk into his skull, and his nose appeared both thinner and smaller. As she watched, his lips drew back, exposing his big, discolored teeth in a frightful grin. Spider exclaimed, "Sphigx shit!"

"He's not the right one," Remora informed Maytera Mint.

She made herself smile.

"This is the one who talks to the one who's not there. The right one was down here with the tall girl. He might be here."

"This is Mucor," Maytera Mint explained to Spider. "She's Maytera's granddaughter. We've spoken before.

"Do you remember, Mucor? You came to tell me our caldé was in danger of capture, and I stormed the Palatine. Afterward, we met in person in the Juzgado."

Remora nodded, his head bobbing like a toy's, lank black hair mercifully concealing his terrible eyes. "Incus is his name. A little augur."

"I don't know him, though His Eminence has told me of him. Mucor? Mucor!"

The death-head grin was fading.

"Mucor, come back, please! If you see Bison or our caldé, tell them—tell either or both—where I am, and that this man is holding us for Councillor Potto."

"You won't be then." The final word was almost too faint to hear. The grin vanished; Remora tossed his hair back as he habitually did, and the eyes his gesture revealed were no longer terrifying. "Not all, hey? Many on our, um, the caldé's."

When no one spoke, he added, "The general's, hey?"

"You want my needler?" Spider asked Maytera Mint.

"Certainly, if you're willing to let me have it."

He presented it butt first. "You wouldn't shoot me, would you, General? Not with my own needler that I gave you."

She accepted it, glanced at it, and dropped it into one of her habit's side pockets. "No. Only if I were compelled to, and perhaps not even then."

"All right. I'm goin' to dig the graves now, see? You two can finish eatin' and watch," Spider stepped out into the empty tunnel, "but if I'm cold 'fore I finish, it's for me. You wrap me and slide me in. Knife's in my pocket."

They followed him down the tunnel until it was blocked by a massive barrier of rusty iron. "Councillor Potto doesn't want anybody to hear," Spider confided, "but I guess it don't matter any more. *Fraus!*"

For a second or longer, nothing happened.

The great barrier shuddered, creaked, and began to creep upward, rolling unpleasantly into itself. Abruptly, Maytera Mint became conscious of the stench of decay, nauseous yet so diffuse that she might almost have believed she imagined it. Remora snorted, sounding surprisingly horse-like, and wiped his nose on his sleeve.

"No fresh air, 'cept when the door's open," Spider remarked as he led them into the dim cul-de-sac the rising barrier had revealed. "It'll air out pretty quick." He stopped to point. "Right here's where the shiprock ends. Have a look."

Maytera Mint advanced to do so, crossing loose earth into which her scuffed black shoes sank. "I'm very glad you let us hear the word for that door. I'd hate to think of our being locked in here, unable to get it open."

"I'm bein' nice to you two so you'll slide me in after it happens. See the rolls of poly?"

"Certainly." She was examining the edge of the shiprock wall. "This is not as thick as I had imagined."

"It's pretty strong, though. There's iron rods in it."

"The—ah—interments." Remora indicated scraps of paper that dotted the sloping earth at the end of the tunnel. "Those, um, are they all?" He counted them silently, his lips twitching. "Eleven in—ah—toto?"

Spider nodded. "Plenty of room left, but we got three in the guardroom, and Paca back in the big tunnel, and me."

"You—ah—depression. A mere, um, state of mind, my son. Emotion, hey?"

"Yes," Maytera Mint agreed heartily. "You mustn't talk as if your death were inevitable, Spider. I mean now, killed by those soldiers. It isn't, and I pray it won't happen."

"That devil you called your sib's granddaughter, General. What'd it say?"

"She is not a devil," Maytera Mint declared firmly. "She is a living girl, one who has been shamefully mistreated."

Spider grunted, picking up a long-handled spade that had lain between two rolls of synthetic.

"This, er, granddaughter, General. An—ah—difficult child?" Remora bit into a strip of dried beef.

Maytera Mint nodded absently, and found herself staring at one of the grim slips of soiled paper. Bending and squinting, she read a name, a date, and a few particulars of the dead man's life. "Is this the most recent one, Spider? The paper seems cleaner than the others."

"Yeah. Last spring."

There was still half a loaf. Deep in thought, she tore away piece after piece, chewing and swallowing slowly, and drank from her bottle.

"I'm about done here." Spider had ceased to dig, leaning on his spade. "Think you two could fetch a cull out for me? Door's not locked."

"I was about to suggest it myself," Maytera Mint told him.

"We—ah—trust, hey? On our honor?"

"I have his needler, Your Eminence. We could go at any time, and I could shoot him if he tried to stop us."

"In that case, um, the circumstances—"

"But he gave it to me, remember? Besides, he knows these tunnels, and we don't."

"Ah—the soldiers."

"I feel certain they'd help us if we could find them, but what if we couldn't? Spider, we'll be happy to bring one of your late friends here for burial. Thank you for your trust in us. It is not misplaced."

He nodded. "Cut off a big hunk of poly. You can lay him on that and drag him, it's real slick. When you get him here, I'll wrap him up in it."

"May I borrow your knife?"

He got it from his pocket and handed it to her, then went back to his digging. Remora held the ends of the smaller roll while she pulled out and slashed free a length twice the height of a man.

As they carried it back to the guardroom, Remora muttered, "You, um, wonders with him, Maytera. I congratulate you."

She shrugged, unconsciously thrusting her hand into her pocket to grasp Spider's needler. "He has no slug gun, Your

Eminence, and without one he would be defenseless against the soldiers. He's hoping our presence will make it possible for him to surrender."

"I, ah—" Remora opened the guardroom door and glanced around. Their stools stood in a circle as they had left them, and the three dead men still sprawled on the gritty shiprock floor, untouched. "One can always, eh? Give up? Capitulate. Not, um, that we—"

"One can always raise one's hands and step into full view of the enemy," Maytera Mint told him. "A good many troopers lose their lives doing it. This one nearest the door, I think. If Your Eminence will unfold that synthetic, we can roll him onto it, poor spirit."

"You, er, concerned, eh?" Remora spread the synthetic winding sheet, holding it down with his knees as he wrestled with the dead man's shoulder. "I observed your demeanor in—ah—there. As you ate."

"Puzzled." She forced her gaze away from the dead man's eyes, wishing that it had been possible to roll him so that he lay face down again. "There was fresh earth on the blade of that spade. At least, I think it was fresh, or fairly fresh. Maytera has a little garden back at the cenoby, Your Eminence. I've helped her with it now and then, hoeing, and spading in the spring. I don't think that Spider noticed it."

"I fail to see the, um, import. Someone else, eh? Could be Councillor Potto, another—hum—subordinate."

"I fail to see it too," she told Remora. "Take the other corner, will you?"

Back at the end of the tunnel, Spider had completed the first grave and begun a second. "That's Hyrax." He produced a stump of pencil and a battered notebook. "I'll write, you two cap for him."

They knelt. Maytera Mint found herself, rather to her own surprise, clasping the cold hand. If things had been different, she thought, we might have been man and wife, you and I. We must be nearly of an age.

The drone of Remora's prayer reminded her of the singsong voices of children in the classroom, reciting the multiplication table, memorizing prayers for meals, for betrothals, for the dead. Had she taught girls this year? Or boys. She could not remember.

We would have kissed and held hands, and done what men and women do, and I would have borne you a child, perhaps, my own child. But when I met Bison . . .

"All right, General, let him go. I got to fold this over him." Suddenly Hyrax was no longer a dead man, but a statue or a picture, still visible but blurred and faintly blue through the synthetic.

"His knife." She rose, dusting loose earth from her black skirt by reflex. "You'll need his knife for the paper."

"I already got it. You want to help, Patera? I could do it alone, but it'll be easier with two." They crouched, one on either side, and Spider said, "Lift when I do, see? A-one and a-two and a-*three!*"

Raising the shrouded corpse to waist level, they slid it into its grave; and he began shovelling earth after it, pausing from time to time to tamp the damp dark face of death with the handle of his spade. He said, "You're wonderin' why we don't dig them down the way you usually do, I guess."

"The, um, papers," Remora ventured. "Stepped upon, eh? Trodden."

"There's that. But mostly it's easier to dig here. Then too, we'd have to walk on the old ones to bury the new ones."

As they were leaving the guardroom with Guan stretched on a fresh sheet of poly, laughter, faint and mad, echoed in the main tunnel. "Wait!" Maytera Mint told Remora. "Did you hear that? You must have!"

He shuddered. "I—ah—possibly."

"Will you do me a favor, Your Eminence?" She did not wait for his assent. "Go back in there and get two packages of that dried meat. One for yourself, and one for me. We can put them in our pockets."

"That—ah—merriment . . ."

"I have no idea, Your Eminence. I have a feeling, a presentiment, if you will, that we may need food."

"If we—er—never mind." Remora vanished into the guard-room.

When he returned, Maytera Mint handed him a needler.

"But I am—er—better, perhaps, with you, eh, General? Your, um, forte."

"That isn't Spider's, it's Guan's," she told him. "Spider said a needler was what he usually used, remember? It didn't really make much of an impression at the time, but afterward, thinking about that poor man who dressed as a woman, it struck me that the other spy-catchers must have done the same thing. They would want some sort of a weapon, and before the rebellion nobody but a Guardsman could walk around the city carrying a slug gun. Then I wondered—this was while we were bringing Hyrax—what they did with them when they got their slug guns. It seemed likely that most of them had simply put them in their waistbands, under their tunics, where they were accustomed to carrying them."

"Most, um, sagacious."

"Thank you, Your Eminence. Anyway, whatever that was we heard wasn't a soldier. Do you agree?"

"I, um, indubitably." Remora stared down at the needler in his hand.

"Or a chem at all, any kind of chem. So a needler should work, and we may need them, just as we may need this meat, for which I haven't yet thanked you. Thank you very much, Your Eminence. It was a great condescension for you to oblige me as you have."

"You must know how to, um, operate? Manage this?" Remora might not have heard her.

"It's not difficult. Push that down," she pointed to the safety catch, "when you wish to shoot. Point it, and pull the trigger. If you want to shoot a second needle, pull it again. I won't show you how to reload now. There isn't time, and we don't have any more needles anyway."

Remora gulped and nodded.

"In your waistband under your robe, perhaps. I believe that's where our caldé must carry his."

"I—ah. It would be, er, inadvisable, hey? When we return to the—ah—up there."

"I won't tell anyone if you don't." Maytera Mint stooped for a corner of the sheet of synthetic on which Guan's body lay. "We'd better go now, and quickly, or Spider will wonder what delayed us."

At the end of the side tunnel she knelt as she had before, trying to keep her mind upon appropriate petitions to the gods. Guan had kicked her shortly before Spider had locked her away with Remora so that he and his men could sleep; the right side of her thigh was still sore and stiff. She had scarcely given it a thought since it had happened, or so she had convinced herself. Now that Guan was dead, now that Guan lay before her, she found she could not free her mind from the memory of that kick. It was easy to mouth *I forgive you,* and to ask the gods, Echidna particularly, not to hold the kick against him; yet she felt that her forgiveness did not reach her heart, however hard she tried to bring it there.

The transparent sheet covered Guan as a sister sheet from the parent roll had covered Hyrax, and Maytera Mint got to her feet. What was the third man's name? He had been the quietest of their captors; she had thought him sullen and marked him as potentially the most dangerous. She would never know, now, whether she had been correct.

"How 'bout if you dig for Sewellel, Patera? I'll go back with General Mint here and fetch him."

"Why, ah—"

She saw Remora assure himself that his needler was in place with a touch of his forearm, and said, "He's not going to attack me, Your Eminence. He would like to speak to me in private, I imagine."

Remora managed to smile. "In that, um, circumstances, I shall—ah—comply. With all good will."

"What it really is," Spider told him, "is I want to see if you can do it right. You'll have to dig for me, see? You seen me do it. Now you do for Sewellel and Paca, and that'll be two for each of us. Let's move out, General."

Obediently, she followed him down the side tunnel. "What

I told Patera's lily," Spider said as they walked. "You know that word? Means the truth."

"Yes, I do, though I've always considered it children's slang. My pupils use it sometimes."

"But that you said, General. That was the lily too."

She nodded, striving to make her nod sympathetic.

"I'm sorry about the way I talk. Sometimes I swear when I didn't mean to. It's just that I always do."

"I understand, believe me."

He stopped abruptly. "Thing is, I don't believe you. Or him, back there. Patera What'shisface."

"Remora."

Spider waved aside Remora's identity. "Echidna made you a general? She talked to you about it?"

"She certainly did."

"Could you see her like you're seein' me now? Could you make out what she was sayin'? She talked to you out of one of those big glasses they got in manteions?"

"Exactly. I can repeat everything she said, if you wish. I'd be happy to." This was a return to familiar ground, and Maytera Mint felt more confident than she had since she and Remora had passed through the ruined gate of Blood's villa.

"I know somebody that says he couldn't really hear the words. He just knew what she meant."

"He had known woman," Maytera Mint explained, hoping that Spider would understand what she intended by *known*. "Or else he had . . . Excuse this, please. The indelicacy."

"Sure thing."

"He had known another man, or a boy, as men know women. That man you told us about? Titi? I should imagine—"

"Yeah, so do I, and the other way, too. Sure he did. Is that the only reason?"

"It is. By Echidna's will, those who have enjoyed carnal knowledge of others may not behold the gods. Nor may they hear them distinctly, though in most cases they understand them. It varies between individuals, and several reasons have been put forward for that. If you don't mind, I won't explain those in detail. They concern the frequency and the specific natures of various sexual relations. You can readily construct them, or similar theories, for yourself."

"Sure, General. You can skip all that."

"I have never known Man. Therefore I saw the face of the goddess exactly as I see yours. More clearly, because her face was very bright. I heard each word she uttered, and can repeat them verbatim, as I said. When I have known Man . . ."

The guilty words had slipped out; she hurried on, conscious that her cheeks were reddening. "I shall no longer be able to see Echidna. No more than your friend could. In the event that I know Man—I mean, have relations with a—with a husband. My husband. Then I won't be able to repeat the words of the gods any more than you could."

"That was the thing I was wanting to talk to you about."

"The words of the goddess? She said—"

Spider waved Echidna's words aside. "You gettin' married and knowin' a man, like you said. I got to tell you."

Her hand closed about the needler in her pocket. "Do you mean yourself, Spider? No. Not willingly."

He shook his head. "Bison. I'm fly, see? I can tell from how you talk about him. It got you worried when I said I got culls you think's yours. You were scared Bison was one."

"Certainly not!" Maytera Mint took three deep breaths and relaxed her hold on the needler. "I suppose I was, a little."

"Yeah, I know. You kept tellin' yourself it couldn't be like that, on account of stuff he's said to you."

She had taken a step backward; she found that her shoulders were pressed against the tunnel's cold shiprock. "I haven't said anything to him, Spider, nor has he said a single such word to me. Nothing! But I've seen—or believed I saw . . . And he, Bison, no doubt has—has. Seen me. And heard me, too. My voice. In the same fashion."

"Yeah, I got you, General." To her surprise, Spider leaned against the wall next to her, sparing her the embarrassment of his gaze. "How old are you?"

"That is none of your affair." She made her voice as firm as she could.

"Maybe it is, and maybe it isn't. How old'd you say I am?"

She shook her head. "Since I decline to confide my age to you, it would be completely inappropriate for me to speculate on yours."

"I'm forty-eight, and that's lily. I'd say you're about thirty-three, thirty-four. If that's queer I'm sorry, but you wouldn't tell me."

"Nor will I now."

"I just want to say it goes awful fast. Life goes by awful fast. You think you know all about that now. The shag you do. I remember all kind of things that happened when I was a sprat."

"I understand, Spider. I know precisely what you mean."

"You just think you do. I've had maybe a hundred women. I wish I'd kept count, but I didn't. There was only two I didn't have to pay, and one was abram once you got to know her."

"It's quite normal for men to think women—" Maytera Mint sought for a diplomatic word. "Irrational. And for women to think men irrational as well."

"Handin' you the lily, I had to pay the other one, too. I didn't give her the gelt, but she cost a shaggy lot more. More than she was worth." Spider shot Maytera Mint a sidelong look. "I got something important to say, but I don't know how to make you believe me."

"Is it true, Spider?"

"Shag, yes! Every word."

"Then I will believe you, even if you don't believe me about the gods. What is it?"

"This isn't it. This's what I should of said back there, see? There was a time when I might of got a woman like you, but that's over. Over and done up, see? Just slipped away. Last year I met one I thought I might like and sort of shaved her a little, you know? And she shaved me back. Then she seen I was gettin' to be serious, and she just froze up. She'd look at me, and her eyes kept sayin' *too old, too old.* It goes so fast. I didn't feel like I'd got old. I still don't."

For a half minute or more, his silence filled the tunnel.

"All right, about this buck Bison."

Maytera Mint forced herself to nod.

"I'm goin' to die. Probably it won't be very long at all. Back there where we bury, I kept hopin' they'd shoot me and I'd get to say it before I went cold, 'cause then you'd believe me. But they don't shoot like that. The way my culls got it, you're chilled straight off, so I got to say it right here. He was one of mine, see? Bison was. A dimber hand."

She could not be certain she had spoken; perhaps not.

"He was supposed to check in every night. I'd meet him, see, in this certain place. But he only come the first time, the first night."

It was possible to breathe again.

"So I sent somebody. I sent this cully we're fetchin', Sewellel. Bison, he told him he was out. He wouldn't tell you anything about us, but he wouldn't tell us anything about you, neither. That's the lily, General. That's how it was. I don't blame you if you don't believe it, and in your shoes maybe I wouldn't. But I'm goin' today and know it, and I'd like you to cap for me when I'm cold."

"Pray for your spirit." She was still trying to wrap her understanding about the fact.

"Yeah. So it's lily. I told you I wouldn't tell you who mine was, the ones you thought was yours. But he's not mine any more. That's what I'm tellin' you."

She found herself entering the guardroom again, with no memory of having resumed their walk. "Shall I go back and cut off a piece of synthetic?" she asked. "I forgot entirely that we'd need another one. If you carry Sewellel on your shoulders, you'll have blood all over you."

"I got it right here," Spider told her. He held it up.

"But I have your knife. You gave me that so . . ."

"I used Guan's, 'fore I wrote for him." Spider smiled, a small, sad smile heart-wrenchingly foreign to his coarse face. "It don't really take three. It don't even take two, see? I been down here by myself and buried a couple times, and that's what I do, 'cause I start by findin' the dead cull's knife."

"Yes," she said. "Yes, I'm certain you must have been the only mourner that those men had, more than once." She thrust her hands into her pockets, found his needler and her beads, and at last his knife. "Take it, please. I don't want to bury you, Spider. I won't. I want to save your life, and I'm going to try. I'm going to try very hard, and I'll succeed."

He shook his head, but she forced the rough clasp knife into his hand. "Close the door, please. I think it would be better if we didn't startle His Eminence."

Striding purposefully now, she crossed the guardroom and entered the storeroom. "I should have gone in here before," she told Spider over her shoulder. "I let His Eminence do it both times, and it was cowardly of me. This locker—I suppose that's what you call it—with the sign of addition on it in red. Is this where the stretcher's kept?"

Behind her, Spider said, "Yeah, that's it."

She turned, drawing his needler. "Raise both your hands, Spider. You are my prisoner."

He stared at her, his eyes wide.

"He may be able to see us. I can't be sure. Raise them! Hold them up before he kills you."

As Spider lifted his hands, the front of the locker swung open; a soldier stepped out and saluted, his slug gun stiffly vertical, his steel heels clashing. Maytera Mint said, "You aren't Sergeant Sand. What's your name?"

"Private Schist, sir!"

"Thank you. There's a dead man in the outer room. I take it you killed him?"

"That's right, sir."

"Take the synthetic this man's holding and wrap him—the dead man out there, I mean. Wrap the dead man's body in that. You can carry it for us."

Schist saluted again.

Spider said, "You knew he was in there all the time."

Maytera Mint shook her head, finding herself suddenly weak with relief. "I wish I were that . . . I don't know what to call it. That godlike. People believe I am, but I'm not. I have to think and think."

She paused to watch Schist through the doorway as he knelt beside Sewellel's corpse. "And even then I ask Bison's advice, and the captain's. Often I find they've seen more deeply into the problem than I have. I suppose it's useless to ask whether you were telling me the whole truth about Bison now. You can put down your hands, I think."

"I was, yeah." From his expression, Spider was relieved as well. "How'd you figure he was in there?"

"From the earth on the spade. There was fresh earth on the blade. Didn't you notice it?"

He shook his head.

From the guardroom, Schist announced, "I got him, sir."

"Good. You'd better walk ahead of us, Spider, and put up your hands again. There are more, you see. They could have rushed you hours ago, but they must have been afraid you'd kill His Eminence and me."

A hundred thoughts crowded her mind. "Besides, if we let you walk behind us, you might decide that your duty to Councillor Potto compelled you to run. Then this soldier would fire."

"I'd hit you, too," Schist said. "I don't miss much." He patted Sewellel's swathed corpse, slung over his left shoulder.

"Can I put my hand down to open the door?"

"Certainly," Maytera Mint told him; and Schist, "Sure."

"I ought to explain that I've spoken with Private Schist's sergeant," Maytera Mint continued as they left the guardroom. "That was on Sphixday, the day after our caldé was rescued. His name is Sand, and he has come over to our side, to the caldé's side, with his entire squad. Or rather, with what remains of it, because several were killed by a talus."

"I know how it feels."

"I realize you do, Spider. Neither you nor I, nor Sergeant Sand, created war. What I was going to say is that our caldé and I, with Sergeant Sand himself and Generalissimo Oosik and General Saba, conferred upon how we might make the best possible use of Schist here and the rest. Of the few soldiers we had. It wasn't a lengthy debate, because all of us found the answer rather obvious. The soldiers knew these tunnels, and none of us did, though our caldé had spent some time in them. Furthermore, down here they might encounter other soldiers whom they could bring over to our side. Plainly then, the best use that could be made of them was to send them back here to scout the enemy's dispositions, and augment their number if they could."

"All right, but how'd you know he was in there from the dirt on my spade?"

"It was fresh, as I said. Still somewhat damp. I asked about the grave that looked most new, and read the date on the paper, and it wasn't nearly new enough. So somebody else had been burying something. I thought of an ear, as they're called, or something of the sort, though to the best of my knowledge Sand didn't have one." She fell silent, listening to their echoing footsteps.

"Go on," Spider urged her.

"Eventually I realized that room back there was a better place. A soldier as intelligent as Sand would surely anticipate that we would stop there to eat and talk. He'd want to know what we said, since you might say something that would be of value to him. He was right, because as soon as we arrived I began asking my questions. At any rate, he had Schist hide and listen, and when we left we were going here."

Already, too soon as it seemed to Maytera Mint, they had passed beneath the great iron door, and Remora was staring at Schist. She called, "It's all right, Your Eminence! We have been rescued, and Spider is our prisoner."

The earth around Remora erupted as two more soldiers freed themselves from it.

Chapter 9

A Piece of Pas

Auk pounded on the door of the old manse on Brick Street with the butt of his needler. Behind him, Incus cleared his throat, a soft and apologetic noise that might have issued from a rabbit or a squirrel. Behind Incus, twenty-two men and women murmured to one another.

Auk pounded again.

"He's in there, trooper," Hammerstone declared. "Somebody is, anyhow. I hear him."

"I didn't," Auk remarked, "and I got good ears."

"Not good enough. Want me to bust the door, Patera?"

"By no means. Auk, my son, allow *me."*

Wearily, Auk stepped away from the door. "You think you can knock better than me, Patera, you go right ahead."

"My knock would be no more effectual than *your own,* my son, I feel quite confident. *Less so,* if anything. My *mind,* however, may yet be of *service."*

"Patera's the smartest bio there is," Hammerstone told the crowd, "The smartest in the whole *Whorl."* They edged forward, trying to peer around him.

Incus drew himself up to his full height, which was by no means great. *"Blessed be this manse, in the Most Sacred Name of Pas, Father of the Gods,* in whose name *we* come. Blessed be it in the name of *Gracious Echidna, His Consort,* in those of their *Sons* and their *Daughters* alike, this day and until *Pas's Plan* attains *fulfillment,* in the name of *Scylla,* Patroness of this Our Holy City of Viron and *my own* patroness."

Hammerstone leaned toward him, reporting in a harsh stage whisper, "They stopped moving around in there, Patera."

Incus filled his lungs again. "Patera *Jerboa!* For you we have the *highest and holiest* veneration. *I* who speak am *like you* a *holy augur.* Indeed, I am *more,* for I am *that augur* whom Scintillating Scylla *herself* has *chosen* to lead the *Chapter* of *Our Holy City.*

"Accompanying *me* are two *laymen* who *themselves* have the greatest of claims to your *revered attention,* for they are *Auk* and *Hammerstone,* the biochemical person and the *chemical* one, *cojoined,* selected by Lord Pas *himself* to execute his will at a *holy sacrifice* at which *I* presided, this very—"

The door opened a hand's breadth, and the pale, affrighted face of Patera Shell appeared. "You—you . . . Are you really an augur?"

"I *am,* my son. But if *you* are *Patera Jerboa,* the augur of this manteion, you are the *wrong* Patera Jerboa, one whom we do *not* seek."

From behind Hammerstone, the foremost of Auk's followers declared, "He ain't no augur! Twig his gipon."

Incus turned back to address him, one small foot blocking the door. "Oh, but he *is,* my son. Do *I* not know *my own kind?* No mere *tunic* can deceive *me."*

"Yeah," Auk put in, "he's a augur right enough, or I never seen one. C'mere, Patera." Catching Shell's wrist, he jerked him through the doorway. "What's your name?"

Shell only stared at him with wide eyes, his mouth opening and shutting.

"He's Patera Shell, my acolyte," announced a white-bearded man who had taken Shell's place; his antiquated voice creaked and groaned like the wheel of an overloaded cart, although he wore a brilliant blue tunic intended for a young man. "I'm Patera Jerboa, and I'm augur here." His rheumy eyes fastened upon Incus. "You're looking for me. I don't hear much any more, but I heard that. Very well." Jerboa stepped through the doorway and traced the sign of addition between Incus and himself, making it both higher and wider than was currently customary. "Do what you came to, but let Shell go."

Auk already had. "You're the cull, all right. You got a Window in your manteion, Patera?"

"It would not be a manteion without one. I've—" Jerboa coughed and spat. "I've served my Window for sixty-one years. I'd . . ." He fell silent, sucking his gums as he looked from Auk to Incus and back. "Who's in charge here?"

"I am," Auk told him, and offered his hand. "I'm what you call a theodidact, Patera. Patera Incus there ought to have told you. I been enlightened by Tartaros. Right now, I'm doing a job for his pa. So're they." He jerked his thumb at Hammerstone and Incus, then held out his hand again.

Jerboa clasped it, his own hand dry and cold, with a grip that seemed oddly weak for its size; for a moment his eyes were bright. "I was going to say that I'd like to die in front of my Sacred Window, my son, but you haven't come to kill us."

" 'Course not. Thing is, Patera, you got a piece of Pas."

Shell, who had relaxed somewhat, stared again.

"He wants it back now. He sent us to get it for him."

"My son—"

"That's the job I been talking about, Patera. That's what he asked me to do for him at the theophany."

One of Auk's followers called, "This afternoon, Patera! We were there!"

"There has been another?" Jerboa lifted his raddled old face to the vanishing thread of gold that was the long sun, and seemed at that moment nearly as tall as Auk.

"At Silk's manteion!" the same follower called.

Auk nodded. "Only this time it was Pas, Patera. You know about that, don't you? You seen him one time yourself, that's what he said."

"He did," Shell announced unexpectedly.

"Dimber here." Auk felt the last lingering doubt melt away, and grinned. "That's good, Patera. That's real good! People talk about how long it's been since any god come to a Window, or they did 'fore Kypris told us we could solve any place we wanted that night. Only they don't never say when last time was, or who it was that got the god to come. Pas said it was you and gave your name, but we didn't know where to find you."

Shell looked beseechingly at Incus. "I don't understand, Patera. The Peace of Pas? Patera's brought the Peace of Pas to thousands, I'm sure, but—"

"A chunk of him," Hammerstone explained. "Like a slice, sort of, or if I was to unscrew one of my fingers."

"We need some animals for him," Auk announced, raising his voice. "A whole herd of 'em. *Listen up, you culls!* We found him. This right here's the holy augur that's got a piece of Pas in his head, a piece that Pas wants back. Our job was to find him. I mean mine and Hammerstone's, and Patera's here."

A sibyl, herself stooped and old, appeared like a shadow at Jerboa's side. "Are they going to hurt you, Patera? I came through the manse. I broke the rule, but I don't care. If you are—if they're going to do something bad to you . . ."

"It will be all right, Maytera," the old augur assured her. "Everything's going to be all right."

Still addressing his followers, Auk told them, "We did our job, and it's your turn. You want to be part of this? Part of the biggest thing that's ever happened yet? You want to bring Pas back for people everywhere in the whorl? You get us those animals now, good ones. Get 'em any way you can, and bring 'em back to this manteion."

"You can't answer your own door," Maytera Marble scolded Silk. "You simply cannot!"

He resumed his seat, vaguely unhappy that the longed-for respite from the stacks of paper before him would be postponed. The city's various accounts at the Fisc totalled—he tapped his pencil in unconscious imitation of Swallow—not much over four hundred thousand cards. In private hands it would have been a vast fortune; but the Guard had to be paid, as did the commissioners, clerks, and other functionaries, to say nothing of the contractors who sometimes cleaned the streets and were supposed to keep them in repair.

His mouth twisting, he recalled his promise—so lightly given—to reward those who had fought bravely on either side.

All four taluses would have to be paid for as well before Swallow would deliver even one; it was in the contract he had signed less than an hour ago. Long before those taluses were finished, the Guard would need food, ammunition, and repairs to five armed floaters. (For the tenth or twelfth time that day, Silk considered using those floaters in the tunnels and rejected it.) Meanwhile, both the taluses the Guard employed currently, the remnant of those it had when the fighting began, would have to be paid as well.

Maytera Marble reentered, bowing. "It's Generalissimo Oosik, Patera. He desires to speak with you at once." Oosik's bulky form was visible in the reception hall beyond the ornate doorway, rocking back and forth with impatience.

"Of course," Silk said heartily. "Show him in, please, Maytera. I apologize for asking you to get the door."

"It was no trouble, Patera. I was glad to do it."

Behind her, Oosik was already marching into the room; he halted before Silk's work table and saluted with a flourish and a click of polished heels. "I trust that your wounds are not too troublesome, Caldé."

"Not at all, Generalissimo. Thank you, Maytera—that will be all."

"Coffee, Patera? Tea?"

Oosik shook his head.

"No, but thank you." Silk waved her away. "Pull up a chair, Generalissimo. Sit down and relax. Have you found—?"

Oosik shook his head. "I regret not, Caldé."

"Sit down. What is it, then?"

"You watched the parade, as I did." Oosik carried over an armless chair that looked too small for him.

"The Guard detachment was amazingly trim, I thought, for having just been taken from the fighting."

"Pah!" Oosik blew aside the detachment. "I thank you, Caldé. You are gracious. But the Trivigauntis? That was the thing to see, Siyuf's horde."

Silk, who had been wondering how to bring up the matters that had occupied his mind earlier in the afternoon, tried to seize the opportunity. "It was what I didn't see that seemed most significant. Sit down, please. I don't like having to look up at you like this."

Oosik sat. "You saw their infantry. I hope you were impressed, as I was."

"Of course."

"Also their cavalry. A great deal of that, Caldé. Twice what I had expected." Oosik wound one end of his white-tipped mustache around his finger and tugged.

"The cavalry was beautiful, certainly, but I was struck by their guns; I'd never seen big guns like that. Do we—do you have any, Generalissimo?"

"A few, yes. Never as many as I would like. What did you think of their floaters, Caldé?"

"There weren't any."

"What of the taluses? I should like your opinion, Caldé."

Silk shook his head. "You won't get it, Generalissimo. There weren't any of those either. That is a matter—"

"Precisely so!" Oosik released his mustache and waved his forefinger to emphasize his point. "I do not seek to embarrass you, Caldé. Every man knows much upon some subjects, little or nothing on others. It cannot be otherwise. No one can predict what will happen in war, yet a commander must try. What sort of fighting does Siyuf anticipate here? A horde shapes itself as a man dresses, at one time to hunt, at another to attend the theater. I have seen her horde now, and I will tell you."

Silk, who had been about to speak at length himself, said, "Please do, Generalissimo."

"She will fight above ground, not in tunnels. Not in the city, either, or little. Infantry, Caldé, for fighting in a city, and to defend one. The guns that so impressed you are for defense also. Mostly she will attack. Thus she brings cavalry, which can go swiftly to a place chosen by herself in her airship and strike without warning. She spoke of mules to free her guns from mud. I overheard your talk, for which I hope you will forgive me."

"Of course you did; you were standing beside General Saba."

"Exactly so. Why not taluses, Caldé? In your Guard, we use our taluses to free mired guns and even wagons, and a talus is stronger than thirty mules. Why will she not use taluses, and tell you so?"

"Because she hasn't got any. I noticed it at the time, and before the parade was over I became very conscious of it. It may be that no one in Trivigaunte knows how to make them, though I'd think unemployed taluses would go there seeking work if that were the case."

"They have kept their taluses at home to defend their city, Caldé. Their floaters, too. Those are best for forcing a city street, however. I would think them best for tunnels, also."

"I agree."

"They would have been destroyed in the tunnels, fighting the soldiers and taluses of the Ayuntamiento. You see."

Silk, who feared that he saw only too well, said, "Not as clearly as I'd like. Go on, Generalissimo."

"My wife visits a woman who professes to reveal the future to her." Oosik tugged his mustache again. "She says she does not believe this, but she does. I have upbraided her without effect. A man without a wife is spared a full half of life's unpleasantness."

"We augurs," Silk said carefully, "profess to reveal the future, too. That is to say, we profess to read the will of the gods in the entrails of their sacrifices. I admit that the intestines of a sheep seem like an unlikely tablet even for a god, but history records many striking instances of accurate predictions."

A slight smile elevated Oosik's mustache. "My change of topic did not discomfit you, Caldé."

"Not at all."

"Good. I mentioned this woman because she and many like her are false, and I do not wish you to think me a false prophet like them. If I predict, with success, the next event of the war, will that increase my credit with you?"

"It can go no higher, Generalissimo."

"Then this will demonstrate that I deserve the confidence you repose in me. Siyuf will send a force of substance into the tunnels. It will bravely engage the enemy, and there will be terrible fighting. You, I think, Caldé, will be taken to see it, if you will go. You will find a tunnel choked with bodies."

Silk nodded thoughtfully.

"Once more in the Juzgado, you will insist that the force be withdrawn, those gallant young girls. Soon it will be, and after that, Siyuf will fight in the tunnels no more."

"You are a false prophet, Generalissimo," Silk told him. "Having heard your prophesy, I won't permit that to happen."

"In which case we must fight there, and because they are narrow, a hundred or two at a time. One by one we will lose our floaters and taluses, and with them scores of troopers. It will be slow work, and while it is done our numbers will grow less each day. These thousands and thousands of troopers of General Mint's, who constitute so formidable a force. Can you afford to pay them?"

Silk shook his head.

"Then what will there be to hold them, if there is little fighting for them? A trooper fights for honor, Caldé, whether he is General Skate's trooper or hers. Or from loyalty. Or for loot sometimes. But he waits for pay. He will not wait without it, because when there is no fighting there is no honor to win, no flag to die for, no loot to gain."

"The Trivigauntis are stronger than we are already," Silk said pensively. "I think so at least, after what I saw today."

Oosik shook his head. "Not yet, Caldé, though Mint's ranks have begun to thin, perhaps. By the end of the winter—"

Oosik was interrupted by chimes, and Horn's hurrying footsteps.

The three augurs had agreed that Jerboa would offer the first victim and the largest. The rest—eight had been led through the chill dusk into the old manteion on Brick Street, and more were expected momentarily—would be divided between Incus and Shell, with Incus offering the second, fourth, sixth, and eighth, and each choosing freely from those available, as long as he did not choose the largest.

Auk, who had been a silent witness to their discussion, watched with interest as Jerboa tottered to the ambion; this feeble frame, this snowy-haired, half-naked skull, contained a tiny fragment of Great Pas, Lord of the Whorl and Father of the Seven. Did it know it was about to be reclaimed?

Shag yes, Auk told himself, it was bound to. He, Auk, had explained the whole thing to old Jerboa, hadn't he? How gods could tear chunks off themselves without getting smaller, and how they could slip those into a cull. The chunk could be jefe then if it wanted to, but it didn't have to. It could, as he had been at pains to make clear, just go along. It was like a buck on a donkey. Sure, he could order it around, make it trot or stop, turn one way or the other—only he didn't have to. Maybe he'd just let go of the reins, hook a leg over the pommel, and snoodge, letting his donkey graze or look for water, or whatever it wanted to. That was what Pas had done for years and years, but how long would he keep it up?

"My very dear new friends," Jerboa began, "I know you have not, any of you—" He coughed and clearly wished to spit, but swallowed. "That you haven't come out here and brought the gods more fine offerings than we've seen since . . . I don't know."

Benevolently, he looked toward the sibyls gathered about the fire that the youngest was kindling on the altar. "Maytera Wood, you've a better memory. They just brought another calf. That makes three. No, four. Four nice calves and four lambs, and a colt. We'll have a bull before we're done, I declare . . . What was I going to ask you about, Maytera?"

"When we'd had better animals," the oldest sibyl told him. "It was when you came from the schola, Patera. Your parents and your aunt bought a bullock and a peacock, and—oh, dear. It was Maytera Salvia who told me. What else did she say?"

"A monkey," Jerboa informed her. "I recollect the monkey, Maytera." He had not liked offering the monkey, and something of that showed in his face after sixty-one years. "It doesn't matter. There were nine, one for each of the Nine."

As if they were a backward class, he fixed his eyes on Auk and Hammerstone, and those of Auk's followers who had returned. "There are nine great gods, as all you young people should know. That's Pas and Echidna, and their children. What my father and my aunt did was to buy a gift for each, for me to give them the first time I sacrificed. On that altar right over there it was. Most were small. Some kind of a singing bird for Molpe, and a mole for Tartaros, and the monkey. I recollect those."

Incus, waiting with Shell, stirred impatiently.

If Jerboa noticed, he did not betray it. "What they were doing was a very important thing. They were starting a young man off—" He coughed again. "Excuse it. The gods' will, I'm sure. I just want to say it's a more important thing that we're doing tonight. A god, not just any god but Lord Pas himself, they say, has told these new gentlemen and Patera— Patera—?"

"Incus," Hammerstone prompted from a front seat.

"What's an incus anyway? I don't think I've offered an incus in all my years. Well, never mind. One of those little things that live in trees and eat the birds' eggs, I imagine." Another cough. "Told them if they'd find me . . . Is that right?"

Incus, who had been on the point of objecting violently a moment before, exerted self-control. "*You* are indeed the augur whom Pas *himself* designated, Patera, if you are that *Jerboa* whom he intended."

Shell added encouragingly, "I'm sure you are, Patera."

"If they'd find me and sacrifice, he'd come again, he said. Have I got that right?"

Hammerstone, Incus, and even Shell nodded confirmation,

as did most of those assembled; there was a stir at the back of the manteion as an immensely tall worshipper led in a tame baboon.

"What I wanted to say while our good sibyls get the fire going is that it's not a little thing. Not a little thing at all. Theophanies over on Sun Street lately, and this you've come from makes three. But I'm no stranger to them, not what you could call a stranger at all."

He turned, shuffling around behind his ambion to address Incus. "You talked to Pas, did you?"

"I *did.*" Incus swelled with pride.

Jerboa faced about again. "He said he was going to come. Well, we'll see. It'll be a great thing, a tremendous thing. If it happens."

Maytera Wood presented him with the knife of sacrifice, the signal that the sacred fire was burning satisfactorily. "I'll have that black calf with the white face," he decided.

"Bird back!"

Bison halted before Silk's table and saluted at the very moment that Oreb, who had been riding on Horn's shoulder, landed upon Silk's head; no slightest twitching of Bison's thick black beard betrayed amusement, although it seemed to Silk that there had been the briefest possible flicker of hilarity in Bison's dark and darting eyes. "I'm early, Caldé," Bison confessed. "I came beforehand because I want to talk to you. If you object, I understand. Go ahead and tell me. But I have to talk to you, and I hope you'll let me when you're through."

"We could have talked at dinner." Silk was thinking about Bison's salute. Bison had not tried to imitate a Guardsman's click, snap, and flourish, which would almost certainly have rendered him ridiculous; yet the salute had conveyed respect for order and the office of caldé, plainly and even attractively.

"Not alone. Part of what I'm going to say . . ." Bison let the thought trail off.

Oosik rose. "We must speak more upon our topic, Caldé. Not now, but soon. I hope you agree."

Silk nodded, causing Oreb to hop from his head to his left shoulder.

"With your permission, I shall look in on my son. I hope he is well enough to attend. I will return at eight."

Silk glanced at the clock; it was after seven. "Of course. Tell your son, please, that all of us hold high hopes for his recovery." Oosik saluted and made an about face.

Stepping aside for Oosik, Horn put in, "Willet's back with Master Xiphias, Caldé. He asked me to tell you."

Silk was on the point of instructing Horn to call Hossaan by his true name, but thought better of it. If Hossaan had called himself Willet, Hossaan had no doubt had a reason.

"Master Xiphias's in the Blue Room. He says he doesn't have to see you before dinner unless you want to see him."

"That's good." Silk smiled. "I'm in dire need of people who don't have to see me. I wish that there were more. You'd better go home now, Horn, or you'll miss supper."

"Nettle and me are going to help. We'll get something."

"Fish heads?" Oreb inquired.

"If there are any, I'll save them for you," Horn promised.

"Very well, Horn, and thank you." Silk returned to Bison. "When I heard you were here early, I hoped that you had come to tell me you'd found Maytera Mint. I take it you haven't."

"No, Caldé, but that's what I want to talk to you about."

"Then sit down and do it. I don't have long before dinner—the other guests will be here soon—but we can finish up afterward if we must."

Bison sat; like Oosik, he seemed too large for the chair. "You've talked to Loris and Potto on a glass, Caldé."

Silk nodded.

"They won't talk to me. I know, because I tried before I came here. But they talked to you, and they might talk to you again. I want you to ask them to let you see General Mint for yourself. They say they've got her. Make them prove it."

"Why do you doubt them, Colonel?"

Bison sighed and leaned back. "I knew you'd ask that. I don't blame you, I would too. Just the same, I kept hoping you wouldn't."

"Poor man!" Oreb commiserated.

"When I ask to see her, they'll want to know why. I must have something to tell them, and the more compelling it is, the more likely it will be that they'll show her to us—assuming that they have her."

"You'll let me watch?"

"Certainly." Silk paused, his forefinger tracing circles on his cheek. "You're emotionally involved. Oreb senses it, and so do I. I hope you won't let your attachment to Maytera Mint, one that I feel myself, goad you into acting rashly."

"I hope so, too, Caldé." Bison clenched hairy fists that looked as big as hams. "You've been down in the tunnels. You said so during that meeting."

"Bad hole!"

"Well, so have I. Maybe I should've told you then, but I didn't because it didn't seem relevant and I didn't want you to think I was showing off. There's a way down in the Orilla, and I'm pretty sure there's more, besides the one under the Juzgado that Sand and his soldiers used."

Silk nodded. It had not occurred to him that Bison might be a thief, and he adjusted his mind to the new information as Bison spoke again.

"I got a hunch after a while. I remembered a place down there, an old guardroom that they used when there were soldiers underneath the city all the time. I had a feeling they might have taken her there, and went in with thirty of my troopers to check it out myself."

"Bad hole!" Oreb repeated; and Silk nodded again. "It is a bad hole, and I'm not in the least sure that what you did was wise, Colonel. I understand why you did it, however."

"We found the place all right." The big hands clasped and seemed intent upon pulling each other's fingers off. "The door was open, and there were bloodstains all over the floor. Fresh blood, Caldé."

"Which could have been anybody's." Silk hoped that his expression did not reveal the dismay he felt. "Horn! Horn, would you come back in here for a moment, please?"

"When we got back to the surface, I tried to talk to the

Ayuntamiento on a glass," Bison continued. "There used to be one in that old guardroom, I think, but it was stolen a long time ago, if there was. Anyway, I tried to talk to Potto, and when he wouldn't, to Loris. Then to Tarsier or Galago. None of them would speak to me. That was when I came here."

"Did you ask your glass to find Maytera for you?"

Bison shook his head. "It didn't occur to me. Do you think they might have her where there's a glass?"

Horn burst in. "Yes, Patera? I mean Caldé."

"It's late," Silk said, "and I'm getting tired. It seems to me that I've been inviting people to dinner all day long, and relying on Maytera to keep track of everybody. Would you ask her, please, as soon as she has time, to write me a complete list of the guests we expect?"

"I can tell you, Caldé. Or write it out for you if you'd rather. I wrote the placecards and put them around."

"Tell me then. If I need a written list afterward, I'll have you do it."

"You, Caldé, at the head of the table. On your right will be Generalissimo Siyuf. Maytera said we had to put her there because the dinner was to welcome her to the city."

Silk nodded. "Quite right."

"Then His Cognizance. She'll be between you and him."

Oreb fluttered uncomfortably; Silk said, "Go on."

"Then General Saba, she's the captain of their airship. Then Colonel Bison."

"I'm Colonel Bison," Bison explained. "I came a little early to speak to the Caldé."

"Good man!" Oreb assured Horn.

"Horn is one of the boys at our palaestra," Silk told Bison. "The leader of the boys at our palaestra, I ought to say, and he's been worth a hundred cards to us. Continue, if you please, Horn."

"Sure. Colonel Bison, then Generalissimo Siyuf's staff officer, whoever she is. And then Maytera at the foot of the table, only I don't think she's going to sit down there much and talk to people, Caldé. She's too excited and worried about something going wrong in the kitchen. That's the chair closest to the kitchen."

"Of course."

"On her right there'll be General Saba's staff officer, then Chenille, then Master Xiphias."

"I'm beginning to lose track," Silk told him. "Where will Generalissimo Oosik sit?"

"On your left, Caldé. Then his son. When he got here, he said please put his son right beside him, because he's been so sick. He's worried about him."

"Naturally," Silk said.

"Then Master Xiphias on the Generalissimo's son's left."

"If I've been following you, there should be five people on the right side of the table and five on the left." Silk counted on his fingers. "Right—Siyuf, His Cognizance, Saba, Colonel Bison here, and Siyuf's staff officer. Left—Oosik, his son, Xiphias, Chenille, and Saba's staff officer."

"That's right, Caldé, and you and Maytera make twelve."

"Bird eat?"

"Yes indeed." Silk smiled, glancing sidelong at Oreb. "I wouldn't think of dining without your company. Unfortunately you'd make thirteen at table the way things stand; you won't, however, because I'm asking Horn to ask Maytera to set one more place to my immediate left—a place for General Mint. Please letter a card for her as well, Horn, and set her place exactly like all the others. It will make the left side a trifle more crowded than the right, but the guests on that side will have to bear it."

"It's a real big table, Caldé. It won't be bad."

"I know, I've seen it. Perhaps General Mint will come. Let's hope so. She'll certainly be welcome if she does."

"Very welcome," Bison rumbled.

"So they—no, wait a moment. What about Mucor? Surely she isn't going to help you in the kitchen. Isn't she going to eat with us?"

Horn looked slightly embarrassed. "Maytera thought it'd be better for her to eat in her room, Caldé. She isn't always— you know."

"Maytera Marble's granddaughter," Silk explained to Bison. "I don't believe you've met her."

Bison shook his head.

"She must certainly eat with us. Tell Maytera I insist upon it. She had better be close to Maytera, however. Put her on the right side, between Maytera and Generalissimo Siyuf's staff officer. That gives us six on each side, and fourteen places—fifteen diners in all, including Oreb. Be sure to letter a placecard for Mucor as well as one for General Mint."

Silk heaved a sigh of relief, feeling better than he had since early that morning; his informal dinner no longer seemed a mere formality, and when the dinner was over the formalities (which he had come to detest) would be over as well. "She may be dead," he told Bison. "With all my heart, I pray she isn't, but she may be."

Bison nodded gloomily.

"Even if she is, however—even if we were to find her body, even if we knew beyond doubt that she was dead—we dare not let the Trivigauntis know it, or even suspect we think it. She has won more victories than any other commander we've got, and the better chance they think we have of winning, the more help they will provide us. Am I making myself clear?"

Bison nodded again. "We mustn't let her troopers know, either. Half would go after her on their own, if they knew the Ayuntamiento's got her."

"Or your troopers. Quite correct." Silk pushed back his chair and stood up. "Come with me; there's a glass in the next room."

The gauntletted hand of old Jerboa withdrew the knife of sacrifice, and the calf fell to its knees and rolled over on its side, its spurting blood captured in an earthenware chalice held by one of the younger sibyls. With more dexterity than Auk would have believed he possessed, Jerboa cut off the calf's head and laid it on the fire. The right rear hoof gave him some difficulty, but he persisted.

A fleeting fleck of color in the Sacred Window caught Auk's eye. He gasped, and it was gone.

The impact of the calf's final hoof sent up a fountain of scarlet sparks; Jerboa faced the Window, hands aloft. "Accept, O Great Pas—" He coughed. "Pas who art of all gods . . ."

The Window bloomed pink, violet, and gold. As Auk watched open-mouthed, the dancing hues coalesced into a face of more than human beauty—one that he saw as plainly as he had ever seen any other woman's. "You seek my lover," the goddess said.

"We do, O Great Goddess." Jerboa's reedy old voice was weaker than ever. "We seek him because we seek to do his will."

Auk blurted, "He said he'd come if we'd find Patera."

The goddess's violet eyes left Jerboa. "So much love . . . So much love here. Auk? You are Auk? Find her, Auk. Clasp her to you. Never part."

"All right," Auk said, and repeated, "All right." It was difficult to argue with a goddess. "I sure will, Kindly Kypris. Only Pas gave us this job. We had to find Patera, so we did. Now we got to find Pas, got to get the two together, like."

"The Grand Manteion. Auk." The goddess's shining eyes left him, opening their bottomless lakes to Jerboa once more. "Will you go, old man? Dear old man, so filled with love . . .? Will you find my lover and your god? Jerboa?"

The old augur struggled to speak. Shell said, "I'll take him, Great Goddess. We'll go together." His voice was stronger than Auk had ever heard it.

Although he could not tear his gaze from hers, Incus, on his knees, scuttled backward. "I am *pledged* . . ."

"To prevent my mischief." Kypris's laughter was the peal of icy bells. "To kill fifty? A hundred children. Or more, that little Scylla may heed you. Homely little Scylla, with her father's temperament and her mother's intellect."

Incus seemed incapable of speech or motion.

"You'll require a sacrifice . . . Auk? Not children."

"Not children," Auk repeated, and felt an immense relief.

"My lover. Pas? My lover is engaged with his wife. At present." This time the precious bells were warm and merry. "Not in making more . . . Brats? You call them sprats. No. Oh, no. Wiping her out of core. Do you know what that means? Auk?" Kypris's smile found Shell. "Tell him. . . ."

"He don't have to, Kindly Kypris. I got it."

"You will need a victim. To get my lover's attention. Not a child . . . Auk? Something unusual. Think upon it."

"A victim in the grand Manteion," Auk repeated numbly.

"Several. Perhaps. Auk. I offer no . . . Suggestions. But tonight. As quickly as you can." For a half second her high, ivory-smooth brow wrinkled in thought. "The piece the old man has may aid him in the fight. I hope so."

As Silk limped into the room, one of the waiters provided by Ermine's pulled out his chair for him. He halted behind it, his hands resting on the back. Bison, smiling broadly, made his way down the table to his seat near the foot.

"Welcome," Silk said. He had intended to welcome them in the name of the gods, but the words died unspoken. "Welcome in the name of the City of Viron, to all of you. I deeply regret that I was unable to welcome most of you when you arrived; but I was engaged with Colonel Bison. Maytera will have welcomed you, I feel sure, in Scylla's name."

At the other end of the table, Maytera Marble nodded.

Xiphias whispered, "Sit down lad! Want your leg worse?"

"In which case," Silk continued, "I welcome you in the name of him who enlightened me, the Outsider, the only god I trust."

"He is right, Caldé." Oosik pushed back his chair. "If you will not, my son and I must rise. We cannot remain seated while our superior stands." The pale cornet on his left was struggling to get to his feet already.

"Of course. That was thoughtless of me, Generalissimo. I beg your pardon, and your son's." Silk sat, finding his inlaid rosewood chair rather too high. "I was about to say that I do trust him, now, though it's very hard for me to trust any god."

"We are like children, Patera Caldé," Quetzal told him, and Oreb flew from Silk's shoulder to perch upon the topmost level of the crystal chandelier. "A child has to trust its parents, even when they're not to be trusted."

The pale cornet looked up with a flash of anger that seemed as much a symptom as an emotion. "What are you two implying!"

"Nothing, Mattak. Nothing at all." His father's big hand covered his.

Siyuf's laugh was clear, pleasant, and unaffected. "So we feel of Sphigx, Caldé. But are we fighting among ourselves so quick as this? At home we make a rule that there is allowed no fighting until the fourth bottle."

"That's a good rule," Bison put in, still smiling. "But the tenth might be better."

The young officer had already relaxed, slumping back in his chair; Silk smiled, too. "I don't know what the proper form is, but this is a thoroughly informal dinner anyway. Generalissimo Siyuf, have you met your fellow diners? I know you know His Cognizance and Generalissimo Oosik."

"There is one I should particularly like to meet, Caldé Silk. That very promising girl who sits with Major Haḍale."

The major, a gaunt, hard-faced woman of about forty, said, "Her name is Chenille, Generalissimo. She's living here in the palace temporarily."

Siyuf cocked an eyebrow at Silk. "I am surprise that you have not seated her next to you. She could fit in very easily here between you and me."

"Good girl!" Oreb assured Siyuf from his lofty perch.

"Major Hadale is correct," Silk told Siyuf. "Her name is Chenille, and she's a close friend. So much has happened since we met that I could call her an old one. She has been helping Maytera here, haven't you, Chenille?"

She stared down at her plate. "Yes, Patera."

"Is there anyone else? What about Master Xiphias?"

"I have not this pleasure." Siyuf's eyes remained upon Chenille.

"Master Xiphias is my fencing teacher and my friend, as well as the best swordsman I have ever seen."

"Rich, too, lad! Rich! You asked me to open the window,

remember? Up there in Ermine's! Everybody heard you! Think they'd stay away after that? Breaking my door down! Doubled my charges Molpsday, tripled them yesterday. It's the truth!"

"I am happy for you," Siyuf told him. "Your Caldé speaks of swordsmen. He has never seen a swordswoman, perhaps. Soon we must cross blades for him."

Silk recalled Hyacinth's feigned fencing with the azoth; to hide what he felt, he said, "We are neglecting the cornet. Neither Generalissimo Siyuf nor I have met you, Cornet. That is our loss, beyond doubt. Are you a swordsman? As a cavalry officer, you must be."

"I am Cornet Mattak, Caldé," the young officer announced politely. "My sword has been drawn against you. I'm sure you know that. Now I long to draw it again, in your service."

"You must recover your health first," his father told him.

Quetzal murmured, "I will pray for him, Generalissimo. We augurs teach others to pray for their foes. We try, at least. We seldom get a chance to pray for ours, because we have so few. I'm grateful for this opportunity."

Maytera Marble was equally grateful for the opportunity to turn the talk to religion. "It's Lord Pas who teaches us that, isn't it, Your Cognizance?"

"No, Maytera." Quetzal's hairless head swayed from side to side above his long, wrinkled neck.

Mattak said, "I want to apologize, Your Cognizance. I've been feverish . . ." His voice faded as he met Quetzal's gaze.

"My son has horrible dreams," Oosik explained to the table at large. "Even when he is awake—" He was interrupted by the arrival of the wine, a huge bottle rich with dust and cobwebs.

"We've an extensive cellar here," Silk told Siyuf, "laid down by my predecessor. Experts tell me a good deal of it may have soured, however. I know nothing about such things myself."

The sommelier poured him a half finger, releasing a light aroma suggestive of wildflowers. "Not this, Caldé."

"No, indeed." Silk swirled the pale fluid in his glass. "I really don't need to taste it. No ceremony could mean less." He tasted it nonetheless, and nodded.

"Except these introductions," Bison said unexpectedly, "if the generalissimo's intelligence is as good as I imagine. I'm Colonel Bison, Generalissimo."

"They are not," Siyuf told him, "yet I hear of you, and I receive a description I find accurate." She let the sommelier half fill her wineglass, then waved him away. "You are Mint's chief subordinate. Not long ago you are upon the same footing as many others. Now you are their superior, answerable to her alone. Is it not so?"

"I'm her second in command, yes."

"So well regarded that Caldé Silk closets himself with you before this dinner. I congratulate you."

Siyuf paused, glancing around the table. "There is but one other I do not know. That thin girl beside my Colonel Abanja. She is also of the caldé's household? Pretty Chenille, you must know her. Tell me."

"Her name's Mucor, and she's Maytera's granddaughter," Chenille explained. "We take care of her."

"This is by adoption, I take it."

Chenille hesitated, then nodded.

"Hello, Mucor. I am Generalissimo Siyuf from Trivigaunte. Are we to hope that you will soon be a fine strong trooper? Or a holy woman like your grandmother?"

Mucor did not reply. The sommelier paused, his bottle poised above her wineglass. Maytera Marble put her left hand over it, and Silk shook his head.

"I see. This is not fortunate. Caldé Silk, you know of my General Saba, and you have heard the names of Colonel Abanja and Major Hadale, also. Will you not tell me of the empty chair at your left? I did not read the little card before sitting.

"Wait!" Siyuf raised her hand. "Let me to guess. Mine is the place of honor. I am your distinguished guest. But in the second is not Generalissimo Oosik as I expect, but another. It is then for someone deserving of exceptional honor, and not one of us, for Crane who saved you from the enemy is now dead."

Surreptitiously, Silk made the sign of addition.

"Tell me if I am right as far as I have gone. If Crane is living and I am wrong, I like to know."

"No, he's dead. I wish it weren't so."

A waiter whose livery differed from the others came in with a tray of hors d'oeuvres; as he set the first small plate before Siyuf, Silk recognized him as Hossaan.

If Siyuf herself had recognized him as well, she gave no indication. "Then Crane must be dismissed. Each officer here was permitted a subordinate. That is our custom, and I think it a good one. For me, Colonel Abanja, for my General Saba is Major Hadale, and for your own generalissimo his son. But there is here also Colonel Bison. Mint herself is not present."

"You're entirely correct," Silk told Siyuf, still studying Hossaan out of the corner of his eye; he handed Maytera Mint's placecard to Siyuf. He had invited Bison himself and forgotten to tell him that he could bring a subordinate, but there seemed little point in mentioning it.

"Bird eat?" The hors d'oeuvres included clams from Lake Limna, and Oreb regarded them hungrily.

"Of course," Silk told him. "Come down and take whatever you fancy."

Oreb fluttered nervously. "Girl say."

"Me?" Chenille looked up at him. "Why Oreb, how nice! I'm flattered, I really and truly am. I always thought you liked Auk better." She gulped, and Maytera Marble directed a searching glance at her. "Only I don't blame you, because I do too. I'll get a bunch of these, and you can have anything you want, like Patera says." Oreb glided from the chandelier.

Siyuf asked Silk, "He is dead, this Auk?"

Silk shook his head.

"He is not, and so this card," Siyuf held it up, "should be for him. Is that not so? He is alive, you say. But your General Mint is as dead as my Doctor Crane."

Quetzal asked, "Are you sure, Generalissimo? I have good reasons for thinking otherwise."

"You have cut open some sheep."

"Many, I fear."

"A god speaks to us, also. Sublime Sphigx cares more for us than any other city. She alone of the gods speaks to us in our ancient tongue, speaking as we did in my mother's house, and as we speak in mine."

Silk said, "The High Speech of Trivigaunte? I've heard of it, but I don't believe I've ever heard the language itself. Could you say something for us? A prayer or a bit of poetry?"

Siyuf shook her head. "It is not for amusement at dinner parties, Caldé. Instead, I shall say what I set out to say. It is that no other city is so close to its goddess as we. Look at you. You have a goddess, you say. Scylla. Yet your women are slaves. If Scylla cared for you, she would care for them."

Mattak started to protest, but Siyuf raised her voice. "We who are near the heart of Sphigx do not butcher beasts to read her will in offal. Each day we pray to her, and do not tease her with questions but offer sincere praise. When we wish to know a thing, we go and find it out. Your Mint has been shot." She looked at Saba for confirmation, and Saba nodded.

"This is not pleasant," Siyuf continued, "and I would like that I am not the one to say it. She went to treat with the enemy, is that not so?"

From Saba's right, Bison answered, "Yes. It is."

"With a holy man to safeguard. The enemy has killed both. Captured, they say, but I have spoken to their leader, this man Loris, and he cannot produce either." Siyuf waited for someone to contradict her, but no one did.

"Your Mint was of greatest spirit. I would have liked to speak to her. Even a bout with practice swords, this old man to see fair play. All I have heard says plainly that she was of greatest spirit, and I am sure that when she, who had come to talk peace, was made prisoner she would resist. Some fool shot her and her holy man also, a filthy crime. I learned of this after our parade and already I have set our Labor Corps to dig. We will find these tunnels, make a new entrance near the big lake, and soon find one that shall lead us to this Ayuntamiento of Viron. Then Mint will be avenged."

Bison glanced at Silk; Silk nodded, and Bison said, "I must tell you, Generalissimo, that the caldé and I saw General Mint in his glass before we sat down. The caldé had a place set for her originally as a sort of signal, I'd say. He wanted to show that we hoped she was still alive."

"That she would return to us soon," Silk added.

"Now that chair," Bison gestured, "is more than a symbol. Caldé Silk got a monitor to show us what it had seen before we questioned it, and it was General Mint, with four other people and some soldiers and animals hurrying along a tunnel. She may join us before the evening's over."

Siyuf pursed her lips. "If your Mint was in the hands of soldiers, is not that the enemy?"

Saba put down her wineglass. "Vironese soldiers protected the caldé when some private guards tried to kill him, sir. I mentioned that . . ." Her voice altered and her mouth assumed a ghastly grin. "I found her, Silk. She was in the market. She bought a little animal that talks. She's taking it where they kill them."

Chapter 10

A LIFE FOR PAS

Sergeant Sand had scrambled up first. Maytera Mint, exhausted and practically suffocated by the ash that filled the air of the tunnel, thought it strange that it should be large enough to admit his bulky steel body. She had purified the altar of the old manteion on Sun Street many times, and although she told herself that she must surely be mistaken, it seemed to her that its chute had been scarcely half as large as this one.

"These victims, eh?" Remora coughed, eyeing the yearling tunnel gods Eland had taken charge of. "For, hem!, Pas. His—er—ah—ghost?"

Schist nodded. "That's what the Prolocutor says."

"You're saying that Pas is dead." Maytera Mint was by no means sure she believed such a thing possible, still less that it had taken place. "He's come back as a ghost?"

"That's it, General."

Shale added, "We're not sayin' it happened, but that's what he says." He jerked his head toward the chute into which Sand's heels had vanished. "Sarge believes him. So do I, I guess."

Urus edged nearer Maytera Mint. "They're abram, lady, all these chems. Look, we're bios, all right? You 'n me, 'n Spider 'n Eland here. Even the long butcher."

She could scarcely make out Urus's features in the ash-dimmed light; yet she could picture his wheedling expression only too vividly.

"We got to stick, us bios. Got to make a knot, don't we? The way they're talkin', we'll all be cold."

"Good riddance," Spider muttered.

Sand's voice ended the conversation, hollow-sounding as it echoed down the chute overhead. "The augur next. Hand him up."

Remora was peering up the chute. "It's a manteion, eh?"

"Big one, Patera. Pretty dark, too. Wait a minute."

Slate had crouched at Remora's feet. "I'm goin' to grab you by the legs, see, Patera? I'm goin' to lift you up 'n in. Get your arms up over your head to steer yourself. When you're in good, I'll push on your feet 'n get you up as far as I can. Maybe you'll have to wiggle up a little more before Sarge can grab hold of you." Abruptly the dark mouth of the chute became a rectangle of light.

It is big, Maytera Mint thought; *it has to be. They have a lot of victims, burn a cartload of wood at every sacrifice.*

Sand's voice returned. "They got oil lamps here. I lit a couple for you."

"Thank you!" Remora called. "My most, um, deepest—ah—sincere appreciation, my son." He looked down at Slate. "I am ready, eh? Lift away."

"You'll be fine, Your Eminence," Maytera Mint assured him.

"You think—ah—fear me apprehensive." Remora smiled, his teeth visible in the light from the chute. "To, um, revisit the whorl of light, Maytera, I should—umph!"

Slate had grasped his ankles and was rising. For a moment Remora swayed dangerously and it seemed he must fall; but Spider pushed his hips to right him, and in another second his arms and head were out of sight.

"Here he comes, Sarge!"

"What it is, see," Urus was nearly at Maytera Mint's ear, "is they think they ought to give Pas somethin'. He put that in their heads, your jefe did."

"His Cognizance." Coughing, she turned to face Urus. "I cannot imagine His Cognizance in these horrible tunnels, though I know he was here with the caldé."

"Me neither. Only, see—"

"Be quiet." Maytera Mint was studying Eland's beasts. "How are we going to get these animals up there, Slate?"

"I been thinkin' about that," Slate said. "Watch this."

Crouching again, he sprang into the chute and scrambled up.

"You two'd better stay here to lift the general and me up," Spider told Schist and Shale.

"Sure thing." With Slate gone, Schist leaned back against the shiprock wall. "We'll pass 'em up just like the slug guns. You'll see."

Shale indicated the opening with a contemptuous gesture. "He's buckin' for another stripe, Slate is. We used to have this corporal from 'H' Company, only he bought it in the big fight with the talus the other day. This time probably they'll promote from inside, and Slate figures he'll cop it."

Slate's voice came from the chute. "Knock off jawin' down there 'n pass them guns."

Schist said, "Sure thing," and lifted the bundled slug guns into the chute. Shale explained, "I strapped 'em together with one of the slings. Makes 'em easier to handle."

The bundle of guns vanished amid scrapings and bumpings. Schist tilted his head back and to the left to grin at Maytera Mint. "He's hangin' in there, see? Sarge's got his feet."

Spider coughed. "Maybe you'd like to go next, General."

"I would," she confessed, "but I'll go last. It is my place as the senior officer present."

"I don't think you can jump up there," Schist objected.

She turned on him. " 'I don't think you can jump up there *sir.*' Or *'General.'* I give you your choice, Private, which is more than I ought to give you."

"Yes, sir. Only I don't think you can, sir, and I'd be glad to stay down here and help you, sir."

"That won't be necessary." Maytera Mint turned to the other soldier. "Private Shale."

"Yes, sir!" Shale snapped to attention.

"You were very ingenious with that sling. After you and Private Schist have passed these beasts up and helped Spider, Urus, and this other convict—"

"Eland," Eland put in, speaking for the first time since they had reached this darkest stretch of tunnel.

"Thank you. And Eland, to climb up, you will contrive a rope of slug gun slings, making a loop at the bottom into which I can put one foot. Can you do that?"

"Sure thing, sir."

"Good. Do it. Than you can pull me up. Last."

Spider ventured, "You're goin' to be down here all alone, for a minute or two, anyhow."

"These—" She was wracked by a paroxysm of coughing. "These animals. I don't know what to call them."

"Bufes," Eland supplied.

"Thank you." Turning her head, she spat. "I will not call them gods. That must stop. More bufes may come, though I hope they won't. I pray they won't. But if they do I'll shoot them. If I don't see them in time, or don't aim well, I will die."

"I'll stay with you," Spider told her.

She shook her head. "Only one—"

From the chute, Slate called, "Gimme a god." Shale lifted a squirming beast over his head and thrust its hindquarters into the opening in the ceiling; its eyes were wild, and blood ran from the sinews binding its muzzle.

"I dunno if I could of trained 'em as big as that," Eland muttered, "only it seems like a shame to waste 'em."

"I caught 'em, sir," Shale explained to Maytera Mint. "The bios and me were back by that dead bio you left behind. We knew the smell would fetch 'em."

Schist added, "That was why Slate and Sarge jumped out of the dirt when they did, probably, sir. Sarge thought you might scare 'em off if you went back for the dead one."

"Perhaps. I can understand how a soldier could capture such an animal. What I cannot understand is how you, Eland, were able to capture others without the help of one."

"Mine was littler when I got 'em." He watched the second beast vanish up the chute. "We killed the big 'uns, we had to. I got behind the little 'uns and got a noose over their mouth."

"It must have been dangerous just the same."

He shrugged, the motion of his skeletal shoulders barely visible. "I want to go up next. Be with 'em. That all right?"

From the chute, Slate called, "Pass up them other bios."

"Certainly," Maytera Mint told Eland. She gestured toward the chute, and Schist lifted him.

"You can't get 'em to like you," Eland said as his head vanished into the chute, "only maybe mine did, a little."

From nearer the top, Slate told him, "Grab on."

"If the bufes don't bring Pas, lady, 'n they won't, I know they won't—"

Maytera Mint shook her head. "You cannot know."

"Then it's us. Me 'n Eland. Him, too," Urus pointed to Spider, "if you let 'em. That sergeant—"

"My son." Maytera Mint stepped so close to Urus that the muzzle of the needler she held gouged his ribs. "I have been most remiss with you. I have let you call me 'lady' or whatever you wished. I must remember to bring it up at my next shriving, if there is a next shriving. In future, you are to address me as Maytera. It means *mother*. Will you do that?"

"Yeah. Dimber here, Maytera."

"That is well." She smiled up at him; she was a full head shorter than he. "As your mother, your spiritual mother, I must explain something to you. Please pay strict attention."

Urus nodded mutely. From the chute, Slate called, "Gimme another one."

"Go, Spider," Maytera Mint said, and turned back to Urus. "I haven't had much time in which to form my estimate of your character, yet I think it accurate. It is not an estimate very favorable to you."

When he did not speak, she added, "Not favorable at all. I

will not compare you to such a man as Sergeant Sand. Though not pious, he is resolute, energetic, loyal, and reasonably honest. To compare him to you would be grossly unjust to him. Nor will I venture to compare you to His Eminence. His Eminence has less physical courage, I think, than many other men. Yet he has more than a casual observer might suppose, as I have seen, and his assiduity and piety have justly earned him a high position in the Chapter. He is intelligent as well, and he labors almost too diligently to put the mental acuity that he received from the gods at their service."

"Have you got the safety on that thing, lady?"

"Call me *Maytera*. I insist on it."

"All right, all right!" His voice shaking, Urus repeated, "Have you got the safety on?" and added, "Maytera?"

"No, my son, I do not." She took a deep breath. "Stop talking and listen. Your life hangs upon it, and we haven't long. I am a general and a sibyl. As a sibyl I try to find good in everyone, and though it may sound less than modest, I generally succeed. I find a great deal in His Eminence, as I would expect. I find more than I expected in Sergeant Sand. There is good in Private Slate, too, and in Private Shale and Private Schist here. Not good of a very high order, perhaps, but abundant in its kind. I have tried to find good in Spider and found more than I dared hope for. The glimmers of good in Eland are hardly discernible, yet unmistakable." She sighed. "I talk too much when I'm tired. I hope you've followed me."

Urus nodded. There was a faint play of light across one cheekbone; it was half a second before she understood that he was sweating, cold perspiration soaking the gray ash black and running down his face like rivulets of fresh paint.

"As a general, it is my duty to defeat the enemy. I must do it by killing men and women. I find that repugnant, but such is the case. You are the enemy, Urus. Do you follow me still?"

From the chute, Slate called, "Ready for the next one."

"That will be you," Maytera Mint told Shale. "Remember what I told you about those slings."

He saluted with a clash of steel. "I'll get right on it, sir."

She returned her attention to Urus. "You are the enemy, I

say. Should I, who have been called the Sword of Echidna, let you live when I have you at my mercy?"

"You're fightin' the Ayuntamiento, right? General, I swear by every shaggy god there is that I never done nothin'—"

"Be quiet!" Angrily, she poked him with the muzzle of the big needler that had been Spider's. "What you say is true, I'm sure. You never served the Ayuntamiento. But ultimately the enemy is evil. Evil is the ultimate enemy of us all."

She fell silent, listening to the faint rattle as Shale was helped up the chute, to the sighing of the ever-present breeze, and to Urus's feverish breathing. "The ash is not so thick in the air as it was," she said.

Schist nodded. "Not so many stirrin' it up, sir."

"I suppose so, and those ugly beasts were struggling." She jabbed Urus as hard as she could, and he yelped.

"This one, too. I'm tired, Urus. I'm awfully tired. I've slept on floors, and walked for leagues and leagues. I forget, sometimes, what I've said, and what I intended to say. You were thinking of snatching my needler a moment ago."

Schist chuckled, a hard dry metallic rattle.

"No doubt you could. No doubt you can. Taking a needler from a tired woman much smaller than yourself, a woman so close that her needler is within easy reach, should be simple for you. For anybody." She waited.

"If you're not going to, you'd better raise your hands. Otherwise some small motion may cause me to pull the trigger."

Slowly, Urus's hands went up.

"As you say, you haven't served the Ayuntamiento. I've talked with Councillor Potto, Urus. Did you know that?"

He shook his head.

"I have. Also with Spider, who served the Ayuntamiento and would serve it still if he could. With a number of Guardsmen, Generalissimo Oosik particularly, who served it for many years. I've questioned prisoners, too. In not one of them did I fail to discover some gleam of good. Councillor Potto is the worst, I think. But even Councillor Potto is not entirely evil."

From the chute, Slate called, "How about the general and that other bio?"

Maytera Mint backed away, then motioned toward the area under the chute. "I give you fair warning. I must see some good in you, Urus, and soon."

His smile was at once pitiable and horrible. "You're goin' to let me get out, lady? Let me go up there?"

"Call me Maytera!"

"M-maytera. Maytera, I figured, see, I'd made it out. Only it w-w-was just the pit, the shaggy pit, 'n then we run back down 'n got into it with the old man—"

Schist lifted him by his ankles. "He ain't got no sores on his legs like that other one, sir. Maybe you saw 'em."

Looking down at the needler, Maytera Mint felt herself nod.

"I had to sorta wash off my hands with ashes." Somewhat violently, Schist shoved Urus's head and shoulders into the chute. "After I lifted him, sir. I got pus on 'em, sir."

"No doubt he'd been nipped from time to time by the beasts he had earlier," Maytera Mint said absently. "Those would be the ones our caldé says Patera Incus killed, perhaps." Eland and Urus might have encountered Auk, in that case; she made a mental note to ask them about it, adding as an afterthought that she must not kill Urus before she had a chance to question him.

"You're goin' to stay, sir?"

"Until Private Shale lets down his slings. Yes, I am. Go ahead, Schist. Anytime they're ready for you."

The safety had been off, as she had said. Did that make her better, because she had told the truth? Or worse, because she had practically nerved herself to killing Urus? Dropping the needler into one of the big side pockets of her torn and soiled habit, she watched Schist's feet disappear into the chute, then sat down in the ash to await Shale's slings, or the beasts that he called gods, and Eland bufes.

Bison put down the untasted leg of a pheasant. "Two cards to every one of them, Caldé?"

Silk nodded, his eyes upon Mucor. "Yes. I hadn't meant to

tell you tonight, Colonel. To be more exact, I hadn't planned to make my decision until morning."

Saba began, "I submit—"

"But if Mucor can locate the manteion to which the woman I've had her looking for is bringing her offering, I'll be busy tomorrow. Besides, it's better that I announce it now, so that Generalissimo Oosik and Generalissimo Siyuf can hear it. We'll send the volunteers home tomorrow, each with a letter of credit worth two cards at the Fisc."

"Caldé . . ." Oosik reached across Maytera Mint's vacant place to touch Silk's arm. "It will take longer than one day merely to collect their weapons."

Silk shook his head. "We won't collect them. They're to keep whatever they have—those are their weapons now."

Saba looked at Siyuf, and when Siyuf did not speak, said, "That's unheard-of. It's folly. Insanity." Chenille caught Silk's eye and nodded. "She's right, Patera. It's abram."

He spoke to Maytera Marble, at the far end of the table. "You told me something earlier that weighed heavily with me, Maytera; there's no one whose judgement I value more, as you know. Would you repeat it for us?"

"I can't, Patera. I don't remember what it was."

Xiphias put in, "Couldn't you just let them keep their swords, lad?"

"I could scarcely take those, could I? Those are their own property already. Chenille, you agree that I shouldn't do this. Why not?"

Saba snapped, "Because they're men, ninety percent of them, and unstable, like all men." Chenille added, "They'll kill each other, Patera."

"Of course they will—they always have." Silk addressed Siyuf. "My manteion is in what we call the Sun Street Quarter. I should explain that our city counts many more quarters than four; a quarter in our sense really means no more than the area served by a manteion."

If she inclined her head, the motion was too slight to be seen. "Fifty thousand, Caldé Silk? All with slug guns?"

"There are more than fifty thousand certainly, but not all

of them have slug guns. Fifty thousand slug guns, perhaps, or a little over."

When she put no further question, he said, "It's a violent quarter; most augurs would say it's the worst in the city. It borders on the Orilla, which is what we call an empty quarter—one without a manteion. A few people from the Orilla come to our manteion, however, just as a few from our quarter go into the Orilla to buy stolen goods. What I was going to say is that there's seldom a week without a killing or two, and there are often three or four. When one man decides to kill another, he does it. If he has a slug gun or a needler, he may use it; but if he doesn't, he uses a dagger or a sword. Or a hatchet, an axe, or a stick of firewood."

Recalling Auk, Silk added, "A big, strong man may simply knock down a weaker one and kick him to death. A group of men could clearly do the same thing; and I know of one instance in which a man who had raped a child was killed by a dozen women, who beat him to death with their washing sticks and stabbed him with kitchen knives and scissors."

Hadale told him, "One woman can kill a man, Caldé. It's common at home, and there's a woman at this table who's killed several."

"It isn't uncommon here, either, Major; and that bears on the thing Maytera told me that impressed me so much. A woman from our quarter came to see her this afternoon, and Maytera asked if she wasn't afraid to walk so far through the city when just about everyone has a slug gun or a needler. The woman said she wasn't, because she had one, too."

Silk paused, inviting comment, and Saba growled, "They'll overthrow you, Caldé, in half a year or less."

"You may well be right." He spread his hands. "But not by force, since they won't have to—I haven't the least desire to retain this office if our people don't want me. That's the chief difference between the Ayuntamiento and our side, really. But I think you've hit on something important. The reason the Ayuntamiento didn't let our people have slug guns or launchers like the one Chenille told me about this afternoon was that they are effective means of fighting soldiers and troopers in armor. The Ayuntamiento believed that if our people didn't have those weapons it could rule as long as it retained the loyalty of the Army and the Guard."

"Very sensible," Saba declared.

"Perhaps, but it didn't work very well. A few days ago, our people overwhelmed hundreds of Guardsmen and took their weapons. I see I have not convinced you."

Saba shook her head.

"Then let me say this. Generalissimo Oosik says that he would need more than a day to collect the weapons of General Mint's volunteers."

Bison added, "If they'd surrender them."

"Exactly. The best troopers would give their weapons up when they were ordered to, but the worst would hide theirs— the precise opposite of the situation we'd prefer. Furthermore, it would take at least as long to reissue those weapons, and we may need the volunteers again any day."

Quetzal, who had been nodding over his untouched plate, murmured, "One hundred thousand cards is a large sum, Patera Caldé. Can you afford that much?"

Silk shook his head.

Xiphias exclaimed, "Then don't, lad! Don't do it!"

"We can't afford to do it, Master Xiphias." Silk smiled wryly. "But we cannot afford not to, either. In the first place, I promised to reward those who fought bravely on either side, and I've done nothing thus far. There may be a thousand things we cannot afford. No doubt there are. But the thing we cannot afford above all—the thing we dare not risk—is to have people come to believe that my promises are worthless. So tomorrow, as I say, every trooper that General Mint and Colonel Bison have is to receive two cards, and permission to return to his or her home and occupation. Those who were given slug guns or other weapons are to be told that the weapons are theirs now. No one will be able to complain that those who fought on our side went unrewarded, at least."

Siyuf smiled. "Like you, Caldé Silk, I think we may need the horde of Mint again, and soon. When you call for them they will come, having been rewarded handsomely for the first time."

"Thank you. Most of our financial troubles result from various businesses—"

Hossaan had entered as he spoke, carrying a huge roast upon a magnificent golden platter. "The people from Ermine's can see to that, Willet," Silk told him. "Please get your floater ready—I'll want it soon."

Oreb flew up the table, circling warily before perching on Silk's shoulder. "Bird too!"

"Of course, if you wish."

"Let me hear the rest, Caldé Silk. I am most interested."

"I was about to say that if the overdue taxes were paid, our city government would be rolling in wealth, Generalissimo. General Mint's troopers will spend the cards they receive very quickly for the most part, and that should produce a wave of prosperity. If we make forceful efforts to collect the overdue taxes then, we may be able to meet our other obligations."

Siyuf looked down the table to Saba. "You have tell me he is mad. He is not mad. He is only more clever than you. It is not the same."

Might not the dead rise and walk again? There were tales of such things, and they flitted through Maytera Mint's mind as she was drawn up the chute.

I was sacrificed, she thought. I should have realized it when Councillor Potto had Spider bend me over his knee. A drop struck me, too. How wonderful it would be if all the rest could come back up through these the way I am!

The top of the chute was a glaring rectangle above her, light so bright that it seemed to her it must surely be noon, with the whole of Pas's long sun pouring golden radiance through the windows of the manteion into which she rose. Fascinated, she watched Slate's metal hands in silhouette as they slowly and steadily hauled her up, each grip succeeded by the next.

Then a hand of flesh, Remora's long blue-veined hand, was reaching for her; she caught it and let him help her climb from the looped slings to a mosaic floor. "There you are, Maytera. I, um, we have been waiting for you. The sergeant is most, er, desirous to proceed, eh?" Remora's face was clean, his soiled overrobe was gone, and his costly robe had be⠀⠀⠀laced by one more costly still.

⠀⠀⠀ooked for the windows she had pictured, expecting to find them glowing with sunshine; but there were no windows, only scores of rock-crystal holy lamps surmounted by long, bright flames, and a fire blazing upon the altar.

"I—ah—kindled the, um," Remora ventured, following the direction of her eyes. "It seemed provident."

"Certainly. You've cleaned up, too. May I ask where, Your Eminence?" Catching sight of Urus edging toward the back of the manteion, she shouted, "Sergeant! Stop that prisoner!"

"An, er, dressing chamber? Cubiculum. Off the sacristy, eh? For sibyls. Cabinets—ah—wardrobes in there. So I, um, given to understand."

"I'll want water and soap," she told him. "Warm water, if that's possible. You've washed, clearly."

Spider interjected, "The sergeant wants to sacrifice right away. He—" From his position between Urus and the door, Sand himself rasped, "The Prolocutor told us Pas would come, sir. I reported that. It's the Plan, and standing orders say it's got higher priority than anything else." Slate nodded agreement.

"Indeed it does. But Pas may *not* come as well. We must be prepared for that eventuality, too. I say that, though I hate putting myself on the same side as Urus, who feels certain Pas won't. But if he comes, as we hope, we must be fit to receive him. Not only I, but all of you as well." She followed Remora onto the sanctuary elevation and past the fire-crowned altar.

"The, um, locality, hey?" Remora was almost grinning.

"What about it, Your Eminence? If you're asking whether I know where we are," she glanced around her, "I haven't the least idea. I didn't know that a manteion like this existed."

They entered the sacristy, thrice the size of Silk's on Sun Street; a shelf held a long row of jeweled chalices, and on a block of fragrant sandalwood a dozen sacrificial knives whose gold or ivory handles flashed with gems.

"I have officiated here, er, innumerable," Remora informed her. "Five hundred, eh? A thousand? I should not contest even so lofty a figure as that. It is the, um, oratorium abolitus, the private chapel beneath the Palace. For His Cognizance's use, hey? And augurs who have—ah—administrative duties, eh? We, er, offer our—ah—seldom-seen? Obscure services to the gods."

He was about to go; she caught the voluminous sleeve of his robe. "The room where I can wash? Where there may be a clean habit I can borrow?"

"Oh, yes, yes, yes! Right—ah—door." He opened it for her. "Should be a bolt, eh? Inside. No doubt, no doubt. Water likewise. Tank, eh?" He pointed at the ceiling. "Under the—ah—in the west cupola."

The room was twice as large as her longed-for bedroom in the cenoby. Gratefully, she shut its door and shot the bolt. Two large wardrobes and a wash basin; a pierced copper hamper, presumably for laundry; a full length mirror on one wall and a glass on another. A table in a corner.

Opening one of the wardrobes, she found half a dozen clean habits of various sizes; she draped the biggest over the glass, then emptied her pockets onto the table, took off her own habit, and dropped it into the hamper. It was probably beyond saving, and the Chapter owed her a round hundred new ones at least.

Grimly stepping out of her soiled underdrawers and removing her chemise and bandeau, she resolved to collect those habits and distribute them to sibyls as poor as she.

It was Mainframe itself to take off her shoes and stockings, although she had to sit on the floor to do it, which made it seem likely there were no clean stockings. She rinsed the ones she had taken off, wrung them as dry as she could, and hung them over the open door of the wardrobe.

The tap to her left gushed water that was at first tepid, then pleasantly steaming. There was a boiler somewhere in the Palace, presumably; Maytera Mockorange, whose family had been wealthy, had spoken of such luxury, although Maytera Mint had never dreamed it might be available to sibyls.

She had to wash her hands three times (with scented soap!) before the suds that streamed from them were no longer black with filth. Even so, small crescents remained under her nails. The point of one of the little projectiles called needles attended to those.

Her small, tired face seemed to her equally dirty, if not worse; gingerly dabbing at the bruises and burns, she washed it again and again, washing her short brown hair too, then sponged her entire body, heedless of the pools that formed on the red-tiled floor.

Remora's querulous voice penetrated the heavy wooden door. "The . . . Sergeant Sand. Sergeant Sand wishes—"

She felt her sly little smile, although she struggled to repress it. "Tell him that I myself wish for sandwiches, Your Eminence, and ask what he knows about court-martials."

"You . . . chaff."

"Not at all. Tell him that and ask him." Her image in the mirror appalled her. If Bison were ever to see her like this!

Not that he or any other man ever would, presumably; but men did not like skinny legs, narrow hips, or small breasts, all of which she possessed to a degree that seemed appalling. Yet she had been pretty twenty years ago; many people had told her so, many of them men.

A pretty girl whose long curls had bordered upon chestnut. Some of those men might have been lying, and no doubt some had been. But all of them? It seemed improbable.

The other wardrobe was divided into pigeonholes; most were empty, but one held two clean chemises and two pairs of clean underdrawers. The underdrawers were several sizes too large, but wearable with the string pulled tight. She could rinse her bandeau as she had her stockings—

In a flurry of rebellion, she flung it into the hamper. A bandeau to cover up what? To hold in what? She had worn one because her mother, and subsequently Maytera Rose, had said she must; she looked no different now in this yellowed chemise than she had in her own in the cenoby.

Snatching the habit from the glass, she clapped her hands. "Monitor? Monitor?" She had used glasses during the past few days, but was not completely comfortable with them.

"Yes, madame." The floating gray face was at once detached and deferential.

"Look at me. I'm lacking an essential item of feminine apparel. What is it?"

"Several, madame. A gown, madame. Hose, and shoes."

"Besides those." She turned sideways and stood on tiptoe. "What is it?"

"I am at a loss, madame. I might offer a conjecture."

"You needn't bother." She took the smallest habit from the first wardrobe. "Do you know who I am?" For an instant she was wrapped in darkness before it settled into place. Still no coif, she thought. Still no coif.

"I recognize you now, madame. You are General Mint. I was ignorant of your identity, previously. Would you prefer that I address you as General?"

"As you like. Has anyone been trying to contact me?"

For perhaps a second, the monitor's face dissolved into darting lines. "Several, madame. Currently, Captain Serval. Do you wish to speak with him?"

She sensed that the name should have been familiar, yet it meant nothing to her. She nodded. Better to find out who he was and what he wanted, and be done.

The monitor's face revised itself, gaining color, a round chin, and a debonair mustache. "My General!" A brisk salute, which she returned almost automatically.

"My General, I have been ordered by Generalissimo Oosik to make you aware of the situation here."

She nodded. Where was "here"?

"It is a detachment of the Companion Cavalry, My General. They have posted sentries who are standing guard with mine as we speak. I have requested that their officer explain this to Generalissimo Oosik, but she refuses."

"I see." Maytera Mint took a deep breath and found herself wishing for a chair. "Let me say first, Captain, that it's good to see you again."

"For me it is a great pleasure, My General. An honor."

"Thank you, Captain. I'm sorry to find that you're still a captain, by the way. I'll talk to the generalissimo about that. You mentioned Companion Cavalry. That is the name of the unit?"

"Yes, My General."

The memory of Potto's boiling teakettle returned. "You'll have to forgive me, Captain. I've been out of touch for the past few days." It had seemed like weeks. "I was told that a Trivigaunti horde was marching toward the city. Am I to take it that this Companion Cavalry is theirs?"

"Yes, My General. An elite regiment."

Regiment was a new term to her, but she persevered. "What was it you wanted this officer from Trivigaunte to explain to the generalissimo?"

"I wish her to explain why she and her women are mounting a guard on our Juzgado, My General, when it is already guarded by my men and myself." (That was "here" then, almost certainly.) "I wish her to explain who has issued these orders and to what purpose."

"I take it she won't tell you either."

"No, My General. She will say only that her instructions are to protect our Juzgado until relieved. No more than that."

"Generalissimo Oosik asked you to make me aware of this situation. Where is he?"

"At the Caldé's Palace, My General. He is dining with the caldé. He informs me that the caldé has seen you, My General, in his glass, and that he has ordered a place set for you at his table. Generalissimo Oosik instructed me to request that you join them there if I reached you, should this be convenient."

"I need sleep more than food." It had slipped out.

"You drive yourself too hard, My General. I have observed this previously."

"Perhaps. Can you tell me what orders you received from Generalissimo Oosik regarding these Trivigauntis?"

"He is of the opinion that they have learned of a threat to the Juzgado, My General. I am to cooperate. There is to be no friction between those of my command and theirs." The captain paused, a pause pregnant with meaning. "Or as little as may be. I am to explore the situation and report once more, should I discover facts of significance."

"And notify me."

"Yes, My General. As I do."

"Also Colonel Bison, I hope. If Generalissimo Oosik did not tell you to notify Colonel Bison, I am ordering you to now. Tell him I consider Generalissimo Oosik's position prudent."

Someone was tapping at the door.

"Colonel Bison is also at the caldé's dinner, My General. Generalissimo Oosik stated that he would inform him."

"Good. That will be all, then, Captain. Thank you for keeping me abreast of things." She returned his salute.

"Monitor, was Colonel Bison one of the people who have been trying to reach me?"

The captain's face grayed and sharpened. "Yes, madame."

"I want to speak to him now. He's at the Caldé's Palace." Vaguely, she recalled seeing it the year before on her way to sacrifice at the Grand Manteion, a huge house upon whose façade files of shuttered windows had risen like stacks of long and narrow coffins; she had shuddered and turned away. "I'll be out in a moment, Your Eminence!"

The monitor said, "I am aware of it, madame. I will ask someone to bring him to the glass there, madame."

She would see him—and he would see her: the tired eyes and bloodless mouth that the mirror had shown her, the wet hair plastered to her skull, the face black-and-blue with bruises, surmounted by a scab. "Monitor?"

"Yes, madame."

"Let me speak to whoever comes to the glass." This was the hardest thing she had ever done, harder even than shutting her eyes during Kypris's theophany. "I needn't speak to the colonel in person."

"Yes, madame."

A minute, then two, passed. The gray features melted and flowed, becoming those of a lean man with hooded eyes.

"Yes, General Mint," he said. "I'm Willet, the caldé's driver. How may I serve you?"

General Saba spoke, looking less like an angry sow than a dead one. "She's coming up here with it, Silk. Coming up the hill you're on."

"This is warlockery," Siyuf declared.

"I disagree, but I haven't time to discuss it now." Silk stood so abruptly that Oreb fluttered to maintain his balance. "Leaving you is the height of bad manners; I know it, and all of you are entitled to be furious with me. I'm leaving just the same. Maytera Marble will remain as my representative. I beg your forgiveness sincerely and fervently, but I must go." He was already halfway down the table,

Xiphias sprang to his feet as Silk strode past his chair. "Alone," Silk said. Undeterred, Xiphias hurried after him, and the door slammed behind them.

Saba's head jerked. She looked around self-consciously.

"We must speak of this," Siyuf hissed. "You must describe to me. Not now."

Major Hadale drained her wine. "I'll remember this dinner as long as I live. What entertainment!"

Maytera Marble whispered to Chenille. "I should have gone, too. He's hurt, and—"

Smoothly, Siyuf overrode her. "General Saba has say to me he suffer a broken ankle, Maytera. Maytera? It is how you are addressed?"

She nodded. "Yes, he did. He does. A week ago Phaesday, I think it was. He fell. But—but . . ."

"He limp. So I observed. He was in greatest haste, he took big steps. No so big of the right leg, however. The old swordswoman—sword-man. He, also, but the left."

"The caldé was shot." Maytera Marble indicated her own chest with her working hand. "That's much worse."

"Not a slug gun, which would have kill there. A needler?" Siyuf glanced around the table, seeking information.

Oosik shrugged and spread his hands. "Yes, Generalissimo. A needler in the hand of one of my own officers. We strive to prevent these terrible mistakes. They occur in spite of all we do, as you must know."

"This is a remarkable young man. We do not breed like him in Trivigaunte, I think. Do you know the—what is this word? The ideas of Colonel Abanja?"

Oosik nodded to Siyuf's staff officer. "I would like to hear them, particularly if they concern our caldé. What are they, Colonel?"

"I am something of an amateur historian, Generalissimo. An amateur military historian, if you will allow it."

"Every good officer should be."

"Thank you. I'm accused of shaping my theory to flatter Generalissimo Siyuf, but that is not the case. I have studied success. Not victory alone, because victory can be a matter of chance, and is frequently a matter of numbers and materièl. I search out instances in which a small force has frustrated one that should have defeated it in days or hours."

Saba had regained her self-possession. "I still say that it is brilliance that's decisive. Military genius."

Maytera Marble sniffed decisively, and Siyuf said, "Colonel Abanja does not think this. Brilliance, it is well enough when the execution of the so-brilliant orders is brilliant also. I do not speak of genius for I know nothing. Except it is rare and not to be relied on."

Bison said, "I have a theory of my own, based on what I've seen of General Mint. I'll be interested to see how it compares to the Colonel's."

"I mention Abanja's," Siyuf continued, "because I think Caldé Silk so fine an example of him. She believe it is not this genius, not any quality of the mind. That it is energy, by clearest thoughts directed. Tell us, Abanja."

"Successful commanders," Colonel Abanja began, "are those who are still acting, and acting sensibly, on the fourth day. They endure. We have a game that we play on horseback. I don't think you play it here, but I've won a good deal of money by betting on the games during the past year."

The ends of Oosik's mustache tilted upward. "Then you must tell us by all means, Colonel."

"It imitates war, as most games do. A cavalry skirmish in this case. The players may change mounts after each goal, but the players themselves can't be changed, or even replaced if one is hurt." Both Oosik and his son nodded.

"There is a twenty-minute rest for them, however, and so we speak of the first half of the game and the second, divided by this rest. What determines the result, I have found, is not which team scores the most goals in the first half, because there's seldom much disparity. The winning team will be the one that plays best and most aggressively in the second. When I see the team I've backed doing that, I double my bet, if I can."

Siyuf nodded. Her head moved scarcely one finger's width, but the nod announced that the time for controversy had ended. "Let us move from the fields where *killi* is played to this city of Viron, where is a so illustrative struggle. Who is winner? It is not too soon to say. One side hide in holes. Above prowl and roars the host of Viron and my horde of the Rani. For the second time I ask you that listen." She paused dramatically. "Who is winner here?"

No one spoke.

"A man? This man Caldé Silk? Can that be? Observe the leg broken, the wound to the chest of which Maytera our hostess speak. Yet he hunt by magic for a woman he require, and when by magic she is found, he leave food and friends and seek her out. Most women, even, would not do this."

Chenille said, "He's going to need a lot more help than one old man. I wish I'd made him take me along."

Across Xiphias's abandoned plate, Mattak said, "Two old men. His Cognizance has gone, too." Surprised, Siyuf stared at the empty chair next to her own.

Under his breath, Mattak added, "I'm glad."

Sergeant Sand spoke for them all. "He didn't come."

Kneeling by the headless, pawless body of Eland's second beast, Remora looked up. "I shall—ah—proceed. I have, um, led astray myself. Enthusiasm. Contagious, eh? But I, um, coadjutor, have not, eh? Seen a god. Possibly the victim will enlighten us."

As the holy knife laid open the beast from breastbone to pelvis, Spider said, "Sure, read it for us, it can't hurt."

It hurt the poor brute, Maytera Mint thought; but its death was swift, at least, and now the pain is over.

Sand had brought his slug gun to his shoulder before she saw Urus, halfway up the convoluted iron stair at the back of the manteion and taking its steps three at a time. She shouted, "Don't fire!" and Sand did not. A moment later the door at the top of the stair slammed shut. "He thought we were going to offer him," she explained to Eland. "Do you? We won't. I will not permit it."

Remora, who had been kneeling by the second victim, rose and strode to the ambion. "Extraordinary, eh? Extraordinary, my, er, sons. And daughter. Nothing, er, initially, and now this." Sand resumed his seat, his head bowed.

"An—ah—preface. Necessary, I think. The offering of persons was practiced in the past in—ah—here. Many of you aware of it. Have to be. Forbidden within, um, by the present holder of the baculus."

O you gods, Maytera Mint thought, he's going to say the entrails order us to sacrifice Eland. What am I to do?

"In practice, children, hey? Almost always. No sense sending a messenger who cannot see the, er, the recipient, eh? The offering of, um, persons, children, by no means usual even then, eh? In dire need. Only then."

Slate shifted his position until he stood behind Eland.

"Before my time. As an augur, eh? I would have—ah—delared . . ." Remora paused, his bony hands gripping the edges of the ambion, his eyes on the headless carcass.

"Never, eh? Couldn't do it. Not a child. Not even, um, Urus. Now—ah—two sides to the entrails. You follow me? One for the congregation and the city. Other the presenter and the augur. For the—ah—Our Holy City, war, death, and destruction. Bad. Calamitous! For the, um, myself, I shall. Offer a person, er, human being. Man. So Pas warns us. Me."

Maytera Mint said firmly, "Eland, can you see the gods?"

He looked at her in mild surprise. "I dunno, General. I never saw any."

There was no time for delicacy. "Have you had a woman? You must have!"

"Sure. Lots of times 'fore I got throwed in the pit."

She turned to Remora. "He is not suitable. I can see that, Your Eminence, and you must—"

Sand stood up. "I am." He jabbed his steel chest with a steel thumb; the noise it made was like the clank of a heavy chain.

"You can't mean it!"

"Yes, sir, I do." With oiled precision, Sand mounted the steps to the sanctuary. "He came. Great Pas came to the Grand Manteion."

Maytera Mint nodded reluctantly.

"He talked to the Prolocutor, and he told him to talk to us. To me. He said for us to get you out, 'cause it's part of the Plan. The Plan's the most important thing there is, sir."

"Certainly."

"You say that," he advanced on her, formidable as a talus, five hundredweight metal. " 'Cause they taught you to in some palaestra. I say it 'cause I know it in my pump. He said get you and sacrifice, and he'd come and tell us what to do next. Pas said that."

Meekly, she nodded again.

"So we caught the bios, and then I thought maybe it's not enough so I made them catch the two gods."

"Bufes, Sergeant."

"Whatever. Only the bufes aren't any good, and now you and him say the bios are no good either, sir." Sand wheeled to face Remora and pushed his slug gun into Remora's hands. "I knew, Patera. 'Fore you read it, I knew. You ever want to die?"

"I? Ah—no."

He's lying, Maytera Mint thought. I know what it is, and so does he.

"I do." Sand gestured toward Schist, Slate, and Shale. "So do they. Maybe they won't say it, but they do. I want to die for Pas, and I'm going to right now." He knelt, staring at the floor, and Remora looked helplessly down at the slug gun.

Maytera Mint murmured, "If you would prefer not to, Your Eminence, it would certainly be permissible for someone more familiar with the weapon to act for you."

"You, er, concur, General?"

She sighed. "Sometimes generals need sergeants to recall them to their duty. So it seems. Whether I learned it in a palaestra or not, Sergeant Sand is right. The Plan is the most important thing in the whorl, and the victim consents."

Still on his knees, Sand muttered, "Thanks, sir."

She knelt beside him. "I've heard it's possible for chems to—to reproduce. You've never done that?"

Slate said, "None of us have, General, and there's hardly any fem chems left." And Sand, "No. Never."

She turned back to Remora and held out her hands for the slug gun. "I've never fired one either, Your Eminence, but I know how they work and I've seen it done thousands of times since this began."

"No, Mayt—No, General."

"Please, Your Eminence. For your own sake."

He silenced her by raising Sand's slug gun and pointing it awkwardly at Sand. "Precisely. Ah—to the point. For my sake, General. If I must, um, officiate, the—ah—holy and um, self-sacrificing. Sole responsibility. Do you follow me? Criminal penalties, hey? Religious, likewise. Removed from the—ah—active clergy."

His wheezing breath seemed to fill the manteion. "But for him—ah—highest god. For Pas!" He jerked at the trigger.

"Not like that, Your Eminence. There's a safety, and if you hold it that way the recoil will cripple you. Or so I'm assured." She positioned the slug gun in his hands. "Grasp it firmly, tight against your shoulder. Then it will merely push you backwards. If you hold it loosely and try to keep it away, it will fly back and strike you like a club."

Sand said, "In the head, Patera. That's the best."

"I am augur here," Remora told him, and fired.

The crash of the shot was deafening in the enclosed space

of the manteion. Sand rose; for an instant Maytera Mint could not see where the slug had hit him. Spinning to face the Sacred Window, he threw up both arms. There was an uncanny sound that might have been a cry of pain or harsh laughter. Black liquid spurted from his throat, spattering the clean black habit she had just put on.

And the Holy Hues began before Sand fell.

She blinked and stared, then blinked again. Not one face but two crowded the Window, one gaping and gasping, the other radiant with power and majesty, just—and more than just—pitiless and nurturing. "My faithful people," intoned Twice-headed Pas, "receive the blessing of your god."

"I see him!" From the voice she thought it must be Spider, although she could not be sure.

Pas's was thunder and a destroying wind. "Carry this most noble of my soldiers to the Grand Manteion. I shall speak—"

Both his faces faded. Tawny yellows and iridescent blacks filled the Window on Mainframe. Serpents writhed across it as scorpions scuttled over their backs; behind them all, Spider and Maytera Mint, Eland and Remora, Slate, Shale, and Schist saw the agonized face of Echidna.

Pas returned as if Echidna had never been. "There our prophet Auk will restore him to us."

Chapter 11

LOVERS

As the floater rose, Hossaan said, "I've a dozen things to tell you, Caldé. I know there won't be time for all of them. It's only four streets."

"I know where it is," Silk snapped. "Hurry!" Xiphias laid a hand on his arm. "Easy, lad!"

Hossaan glanced at the small mirror above his head, and his eyes met Silk's. "So I'm going to tell the most important one first. You think there won't be anybody at the Grand Manteion when Hy gets there, and you're afraid she'll leave."

"Yes!"

"That's not right. I told you I had to talk to General Mint on your glass, and that was what made me late." Heeling like a close-hauled boat, the floater swerved around a gilded litter with eight bearers.

"I said we'd discuss it later."

"Right. Only because of what she said, I thought it might be smart to have a look at the Grand Manteion. There's three augurs in there and a couple thousand people."

"Did you see Hyacinth?"

Hossaan shook his head. "But I could've missed her pretty easily, Caldé. She's not as tall as the redhead, and there was a bunch of women with animals."

Orb muttered, "No cut."

"She's probably still outside, Caldé. If she was climbing the Palatine when Mucor said she was, she can't have gotten to the Grand Manteion yet."

Xiphias asked, "Why's everybody there, lad?"

"There's been another theophany—there must have been. Do you know about Pas appearing to His Cognizance?"

"No, lad! Never heard about it!"

"I have," Hossaan said. "There's a rumor, anyhow. Do you think that's brought them?"

Silk shook his head. "It was Molpsday, and would be stale news now." Half to himself he added, "What does it mean, when a dead god rises?"

No one answered him. The floater sped on.

A surging crowd filled Gold Street. "Stop!" Silk ordered Hossaan. "No! Higher if you can. I saw her. Turn around."

"Near us, Caldé?" They rose, blowers racing.

"Cut!" Oreb exclaimed. "Cut cat!"

"Two or three streets down the slope. Turn!"

The floater darted forward instead. "Your bird's right," Hossaan told Silk. "It would take too long to get through that mob, but we can duck down here—" He swerved onto a steep and narrow street bordered by high walls. "And cut across to Gold so we come up behind her. We'll be moving with them, and that will make it a lot faster."

Silk drew breath and exhaled. The aching weakness in his chest was fading, but it seemed to him that he had not filled his lungs properly for days. "You told Horn that your name was Willet, Willet. Also you found clothing—somewhere in the Caldé's Palace, I suppose—similar to the waiters', so that you could help them serve."

"I like to be useful, Caldé."

"I know you do, and it may be useful for you to tell me why you did those things before we locate Hyacinth—if we do.

You say you have a dozen items to relate. That should be the next."

Still steering their floater expertly, Hossaan glanced over his shoulder at Xiphias.

"If Master Xiphias and Maytera Marble can't be trusted, no one can. If I explain your actions—I believe I can, you see—will you tell me whether I'm correct?"

They spun around a corner as though it were an eddy. "I'm afraid not. General Mint says Siyuf's surrounded the Juzgado. That's why I thought I ought to check on the Grand Manteion."

"Where was she, and how did she learn of it?"

"I don't know, Caldé. She didn't say, and I didn't ask. She said one of Oosik's officers told her. Oosik had told him to try and get in touch with her."

Xiphias said, "He left when Willet here was handing out those appetizers, lad! Another waiter fetched him, remember?"

"Later than that—after I had asked Mucor to find out to which manteion Hyacinth was bringing her offering."

Their floater tacked on Gold, pushing through chattering pedestrians.

"You know what she looks like," Silk muttered. "She had on a black coat, and was carrying a large rabbit, I believe."

"Cat talk," Oreb informed him. "Talk bad."

"The bird's right, lad! The skinny girl said it talks!" Before Xiphias had finished speaking, their floater was slowing and stopping; the canopy slid into its back and sides.

For the space of a breath, Silk thought there had been a mistake. The hurrying young woman with something orange-furred tucked under her arm seemed too tall and too slender until she turned with their cowling nudging her leg, and he saw her face.

"Hyacinth!" He stood up by reflex, and for a moment he was half outside the floater (and she more than half in it) as they kissed.

When that kiss ended, they lay face-to-face on the soft leather seat, she crowded against its back and he practically falling off, with Xiphias standing over them and waving his saber to force passersby to keep their distance. They sat up, but their hands would not part. "I was afraid you were dead," Silk confessed.

And Hyacinth, "I shaggy near was, and I—but I . . ." Her eyes swam with tears. "Can't we put up the top?"

"I don't know how."

"I do." She freed her hand, and with a flurry of skirt and ruffled underskirt, and a flash of legs and spike-heeled scarlet shoes, was in Hossaan's seat. Xiphias ducked, and the canopy flowed up and darkened until it was nearly opaque.

She wiped her eyes. "Now I'm coming back. Catch me." She rolled over the back of the front seat so that Silk had to, and lying in his arms kissed him again. With no need of speech, her kiss said, *Beat me, shame and starve me. Do as you want with me, but don't leave me.* I'll never do those things, he thought, and tried to make his own kiss tell her so.

When they parted, he gasped, "Where do we start?"

She smiled. "That WAS the start. I love you. Let's start from there. I haven't felt this way since—since you jumped out my window."

He laughed, and she turned to Xiphias. "This time I know you from a rat. You teach sword fighting, and I want lessons. Do you always go around with him?"

"Much as I can, lass!"

Silk asked her, "Where have you been? I've had people searching everywhere."

"In a horrible old building in the Orilla, with a soldier as big as this floater watching me for Auk. You must know Auk, he says he knows you. Tartaros turned me loose." Hyacinth grinned like a twelve-year-old. "You believe in the gods, but you won't believe that. I don't, and I know it happened. Do you mind if I don't call you darling?"

Silk shook his head. "Not in the least."

"I've called too many men that. I'll find something else, something good enough, but it may take a while." She turned back to Xiphias. "There's jump seats that fold down out of the back of that one. You'd be more comfortable."

"Feel better outside, lass! Know how to get this plaguey door open?"

She laid her hand on his. "You stay in here or we'll get all naked and sweaty, and we ought to do that someplace nicer. Where's the driver?"

"Hunting!" Xiphias jerked down a seat, sat, and contrived to sheath his saber. "Hunting your cat with Silk's bird!"

"That's right, I dropped Tick, and he cost five cards."

Silk said, "When you got free—and I'll be grateful to Tartaros forever—you should have come to me."

Hyacinth shook her head.

"I understand. You didn't know where I was, either."

"No, you don't. I did. I knew exactly where you were. At the Juzgado or the Caldé's Palace. Everybody I asked wanted to talk about you, and everybody said one place or the other. But I looked, well, like every other slut in the Orilla, only worse, and I stank. I couldn't wash, or only a little. I tried, but when the water's dirtier than your face it doesn't help much. I wanted perfume and powder, and a comb to hold my hair, except I had to wash it first and dry it. I tried to go back to Blood's. Do you know about Blood?"

"About your trying to go back there? No."

"And clean clothes, clean underwear and a bunch of other things. You know what I'd look like without all this stuff?"

"Yes," Silk declared. "Like Kypris herself."

"Thanks. Like a boy, only with tits down to my waist. You saw me naked."

Silk felt his face flush. "They weren't. Not nearly."

"That's the trouble with big ones," Hyacinth explained to Xiphias. "The bigger they are the lower they go, unless you've got something to hold them up. Will that make it hard for me to sword-fight?"

"Will if they bounce, lass! But there's ways! Think I don't know 'em, long as I've been at it?"

"I put myself in your hands, Master Xiphias." She gave him a sly, sidelong smile, then brushed Silk's cheek with a kiss. "I was going to see about lessons that time I came to meet you, I mean before I found out it was so bad here, before we left

Blood's. When we got out of bed I said wouldn't I be a good sword-fighter, and you said you'd back a dell with shorter legs that wasn't so fond of her looks, or something like that. So I thought I'd learn and surprise you."

He nodded, speechless.

"I'm a good dancer, I really am, and I never had lessons, so I think with lessons I could learn. Only it's a long way to Blood's and Auk took my money, and I looked like a slut, so I turned around and went to Orchid's. She loaned me gelt and let me wash and, you know, fix up. But she says Blood's for ice. This was only about, oh, before I went to the market. Did you know? That Blood was dead? Since Phaesday, she says."

"Yes. I killed him." Hyacinth's eyes widened, and Silk felt pride, coupled with a deep shame in it. "I killed him with a sword Master Xiphias had loaned me, and destroyed the sword in the process. I'd rather not discuss the details. I understand why you wanted to return, or at least I believe—"

"All my things are out there! My clothes, my jewelry, everything I've got!"

"Also, you thought your driver would have gone back there, I'm certain. I also understand why you went to Orchid's; you anticipated help from her, and you received it. I went there myself for the same reason a few days ago, and I was helped as well—I found Chenille there. Which brings me to a point I ought to have raised sooner. What was the soldier's name? The one who watched you for Auk?"

"Hammerstone." Two tiny lines had appeared on Hyacinth's forehead. "It was Corporal Hammerstone, and he had stripes on his arm like a hoppy corporal, but painted on. All of a sudden you're worried, I can see it. What is it?"

"It would take an hour to explain it all." Silk shrugged. "I'll try to be brief. I love you very, very much."

"I love you, too!"

"Because I do, I have something to lose, someone—you—I must protect. Most men live their entire lives like this, I suppose, but I'm not accustomed to it."

"I'm sorry. I'll try to help. I really will."

"I know you will. You'll put yourself at risk, and that worries me more than anything else."

There was a tap on the canopy.

"You see, I've forgotten some of my obligations already. I promised Chenille I'd help her find Auk, and Auk took you from me. Do you know where he is, or where this Corporal is? Patera Incus is anxious to locate him, I know."

Xiphias interjected, "Don't you think that's that Willet outside knocking, lad?"

"Let him in, please."

"I don't know how to work this soggy door!"

"Then that will give us a little more time. You'll solve it soon, I'm sure."

Hyacinth giggled. "You've been around people like me too much. That's what Auk says about houses. And I know where he is, too, or anyway I know where he was, at a reedy old manteion on Sun Street. Was that yours? That's what somebody said when we were going over there."

"It was." Silk found that he was smiling. "It's old and run down, just as you say; but I used to love it, or thought I did. In a way I suppose I still do."

Scarcely visible on the other side of the darkened canopy, Hossaan tapped again. This time his taps were followed by a series of sharper ones.

"That's where Kypris came to your Window? Orchid told me. It was at Orpine's funeral, she said. I knew Orpine, and I wish I'd been there. I've got a shrine for Kypris . . ." Hyacinth paused, teeth nibbling her full lower lip. "Or I did. Is the house really wrecked? That's what Orchid said."

Silk recalled Blood's villa as he had seen it during his rescue. "It's badly damaged, certainly."

"If it was just damaged we've got to go there!"

He gestured toward the canopy. "Even with Willet outside knocking? Willet used to be one of Blood's drivers. You must know him—he drove you to the city so that you could meet me at Ermine's."

"That's wonderful! He can take us."

Xiphias exclaimed. "Think I've got it! Want me to let him in, lad?"

Silk nodded, and the door opened. Hossaan reached through it to unlatch the one in front, and Oreb shot past him to land upon Silk's shoulder, a-flutter with excitement and indignation. "Bad cat! Cut cat!"

Hossaan slid into the driver's seat as the orange-and-white animal he held spat, "Add word!"

"He led us quite a chase, Hy," Hossaan said, "but we got him in the alley trying to wriggle through a hole."

"You're bleeding!"

"He put up a fight. If somebody else will hold him, I'll get out the aid kit."

"Add, add word!" the little orange-and-white catachrest reiterated. "Pack! Itty laddie, peas dun lit am kilt may!"

"She won't, for an hour or two at least," Silk told him. "Willet, I want you to take us out to Blood's and help us collect Hyacinth's belongings." For a moment, Silk paused to gaze upon Hyacinth. "Then to the Prolocutor's Palace." As the floater slid forward, he added, "We may well need weapons, but we'd have to go back to the Caldé's Palace, and we can't afford that. I'd never get away."

Xiphias accepted the small catachrest from Hossaan. "I've my sword, lad!"

Silk nodded absently as the song of the blowers strengthened to a muted roar. "Let's hope it will suffice."

"We might have these drinks I wish in the bar, perhaps," Siyuf told Chenille, "but in my lodging would be more nice, do you not think also?"

"I had three with dinner." By intent, Chenille spoke too loudly. "If I'm going to start falling down and taking off my clothes, I'd a whole lot rather do it in private." She looked around Ermine's sellaria with interest. "Only we've got to get a room, don't you?"

"My staff has arrange this for me while I watch our parade with your friend the caldé." Siyuf stopped a liveried waiter.

"My lodging will be up the big stairs, I think? Number seventy-nine?"

He shook his head. "We don't have a room seventy-nine at Ermine's, General."

"Generalissimo. Wait, I will show you." While Chenille smiled and strove to appear innocent, Siyuf fished a key from her pocket.

"Ah!" The waiter nodded. "Number seven nine. That's a double room, we call it the Lyrichord Room, Generalissimo. On your right at the top of the Grand Straircase. You can't miss it."

"A room you say. More, I understood."

The waiter lowered his voice confidentially. "Our suites are four, five, or six rooms, depending. We call them rooms for convenience. Your room, the Lyrichord Room on account of the instrument in the music room, is a double suite with eleven rooms and three baths, besides balconies and so forth. Three bedrooms, sellaria, cenatiuncula for formal dining, breakfast cosy, drawing room—"

She waved him to silence. "You have here a wine waiter, one good and knowing?"

"The sommelier, Generalissimo. He's at the Caldé's Palace just now, I believe."

"I come from there. He too, I think. Send him to me when he arrive."

Siyuf turned away, motioning to Chenille. "Men are so stupid, do you think also? It is what renders them less than attractive, even the most fine. One thing, better I had say, one thing from many. Men are duty. So we are taught in my home. Girls are pleasure."

Chenille nodded meekly, blinking to show that she was assimilating this information. "In Trivigaunte, you mean? That's where your home is? I still can't get used to liking somebody from someplace so far away."

"This is natural. I have a house there bigger than this Ermine of your Viron's, the house which was my mother's. Also outside our city, a farmhouse made large for rest and educating my horses. For the hunt two houses also, one in a cave where is more cool. Do you perhaps hunt? I will show it to you. You will be very delighted I think, but there are places where you could not stand so straight, perhaps."

"I'd like to learn. Only I thought all of you were east of here. The caldé, I call him Patera, said something about tents out there. Anyway, it's really nice you've got this suite too, only I never would have guessed."

Arms linked, they started up the broad staircase. "I have my tent outside your city, and my headquarters, which I bring closer soon. Also this is convenient, as we see. I have good hunting there, so perhaps I will not have to take you home to teach. Already we kill three wing people and catch one also."

"Four Fliers?" In her astonishment Chenille forgot to sound admiring. "I didn't think anybody could."

Siyuf laughed. "Nine years in Trivigaunte another kill a wing person, but she does not catch the round thing on the back that push forward. I forget this word."

"I have no idea."

"By this we put wings on my pterotroopers. This time it is me that kill and I have catch the things that push also, but he does not yet tell me how it go."

Siyuf moistened her lips, and for the first time Chenille felt frightened. "Not yet he will not tell. But soon. He is like all men stupid, and not fine even but small and thin. We take his clothes and do other things until he is our friend. This is not confusing to you, I hope?"

"I think I get it."

"We take the clothes, and look, he is nothing. I have five husbands, all are more fine. Perhaps you would like him? When we have finish, I will give him to you."

"Oh, no! I don't want him, Siyuf."

"Good."

"I really don't like men at all, except Patera and one other one."

They had reached the top of Ermine's sweeping and richly carpeted Grand Staircase. Siyuf glanced to her right and down at her key. "My husbands I like sometimes, but so one like a hound. For me, tall girls and strong over all else. I enjoy, you see, at first a certain resistance."

Maytera Marble paused to stare at the strange procession crossing Manteion Street; although it was some distance away, Maytera Rose's legacy had improved her eyes out of reckoning. In the streetlights' glow, she saw a large and rough-looking man, accompanied by a smaller man so thin that he seemed a mere assemblage of sticks. After them, three soldiers, large and handsome like all soldiers, two of whom appeared to be carrying a fourth. Behind the soldiers, a tall augur and—and . . .

"Sib! Oh, sib! General, General Mint! It's me, sib!" In her joy Maytera Marble actually sprang into the air. The diminutive sibyl walking beside the tall augur looked around, and her mouth dropped open.

Maytera's eyes were not the only things Maytera Rose's legacy had improved; Maytera Marble dashed up Manteion Street as though winged, and Oreb himself could not have covered the distance more rapidly. Her good hand clutching her coif, she shot between the rough men, collided with the leading soldier with a clang and a fluster of elided apologies, and threw her arms about Maytera Mint.

"It's you, it's really you! We've been so worried! You don't know! You can't, and when Patera said you were all right I thought that's just when it happens, when everyone's saying the danger's over, that's when they get killed, and, and—oh, Hierax! Oh, Scylla! Oh, Thelxiepeia! I simply couldn't stand it. You were the light of my existence, sib. I know I never told you but you were, you were! If I'd had to live by myself in the cenoby with just Maytera Rose and that chem I couldn't have stood it. We'd have gone mad!"

Maytera Mint was laughing and hugging her and trying to lift her off the ground, which was so ridiculous that Maytera Marble exclaimed, "Stop, sib, before you hurt yourself!" But it really did not matter at all. Maytera Mint was right there, laughing, and was the same dear Maytera Mint but better because she was the Maytera Mint who had come back from

Tartaros knew where and there was no mother and daughter, no grandmother and granddaughter half so close as they, and no child or grandchild half so dear.

"I'm happy to be back, Maytera," Maytera Mint declared when she could stop laughing. "I hadn't really known how happy till now."

"Where have you been? Dear, dear sib, dear girl! Patera said they'd got you, they had you in some horrible place under the city, and then they didn't, you were with soldiers, but the generalissimo, not the fat one, the other one, said you were dead and—oh, sib! I missed you so much! I wanted you to meet Chenille. I still do, because Chenille's been a second granddaughter to me, but nobody, nobody in the whole whorl can ever mean as much to me as you!"

The tall augur said, "The—ah—all Viron. Feels as you do, eh, Maytera? Just look at them."

Already heads were turning and people pointing.

"You—ah—speak to them, General? Or, um, I myself—"

Maytera Mint waved both hands and blew the onlookers half a dozen kisses; then the silver trumpet sounded, the trumpet that Maytera Marble had heard in Sun Street on that never to be forgotten Hieraxday when the Queen of the Whorl had manifested during her final sacrifice, ringing from every wall and cobble like a call to battle: "I am General Mint! His Eminence and I have been down in the tunnels where the Ayuntamiento's hiding, and Pas himself has given us instructions. We're going to the Grand Manteion! All of you are going there, too, aren't you?" She pointed with a wide gesture that was like the unsheathing of a sword.

There were cheers, and several voices shouted, *"Yes!"*

"Lord Pas's prophet, Auk, will be there. We know, because Lord Pas told us. Please! Do any of you know him?"

A giant, taller even than Remora, waved. He held a ram under his left arm, and a tame baboon trotted after him as he pushed through the crowd; Maytera Marble thought that she had never seen so big a bio, a bio nearly as big as a soldier.

"I do." His voice was like the thudding of a bass drum. "I know you, too, General. Know you a dog's right, anyhow, but me an' Auk's a old knot." Legs like two pillars devoured the distance between them with swinging strides.

For a second time, Maytera Mint's small face went blank with surprise. "Gib! You're Gib! We charged the floaters on Cage Street together!"

"Pure quill, General." The giant dropped to one knee, eliciting an enraged bleat from the ram. "I'm Gib from the Cock, an' I was tryin' to stick by you, but that sham horse couldn't keep up. Too much weight's what Kingcup says. Then he took a slug an' down we went." He held up his free arm to show a cast, then touched the ridge above his eyes with the fingertips protruding from it. "So I can't salute like I'd like to, but Bongo here can. Salute the General lady, Bongo. Salute!"

The baboon rose on his hind legs, his forepaw seeming to shade his startlingly human eyes.

Maytera Mint demanded, "But you know Auk, Gib? I mean Pas's prophet named Auk?"

Maytera Marble sensed her uncertainty. "She knows a man called Auk who went to our palaestra; but I don't believe she's sure he's the one Pas—Pas told you about this Auk, sib?"

"Yes!" Maytera Mint nodded so hard her short brown hair danced. "Just now, a few minutes ago, down in a chapel under the Palace. He came to the Window there, Maytera, and all of us could see him, even Spider and Eland. It was wonderful!"

The soldier carrying the feet of the fourth soldier said, "He talked about our sergeant. We gave him to Pas."

The third soldier objected, "He gave himself, that's how it was. Now Pas wants him fixed. Not 'cause he don't want him but 'cause we need him. Pas don't want to scrap him."

The augur tossed back a lock of lank black hair. "It—ah—*gave*. Sense of the word, hey? I myself—"

Maytera Mint was not to be distracted. "Do you know Auk the Prophet, Gib? Yes or no!"

"Sure do, General."

"Describe him!"

"He's part owner in my place, he's maybe forgot but he is.

Pretty big cully." Gib waved his cast toward the larger of the rough-looking men. " 'Bout like him, only not so old. Got more hair than he needs an' ears that stick out of it anyhow."

"A strong, forthright jaw!" She was fairly dancing with anxiety and impatience.

"That's him, General. You could hang your washing on it." Gib chuckled, the laughter of a happy ogre hiding in his barrel chest. "I was wantin' to say he looks like Bongo here. Auk's my ol' knot an' wouldn't mind. Maybe you would of, though, an' maybe the god that's tapped him. Tartaros is what he says."

"This, er, hiatus, General . . ."

Maytera Mint nodded vigorously. "He's right, Gib. Stand up. You needn't address me as if I were a child, just because I'm not tall."

She trotted forward, drawing the giant behind her like a magnet. "Let's see . . . You don't know anybody here except me. Neither does poor Maytera, whom I ought to have introduced. Or have you been introduced to His Eminence, Maytera?

"Your Eminence, this is my senior and my dearest friend, Maytera Marble. Maytera, this is His Eminence the Coadjutor, Patera Remora."

Maytera Marble, hurrying after them, paused long enough to bow in approved fashion.

"An honor, eh? For me, Maytera. For me. Very much so. Um—privilege. We begin our acquaintance under the most— ah—propitious circumstances. You, um, concur?"

"Decidedly, Your Eminence!"

Maytera Mint never broke stride. "This is Gib, as you heard, a friend of Auk's and a comrade-in-arms of mine. The soldier with his slug gun pointed at our prisoners— Slate, you really don't need to do that. They're not going to run."

She glanced back at Maytera Marble. "Where was I? Oh, yes. That's Acting Corporal Slate. I've put him in charge of his fellow soldiers till Great Pas, as he promised, restores Sergeant Sand to us by Auk's agency."

Catching up to her, Maytera Marble ventured, "That must be poor Sergeant Sand they're carrying?"

"That's right, and Schist and Shale are carrying him. Our prisoners—they're friends now, friends of mine at least, and His Eminence's too, I'd say—are Spider and Eland." She had reached the milling crowd before the Grand Manteion and stood on tiptoe in the hope of catching a glimpse of Auk.

Xiphias had found a candle and lit it; Silk drew Hossaan away from its light and out into the darkness of the corridor. "Master Xiphias can help her look—hold the light, at least, which is all she needs. You and I have things to talk about."

"Good man!" Oreb assured Silk.

"I employed you—knowing you are an agent of the Rani's—because you Trivigauntis are our allies. You realize that, I'm sure."

"Certainly, Caldé."

"You owe nothing to Viron, and nothing to me. But if you want to remain, you'll have to be more forthcoming than you've been thus far."

"Only because the old man was listening, Caldé. I know you trust him, and you probably can. But I'm not you. I try not to trust anybody more than I've got to."

"I understand. Do they trust you? I mean the officials to whom you report."

There was a momentary silence; it was too dark for Silk to see Hossaan's face, but he sensed that it would have done little good. Then Hossaan said, "No more than they have to, Caldé. I don't mind, though. I'm used to it."

"I'm not. No doubt I must become used to it, too; but I'm finding that difficult. You're deceiving them. That was the reason you had Horn—and others, no doubt—call you Willet, the name you had used here. That was also why you helped serve dinner. You wanted to show someone at my table that you had penetrated my household—someone who would recognize you at once. Isn't that correct?"

Hossaan's only answer was an eerie silence. On Silk's shoulder, Oreb croaked and fluttered uneasily.

"That person will assume, of course, that I am not aware you're a Trivigaunti—"

"Let's not dodge words, Caldé. I'm a spy. I know it and you've known it since you spotted me on the boat."

"You will be applauded and rewarded."

Hossaan started to speak, but Silk cut him off. "I'm not finished. While you took us out here, I was thinking about your deception and your position as my driver. Please don't tell me that your lie is essentially the truth because I'm the only one who knows and you intend to inform your superiors that I do. It would only be a further lie."

"All right, I won't."

"Then I say this. You may tell your superiors everything you learn. I've assumed that you would from the start, and since I haven't the least intention of betraying the Rani, it can do Viron no harm. But you must afford me the same courtesy Doctor Crane did—you must tell me everything I want to know about what you're doing and reporting. In return, I'll keep your secret."

A second crept by, then two. "All right, Caldé. But I've always been willing to tell you whatever you needed to know."

"Thank you. Earlier I asked whether Generalissimo Siyuf or General Saba knew you by sight. You said neither did, and I believed you." For a moment, it seemed to Silk that something stealthy moved through the darkness. He paused to listen, but heard only the sudden flapping of wings as Oreb launched himself from his shoulder.

"I ask again—was it the truth? Does either know you?"

"It is, Caldé. I've never spoken with them, and I doubt that they know what I look like, either one of them."

"There was someone at my dinner who does. Who was it?"

"Colonel Abanja. Didn't you ask what she does on Siyuf's staff? She's intelligence officer."

"Do you report to her?"

"I will now, probably. You still don't see—"

Soft candlelight had appeared in Hyacinth's doorway. Oreb announced, "Cat come!" from Xiphias's shoulder.

Silk asked, "How are you faring, Master Xiphias?"

The old man shook his head. "Not a thing, lad! Want a bit of silver chain? Ring worth half a card?"

"No, thank you."

"Me neither! But we found 'em! Think she'd keep 'em? Threw 'em on the floor! Fact!"

Oreb confided, "Girl cry."

"You shouldn't have left her in the dark," Silk muttered.

"Chased me out, lad! Candle and all!"

Feeling the pressure of Hossaan's hand on his back, Silk said, "You're right, of course, Willet. I must go in to her. I don't know that I can help, but I must try."

Alone, he walked down the dark corridor and turned into the darker doorway of what had been Hyacinth's suite. Here there had been a dressing table inlaid with gold and ivory, wardrobes crammed with expensive gowns and coats, and a summonable glass. Only darkness remained, and the melancholy sweetness of spilled perfume. One door had led to Hyacinth's balneum, Silk reminded himself, another to her bedchamber. In vain, he tried to recall which was to the left and which to the right, although with her sobs to guide him he did not really need to know. By touch, he located the correct door and found that it was open.

After that, there was nothing for it but to walk in, with the ghost of the Patera Silk that he had been.

"Halt!" The voice was male, accompanied by the rattle of sling swivels and the click of the safety; Siyuf's intelligence officer raised her hands while trying to make out the sentry in the cloud-dimmed skylight. "I am Colonel Abanja, in the Rani's service."

Whispering. There were two or more sentries, clearly. "Advance and give the password."

Abanja moved forward slowly, hands still in the air. If these nervous men were from the Caldé's Guard, they were (or at least ought to be) disciplined troopers. If they were General Mint's volunteers, they might fire without warning.

"Halt in the name of the Rani!"

Abanja stopped again and identified herself a second time.

Somewhere behind her, a voice hissed, "They're shaggy shook up, lady. I wouldn't stand between 'em."

"Thank you," she murmured. "That's good advice, I'm sure."

A lanky trooper of the Companion Cavalry stepped from a shadow; Abanja was happy to see that the muzzle of her slug gun was lowered. "You must give to me our password also, Colonel."

"Boraz." Now she would see whether this trooper's lack of familiarity with the Common Tongue, with its implication of aristocracy, was real or feigned.

"You can pass, sir."

Feigned.

"*Halt!*" It was the caldé's men again. Abanja said, "I've already halted for you once."

"Do you have our password?"

Inwardly, she sighed. "I didn't know one was required. I have to speak with the officer in charge of our detachment."

"You can't go in the Juzgado without our password."

"Then you must give it to me."

Another whispered conference. "It's against regulations, Colonel."

Her eyes were adapting to the darkness; both male sentries were visible to her now, skylight gleaming on their waxed armor. "If it's against regulations to give it to me, you can't expect me to know it." She spoke to the cavalry trooper. "Go get her. You have my permission to leave your post."

Too softly for the men to overhear, the voice behind Abanja hissed, "There's a nice place, Trotter's. A street down 'n turn west. We can have a drink. Tell these hoppies to send her when she comes."

Abanja shook her head.

"Lady, you need me worse'n I need you."

Without looking around Abanja murmured, "Do I? I hadn't realized it."

"I could of got you in without a hitch. Shag, I still will. Tell 'em *Charter.* This's for free."

"Sentry!" Abanja called. "I remember your password now. Your caldé told me at dinner."

Both advanced with leveled slug guns. "Give it."

She smiled. "Unless someone's changed it without notifying your caldé, it's Charter."

"Pass, friend."

"Thank you again," Abanja murmured.

The hiss was scarcely audible. "Back room. Name's Urus."

"All g-gone." Slowly, Hyacinth's sobs had subsided into sniffles. "All the times. All that smiling. Cream and lotion. Beggar's root and rust, do this and do that. N-nothing left." The sobs returned. "Oh, K-k-kypris! Have pity!"

Silk muttered, "I think perhaps she already has."

"Bake here shop!" It was the catachrest. "Cuss-cuss."

He did, kissing Hyacinth's ear and the nape of her neck, and when she raised her face to his, her lips.

"Niece! Mow cuss!" The little catachrest attempted a smacking that emerged between the intended kiss and a squall.

The third cuss was not yet over. When it was, Hyacinth said, "Wipe your face. I got snot all over you."

"Tears." Silk took out his handkerchief.

"B-both. I was crying so hard my nose ran. Don't think I can't cry pretty when I w-want to."

"Itty laddie, done! Shop!"

"I've got certain things I think about, and here it comes. Know what I had when I left h-home?"

He shook his head, then said, "What was it?" realizing that she could not have seen the motion.

"Two gowns M-Mother made and her umbrella. She didn't have a-anything else to give me, so she gave me that. A big green umbrella. I kept it for years, and I don't know what happened to it. H-Here's what I've got now. The clothes I've got on and a gown Orchid promised to get cleaned, Tick here, and one card. But I owe her seven. That's w-way too much for what I got, but what could I say?"

Silk stood. "That you'll repay her later. You can say that again, too."

"Y-y-you know . . ." A stifled sob. "You're learning, you really are. Listen, I'm not through crying about all this yet. I'll cry m-m-more—cry some m-more . . ."

"Shop!"

"Tonight. Before I go to sleep. I just about always cry then, and when I'm asleep, too, s-sometimes. Well, by Thelx!"

"What is it?" Silk inquired.

"Go stand in the doorway. Shut it behind you. Don't ask, do it quick."

He did, and heard voices in the dark: "Tick? Tick, are you still in here?" "Puck Tuck ape no!" "All right, quit pulling my skirt." "Nod heavey." "Did I say why I got him? You can open the door again. I was going to give him to Kypris and ask her to give me you."

Once more, Silk was speechless.

"The market was closed, but some animal culls are always in there, and I gave the watchman a card to let me in and got Tick. The cull said talking animals are the best."

"So I've been told—by the same seller, I'm sure."

"I had a string around his neck, and I held it while I was looking for my things. Sometimes I held it in my teeth. When I got to crying I put my foot on it, but he got it off. Untied it or got it up where he could bite it, I guess."

"Nod rum."

"No, you didn't run, and I know you knew what I was going to do, 'cause you kept on begging me not to." To Silk, Hyacinth added, "Then everybody was going to that big man-teion uphill, so I did, too."

"I understand."

"But when he got loose he didn't beat hoof. Why not, Tick?"

"Say wharf laddie."

"I guess." Abandoning Tick, she addressed Silk. "What I'm trying to say is I know you're really religious. I'm not, but you could teach me."

He could not escape the thought that it would be better if

she taught him. "I'm far from being the best possible teacher, but I'll try if you wish it."

"You said we'd go to the Prolocutor's when we were done here. If it was for me, we don't have to."

He smiled. "You're not going to offer Tick?"

"I will if you want me to."

Tick protested, "New!"

"I see no point in it." Something large and soft pressed Silk's leg; he groped for it in the dark, but there was nothing there. "You want me to teach you. The gods—this is what I've found—aren't greatly influenced by our gifts. When they give us what we ask—" The soft pressure resumed, practically pushing him off his feet.

"What is it?"

"That's what I was wondering myself, but now I believe I know. Oreb tried to tell me out in the hall; and I should have guessed when he flew the first time I heard it. Mucor calls them lynxes. There's one in the room with us."

"Are they like bats?" Hyacinth sounded alarmed.

"They're cats."

"Have—something touched me. As big as a big dog."

"That's it; but there's no point in my describing them, when you could see this one for yourself." Silk raised his voice. "Master Xiphias, bring your candle, please."

"Are they the big cats the talus used to let out at night?" Hyacinth sounded more frightened than ever.

"Mucor controls them, to her benefit and ours." Silk tried to sound reassuring. "I'd imagine that this one would like us to bring it to the Caldé's Palace, where she is."

There was a muted yowl, far too deep and reverberant to have proceeded from Tick.

Abanja glanced around Trotter's, which seemed deserted except for an old man asleep at a table and a fat man washing earthenware mugs. "Barman?"

"Yeah, sister. You need a drink?"

She shook her head. "I'm addressed as Colonel. Since I want something, you may call me sister. When you want something from me, call me Colonel. You might get it if you do."

The fat man looked up. "Hey, I'll call you Colonel right now, sister."

"Though I don't think so. You have a patron named Urus."

"Couple, anyhow," the fat man said. "Three I can lay hand to, only one got the pits."

"Urus is in your back room, and he's expecting me. Show me where it is."

"Nobody's in my back room, sister."

"Then I'll wait there for him. That yellow bottle." She pointed. "I take it that's sauterne?"

The fat man shrugged. "S'posed to be."

"Bring it, and two clean glasses."

"I got some that's better, only it's twenty-seven bits. That up there's sixteen."

"Bring it. You keep accounts for patrons? Start one for me. My name is Abanja."

"You mean you'll pay later? Sister, I don't—put that thing away!"

"You men." Abanja smiled as she stepped behind the bar. "How are you to face lances if one small needler terrifies you? Get the good sauterne and the glasses. Are you going to send for the Caldé's Guard when you leave me? They won't arrest an officer of the Rani's, but I don't think my friend Urus will like it."

"I never do that, sister."

"Then it won't be necessary for me to have you arrested when they come. Nor will I have to shoot you. I admit I had thought about it." Abanja smiled more broadly, amused by the clinking of the glasses in the fat man's hand. "Lead the way. If you don't misbehave, you have no reason to be frightened."

With her needler in his back, he pushed aside the dirty green curtain that had concealed the entrance to a dark and narrow hall. She said, "You know, I think I understand this Trotter's of yours. Are you Trotter?"

He nodded.

"Your courts meet in the Juzgado, and this is where the accused drink before they go there. Or if they're discharged. It's empty because your courts are not in session."

"The back room's empty, too." Trotter had stopped before a door. He gulped. "You can wait if you want to, only I close—"

She shook her head.

"When you leave. After that, all right? If anybody called Urus comes in, I'll tell him you're here." Trotter opened the door and gaped at the filthy, bearded man at the table inside.

With exaggerated politeness, Urus rose and pulled out a chair for Abanja. As she sat, Trotter mumbled, "I forgot the caldé let 'em out. A lot can't hardly walk."

"I sprung myself," Urus told him. "Get me somethin' to eat. Put it on her tab."

Still smiling, Abanja nodded.

When the door had closed behind Trotter, Urus said, "Thanks for gettin' the bottle 'n standin' me a meal. You're the dimber damber, lady." His voice became confidential. "What I got to tell you is I'm all right too. You treat Urus brick 'n he'll treat you stone. Ain't you goin' to put your barker up?"

"No. Trotter didn't know you were in here."

"He'd of wanted me to drink, 'n I didn't have the gelt. Lily with you, see? Yeah, I been in the pits. I just got out. Yeah, I'm flat. Only you need me, lady, so you're goin' to give me ten cards—"

She laughed.

" 'Cause I'm goin' to tell you a lot. Then I'm goin' to find out a lot more, 'n you 'n me'll knot up again, see?"

"Open that and pour yourself as much as you want," she told him. "I feel sorry for you, so I'm giving you a drink, and food if the barman has any."

"You know who Spider is?"

"Should I?"

"Shag yes. You got spies here. Spider knows 'em all. He knows me, too, only he don't know I'm workin' for you."

"You aren't. Not yet. To whom does this Spider report, assuming that he exists?"

"Councillor Potto. He's Potto's right hand. You ever hear of Guan? How 'bout Hyrax? Sewellel? Paca?"

Abanja looked thoughtful. "Some of those names may be familiar to me."

"They're dead, all of 'em, 'n I know what happened to 'em. Spider was their jefe, 'n he ain't. I know where he is 'n what he's doin'. I could bring you. I don't scavy you'd want me to, only I could. You twig they nabbed General Mint?"

"She's free now." Abanja holstered her needler. "That's what I've been told."

"You don't cap to it."

"I believe what I see."

Urus grinned. "Pure keg, lady. All right, it's the lily, she's loose. I could show her to you 'n throw in Spider, 'cause they're together. Only I'm like you, see? 'N what I want to see's gelt."

Abanja took a card from her card case and pushed it toward Urus, across the stained and splintered old table.

With a furtive glance into the next room, Chenille tapped the surface of the glass with her forefinger. A floating gray face appeared. "Yes, madame."

"Keep your voice down, all right?" Chenille herself was whispering. "There's somebody asleep in the big bed."

"Generalissimo Siyuf, madame. She is well within my field of view."

"That's right, and you wouldn't want to wake her up, would you? So keep it down."

"I shall, madame. I suggest, however, that you close the door. It would provide additional security, madame."

Chenille shook her head, her raspberry curls bobbing. "I got to know if she's waking up. Pay attention. You know the Caldé's Palace?"

"Certainly, madame."

"I've asked three or four times on the glass there, see? He let me, the caldé did, I'm a friend of his. What I want to know is are you the same one? The monitor I talked to there?"

"No, madame. Each glass has its own, madame, though I can utilize others, and consult their monitors if need be."

"That's good, 'cause he couldn't find Auk for me, ever, and I saw this glass of yours when me and Generalissimo Siyuf came in, and I've been wanting to try it ever since, only not where she could hear 'cause I'm looking for Auk. I know there's a lot of Auks. You don't have to tell me that. The one I want's the one that lives in the Orilla, the one they call Auk the Prophet now. Real big, not too bad looking, broken nose—"

"Yes, madame. I have located him. It was a matter of no difficulty, the word *prophet* being a sufficient clue. Do you wish to speak with him?"

"I—wait. If I speak to him, he can see me, right?"

Like a floating bottle disturbed by a ripple, the gray face bobbed in nothingness. "You might postpone your conversation until you are dressed, madame. If you prefer."

"That's all right. Just tell me where he is."

"In the Grand Manteion, madame. It is two streets north and one west, or so I am informed."

"Yeah, I know. Listen, he's there now? Auk's there right now, in the Grand Manteion?"

"Correct, madame."

"Is he all right? He's not dead or anything?"

"He appears somewhat fatigued, madame. Otherwise I judge him in excellent health. You do not care to converse?"

"I think it would be better if he didn't know about me and the generalissimo. Better if I don't shove it at him, anyhow, and even if I close the door he's bound to want to know what I'm doing here."

The gray face nodded sagely. "Prudent, madame."

"Yeah, I think so. Wait up, I got to think."

"Gladly, madame." For nearly a minute, there was no sound in the Lyrichord Room save Siyuf's hoarse respiration.

At last Chenille announced, "This is going to be one tough job for you, Monitor."

"We thrive upon adversity, madame."

"Good, I've got some for you. I want to get word to a lady

named Orchid. Get her, or get anybody that might be able to get a message to her. What time is it?"

"Two twenty-one, madame. It is Phaesday morning, madame. Shadeup is less than four hours distant."

"That's what I was afraid of. If you can't do it, just tell me. I won't blame you a bit."

"I shall make the utmost effort, madame, but *Orchid* is also a widely employed appellation. Additional information may be of assistance."

"Sure. This Orchid's got a yellow house. It's on Lamp Street. Music runs right in back, and there's a pastry shop across the street. Across Lamp Street, I mean. She's a big fat woman, I guess forty or forty-five."

"That is sufficient, madame, I have identified her. There is a glass in her private apartments, and she is preparing for bed in the room beyond. Shall I summon her to her glass?"

"I know that glass and it doesn't work."

"To the contrary, madame, it is fully operational, though it was out of service for . . . eighteen years. Would you care to speak with Orchid?"

Chenille nodded, and in half a minute saw Orchid standing in front of her own glass in lacy black pantaloons and a hastily assumed peignoir. "Chen! How'd you get this thing turned on?"

"Never mind, it just is. Orchid, I need a favor, only there'll be something for you. Maybe a card. Maybe more."

Orchid, who had been eyeing the rich furnishings of the Lyrichord Room, nodded. "I got my ears up."

"All right, you see the mort in doss in the next room? She's the Trivigaunti's generalissimo. Her name's Siyuf."

"You always were lucky, Chen."

"Maybe. The thing is, I got to beat the hoof. Is Violet riding pretty light?"

Orchid shrugged, plump shoulders rising and falling like pans of dough. "Pretty much. You know how it is, Chen. Where are you?"

"Ermine's. This's Room Seven and Nine, get it? It's a double room, so seven and nine too. Right at the top of the big

stairs. Siyuf likes tall dells, she would've given me five easy.
Five's nothing to her. Violet ought to get more if she soaps
her. Tell her to come uphill and play spoons, tell Siyuf she's
my pal and I told her what a nice time I'd had, so she thought
she'd drop by and party. I'll leave the door unlocked when I
go out." Chenille's voice hardened. "Only I get half. Don't
think you're going to wash me down."

"Sure thing, Chen."

"The way I'm set with the caldé—" groping the carpet at
her feet, Chenille found her bandeau, "I ought to be able to
throw something your way pretty often. Only don't try to
wash me, Orchid. The word from me could shut you down."

Under her breath, Hyacinth asked, "Do you really want to go
through with this?"

It seemed too foolish to require a reply, but Silk nodded.
"Your Cognizance, you and His Eminence, with Patera Jerboa and Patera Shell, are more than sufficient, surely."

From Echidna's dark chapel behind the ambulatory,
Maytera Marble called, "Just one moment more, please, Patera. Patera Incus is working as quickly as he can, and—
and . . ."

Like a rumble of thunder, Hammerstone's deeper voice
added, "She wants to be there, and there's another reason.
Hold on, Caldé. Patera's about finished."

Hyacinth whispered, "We really don't have to. We could
just go somewhere and do it all night. It doesn't matter to me,
honest." Tick added, "Goo no!" from her arms.

"I've revoked your vow of chastity," Quetzal said; it was
impossible to say whether he had overheard her. "You're still
an augur. Is that clear?"

"Perfectly, Your Cognizance."

Remora smiled in a way he meant to be reassuring. "Can't,
eh? Not even Quetzal. Indelible, hey?"

The Prolocutor himself nodded. "I could enjoin you from
augural duties, but you'd still be an augur, Patera Caldé."

"I understand, Your Cognizance."

"I'm not doing it. You're relieved of the requirements. You

need not say the office and sacrifice, but you can if you want to. You can and should wear the robe. Our citizens have chosen an augur, believing the gods chose for them. We must keep it so. We must sustain their faith. If necessary, we must justify it."

He glanced at Maytera Mint, who said, "Your Cognizance is wondering whether I retain mine after Pas failed to appear. I don't know, and it may be weeks before I do. Years, even. I wish Bison were here."

Spider nodded. "Me, too."

Spokesman for his master, Oreb croaked, "Do now!"

Hoping his bird had been understood, Silk said, "You told me what took place, General, but I'm afraid I wasn't listening as closely as I should have been. I couldn't think beyond my need to obtain His Cognizance's permission and persuade Hyacinth to accept me. Did Pas actually say that he would grant you a second theophany when you got here?"

"I . . ." Maytera Mint sighed, her face in her hands. "To tell you the truth, I don't remember. I thought so."

Slate put in, "No, he didn't, sir. He said you take the sarge to the Grand Manteion, 'cause my prophet Auk's there and I mean to tell him how to fix him up. He didn't say nothing about right away."

Remora nodded.

Auk said, "He told me he'd teach me, and he will. Only he ain't yet." Auk cleared his throat. "This was as queer for me as for Maytera. Worse, when I had to watch what it did to her. Pas had us fetch Patera Jerboa there—that's Hammerstone and me, and Patera Incus. All right we did, only nothing's happened yet. I had all my people up here and they're not here any more, so I guess you know what they think about me after this."

Oreb sympathized. "Poor man!"

"Only that don't matter." Defiantly, Auk looked around at the rest of the impromptu wedding party. "They still think more of me than what I do myself. It's what they think about the Plan, and that's what's hardest, harder even than Maytera.

But I'm sticking. If everybody goes, that's all right, only not me. I'm here, like Pas said, and I'm sticking."

From deep within the vast nave, far from the light of the dying altar fire, a voice rumbled, "This's my fault, Caldé." A man taller even than Auk rose, and as he did a misshapen figure sprang to the top of the pew before him.

From his position behind and to the right of Quetzal and Remora, old Patera Jerboa quavered, "My son . . ."

"Probably you don't remember me, Caldé, only I gave you one on the house once, 'cause you said Pas for Kalan. I'm Gib from the Cock."

Silk nodded and smiled. "Of course I remember you, Gib; though I admit I didn't expect to meet you here, and I thought we'd met everyone. Have you been praying?"

"Tryin', anyhow." Gib strode down a side aisle, his tame baboon leaping from one pew to the next.

Auk said, "Muzzle it, Gib. You didn't do anything."

Silk nodded again. "If by 'fault' you mean this delay, the fault certainly isn't yours, Gib. If anyone is at fault, I am the person. I should have acted much more expeditiously to have Maytera's hand repaired."

Tick said, "Ale rat, nod rung." And Hyacinth, "You always blame yourself. Do you really think you're the only one in the whorl that makes mistakes?"

"I tagged along after Auk when he went to your place over on Sun," Gib explained. "Me an' him's a old knot. I'd got Bongo here when I broke my flipper, see, Caldé? I can't pluck proper. He'll do for anybody I say. I figured to sell him when it was fixed."

"I believe I'm beginning to understand," Silk said.

"Then Auk says to fetch animals, so I fetched him. Bongo here, that is. Then comin' up here I thought maybe—"

Jerboa's trembling hand motioned him to silence. "It was I, Caldé. I—" his thin old voice trembled and broke, "have an aversion to offering them. Just an old fool."

"It isn't, Patera," said a sibyl who seemed at least as old. "Caldé, they remind him of children. I don't feel that way, but I know how he feels. We've talked about it."

Patera Shell stepped forward. "Someone brought one once for Thelxiepeia, Caldé, a little black monkey with a white head. Patera had me offer it."

Silk cleared his throat. "In your youth—I understand, Patera Jerboa. Or at least I believe I do. Let us say that I understand as much as I need to. You dissuaded Gib."

"While we were walking—" Jerboa coughed. "It's a long, long way. He helped me along. He's a kind man, Caldé. A good man, though he doesn't look it. I asked him to refrain for my sake. He said he would, and left us to buy a ram. I offered it for him tonight."

Gib said, "Only I think that's why Pas won't come. They kill stuff at weddin's, don't they? So you—"

"*Auk!*" Silk recognized Chenille's voice before he saw her. "Auk, is this a wedding?" Holding up her skirt, she sprinted down an aisle. "Hello, Patera! Hi, Hy! Congrats! Are you going to marry them, Your Cognizance?"

Quetzal did not reply, smiling at Hammerstone and Maytera Marble as they emerged from Echidna's chapel. She knelt before him. "I begged your predecessor, Your Cognizance . . ."

Quetzal's hairless head bobbed upon his long, wrinkled neck. "My predecessor no longer holds the baculus, Maytera."

"I begged him to. I implored him, but he wouldn't. I should tell you that."

Maytera Mint looked down at her in amazement.

"Your Eminence, you said a moment ago, I overheard you, that not even His Cognizance can unmake an augur. It's true, I know. But—but . . ."

"Their vow, eh?" Remora spoke to Silk. "Not indelible, hey? Not as—ah—serious."

Quetzal inquired, "Do you want me to free you from your vow, Maytera? Yes or no will suffice."

"Yes, but I really ought—"

"To explain. You're right. For your own peace of mind, you must. You've good sense, Maytera, I've seen that. Doesn't your good sense tell you I'm not the one to whom you owe

your explanation? Stand, please. Tell your sib Maytera Mint.
Also Maytera Wood and her sibs. Be brief."

As Maytera Marble got to her feet, Hammerstone said,
"We knew each other a long time ago. You remember, Caldé?
I told you before you gave me the slip. Her name was Moly
then."

Maytera Marble spoke to Maytera Mint and the other sibyls
in a voice so soft that Silk could scarcely hear her. "I was the
maid, the sibyls' maid, when the first bios moved into the city.
I got our cenoby ready for them, and in those days I used to
look like—like Dahlia, I nearly said, sib, but you never knew
Dahlia. Like Teasel, a little." She laughed nervously. "Can you
imagine me looking like Teasel? But I did, then."

Still staring, Maytera Mint managed to nod.

"There were six then. Six sibyls on Sun Street. I didn't have
a room, you see. I don't really need one. But there were never
more than six, and as time went on, fewer. Five and then four,
then three. And then—and then only two, as it was with us,
dear, dear sib, after I died."

The youngest sibyl from Brick Street started to object,
glanced around at the others, and thought better of it.

Maytera Marble displayed a string of yellowed prayer
beads. "Just Maytera Betel and I. These were hers. They're
ivory." She lifted her head, a smile and a plea. "The chain is
silver. She was a fine, fine woman."

"Girl cry," Oreb informed Silk, although no tears streaked
Maytera Marble's smooth metal face.

"We couldn't do it all. There was just the two of us and
young Patera Pike. And ever so many children, and so
Maytera called—called upon . . ."

Hammerstone explained, "She drafted Moly."

"Upon me. I knew arithmetic. You've got to, to keep any
sort of house. How much to buy for so many, and how much
you can spend, that sort of thing. I kept a—a diary, I suppose
you call it, to practice my hand, which was really quite good.
So I could teach the youngest their sums and letters, and I did.
Some parents complained, and . . . There wasn't any reason
not to. I put my hand on the Writings and promised, and

Maytera and Maytera Rose witnessed it and kissed me, and—and then I got new clothes."

She looked at Hammerstone, begging his understanding. "A new name, too. I couldn't be Moly any more once I was a sibyl, or even Maytera Molybdenum. We all take new names, and you were gone. I hadn't seen you in years and years."

"He *slept*," Incus told her. "He was so *ordered.*"

"Yeah, I did," Hammerstone confirmed. "For me a order's a order. Always has been. Only now Patera says it's all right. If he'd of said no—" Slate slapped him on the backplate, the clang of his hand startlingly loud in the religious hush of the Grand Manteion.

Xiphias nudged Silk. "Double wedding, lad!"

"Your Cognizance must think this terribly strange," Maytera Marble ventured.

"Perfectly natural," Quetzal assured her.

"We—we're not like bios about this. It matters terribly to you how old somebody is. I know, I've seen it."

"Her and me are really about the same age," Hammerstone confided. "Only I slept so much."

"What matters to us is—is whether we can." Maytera Marble raised her right hand to show Quetzal the weld that had reattached it, and moved her fingers. "My hand's well again, and I've got a lot of replacement parts, and I can. So we're going to. Or at least we want to, if—if Your Cognizance—"

"You are released," Quetzal told her. "You are a laywoman again, Molybdenum."

"Like a story, right, lass?" Xiphias edged toward Hyacinth and spoke in a tone he intended as confidential. "Must be the end! Everybody getting married! Need another ring!"

Chapter 12

I'M AUK

It was, Silk thought, no time to be wakeful.

Or more persuasively, no time to sleep. Careful not to awaken Hyacinth, he rolled onto his back and put his hands behind his head. How many times had he daydreamed of a night like this, and thrust the dream away, telling himself that its reality could never be his? Now . . .

No, it was no time to sleep. As quietly as he could, he slipped from their bed to bathe and relieve himself. Hyacinth, who wept before sleep, had wept that night; he had wept too—had wept in joy and pain, and in joy at his pain. When tears were done and their heads rested on one pillow, she had said that no man had ever wept with her before.

Two floors below them, their reflected images knelt in the fishpond at Thelxiepeia's feet, subsistent but invisible. There she would weep for him longer than they lived. He lowered his naked body into a rising pool, warm and scarcely less romantic.

Ermine's, Silk discovered when he rose from it, provided everything. Not merely soap, water, towels, and an array of perfumes and scented powders, but thick, woolly robes: one pale and possibly cream or pale yellow, and a longer, darker one that might have been blue had he dared clap and rouse the dim sparks that circled one another on the ceiling.

After drying himself, he put on the longer robe and tied its belt, returned to their bedroom, and covered Hyacinth's perfect, naked body with infinite gentleness. Then, standing outside upon air, watched himself do it, a darker shadow with tousled hair pulling up sheet and blanket to veil his sleeping wife's long, softly rounded legs and swelling hips—Horn and Nettle huddled in a musty bed in a small, chill room in the Caldé's Palace.

—Patera Pike cutting the throat of a speckled rabbit he himself had bought.

—a ragged child weeping on a mattress of straw.

—a blind god metamorphosised from a blind man who remained a blind man still, and was struck.

—a man scarcely larger than the child lying naked on the ground, his stark ribs and emaciated face black with bruises, his arms chained around a tent pole.

—a madman among tombs, howling that the sun would die.

—Violet embraced by Siyuf in the room below.

—Auk asleep on his back before the smoking, unpurified altar of the Grand Manteion.

"Auk? Auk?"

He sat up blinking, and rubbed his eyes. Chenille slept at his side, her head pillowed on muscular arms, her skirt hiked to her knees. Sergeant Sand slept in death at the foot of the Sacred Window; about him lay Pateras Jerboa, Incus, and Shell, Incus face up and snoring.

On the farther side of the lofty marble ambion, Spider and Eland slept as well, watched by three soldiers; Slate nodded in friendly fashion and touched his forehead. In the third row of pews, Maytera Mint knelt in prayer.

"Somebody call me?" Auk asked Slate softly.

Slate's big steel head swung from side to side. "I'd of heard. Must of been a dream."

"I guess." Auk lay down again; he was as tired as he could ever remember being, and it was good not to have been called.

Sciathan soared above a leafless plain at sunset. Far ahead, Aer flew a little higher and a little faster. He called to her aloud, knowing somehow that her helmcom was out or had been turned off. She looked back, and he glimpsed her smile, the roses in her cheeks, and a tendril of flaxen hair that had escaped her helmet. *Aer!* he called. *Aer, come back!* But she did not look back at him again, and his PM was overheating. Moment by moment, over a long hour of flight, he watched her dwindle into the dark sky ahead.

"Auk? Auk!"

He sat up stiffly, conscious that he had slept for hours. The great arched windows of the Grand Manteion, which had been featureless sheets of black by night, showed vague tracings now—gods, animals, and past Prolocutors half visible.

He stood, and Maytera Mint looked up from her vigil at the scrape of his boots on the floor. Leaving the sanctuary, he knelt beside her. "Did you call me? I thought I heard you."

"No, Auk."

He considered that, rubbing his chin. "You been awake all this time, Mother?"

"Yes, Auk." (A tiny spark of happiness appeared in her red-rimmed eyes; it warmed him like a blaze.) "You see, Auk, I swore I would wait here in prayer until Pas came, or shadeup. I'm keeping that vow."

"You've kept it already, Mother. Look at those windows." He gestured. "I was so tired I lay down with my boots on, see? I bet you were just as tired, but you haven't slept a wink. You know what I'm going to do?"

"No, Auk, how could I?"

"I'm going to lay down again and sleep some more. Only first I'm going to take off my boots. Now you lay down and sleep too, or I'm going to make a fuss and wake up everybody. The job's done. You did it just like you promised."

Hyacinth woke and went to the open window to examine her ring in the faint gray light of morning—a tarnished silver ring like a rose with a woman's tiny face at its heart, framed by petals. She had bought it because a clerk at Sard's had said it resembled her, never guessing that she was buying her own wedding ring. She had worn it once or twice, tossed it into a drawer, and forgotten it.

It didn't really look like her at all, she decided. The woman in the rose was older, at once more come-on and more . . . She groped for a word. Not just pretty.

Though Silk thought her beautiful, or said he did.

She kissed him as he slept, went into the dressing room, and tapped the glass.

"Yes, madame."

"Show me exactly the way I look right now. Oh, gods!"

Her own face, puffy-eyed and retaining traces of smeared cosmetics, said, "You are actually quite attractive, madame. If I might suggest—"

She waved the suggestion away. "Now look at this face in my ring. See it? Make me look just a tiny little like that."

For a few seconds she studied the result, turning her head left, then right. "Yes, that's good. Hold that." She picked up the hairbrush and began a process that Tick the catachrest watched approvingly.

"Auk! Auk!"

He sat up and stared at the Sacred Window. The voice had come from there—this time he was certain of it. He got up, grasping his hanger to keep the brass tip of the scabbard from rattling on the floor, and padded across the sanctuary. Shell and Incus were clearly sound asleep, but Jerboa's eyes were not quite closed. Old people didn't need much sleep, Auk reminded himself.

He squatted beside Jerboa. "It's all right, I wasn't going to nip your case or anything, Patera. Is that what you thought? Anything you got you can keep."

Jerboa did not reply.

"Only somebody over here's been calling me. Was that you? Like when you were dreaming, maybe?"

Shell grunted something unintelligible and turned his head away, but Jerboa did not stir. Suddenly suspicious, Auk picked up Jerboa's left hand, then slid his own under Jerboa's tunic.

He rose, wiping his hands absently on his thighs; it would be well, certainly, to move the old man's body to some private spot. The sibyls were sleeping in the sacristy; that, at least, was where Maytera Mint had gone when he had persuaded her to lie down for an hour or two, and Auk thought he recalled old Maytera Wood and the others—sibyls whose names he had not learned—going in there at about the time he had stretched himself on the terrazzo floor.

Squatting again, he picked up the old augur's body and carried it to the ambulatory. Schist straightened up as they came into view. "He dead?"

"Yeah," Auk whispered. "How'd you know?"

Schist's steel shoulders rose and fell with a soft clank. "He looks dead, that's all."

Shale asked, "How's Pas supposed to get his part back if he's dead?"

Without answering, Auk carried the body into the chapel of Hierax and laid it on the altar there.

Slate inquired, "You goin' back to sleep?"

"Shag, I don't know." Auk discovered that he was wiping his hands again and made himself stop. "I think maybe I'll fetch my boots and walk around outside a little."

"I thought maybe you could wake the rest of 'em up." Slate waited longer for his reply than a bio would have, then asked, "What you lookin' at over there? Must be shaggy interesting."

"Him."

Slowly, Slate clambered to his feet. "Who?"

"Him." Auk turned away impatiently, striding toward the Sacred Window. "This soldier. He got it in the autofunction coprocessor, see?" Auk knelt beside Sergeant Sand. "Only his central could handle that stuff if it had to. There's lots of redundancy there. His voluntary coprocessor could, even."

He fumbled for his boot knife, discovered that he was not wearing his boots, and got it. "Look alive, Patera!" He shook Incus's shoulder. "I need that gadget you got."

"Up!" A boot prodded the captive Flier's ribs. "Reveille an hour ago. Didn't you hear it?"

Blinking and shivering, Sciathan sat up.

"You speak the Common Tongue well," the uniformed woman looming over him said. "Answer me!"

"Better than most of us, yes." Sciathan paused, struggling to clear his brain of sleep. "I did not hear it, that word you used. I know I did not since I heard nothing. But if I heard it, I would not know what it was."

The woman nodded. "I did that to establish a point. Any question I ask, you are to answer. If you do, and I like your answer, you may get clothes or something to eat. If you don't, or I don't, you'll wish you'd been killed, too." She clapped. "Sentry!"

A younger and even taller woman ducked through the door of the tent and stood stiffly erect, her gun held vertically before her left shoulder. "Sir!"

The first woman gestured. "Get him off that pole and lock the chain again. I'm taking him to the city." As the younger woman slung her gun to fumble for the key, the older asked, "Do you know my name? What is it?"

He shook his head; a smile might have helped, but he could not summon one. "My name is Sciathan. I am a Flier."

"Who questioned you yesterday, Sciathan?"

"First Sirka." His hands were free. He held them out so that the younger woman could refasten his manacles.

"After that."

"Generalissimo."

"Generalissimo Siyuf," the older woman corrected him. "I was there. Do you remember me?"

He nodded. "You did not speak to me. Sometimes to her."

"Why did your people attack Major Sirka's troopers?"

Here it was again. "We did not."

She struck his ear with her fist. "You tried to take their weapons. One escaped, three were killed, and you were captured. Why did you break your wings."

"It is what we do."

"How did you disable your propulsion module?"

He shrugged, and she struck him on the mouth. He said, "We cannot do it. Mechanisms have been proposed, but would increase weight."

She smiled, surprising him. "Aren't you going to lick that? My rings tore your lip."

He shrugged again. "If you want me to."

"Get him a rag he can tie around his waist," she ordered the taller, younger woman. Turning back to him, she said, "I'm Colonel Abanja. Why did you attack Sirka's troopers?"

"Because they were shooting at us." He could not actually remember that, but it seemed plausible. "I made a face. I do not know why."

"Did you now?" For a fraction of a second Abanja's eyes widened. "What kind of face?"

He was able to smile when he reflected that this was vastly preferable to talking about the propulsion modules. "With lips back."

"You don't know why you did that. Perhaps I do. Are you saying we shot your people because you grimaced? You yourself weren't shot at all."

"Aer saw it and screamed. They shot her then. We tried to take their guns so they could not shoot."

Abanja stepped closer, peering down at him. "She screamed because you made a face? Most people wouldn't believe that, but I might, and perhaps Generalissimo Siyuf might. Let's see you make a face like that for me."

"I will try," he said, and did.

The click of booted heels announced the younger woman's return. When Abanja turned toward her, she held up a scrap of cotton sheeting that had been used to clean something greasy. "Will this do, sir?"

Abanja shook her head. "Get the coveralls he was wearing.

Bring a winter undershirt and a blanket, and tell the cooks to give you something he can eat on horseback."

She returned to Sciathan. "Stop grinning, it's making your lip bleed. You came here looking for a Vironese, a man. That's what Sirka told us. You gave his name, and it was one I think I heard last night. Say it again for me."

"Auk," Sciathan said. "His name is Auk."

Sergeant Sand's arm stirred, then struck the floor of the Grand Manteion hard enough to crack it. Chenille shouted a warning. "Don't worry," Auk told her, "just a little static, like. I got it fixed already."

Behind him, a voice he did not recognize said, "I only wish Patera Shell could watch. He'll be *so* disheartened when we tell him what he missed."

"So will His Eminence," Maytera Mint murmured. "But it's his fault for going back to the Palace, if that can be called a fault. We're certainly not going to wait to carry out Pas's instructions, nor would His Eminence want us to. You didn't see Pas, Auk? Are you certain?"

"No, Maytera, I ain't." Auk squinted, still bent over his work. " 'Cause he must've showed me this stuff some way, after I talked to you, probably." Inspiration struck. "Want to know what I think, Maytera?"

"Yes! Very much!"

"I think it was you keeping your promise the way you did that swung it. I think he was asking himself if we were worth all the trouble he was taking, till then. Wait a minute, I got to tie in his voluntary."

Auk made the last connection and leaned back, easing aching muscles. "Think you could fetch one of those holy lamps over here, Patera? I'm going to need more light."

Incus scurried away.

"Patera Shell is hoping to engage a deadcoach to return Patera's body to our manteion." The owner of the unknown voice proved to be a young and pretty sibyl. "Maytera said nothing would be open, but he said they *would* be by the time he got there, or if they weren't he'd wait. It was a great temptation, Maytera admitted this to me, to ask His Cognizance to permit Patera's final sacrifice to take place right here in the Grand Manteion, since he ascended to Mainframe from here. But the faithful of our quarter would *never*—"

Incus, returning, knelt beside Auk. "Is this *sufficient?* I can pull up the *wick,* should *more light* be needed." He held up a flame-topped globe of cut crystal.

"That's dimber," Auk told him. "I can see the place and the register, and that's all I got to see." Delicately, he eased the point of his knife into Sand's cranium. "Muzzle it, everybody. I got to think." He counted under his breath.

And Sand spoke, making Maytera Mint start. "V-fifty-eight, zero. V-fifty-eight, one. V-fifty-nine, zero. V-fifty-nine, one."

"Those are *voluntary* coprocessor inputs," Incus explained in an awed whisper. "He's *enabling* them."

When Auk showed no sign of having heard, the young sibyl from Brick Street whispered, "I simply can't believe that your Maytera—she was, I mean. That Molybdenum and that soldier are going to do all this, and where are they going to buy these coprocessor things?"

"They must *make* them, Maytera," Incus explained, "and *I* shall assist them." Maytera Mint shushed him.

Auk returned his knife to his boot. "Don't froth, Maytera. He's all right. He just don't know it yet."

As if on cue, Sand raised his head and stared around him.

"Hold that right there," Auk told him. "I got to put your skull plate back. How was Mainframe?"

The crack-crack-crack of a needler was followed by a savage snarl, more shots, and the boom of a slug gun. In the choir high above them, a nephrite image of Tartaros fell with a crash.

"Is that warm?" Abanja asked as she watched Sciathan pull on his flight suit.

Smiling was easy now. "Not as warm as I wish, sometimes."

"Then you better put the undershirt over it. It's wool and

should be a lot warmer than that thing. Once you're on your horse you can wrap the blanket around you." She fingered the needler in her holster. "Can you ride?"

"I never have."

"That's good," Abanja told him. "It may save your life."

In the cutting wind outside, two bearded men held a pair of restive horses. Abanja said, "That's mine," and to Sciathan's relief pointed to the larger. "The other one's yours. Let's see you mount."

She watched him for five minutes while the bearded men struggled to contain their mirth. At last she said, "You really can't ride, or you're a marvelous actor," and ordered them to help him. As they lifted him into the seat, she swung herself up and onto her own tall horse with a practiced motion that seemed almost miraculous. "Now let me explain something." She leveled her index finger. "It's two leagues to the city, and when we're halfway you're liable to think that all you've got to do to get away is clap your heels to that horse."

He shook his head. "I will not."

"I could chain you to your saddle, like you were chained to that pole. But if you fell, you'd probably be dragged to death, and I don't want to lose you. So listen. If you start that horse galloping, you're going to fall and you could be killed. If you're not I'll catch you, and I'll make you wish you'd died. Don't say I didn't warn you." She slapped her horse with its own control straps, and it stalked away a great deal faster than Sciathan had ever wanted a horse to go.

"I will not ride quicker than you," he promised.

For a moment it appeared he would not ride at all. Then one of the bearded men shouted, *"Hup!"* and struck the horse with something that made a popping sound, and he felt that he was being blown about by the wildest gale in the *Whorl.*

Abanja pulled up and looked back at him. "Another thing. This is a good horse. Yours isn't. Yours is old, a common re-mount nobody wants. Your horse couldn't gallop as fast as mine if a lion were after it."

Shaken too hard to nod, he clutched his blanket.

"If you're fooling me—if you really can ride, and you gallop off when you see your chance—I'll shoot your horse. It's not easy to bring down an animal as big as a horse with a needler, but half a dozen ought to do it. I'll try not to hit you, but I can't promise."

He gasped, "You are a kind woman."

"Don't count on it." After a moment she laughed. "It's just that you may be useful. Certainly it will be useful for you to show Siyuf what you showed me. I take it women aren't kind among your people."

"Oh, no!" He hoped his shock showed in his face. "Our women are very kind."

"That Aer who screamed, wasn't that a woman? You said, *her.* Stand in the stirrups if you're getting bounced."

He tried. "Yes, a woman. A kind woman."

"You loved her." There was a note in Abanja's voice he had not heard before.

"Very much. If I may say this, Mear loved Sumaire also. In the tent last night I thought about them. How stupid I was! I did not know they loved until they died."

"Mear, was that the woman who killed the troopers?"

For the first time since his capture, Sciathan felt like laughing. "Mear is a man's name. It was Sumaire who killed the women with guns, and they killed her."

"Just trying to take away their weapons."

Aer had been shot before Sumaire killed the troopers, but arguing would be worse than useless. Sciathan remained silent.

"She was your leader?" Abanja slowed her horse.

"Thank you." He was genuinely grateful. "We do not fly like that. Each flies for himself. Sumaire was the best at *gleacaiocht*, the best at fighting with hands and feet. I do not know your word."

"I saw her body," Abanja told him, "but I didn't measure it. I wish I had. The blonde?"

By now Sciathan was able to shake his head. "Dark hair. Like yours."·

"The little one?"

He nodded, recalling how cheerful Sumaire had always

been, most cheerful when storms roared up and down the hold. When Mainframe had needed information and not excuses, it had sent Sumaire.

It would send her no more.

"Answer me!"

"I am sorry. I did not intend to be rude." Unconsciously, Sciathan looked down the unpaved track and over the wind-scoured fields, seeking something that would render his loss bearable. "The small one, yes. Smaller than Aer."

"But taller than you."

He looked at Abanja in some astonishment.

"Was she smaller?"

"Yes, much." He considered. "The top of Aer's head came to my eyes. I think the top of Sumaire's head would have come to Aer's eyes, or lower. To my mouth or chin."

"Yet she killed troopers a long cubit taller."

"She was a fine fighter, one who taught others when she was not flying."

Abanja looked thoughtful. "What about you? Do you know this kind of fighting? I forget the word you used."

"*Gleacaiocht.* I know something, but I am not as quick and skillful as Sumaire was. Few are."

When Abanja said nothing, he added. "We all learn it. We cannot carry weapons as you do. Even a small knife would be too heavy." Now that he was no longer being shaken so much, he had begun to feel the cold. He shook out the rough blanket he had held onto so desperately and wrapped himself in it as she had suggested, contriving a hood for his head and neck.

"In that case you can't carry food or water, can you?"

"No, only our instruments—" He had been on the point of saying "and our PMs." He substituted, "and ourselves."

"Have you seen our pterotroopers? Troopers with wings who fly out of the airship?"

"I have not seen these. I was told, and I have seen your airship if it is what I think."

"You can see it now." Abanja pointed. "That brown thing catching the sun above the housetops. Our pterotroopers carry slug guns and twenty rounds, but no rations or water. We tried field packs, but they left them behind whenever they could."

"Yes," Sciathan said.

"You would too, you mean. So would I, I suppose, though I've never flown. I doubt that our wings are much better than yours, and they may not be as good. I hadn't thought about how you'd fight, but I should have. Do you have to break your wings if you're forced down? You said that."

He nodded. "We must."

"The others didn't. We've got them. Siyuf is sending a pair back to Trivigaunte for study, the blond woman's wings and her propulsion module. Is that what you call it?"

"In the Common Tongue? Yes."

"What about in your language?"

He shrugged. "It does not matter."

Abanja stopped her horse and drew her weapon. "It does to you, mannikin, because I'll shoot if you don't answer. What do you call it?"

He chose the least revealing word. "The *canna.*"

"Her *canna.* You don't know how they work, you say."

"I do not. Shoot me and end it."

Again, her smile surprised him. "Shoot you? I've hardly started on you. Who makes them?"

"Our scientists. I do not know the names."

"You have scientists."

"That may not be the correct term." He had said too much, and knew it. "Makers. Mechanics. Is that not what it means?"

"Scientists," Abanja said firmly, then changed the subject with an abruptness that startled him. "You loved Aer. Were you planning to be married?"

"No, she was a Flier."

"Fliers don't marry? Here the holy women don't, which seems pointless to us."

"Marriage is so that there shall be children, new Fliers, in the next generation." He was floundering. "I do not talk of you or, or—" He pointed. "People in the house upon this small hill. But for us, for Crew, it is for children. A Flier woman cannot, because she could not fly. She may when she no longer flies. Some give up wings for marriage." He hesitated, remembering. "They are not happy soon."

"But you can marry. Are you?"

"Yes. One wife." If he had succeeded in this, he would have been given one more at least, and perhaps as many as four; he thrust the thought aside.

"But you loved Aer. She must have been handsome when she was alive, I could see that. Did she love you?"

He nodded slowly. "When she was alive, I wondered. She did not like to say. She is dead, and I know she did."

"I know this must mean a whole lot to you, Patera, and I really am sorry." Chenille's face, framed by the metal margins of the glass, was almost comically apologetic.

"Why?" Silk seated himself in the low-backed chair facing it. "Because my egg will get cold? The kitchen here will send up another if I want it, I feel sure."

"We all got together," Chenille drew breath, her formidable breasts heaving like capsized boats. "That's Auk and me, and General Mint and Sandy and the other soldiers, and Spider and Patera Incus, and those sibyls. Maytera Wood and Maytera Maple, and the rest of them. I don't remember who most of them are."

"I doubt that it matters," Silk told her. "What were you getting together about?"

"Everything, but especially the shooting. So much's been— oh, hi, Hy! I'm sorry about this, truly I am, only Patera said you were finished and having breakfast."

"Bird eat," Oreb announced from Hyacinth's shoulder; Tick countered with, "Ma durst, due add word!" She hushed them, setting Silk's plate and the toast rack before him. "Hi, Chen. Did you and Auk get married too?"

"We talked about it, but we want Patera to do it, so just Moly and her soldier."

"I know that soldier," Hyacinth positioned Silk's egg cup, "and I know your Auk, too. Kypris's kindness on both of you. You're going to need it."

"Auk's all right." Chenille winked. "You've got to know how to handle him."

Silk cleared his throat. "You mentioned shooting, and that sounds very serious. Who was shot?"

"Eland. Only I'd better start at the beginning, Patera—"

He raised his hand. "One question more, before you do. Who is Eland?"

"This cull General Mint nabbed when she was down in the tunnels where me and Auk were."

Oreb whistled. "Bird see!"

"Yeah. Oreb, too. She had these culls, Spider and Eland, and the soldiers were watching them for her. Spider's the fat cull, and the skinny one was Eland, only he's dead."

Silk's forefinger drew small circles on his cheek. "I said I would ask only one question, but I'd like a point verified as well. When you listed those who participated in your impromptu conference, did you include Sergeant Sand?"

"That's the pure quill, Patera. Auk brought him back, just like General Mint says Pas said he would."

"I see. I ought to have had more faith in Pas, though at the time it appeared to me that Maytera Mint had originally had more than enough for both of us, and had been disappointed."

"Yeah, Auk was too. He got all these culls sold on him and said Pas would come, so after the animals were used up and Pas never did, they cleared out. Except Gib. Then when you and Hy went, and Moly and Hammerstone, Gib did too. I said I'd start at the beginning. I guess I have already."

Silk nodded. "Tell me everything, please."

"When you and Hy went, the old man sort of followed you. Master Xiphias, only I don't think he went home. I think he's probably hanging around there to watch out for you. Then His Cognizance and the augur that talked to us that time in your manse left. Maybe it would be easier if I said who didn't, who was still there."

"Go ahead."

"I'll try not to make it so long. Auk stuck, so I did too. We slept on the floor and didn't do anything. Everybody from Brick Street stayed, and Patera Incus, like I said, and General

Mint and the soldiers, only Sandy was dead, and those culls the soldiers were watching. I think that's everybody.

"It was a soldier shooting that woke me up, Slate his name is. There was somebody way up in the balcony, and he'd shot Eland. Patera Incus said Pas for him. Slate saw him up there and took a shot at him, only he doesn't think he got him. He broke a beautiful statue, is all. Auk went up there with him to look, and they brought back a great big dead cat. I thought it was Gib's baboon at first, but it wasn't. It was spotted, sort of like a big house cat only with a little beard and a little short tail."

Hyacinth said, "We brought it in the floater," to which Tick added, "Add cot!"

"I was sort of scared of it," Hyacinth continued, "but Silk said it wouldn't hurt us, and it didn't." He put down his cup. "His name was Lion, and he belonged to Mucor. We stopped at the Caldé's Palace and let him out, thinking he would go to her; it's only a few streets from the Grand Manteion, of course. Am I to take it that Lion was with the person who shot Eland, and that this Slate hit Lion when he fired at Eland's murderer?"

Chenille shook her head, her raspberry curls dancing. "It wasn't a slug gun that did for it, it was a needler. We think when it saw this cully shoot Eland it went for him and he shot it, too. Auk says he heard it before Slate shot, and a needler shooting four or five times up there. That's what got everybody worked up, mostly. That and Pas, only nobody saw him, and Auk bringing back Sandy. Only Sandy's kind of mixed up, on account of being dead."

"I would like to speak to him," Silk said. "I will, at the first opportunity. Before you proceed, did you know Eland, other than as a prisoner of Maytera Mint's? Did you, Hyacinth?"

Both said they had not.

"Since Maytera Mint captured him, I assume he was one of our citizens who remained loyal to the Ayuntamiento. If that's the case, he may have been shot by someone who considered that treachery; but there are a dozen other possibilities. What took place after that?"

"Did I tell you the old augur from Brick Street's dead? He'd gone to Mainframe when I woke up, only he wasn't shot or anything. It looked like he'd just gone to sleep."

"When Pas came," Silk murmured.

"I guess it could've been, yeah. Auk says Pas showed him that stuff about Sandy, only he doesn't remember seeing him."

Silk broke the corner of a slice of toast, and dipped it into his egg. "Others have been visited by gods, though they did not see them. Patera Jerboa was safeguarding a fragment of Pas—or so Hyacinth and I were told."

Hyacinth said, "Something's bothering you. What is it?"

Much as Sciathan was just then shrugging in response to a question from Abanja, Silk shrugged. "I was thinking that the fragment of Pas which Patera Jerboa was safeguarding may have been responsible for his long life, and that its retrieval may have been responsible in his death—not because Pas willed it, but simply because that fragment of Pas was no longer present to maintain him in life."

Silk put the egg-soaked toast into his mouth, chewed it reflectively, and swallowed. When neither woman spoke, he said, "After that, logically enough, I began to wonder which god it is who maintains the rest of us. I believe I can guess, but we have other things to talk about. Naturally you were agitated, Chenille. No doubt all of you were."

"That's right, and General Mint said we ought to find you and tell you, only we thought you'd come here. The sibyls from Brick Street—"

"Wait. You're at the Caldé's Palace?"

"Right. We thought you and Hy probably came here, so we walked over, except the sibyls. They stayed to watch the old man's body, and there's a deadcoach supposed to come. Only you and Hy weren't here. I went in here where this glass is because I thought the monitor would probably know where you went."

Hyacinth exclaimed, "It couldn't!"

"Last night Hyacinth instructed our monitor not to reveal our whereabouts to anyone," Silk explained. He looked to her for confirmation, and she nodded vigorously.

to eat later." The warder paused. "Hoppies didn't rough you up much."

"You're a hoppy yourself," the newcomer told him.

"They don't think so."

"Sure you are. You just don't get the green clothes." The newcomer craned his neck to look up at Sciathan. "Remember what I said about his name? It's 'cause his whole family's hoppies, just about. They want their sprats to be hoppies, too, so they give 'em those names, Peeper and like that."

The warder said, "I got a brother named Buffo and he's a hoppy all right, but not me."

"Pardon." Sciathan leaned over the edge of the upper bunk to look at the laden tray that held the newcomer's meal. "I do not understand."

"He's foreign," the warder informed the newcomer. "They got queer ways in Urbs and places like that."

The newcomer was unwrapping napkins to reveal a loaf as long as Sciathan's arm. "What's itching you, Upstairs? You figure they don't feed everybody this good?"

The warder laughed.

"Your food was not prepared here."

The newcomer shook his head. "There's a place over on the other side of Cage Street. Peeper went over there for me and told 'em what I wanted, then after he locked me up he went back and got it. I fronted him a card, and he gets half for doing it for me. That's how we do here."

"You have just arrived," Sciathan objected. "There could not be time to prepare so much."

"He was in the hot room," the warder explained, "only they made it easy for him, it looks like, and they let me come in to see if he wanted anything."

"They know me, too," the newcomer said.

Sciathan glanced at the snowflakes drifting down beyond the small, barred window, and drew his blanket about his shoulders. "It is warmer in there?"

Both big men laughed, and the newcomer said, "It's where they ask you questions, only they're pretty easy on everybody today, I figure."

"On myself as well. It may be so. It will be worse the next time, I am sure."

The newcomer was spreading butter over a quarter of the long loaf. He said, "They have you in the hot room today?"

The warder shook his head.

"I do not think the hot room. I was questioned on a horse by Abanja, which was not as bad as I feared. Afterward here by Siyuf, Abanja, and others whose names are not known to me. It was worse then. Siyuf is a hard woman."

"That's this Trivigaunti that's taking over," the warder explained to the newcomer. "Generalissimo Siyuf, and she's got the caldé doing everything she says."

"They're supposed to be here helping us out," the newcomer protested.

"They're helping themselves, if you ask me."

The newcomer raised his buttered quarter-loaf. "Here, try some, Upstairs. You hear what we just said?"

"Thank you. I could not fail to do so."

"Well, that's why the hoppies made it easy for me. They ain't sure where they stand yet."

"This is your police? Vironese police?"

"Yeah. Only all of a sudden they're working for the Rani, maybe. They don't know, and neither do we."

The warder cleared his throat. "Anyhow, it's all here. Red in the bottle, and here's your tumbler on top. There's pigs' feet, too, in the square dish, and lots of other stuff. Yell if you want anything."

"I sure will," the newcomer told him, and chuckled as the iron door closed behind him. "Keep a sharp eye on me, Peeper. Make sure I don't get out."

"This is good bread," Sciathan said. "Very good. I thank you for it."

"Sure." The newcomer was heaping noodles and brisket onto his plate.

"I wish that I could repay you. I have no means."

The newcomer looked up at him. "You been in clink before?"

"Last night. My arms were chained about a pole, and I was

made to sleep upon the ground. There was grass, not as hard as your floor, I am certain."

"Only a lot colder. Had to be. I was pretty warm, even on the floor."

"Cold, yes." Sciathan took another bite of bread; it was soft and white, with a thick brown crust that required chewing.

"I had my mort with me, too, and she kept me warm. You say you ate already?"

It was a moment before Sciathan was able to swallow. "On a horse. A slice of gray meat between bread, bread not as good as this. We had spoken about the Common Tongue, Abanja and I, this language in which you and I converse. She said that my meat was also common tongue, which she thought amusing."

"Wait a minute." The newcomer poured the extra sauce from its small side dish into his plate. "Want me to put you some noodles in here? You'll have to eat 'em with your fingers. We only got the one fork."

"I should not." Sciathan wrestled against temptation. "I must tell you there have been many, many days on which I have eaten less than the gray meat. Always we eat little, and often we do not eat at all." He swallowed again, this time only his own saliva. "But, yes. I would like these noodles very much, and it will not trouble me to eat them with my fingers."

"You got it." The newcomer forked noodles into the sauce dish. "You know, I been wondering why you're so weedy, and I hear the rice is bad in Palustria. You come looking for food?"

"Eating makes one heavy." The concept was so simple and so basic that Sciathan had trouble formulating it. "One no longer flies well. I am a Flier. That is your term."

The newcomer gave him a sceptical look. "They don't never come down, and they're spies anyhow, everybody says."

"I am not a spy. Even Siyuf does not think that."

"Then you better muzzle that clatter about being a Flier. Somebody might believe you." The newcomer passed the sauce dish up to Sciathan. "I put a little bit of smoked turtle on top there for you. They give me a little bit of that, too, smoked turtle and onions. If it makes you too thirsty, we can get Peeper to fetch water."

"I have never eaten this." Sciathan dipped up the brown concoction with two fingers and tasted it. "It is delicious."

"Maybe I ought to try some myself."

"I have spoken of becoming heavy," Sciathan muttered, "but why should I not? My wings will not fly again."

The newcomer peered at him. "You really are a Flier, huh? They go up in the big airship and catch you?"

Sighing, Sciathan shook his head. "We landed to question them. I knew that it would be hazardous." More swiftly than a conjuror's transformation, his wizened face twisted to display a corpse's rictus. "Hello, Auk."

"Hi. You really can do this. Jugs and Patera swore you could, but I guess I didn't believe 'em."

"Do you need help?"

"Nah." Finding the empty stare that had become Sciathan's unsettling, the newcomer returned to his plate. "Tell 'em it's going fine, and I'll give a signal when I know which one." He mopped up sauce with a piece of beef, hoping she would be gone before he finished. "I'll send Peeper to fetch something, too. Be better to get him out of the way."

"So hungry, this tiny man."

The newcomer chewed brisket into submission. "He's got more meat on him than you."

"I'd like some soup. I'll ask Grandmother."

"Do that," the newcomer said.

Sciathan blinked and grabbed, discovering that the sauce dish was about to slide off his lap. He made himself breathe deeply. "This is not expected."

The newcomer nodded without looking up. "What's that?"

"When one flies too high, one grows faint. Now too I felt faintness. Could your food be drugged?"

"No," the newcomer said.

"You spoke to me several times. I replied, but I do not recall what you said, or what I said."

"Doesn't matter."

Sciathan finished his smoked turtle and started in on his noodles. "I have no reason to trust you. You might be a spy."

"Sure."

"I have received good food from you, for which I thank you very much. It is better to be spied upon than beaten."

"You can say that again."

"There is nothing I know that I have not told Siyuf and Abanja. Why am I confined?"

The newcomer lifted the lid of another dish. "You like cheese? He gave me some of that, too."

"I have eaten more than suffices already. I have not even finished the bread you gave."

"Here." The newcomer offered a blue-streaked, whitish lump. "Try some of this with it."

"Thank you. We make good cheese in my home, but I have not eaten any in a long while."

"Now you listen up, Upstairs." The newcomer poured four fingers of brandy into his tumbler. "These Trivigauntis you talk about, Abanja and Siyuf? I never seen either one of 'em. I don't know 'em from dirt, but I know about this place here, and the hot room, and the courts and beaks, and all that. If you want to tell me what you did and what's going on with you, I just might be able to scavy you a couple answers. If you don't want to, dimber here. Only don't ask me stuff I don't know, why I'm confined and that clatter."

"You desire to know my crime. I have done nothing wrong."

"Then if they're keeping you here, it's 'cause they're afraid of what you'd do if you got out. What's that?"

"I would resume my searching for the man called Auk. That is all. They know this."

"You going to chill him when you find him?"

Sciathan leaned over the side of his bunk to look down at the newcomer. "Is this equivalent to *kill?* The softer sound instead of the hard sound at the top of the mouth?"

"Yeah. It's what this holy sibyl that taught us would say was an alternate pronunciation."

"No, I would not chill him. I would tell the masters of the

airship above this city that they must take me, with this man Auk and those he chooses, to Mainframe."

"Wait up." The newcomer cleaned his ear with the nail of one forefinger. "To Mainframe? I ain't sure I heard you right. Say it again."

"I am from Mainframe. This is where we live, we Crew. It is our director, it shelters us and we repair it as it directs, when repairs are needed."

"A real place." The newcomer sipped brandy.

"Mainframe is where we live. Viron is where you live."

"If you live there, why are you shaggy flying over here all the time making it rain?"

"Because Mainframe directs it. It is the director of the *Whorl*, not ours alone. If rain did not fall, you Cargo would perish. Or if too much falls. Mainframe has many sources of data. We are one, not the least."

"You want some red?" The newcomer offered his tumbler. "You still feel like fainting, it might be good for you."

"No, thank you."

"All right, what's this about cargo? Like on a boat?"

"You people, the animals, and the plants. It is the same as a boat, yes, because we are in a boat, we as well as you."

"We're the cargo?" Staring up at Sciathan, the newcomer tapped his own chest. "Me, and everybody I know?"

"That is it with precision." Sciathan nodded emphatically. "Abanja and Siyuf also. So you see that I would not chill Auk. It is our duty to preserve the Cargo, not to chill it."

"Mainframe told you to do this?"

"To preserve the Cargo? Yes, always." Sciathan's voice dropped. "It is increasingly difficult. The sun no longer responds well, not even so well as in my father's day. Heat accumulates, another difficulty, because the cooling no longer functions efficiently. Mainframe may be compelled to blow out the sun. Is that how you say it? Interrupt its energy. It has warned us, and we have done what we can to be ready."

The newcomer put down his tumbler. "You're getting me dizzy enough without this." He rose, stepping to the small barred opening in the iron door. "Hey! Peeper!"

"You think that I am deceiving you. You will seek to have me removed."

The newcomer turned to face him. "Cost me two cards to get this pad, and now I scavy you're cank. It's getting too hot, you said. The whole whorl's getting too hot."

Sciathan nodded. "There are other difficulties, but that is worst."

"So you're going to shut off the cooling—"

"No, no! The sun. Until the *Whorl* can be cooled. I will not do this, you must understand. I could not. Mainframe must, if it must be done. It will be a terrible darkness."

" 'Cause the whorl's getting too hot." The newcomer strode to the window. "You take a look out there. That's snow."

"You will not credit me." Sciathan sighed, studying the newcomer's coarse, bearded face for some sign of belief. "I cannot condemn you, but you have fed me and been kind. I would not deceive you. It was difficult to make the winter this year. Mainframe struggled, and we flew many sorties."

"It had to make winter. Mainframe had to make it?" The newcomer pointed to the window. "I always figured winter was just natural."

"Nature is a useful term for processes that one does not understand," Sciathan told him wearily. "Once already the sun has blown out because Mainframe was trying to make this winter. This was not intended."

"Yeah. I heard about that." The newcomer sounded less argumentative. "Then the sun came back, only real bright for a minute. It set fire to some trees and stuff. A cull I know asked Patera about it. Caldé Silk. He said it was another god talking and he knew which one, only he didn't say."

"It was not a god," Sciathan asserted. "It was the sun's restarting. Restarting must be at maximum energy."

"Anyhow, that's not why you're here." The newcomer pulled his tunic over his head, revealing a red wool undershirt that he removed as well. "Mainframe told you to find this cully Auk."

The warder's face appeared in the opening in the door. "What you need?"

"I want you to go to Trotter's for me," the newcomer told him, and handed him two cards. "You tell him any friends of mine that come in, the first one's on me. Have him tell 'em I'll be back real soon, and I'll see 'em at the Cock. You got it? You got to go straight away."

"Sure. You too hot in there?"

"I got a itch is all. You tell Trotter, then maybe I'll have another little job for you."

When the warder had gone, Sciathan began, "Is it known here . . . I do not wish to offend religious sensibilities."

"You won't," the newcomer told him, " 'cause I ain't got any. I got religion, and that's different."

"Is it known that all the gods are Mainframe?" Sciathan awaited an explosion with some anxiety; when it did not come, he added, "Equally is Mainframe all gods. Mainframe in its aspect of darkness, which in this tongue is termed Tartaros, issued my instructions."

After knotting its sleeves around one of the bars, the newcomer pushed his undershirt out the window. "You know, I wish you'd told me that sooner, Upstairs."

He picked up his fork, bending its tines with powerful fingers. "What's your right tag, anyhow?"

"I am Sciathan. And you?"

"I ain't going to tell you, Sciathan. Later I will, only not now, 'cause I scavy it might slow us down. You know where the keyhole is in this door? About where it is, anyhow?"

Sciathan nodded.

"Dimber. Look here. See how I twisted the one funny and bent the other two up out of the way? I want you to stick your arm through the peephole there. I could maybe do it if I was to rub butter on my arm, but you can do it easy. Sort of feel around for the keyhole with your kate, that's the funny-looking one. When you find it, stick your kate in and twist."

Sciathan accepted the fork. "You are saying this will open the door. You cannot know it."

"Sure I do. I seen the key when he was letting me in, and I know how these locks work. I know how everything works soon as I see it, so get cracking. I don't want to keep 'em waiting outside."

Slowly, Sciathan nodded again. "Then you will be free, and I free to pursue my search for Auk, but clothed as I am, and ignorant of the customs of this city."

"We're going to take care of you," the newcomer told him briskly. "Clothes and everything, and we'll teach you how to act, all right? Do it!"

Standing on tiptoe, he was able to thrust his arm through the space between two bars. The strangely bent tine scratched the door for the lock plate, then scratched the lock plate for the keyhole. "I am fearful that I may drop it," he told the newcomer, "but I will try to—" He had felt the bolt retract. "It is unlock!"

"Sure." As Sciathan withdrew his arm, the newcomer pushed the door open. "Come on. There's a couple mort troopers on the outside door already, so we best bing. Wrap that blanket so they can't see your kicks."

He led Sciathan along the corridor and down a stair to a massive iron door. "They ought to of had 'em inside too," he whispered, "only they figured it was all rufflers and upright men, so nothing would happen. It don't matter what's afoot, it gets queered when some cully figures nothing's going to happen."

"I understand this," Sciathan told him; and wanted to add: *Yesterday that was I.*

"Only that's the way I'm figuring too, 'cause I got to. They'll have slug guns out there, and if we beat hoof they'll pot us sure. So we're going to walk easy going out, and just keep going till we're 'cross the street. And maybe nothing will happen. If they holler or say something, don't you stop or even look back at 'em. You got it?"

"I will try. Yes."

"Dimber." The newcomer pressed his ear to the iron door. "Long as you do, you don't have to worry. We'll take care of the rest."

There followed a lengthy silence; at last the newcomer said, "Pretty quiet out there. Get set."

The motion of the door seemed much too quick as Sciathan stepped, half blinded by winter sunlight, through the doorway at the newcomer's side. From the corner of his eye he glimpsed the towering woman whose thick sand-colored greatcoat his blanket brushed.

The wide street was freezing mud, rutted by the wheels of carts and wagons, and almost empty. Snowflakes whirled before his eyes, a few sticking to their lashes.

"You two!" a woman's voice bawled. *"Halt!"*

So fast that it seemed sure to strike them, a black vehicle swooped toward them, roaring like a storm. He was airborne once more, out of control and without wings. For an instant he saw the startled face of a man in black with whom he collided full tilt, after which something huge and heavy struck his back.

A bang—like a slamming door—and the roar mounted to a deafening crescendo. Acceleration pushed him backward into two obstacles he did not at first realize were the shins of the man in black. As though by some mysterious device of Mainframe's, the roar was muffled; above and behind him the newcomer growled, "Just the one shot. Pretty good."

A new voice, that of the man in black, said, "Even one is too many."

And then, as the pale hands of the man in black and the muscular hands of the newcomer lifted him onto a padded seat, "Welcome to Our Holy City of Viron, in the names of its people, its patroness, the Outsider, and all the other gods. I'm sorry we couldn't do this with less violence and more ceremony. Are you hurt? I'm Caldé Silk."

Sciathan wiped his mouth with his fingers, finding to his surprise that it was not bleeding. "I am somewhat bruised, but from blows and not from this escaping. I am Sciathan." Beyond their enchanted tranquility, snow swirled and homely blank-faced buildings raced like camels. He blinked, looking from this pale Cargo to the newcomer and back. "Are we safe?"

"For the time being at least," the pale Cargo called Caldé Silk assured him.

"I am your prisoner, instead of that of the tall women?"

Caldé Silk shook his head. "Of course not. You may come and go as you wish."

The newcomer added, "Anyhow, we like you."

Sciathan smiled; it was very good now to smile, he found. "Then I am free to search again?"

"Yeah," the newcomer told him, "only it ain't going to take you long. I'm Auk."

Chapter 13

MAKING PEACE

"Good man!" Oreb assured everyone at the table.

"This is Sciathan." Silk indicated the tiny man on his left. "Sciathan landed near the Trivigaunti camp on Thelxday, with four of his fellow Fliers—I believe while the parade was still in progress. The Trivigauntis shot three of them and captured him. One escaped."

Potto nodded, his round, cheerful face mirrored in the waxed and polished wood. "And he escaped yesterday with your help. I won't congratulate you on that operation, just on its success. We could have managed it much better."

Halfway down the table, Spider concurred. "Shag, yes!"

"It was hastily improvised," Silk admitted. "We knew only that Sciathan had come to find Auk; we couldn't even guess why he wanted him. Fortunately Generalissimo Oosik was able to get through to the Guardsmen on duty in the Juzgado—"

Loris interrupted. "They've been replaced."

"That's good. I'm glad nothing worse was done to them. On Generalissimo Oosik's instructions, they pretended that they had arrested Auk, and he was able to bribe a turnkey to put him in Sciathan's cell. Quite frankly, we thought it likely that Auk would leave him there after he had talked to him, at least for the time being. We were extremely reluctant to worsen our relations with the Trivigauntis."

Silk scanned the faces beyond Hyacinth's. Maytera Mint looked angry; Bison, beside her, angrier still. Oosik, eager and expectant, a slug gun across his lap; he had wanted both councillors killed, and might conceivably have a subordinate stationed somewhere to kill them.

"If things had gone as we expected," Silk continued, "The rest would have been easy. Auk would have been escorted out by Guardsmen, and Siyuf's sentries would have assumed that he had been questioned and was being released."

Auk himself said, "Only I couldn't. We got to get to Mainframe. That's him and me and everybody that's going with me." He glanced at Quetzal and Remora, seeking support.

Potto smiled more broadly than ever. "I congratulate you again on the outcome. It was all we could wish for and more. Just the same, our enemies retain four propulsion modules, and three undamaged pairs of wings."

Hyacinth said loudly, "You're the enemy!"

Maytera Mint shook her head. "They were the enemy, up to Thelxday night. Now we've been betrayed, and we're no longer sure. I doubt that the Trivigauntis are either. We're all Vironese here, everybody except the Flier. If Councillor Loris is really here to make peace, we ought to welcome it."

She closed her eyes. "I do. Echidna, forgive me!" On the other side of the table, Remora nodded emphatically.

Silk asked, "Have you come to make peace, Councillor Loris? Councillor Potto?"

"Our azoths have been confiscated." Potto giggled. "I was searched! Me! It was absolutely hilarious, but calling this a peace conference is funnier."

"I didn't say it was a peace conference," Maytera Mint snapped, "I implied it could become one. It should, if there's any chance for peace. As for taking your weapons, His Eminence and I went to parlay without any, and you know what you did to us. Because of that, this parley is being held on our ground with us armed and you disarmed. I will insist upon the same arrangements for any future parleys as well."

Loris snarled, "Your troops are melting away as we speak!" to which Potto added, "It was worth it to see your face, my dear young General, when I threatened you with the teapot. I'd do it again, just for that. But you have no right—"

Oosik interrupted him, drawing his needler and holding it up. "Here is one of my weapons. It will kill me, or General Mint, or even Caldé Silk. Do you want it?" He laid it on the polished tabletop between them, and gave it a push that sent it past the middle of the table.

While Silk counted three beatings of his heart, no one spoke. Potto stared at the needler before him, and at last shook his head.

"Then do not complain to us about your weapons," Oosik told him.

Silk rapped for order. "Like you, Generalissimo, I do not believe that Councillor Potto is entitled to complain about the loss of his weapons. We are entitled to complain about the projected loss of ours, however, and I'm not at all sure that Councillor Potto—although he is inclined to be proud of his information—knows about that. Councillor Loris seems to be less than current with regard to General Mint's volunteers."

He addressed Potto directly. "Councillor Loris said they were melting away. Colonel Bison reports that they've melted altogether. We had to hurry it, and hurry it we did. Do you know why?"

Loris said, "He doesn't, but he'll never admit it. I'm not so pigheaded. Why, Caldé?"

Silk nodded to Bison, who said, "Generalissimo Siyuf has ordered the Guard to collect our peoples' slug guns and store them in the Juzgado." Bison leaned forward, his eyes on Loris and his face tense. "It was exactly—exactly!—the right order to split the Guard and our people, and she didn't even try to route it through Generalissimo Oosik. She sent it to the individual officers in command of the brigades."

Potto put in, "Except Brigadier Erne."

"Except for Erne. That's right. We were lucky, in that the brigadiers wanted to clear those orders with Generalissimo Oosik. He countermanded them, naturally. Now we've dispersed our people so that it will be impossible for the Trivigauntis to disarm them themselves."

Potto's giggle mounted to a shrill laugh. He slapped his thigh. "You can't use them against us unless you call them up again. And you won't dare call them up because your friends from Trivigaunte will disarm them. You're in a pickle!"

Maytera Mint told him, "Yours is worse."

She glanced at Silk, who told Potto, "We have a strategy, you see—one that you cannot frustrate. The Trivigauntis are preparing to mount a vigorous offensive against you. You know that, I'm sure."

Loris nodded.

"I listened to Generalissimo Siyuf outline her plans last night, and I've been thinking about our options all day. In order to win, all that we have to do now is sit back and let them carry out those plans. She is a rigid disciplinarian, and she's never been down in those tunnels. Furthermore, she's not greatly concerned about the lives of her troops, especially her infantry, which consists largely of conscripts."

Silk leaned back, his fingers joined in a pointed tower. "As I said, all we have to do is to let her do as she plans. There will be a terrible war of attrition, fought underneath the city between foreigners and soldiers most of the men and women who live in it have scarcely seen. In the end, one side or the other will triumph, and it won't make much difference which it is, since the winner will be too weak to resist General Mint's horde when we reassemble it. Either way, we'll be masters of the city. And either way, you will both be dead."

Potto sneered. Loris said smoothly, "A few minutes ago somebody was saying we're all Vironese here, with a single exception. Was it you, General? You, whose troops are to complete the destruction once Viron's army has defeated the Trivigauntis for you?"

"Yes," she told him. "It was."

Silk said, "There are at least three major objections to the strategy I have just outlined, Councillor, though I do not doubt that it would succeed—that it will, if we choose to employ it. You've voiced the first yourself: it entails the destruction of Viron's army. The second is that it will take at least half a year, and very possibly several years; either would be too long, as we'll explain in a moment. The third is that there is one part of Siyuf's force that we must have, and it is exactly the part that would almost certainly escape us. I refer to General Saba's airship.

"Sciathan, will you please tell these councillors what you told me?"

The Flier nodded, his small, pinched face solemn. "We of Mainframe, we Crew, were visited by the god you call Tartaros. It was the morning of the day on which I was captured."

Auk put in, "Right after he left me, see?"

"His instructions were urgent. We were to find this man Auk," Sciathan pointed, "and bring him and his followers to Mainframe, so that they can leave the *Whorl* to journey to a short-sun sphere outside." Sciathan turned to Silk. "They do not believe me."

"They need only believe that I believe you," Silk told him, "as I do. Continue."

"This very wise man Caldé Silk has spoken to you of the airship, the great vessel that flies without wings, stirring the air with wooden arms. The god also spoke to us of this airship. We were to employ it to carry back this man who is my friend now, and those who wish to accompany him."

Profound conviction lent intensity to Sciathan's voice. "It cannot be accomplished otherwise. No, not though a god should demand it. He cannot fly as we do, nor can the others who wish to accompany him. For them to walk or ride animals would consume many months. There are mountains and deserts, and many swift rivers."

"We'd need enough bucks with slug guns and launchers to fight our way past anybody that tried to stop us," Auk added. "We ain't got them." Seeing Chenille enter with a tray, he inquired, "What you got there, Jugs? Tea and cookies?"

She nodded, "Maytera thought you might like something. She's busy with Stony and Patera, so Nettle and I baked."

"There is too much eating here," Sciathan protested in a whisper, "also, too much drinking. Behold that one." He indicated Potto with a nod.

"I agree," Silk said, accepting a cup of tea, "but we must consider hospitality."

"In short," Loris was saying, "you want us to help you take over the airship. I won't argue about your reason for wanting it, though I might if I thought we could do it. I doubt that we can."

Potto rocked from side to side, bubbling with mirth. "I might. Yes, I might! Silk, I'll make you an offer on behalf of my cousins and myself, but you'll have to trust me."

Maytera Mint shook her head, but Silk told her, "This is progress, whether we accept it or not. Let's hear it."

"I'll seize the airship for you within a month, capturing as many of the technicians who operate it as possible. I'll turn them over to you after they've agreed to cooperate with you in every way." He tittered. "They will, I promise you, when I've had them for a few days. Ask the general there."

He turned to Chenille, who was serving Remora. "May I have a cup of your tea, my dear? I can't drink it, but I like the smell."

Maytera Mint snorted.

"I do, my dear young General. You think I'm mocking you, when I'm simply indulging the only pleasure of the flesh left to me." As Chenille poured, he added, "Thank you very, very much. Five bits? Would that be acceptable?"

Chenille stared. "Is this . . . I don't—"

Silk said, "Councillor Potto is merely using you to make a point, Chenille. He prefers to make his points in the most objectionable way possible, as General Mint and I can testify. What is it, Councillor?"

"That even trivial things are seldom free." Potto smiled. "That there is a price to pay, even when it's a trivial price. Want to hear mine for the airship?"

Silk nodded, feeling Hyacinth's hand tighten about his.

Loris said, "I've no idea what he has in mind, but I'm going to attach one of my own first. You're to do nothing to interfere with us during the month specified. No attacks on any position of ours, including Erne's."

Silk said, "We wouldn't, of course—if we accepted. But it's your cousin's price that concerns me."

"Two men." Potto held up two fingers. "I want to borrow one and keep the other. Can't you guess which they are?"

"I believe so. Perhaps I should have made it clear that I haven't the least intention of accepting. Even if you had offered to do it for nothing, as a gesture of goodwill, I still could not have accepted."

Auk started to protest, but Silk cut him off. "Let me say this once and for all, not just to you, Auk, and not just to these councillors; but to everyone present. Trivigaunte is our ally. There has been friction between us, true. I daresay that there is always friction in every alliance, even the small and simple alliance of husband with wife."

Hyacinth's lips brushed his cheek.

"I did not ask the Rani to send us help, but I welcomed it with open arms when she did. I have no intention of turning against her and her people now, because of a little friction. Maytera Marble often tells me things she's learned from watching children's games, and I received the greatest lesson of my life during one such game; now I want to propose a game for us. Let us pretend for a few minutes that I'm Generalissimo Siyuf. Will all of you accept that, for the sake of the game?"

His eyes went from face to face. "Very well, I am Siyuf. I understand that some of you are nursing grievances in spite of my long and swift march to your rescue, and in spite of the aid I brought you. Let me hear them now. There is not one I cannot dispose of."

Loris said, "I hope you're not so deep in your part as to shoot me."

Silk smiled and shook his head.

"Very well then, Generalissimo Siyuf. I have a complaint, exactly as you said. I'm speaking as the presiding officer of the Ayuntamiento, the legitimate government of this city. You and your troops are interfering in our internal affairs. That is an act of war."

Silk heaved a sigh, and his gaze strayed to Chenille, who was pouring tea for Maytera Mint. "Councillor, your government was never legitimate, because it was established by murdering your lawful caldé. I can't say which of you ordered his murder, or whether you acted jointly. For the purposes of discussion, let's assume it was Councillor Lemur, and that he acted alone. You nevertheless—"

"I didn't intend to get into this," Loris protested. His craggy face was grim.

"You introduced the subject yourself when you referred to yours as the legitimate government, Councillor. I was about to say that though you searched for the adopted son Caldé Tussah had named as his successor, as your duty required, you did not hold elections for new councillors, as your Charter demands. My ally Caldé Silk governs because the people of your city wish it, and so his claim is better than yours. Aid given by a friendly power is not an act of war. How could it be? Are you saying that we of Trivigaunte attacked your city? It welcomed us with a parade."

Silk waited for a response; when none came, he said, "You have already heard that I know the contents of your previous caldé's will. I found a copy in your Juzgado. Let me say, too, that in my opinion the adopted son you searched for with so much diligence did not exist. Caldé Tussah invented this son to draw your attention from another child, an illegitimate child who may or may not have been born before his death. If she had already been born, referring to an adopted *son* was doubly misleading, as he doubtless intended it to be." Silk sipped his tea. "Don't go, Chenille."

Potto sprang to his feet. "You!"

"Did you kill my father, Councillor?" Chenille's dark eyes flashed. "The real one? I don't know, but I don't think it was really Councillor Lemur. I think it was you!"

Oosik raised his slug gun, telling Potto to sit down.

"If you did and evidence can be found," Silk continued, "you will have to stand trial. So far we have none."

"Are you Silk or Siyuf?" Potto demanded.

"Silk at present. I'll resume the game in a moment. Your Cognizance, will you speak? I ask it as a favor." Upon Silk's shoulder, Oreb fluttered uneasily.

"If you want me to, Patera Caldé." Quetzal's glittering gaze was fixed on Potto. "Not many of us knew Tussah. Patera Remora did, and Loris. Did you, Generalissimo?"

Oosik shook his head. "Twenty years ago I was a captain. I saw him several times, but I doubt that he knew my name."

"He knew mine, eh?" Remora cleared his throat. "I had, er, was coadjutor in those—um—happier days. Ah—mother still living, eh, General? It, um, sufficient in itself, hey? Though there were other favorable circumstances."

Chenille, who had stopped pouring tea, murmured, "I wish I knew more about him."

"I, um, disliked him, I confess," Remora told her. "Not hatred, you understand. And there were times, eh? But I was, er, substantially alone in it. Wrong, too, eh? Wrong. I, um, concede it now. Loud, brawling, vigorous, and I was—um— determined, quite determined secretly, to be offended. But he, er, put the city first. Always did, and I—ah—accorded insufficient weight to it."

"He wouldn't flatter my then coadjutor, Patera Caldé," Quetzal explained. "He flattered me, however. He flattered me by confiding in me. He never married. Are you both aware of that?"

Silk and Chenille nodded.

"Clergy take a vow of chastity. Even with its support, chastity is too severe for many. He confided to me, as one friend to another, that his housekeeper was his mistress."

"Not—ah—under the Seal, eh?"

Quetzal's hairless head swayed on its long neck. "I don't and won't speak of shriving, though I shrove him once or twice. This was at dinner, one at which only he and I were present. If he were alive I wouldn't speak of it. He's dead and can't speak for himself. He introduced the woman to me. He asked me to take care of her should he die."

Chenille said, "If that was my mother, you didn't."

"I did not. I couldn't find her. Though she was good-looking in her way, she was an ignorant woman of the servant class. I know she disliked me, and I think she was afraid of me. She was guilty of adultery weekly, and unable to imagine forgiveness for it."

Silk said, "You searched for her as soon as you heard Caldé Tussah was dead?"

"I did, Patera Caldé. Not as thoroughly as I should, since she was alive and I failed to find her."

Loris said, "I remember her now. The gardener's wife. She oversaw the kitchen and the laundry. A virago."

Quetzal nodded frigidly. "She was the type he admired, and he was the type she did."

Auk began, "This gardener cully—"

"A marriage of convenience, performed by my prothonotary in five minutes. There would have been talk if Tussah had a single woman in this palace. His gardener wasn't intelligent, though a good man and a hard worker. He was proud to be seen as married, as a man who'd won the love of an attractive woman. I imagine she dominated him completely. I thought they would look for new employment when Tussah died, and I planned to make places for them on our staff. They didn't. I know now, thanks to Patera Caldé, that they became beggars. At the time I assumed they'd known something about Tussah's death, and had been silenced."

Chenille said, "We sold watercress. But if somebody wanted to give us money, we took it. I used to ask for money, too, and run errands. Do little jobs." She swallowed. "After a while I found out there were things men would give me half a card for. It was a fortune to us, enough food for a week." She stared at her listeners, challenging them.

Loris smiled. "Blood will tell, they say."

"Blood won't," Silk declared. "Blood's dead—I killed him. But if Blood were alive, he might tell you that it was good business to give rust, at first, to the young women at Orchid's, and to sell it to them afterward—to keep them in constant need of money, and thus keep them there for as long as he and Orchid let them stay. The Ayuntamiento let him bring rust and other drugs into our city, in return for what I must call criminal services."

Hyacinth said, "I use it sometimes, and I've been telling myself that if Chen can kick it so can I, and I hope it's true. But it's hard, don't ever believe anybody who says it's not."

Quetzal gave Loris a lipless smile. "Blood does tell, my son."

"Watch out!" Oreb advised; it was not clear to which he spoke.

Maytera Mint asked, "Do you know why they didn't try to find another situation, Caldé?"

"I don't; but I believe I can guess. Chenille's mother had recently given birth to the caldé's child, or if she had not, she was carrying that child—and it was her child, too. She must have guessed, or known, that the caldé had been murdered. At that time, the Ayuntamiento was searching everywhere for the adopted son mentioned in the caldé's will; and she would have supposed, as I believe most people did, that it would kill him if it found him. She needn't have been an educated woman, or an imaginative one, to guess what would happen to another child of the caldé's, if it learned that she existed."

Silk filled his lungs, feeling a twinge from his wounded chest. "We've gotten far off the subject, but since we're here, let's finish what we've begun. Caldé Tussah left a substantial estate. I have it now as trustee for his daughter; I'll turn it over to Chenille as soon as she reaches twenty, the legal age of maturity."

"Good girl!" Oreb assured everyone.

Loris told Silk, "That will have to be adjudicated by the courts, I'm afraid."

He shook his head. "Our government is sorely in need of funds, Councillor. We have a war to prosecute, in addition to all the usual civic expenses; and we gave each of General

Mint's troopers two cards, as well as his or her weapon, before we sent them home."

Loris said, "You're generous with the taxpayers' money."

"In order to do it, we've taken control of the Fisc; the city assumes responsibility for inactive accounts, and for the accounts in trust, such as Caldé Tussah's. We've sequestered the accounts of the members of the Ayuntamiento, as you know. Do you want to talk about it now?"

Sciathan said, "We must speak more of the airship. It is urgent. This Potto says he will get it, but in one month. We have a few days at most. Not more."

"Why?" Hyacinth asked him, speaking across Silk.

Auk told him, "Let 'em jaw about the money first. If you don't, they'll keep going back to it."

"Wise man!" Oreb exclaimed.

Silk rapped the table. "Which will it be, the airship or your accounts? Personally I'd prefer to deal with Generalissimo Oosik's complaints against Generalissimo Siyuf, and General Mint and Colonel Bison's. It's usually best, I've found, to consider minor matters first and get them out of the way. Otherwise they cloud everyone's thinking, as Auk says."

"We knew you'd stolen our money," Loris told him, "but we also knew it would be useless to protest the theft."

Maytera Mint declared, "You want to make peace after all."

"Hardly. But we're prepared to offer you new terms of surrender, much more liberal terms than those I proposed at Blood's, which were intended merely as an opening point for negotiations."

"You said at the time that they were not negotiable," Silk reminded him.

"Certainly. One always does. You were willing to listen to Potto's proposal. Will you hear ours as well? Our joint proposal?"

"Of course."

"Then let me first explain why you should accept it. You assert that you have a strategy that will assure your victory, though you are loath to follow it. You are mistaken, but we are not. We have a strategy of our own, one that will assure your defeat in under a year."

Oosik said, "Clearly you do not, or you would follow it," and Silk nodded.

"You have been assisting us with it," Loris continued, smiling, "for which we are appropriately grateful."

Potto grinned. "We're giving away slug guns too!"

"We are," Loris confirmed, "and other weapons as well, needlers mostly. We still have access to several stores of weapons. I hope you will excuse my keeping their locations confidential."

"Giving them to who?" Bison inquired.

"In a moment. Some preparation is necessary. You were underground not long ago, Colonel. The tunnels are extensive, are you aware of it? You saw not a thousandth part of them."

"I've been told the caldé went into them from a shrine by the lake, and that General Mint went in from a house north of the city and came out on the Palatine. If those she saw and those he saw belong to the same complex, it's pretty large."

Maytera Mint told him, "Much larger than that, according to what I've learned from Spider."

"I want him," Potto put in. "I want him and the Flier. I offered the airship and you refused it. Name your price."

Silk sighed. "I said that trivial points tend to obscure discussions. This is just such a point, so let's dispose of it. Spider is our prisoner. We will exchange him for one of equal value, during this truce or another. Have you a prisoner to offer us? Who is it?"

Potto shook his head. "I will have, soon. Give him back, and you'll get double value as soon as I have it."

"No!" Maytera Mint struck the table with her small fist, and Hyacinth's catachrest thrust his furry little head above the tabletop, saying, "Done bay saw made, laddie."

"Of course not," Silk told Potto, "but may I propose an alternative I believe workable?"

"Let's hear it."

"In a moment. You also want Sciathan."

"Only temporarily." Potto giggled. "I'll pay you a fine for

every day I keep him over a fortnight, how's that? Like a library book. I still have a lot more money than you stole."

Auk declared, "I heard about you from Maytera, and you ain't taking him."

"Auk speaks for me as well," Silk said, "and for all of us. Sciathan is a free individual—"

"A free *man,*" Loris amended.

"Precisely. He is not mine to give or keep. He is here in this palace as my guest, and nothing more—nothing less, I ought to say. If you believe he's under restraint, ask him."

Remora tossed back his lank black hair. " 'Sacred unto Pas are the life and property of the stranger you welcome.' "

"Furthermore, he would disappoint you. He's been beaten and interrogated already by Generalissimo Siyuf, who hoped to learn how the Fliers' propulsion modules operate. Councillor Lemur killed Iolar, who was another Flier, for the same reason; I shrove Iolar before he died. Since Lemur himself died soon after, you may not be aware of it. Are you?"

Loris shrugged. "We were aware of his capture, of course. What Lemur learned from him died with Lemur, unfortunately."

"Lemur learned nothing from him; that was why Lemur killed him. I discussed the propulsion modules with Sciathan today. He freely conceded that their principle is important; that it would be valuable to our city or any other is obvious; but he doesn't have it, and neither did Iolar.

"The scientists who make them remain in Mainframe, safe from capture. The Fliers who use them are kept ignorant of the principle, for reasons they understand and approve. It's an elementary precaution, one that you and your fellow councillors ought to have anticipated. It would have been anticipated, surely, by anyone not blinded by the itch for power. If you want to find out how they operate, you might capture one of those the Trivigauntis have and take it apart; but I doubt that I could tell leaf from root."

"Naturally you couldn't." Potto giggled. "Have you got one? Name your price for Spider. A hundred cards? I want to hear it, and the price of the propulsion module, too, if you've got one."

"We don't. Councillor Loris, Councillor Lemur told me that he was a bio, not a chem. Are you?"

"Certainly."

"Despite the marble bookend you crushed at Blood's?"

"This is not my natural body. Physically, I'm on our boat, well out of your reach. This body," Loris touched his black velvet tunic, "is a chem, if you like. To simplify matters, I won't object to your calling it that. I manipulate it from my bed, making it move and speak as I did when I was younger."

Maytera Mint told Silk, "I explained all this, I think."

"Yes, you did, Maytera; I'm very grateful. Spider should be grateful as well."

"If it gets me loose," Spider grunted.

"It very well may. From what General Mint has reported, counterintelligence has been your chief concern. I'm not so naïve as to think that your organization—what remains of it— could not be put to other uses, however; and I noticed that Councillor Potto wanted you back when he was planning to seize control of General Saba's airship."

Potto said, "I do anyhow. He's valuable to us."

"Clearly. Primarily in frustrating spies?"

Loris said, "Primarily, yes."

"Spider, General Mint says you're a decent man, a patriot in your way. If I were to release you to Councillor Potto, as you wish, would you be willing to give me your solemn promise that in so far as our forces are concerned, you would confine your activities entirely to counterintelligence? By 'our forces' I intend those headed by Generalissimo Oosik and Auk—not only the Guard, but General Mint's volunteers, including those commanded by her through Colonel Bison."

Spider licked his lips. "If Councillor Potto don't tell me I can't, yeah, I will."

Potto raised a hand. "Wait. I think I heard something funny. Does your friend Auk have a private horde now?"

Auk grinned. "The best thieves in the whole city, the ones

that's going with me and Sciathan. A month for the airship, you said. I figure we might nab it a whole lot sooner."

Sciathan stood up. "We must! If the Cargo will not leave the *Whorl,* Pas will drive everyone out as one drives a bear from a cave. He will starve and afflict Crew and Cargo until we go."

Loris's icy blue eyes twinkled. "A rain of blood. The Chrasmologic Writings speak of such things, I'm told."

Remora nodded solemnly. "Ah—worse, Councillor. Plagues, hey? Famine, er, likewise."

"Listen to me!" Sciathan's excited tenor cracked. "If a landing craft leaves, even one, Pas will wait for more. But if none leave, everyone will be driven out. Do you understand now? We Crew have a craft ready, but so much Crew cannot be spared so early in the Plan. For this reason Tartaros has readied Auk for us, and we must have them!"

"Me and my knot," Auk explicated.

Chenille added, "That's me. I hope you don't mind that I stayed to listen, Patera. But when Auk goes, I go too."

"With my blessing," Potto chortled. "Oh, yes! Very much so. I'll be delighted to lose my accuser, and have the enemy lose its airship."

He turned to Silk. "Will Spider be free to act in any way we choose against your cherished allies? That's what it sounded like. You didn't expect me to miss that, did you?"

"No." Silk's expression was guarded. "But if you had, I would have mentioned it to him. You may not be aware of it, but Maytera Mint left the tunnels with two other prisoners. One was a convict named Eland. Eland was murdered yesterday morning in the Grand Manteion."

"A mystery!" Potto clapped his pudgy hands like a happy child. "I love them!"

"I don't. I try to clear them up when I can, and I've been trying to clear up this one. My first thought was that this man Eland had been killed by some old enemy, most plausibly someone who had attended the sacrifice there the previous night and had seen him. I asked Auk to find out who that enemy might be, and had one of General Skate's officers inquire as well."

Silk shifted his attention from Potto to Spider. "The harder they looked, the less probable it appeared. Eland had not been a thief, as I had assumed, but a horse trainer who had killed his employer in a fit of rage. Presumably there was some public sympathy for him, since he was not executed. Auk could find nobody who knew of anyone who bore him a murderous grudge."

Maytera Mint asked, "Did you consider Urus, Caldé?"

"We did, but we quickly dismissed him. Eland had been a useful subordinate in the tunnels, where Urus would have had any number of opportunities to kill him in complete safety. Why wait? Why run the risk of being shot by Acting Corporal Slate, as the killer very nearly was? Besides, I've gotten a sketchy description of the killer, and if it's even roughly correct, he was neither dirty nor dressed in rags. I'll tell you later how I obtained it."

"Got to protect his sources," Spider explained. "That's how it is, Maytera."

"Most of Eland's friends and relatives had assumed he was dead long ago," Silk continued, "yet someone with a needler had quite deliberately climbed into the choir of the Grand Manteion to shoot him. Why? After I'd turned over the question for an hour or two, it occurred to me that someone might have made a mistake—that he might have intended to shoot another person entirely, and mistaken Eland for that person. Chenille here was able to tell me in considerable detail how everyone present had been dressed, and Auk and Spider appeared to be the only possibilities."

Eyeing Spider, Oreb whistled.

"There were a number of sibyls present. All wore habits, and could be dismissed at once. So could Patera Incus and the body of Patera Jerboa—both were robed in black, as I am. No one could mistake a man for Chenille, and so on. If an error had been made, the intended victim was clearly Auk or Spider."

Auk said, "I don't think he was shooting at me."

"Neither do I," Silk told him. "You were near the altar, and thus somewhat nearer the killer. Furthermore, you were in a relatively well lit area. Spider and Eland were in a chapel behind the sanctuary, a more distant area as well as a more dimly lit one. I would guess that the killer had been given a verbal discription of Spider, and had been told that he was being guarded by soldiers."

Silk turned back to Spider. "Were you and Eland awake when he was shot?"

Spider nodded.

"Were you standing up?"

Spider shook his head. "We were sittin' on the floor. That soldier wouldn't let us get up unless we had a reason."

"There you have it." Silk shrugged. "At least, you have as much as I do. Sitting would tend to conceal the difference in size. Slate was guarding both of you, and from what I've heard, neither of you had been given an opportunity to wash and change clothes, as General Mint and Patera Remora did. In the dim light of the chapel, the killer may not have seen you at all. Or he may simply have felt that Eland corresponded more closely to the description he had been given.

"The question then became, who would want to kill Spider? Plausibly, the Ayuntamiento or the Trivigauntis. The first because he knows a great deal about its espionage and counterespionage activities, and about the tunnels under the city, information that he might pass on to Generalissimo Oosik, to General Mint, or to me."

"I'd know about it. I'd have ordered it." Potto giggled. "I didn't."

Silk nodded. "And you could easily have found an assassin who knows Spider by sight, I would think. The Trivigauntis are our allies—but they are Spider's enemies, and he is said to know a great deal about their spies in Viron." He fell silent.

Maytera Mint said, "You can't be sure this is true."

"No, I can't; but I believe it very well may be. We stole a prisoner from Generalissimo Siyuf. Is it absurd to suppose that she might try to kill one we had? Since that may have been the case, it would be manifestly unjust to limit Spider's activities with regard to Siyuf and her horde."

"They went after me, so I can go after them," Spider said.

"Exactly."

Hyacinth touched Silk's arm. "I don't understand. Are we for them or against them?"

Maytera Mint was staring at Silk. "I feel this is almost ancient history, but before all this started—before poor Maytera Rose passed on, I felt that I understood you, just as I felt I understood myself. In the past ten days or so you've become somebody else, somebody I don't understand at all, and so have I. You're married now, I witnessed the ceremony, and I'm thinking about marrying too."

A change in her expression told Silk that Bison's hand had found hers.

After a moment of silence she added, "You've lost your faith, or most of it, I think. What's happened to us?"

Potto laughed loudly.

Quetzal, seated between Oosik and Loris at the other end of the table, murmured, "Circumstances have changed, Maytera. That's all, or nearly all. There is an essential core at the center of each man and woman that remains unaltered no matter how life's externals may be transformed or recombined. But it's smaller than we think."

Silk nodded his agreement.

"If I—ah—permitted." Remora pushed back the errant lock of lank, black hair. "The General and I were companions in, um, adversity. The—ah—spirit. The inalterable core, as His Cognizance has, um, finely. The spirit that survives even death. It grows when trod upon, like the dandelion. I have learned it, eh? So may you, if you—um—reflect."

He stared down at his long, bony hands. "Wouldn't have killed Spider, hey? In those tunnels? Would've, er, failed. But I wish now I had tried, or very nearly. And here, eh? No longer coadjutor. Got my own manteion, hey? After all these years. Moved in today."

He spoke to Silk. "I, er, necessary that I talk to you about it, eh, Caldé? Sun Street. Accounts and so on. When we're, um, we've adjourned."

Silk managed to say, "Gladly, Patera."

"Stripped of, er, power. That's the expression. Smaller, outside, growing, inside. I—ah—feel it." He held up the gammadion he wore; it was of plain iron.

As much to cover his embarrassment as her own, Maytera Mint asked Silk, "You said everything Siyuf's done since her horde arrived could be defended, and she's our ally, and yet you're letting Spider go? Free to attack her and the rest of the Trivigauntis in any way Potto chooses?"

Potto rocked with merriment. "Be her again, Silk, and you can shoot yourself."

He shook his head. "I'm not being asked to defend Siyuf's actions now, but my own. I have changed, I suppose, General, as you say; but I don't think I've changed as much as you may imagine. The faith I had, I had learned as one learns other lessons—from reading and lectures and my mother's example and conversation. I'm in the process, I believe, of replacing it with new faith gained from experience—from circumstances, as His Eminence says. You have to wreck the old structure, or so it seems to me, before you can build the new one; otherwise, it's always getting in the way."

He held out his hand to Hyacinth, who took it.

"We're married, as you say. I don't believe my mother ever was. Did I tell you that?"

Maytera Mint shook her head.

"I told Maytera Marble, I'm sure. I know now, or think I know, how—how I came to be, as a result of something that happened to me in the tunnels, or at least underground. You don't understand me, I know."

"Certainly I do! You don't have to talk about that, Caldé, or anything. But I certainly wasn't asking about that."

Silk shook his head. "You don't, you merely suppose you do. Councillor Potto, here's a mystery for you. Can you solve it? I've lied about it once already tonight, I warn you; and I'll lie again if I must."

Maytera Mint objected, "You don't tell lies, Patera."

Silk shook his head. "We all do when we must. When we're asked about something we heard in shriving, for example. We say we don't know. This is something I have to lie about, at least until it no longer matters, simply because everyone would think I lied if I told the truth."

Maytera Marble's voice surprised him. "Not I, Patera."

He turned in his chair to look at her.

"Chenille brought in tea and cookies, the ones she and Nettle baked, and she never came back. Horn seems to have disappeared, too. I thought something might be wrong."

"A great many things are, Moly," Silk told her, "but we're trying to set a few right. Do you remember what I told you about my enlightenment? I saw Patera Pike praying, praying so very hard year after year for help for his manteion, remember?"

She nodded.

"Until the Outsider spoke in his heart, telling him his prayer was granted. When I had seen that, I waited, waited full of expectation, to see what help would be sent to him."

Maytera Marble nodded. "I remember, Patera."

"It arrived, and it was me. That was all it was. Me. Laugh, Councillor."

Potto did not oblige.

"But for a moment, ever so briefly, I saw myself as Patera Pike had seen me then. It was a humbling experience. Better, it was a salutary one. I'm emboldened by the memory now, when I find myself having to reckon with councillors and generalissimos, people whose company is alien to me, and whose opposition I find terrifying."

Maytera Marble nodded, "As they find yours, Patera."

"I doubt it." Shaking his head, Silk addressed Loris. "We're prepared to offer you a very good bargain, Councillor—an exceptional one. Spider has promised he'll confine himself to counterespionage as regards our forces if we will release him. We ask no oath on the Writings, no ceremony of that kind; a man's word is good or it isn't, and General Mint has indicated that his is. In exchange, we ask only your present self. I emphasize *present*—the Councillor Loris here with us. You can divert your consciousness to another such body as soon as we're through conferring, and I assume that you will; it won't be a violation of our bargain. Do you agree to the exchange?"

"No," Loris said. "I have no second body available."

Potto exclaimed, "I will!"

"I'm afraid not, Councillor. When you have a prisoner of similar importance, an exchange can be effected. Until then, Spider must remain with us. Councillor Loris, are you certain you won't reconsider?"

Loris shook his head—then stared at Remora, who was seated to Potto's right.

Quetzal murmured, "He has these fits occasionally, poor fellow. I think Patera Caldé witnessed one last week."

"I did, shortly before my bride and I were reunited at Ermine's." Longing to embrace her, Silk tore his gaze from Hyacinth's.

"They're coming, Silk." Remora announced in a flattened voice. "A colonel and a hundred cavalry troopers."

Oreb whistled sharply.

"Thank you. Auk, I'm afraid this means we have very little time. You and Sciathan must leave at once by a side door. Your followers are meeting at the Cock? Warn them that Trivigaunti patrols may search for them. Chenille had better go with you; otherwise they're liable to take her to get you."

Loris stood. "We'd better leave, too."

"Not with us," Auk snapped. "Out the front, if you're going. C'mon, Upstairs. C'mon, Jugs."

Potto rose, giggling. "He doesn't share Silk's love for you, Cousin Loris."

Silk motioned for both to sit again. "You have come under a flag of truce. They'll respect that, surely."

"So did we," Maytera Mint told him.

He ignored it. "You and Colonel Bison are affronted now because Generalissimo Siyuf wished to confiscate the weapons you gave your troopers. If she were here, she might explain that she acted in support of our government, the one opposed to the Ayuntamiento that Echidna ordered you to establish and that you have established. She probably feels sure, as General Saba and Chenille did Thelxday night, that once freed of the restraint of discipline your troopers will use their weapons to overturn it. Remember that, when we talk to these Trivigauntis."

Silk addressed Oosik. "You, Generalissimo, are piqued because Generalissimo Siyuf bypassed you and Skate, issuing orders to the commanders of the brigades."

Oosik nodded, his face grim.

"Bear in mind that when she tried to collect those weapons she was doing what you would have, had you not been restrained by my orders; and that she's shown clearly that she thinks it useless to try to suborn your loyalty."

"I—er, um?" Remora gaped at Quetzal's vacated chair.

"His Cognizance has left us," Silk explained. "I suppose he went with Auk. You dozed off for a moment, I believe.

"Councillor Loris, Councillor Potto, you said you'd come to demand my surrender, with new terms. Let's not trouble about the terms now. Explain briefly, if you will, how you know that we and our allies will be defeated."

Loris nodded. "Briefly, as you ask. Siyuf's been sending patrols into the countryside to forage for food. They take whatever our people have and leave promissory notes in which our people have no confidence. Notes that are almost certainly valueless, in fact. Our farmers have begun hiding what food they have and organizing bands to resist—"

Oosik interrupted him. "You gave your permission, Caldé, at the parade. I was thunderstruck."

Hyacinth said, "You think you're terribly clever, don't you, Oosie. What would you have done?"

Oosik started to speak, but thought better of it.

"He would have told Generalissimo Siyuf that she'd have to buy what our farmers brought her—or so I imagine." Silk shrugged. "They wouldn't have brought enough, or nearly enough, and they wouldn't have accepted promises to pay later. Soon she would have had to send out patrols, as she's doing now, or shut her eyes to the fact that unit commanders were foraging for themselves. In either case, we would have had to stop them, or anyway we would have had to try. Within a short time we'd have been fighting Trivigauntis in the streets. I hoped to prevent that, or at least postpone it; but I'm afraid that I gained very little time for us, and it may be that I gained none at all."

"We could have sent out foraging parties of our own," Bison suggested.

Maytera Mint shook her head. "Then the farmers would have hated us instead of them. If they must hate somebody, it's far better that they hate Siyuf and her Trivigauntis."

"The point," Loris interposed, "is that they're beginning to resist. You've helped them, and we're helping them more."

Potto grinned at Silk. "Cementing their loyalty to us, you see. We're the government of the good old days, coming up out of the ground with armloads of slug guns, and giving them away." He tittered. "We get food aplenty for our bios. It's mostly chems with us down below, and they don't need it."

"We estimate that fifteen thousand of General Mint's fifty thousand odd were countryfolk," Loris continued. "They're armed now, thanks to you. We've armed another four thousand thus far, and we continue to distribute arms. This sibyl—"

"I'm a laywoman again," Maytera Marble told him.

"This officious laywoman once boasted that though others might be tempted to lie, her figures were accurate. So are mine. Inside of three months, Siyuf will be unable to feed her troops, to say nothing of her horses, mules, and camels. Having no alternative, she'll return to Trivigaunte. By then half the city will have abandoned your rebellion. We came to inform you of that, and demand that you restore our personal accounts."

"And keep your hands off the Fisc," Potto subjoined.

"That will be guaranteed by their surrender." Loris looked around the table, a councillor so rich in wisdom and experience that even Maytera Mint was inclined to accept everything that he said. "Would you care to hear our terms?"

"No." Silk paused, listening to the sounds of hurrying feet in the foyer. "We haven't time. I accept. We surrender.

We can discuss terms when we have more leisure. That was why I hoped you'd remain, Councillor. It would have facilitated—"

At that moment I burst into the room. "They're coming, Caldé, like you said. A couple of hundred, some on horses."

"Thank you, Horn." Silk smiled sadly. "They'll knock, I believe—at least I hope they will. If they do, delay them as long as you can, please."

Potto was on his feet again. "We accept your surrender. Let's go, Cousin!"

Maytera Marble stepped into their path. "Let me remind you of what I told you at my son's. Caldé Silk's surrender is valid and binds everyone. Patera Silk's means nothing at all. Do you accept him as Caldé? For life?"

The door to the kitchen flew open then, and Hossaan strode in with a needler in each hand; behind him came a dozen women brandishing slug guns. "That life may be short," he told Silk. "It will be, unless you get your hands up. The rest of you, too."

One by one Hyacinth, Silk, Remora, Potto, Spider, and Horn complied, Maytera Marble and Bison raising their hands last, and together. Silk said, "You realize, I hope, that this is fundamentally a misunderstanding, a falling out among friends. It can be smoothed over, and soon will be."

"Spread out," Hossaan told the women who had entered with him. "Each cover a prisoner." He smiled at Silk, a smile that did not reach his hooded eyes. "I hope you're right, Caldé. On the personal level, I like you and your wife. I'm carrying out Colonel Abanja's—"

The crack of a needler cut him off. Ragged fire from the slug guns ended in a choking cloud of plaster dust and an ear-splitting roar as most of the west wall fell, severed from its foundations by the azoth Silk had received from Doctor Crane and given to Maytera Mint.

Chapter 14

THE BEST THIEVES IN THE WHORL

"Patera?" Horn inquired softly. "Caldé?"

Silk sat up. "What is it?"

"Nettle's asleep. Just about everybody is, but I knew you weren't. I could see your eyes."

Silk nodded, the motion almost invisible in the darkness of the freezing tent. "You're right, I wasn't; and you're afraid, as we all are, and want reassurance. I'll reassure you as much as I can, though that isn't very much."

"I have some questions, too."

Silk smiled, his teeth flashing in the gloom. "So do I, but you can't answer mine. I may be able to answer a few of yours. I'll try."

Nettle whispered, "I'm not asleep. Horn thought I was, but I was pretending so he'd sleep." Horn took her hand as she said, "I've got a question too."

"Reassurance first," Silk told them. "You may need it more than you realize. It's quite unlikely that Generalissimo Siyuf will have you executed or even imprisoned. Hossaan—that's Willet's real name, he's a Trivigaunti—knows that you and

Horn were at the palace to help Moly. Besides, you're hardly more than children. Siyuf's a harsh woman, but not a cruel one from what I've seen; she wouldn't command the loyalty she does if she were. I can only guess, but I believe that you and Horn will be questioned and released."

Horn asked, "Is there anything you don't want us to tell?"

"No, tell them everything. Nothing you can say can harm Hyacinth or Moly or me. Or Patera Remora and Patera Incus, or even Spider. Nor can anything you say harm you. The better they understand your place in all this, the more likely it is that you'll be set free once they've learned all they can from you—or so it seems to me."

In a whisper, Nettle asked, "Does this mean we've failed, Patera?"

"Of course not. I'm not sure what you're asking about—whether you're afraid we've failed as human beings—"

"Failed the gods."

"No." There was resolution in Silk's voice. "How old are you?"

"Fifteen."

"I'm eight years older. It seems an enormous separation to me, as no doubt it does to you. How does it appear to His Cognizance, do you think?"

Horn said, "Like nothing. His Cognizance was an old, old man when we were born."

"When I was, too. Consider then how young we must appear to Pas, who built the whorl—or to the Outsider, who shaped our forebears from the mud of the Short-Sun Whorl." Silk fell silent, listening to the slow pacing of the sentries outside, and Remora's soft snores.

"Since the Outsider began us, let us begin with him. I've never seen him, except in a dream, and even then I couldn't see his face clearly; but he's seen me from the beginning—from before my own beginning in fact. He knows me far better than I know myself, and he chose me to perform a small task for him. I was to save our manteion from Blood.

"Blood is dead. Musk, who was the owner of record and who I once considered worse than Blood, is dead too. Patera

Remora over there is the new augur on Sun Street—I believe that may be the Outsider's way of telling me the task is done. You both helped do it, and I'm sure he's grateful, as I am."

Horn muttered, "We didn't do anything, Patera."

"Of course you did—but listen. I may be wrong, wrong about having saved our manteion, and wrong about the sign. I may fail after all; I can't be sure. But I can be sure of this— he will forgive me if I fail, and he would surely forgive you. I know him more than well enough to be certain of that."

Nettle said, "I was mostly thinking about Echidna. I saw her, when she talked to Maytera Mint? I was there."

"So was I. Echidna told her to destroy the Alambrera. It has been destroyed, and the convicts have been freed. I freed them."

"Yes, but—"

"Echidna also ordered the destruction of the Ayuntamiento. It is still in existence, if you like, but consider: Lemur, who headed it so long, is dead; so is Loris, who succeeded him."

"Maytera says that wasn't really him," Nettle objected. "She says Maytera Mint said Potto just works the councillors that we see, like you'd work a puppet."

Silk chuckled, a small, cheerful sound in the darkness. "Like the wooden man that Horn had when you were small."

"Yes, Patera."

"That's true, I'm sure; and I'm equally sure that at one time it was true of all five councillors. Before Doctor Crane killed Lemur, however, we learned that the real Lemur had died some time before—years before, probably. The manipulated body had become Lemur, the only Lemur in existence, though it thought itself still manipulated by the corpse in Lemur's bed. Do you follow this, Horn? Nettle?"

Nettle said, "I think so, Patera."

"When I had time to think about that, which wasn't until Doctor Crane and I had been pulled out of the water, I wondered about the other councillors. If Councillor Loris had remained with us as I asked, and if he had found it impossible to divert his consciousness to another chem, I would have known—and we would have held the presiding officer of the

Ayuntamiento. As it was, I would guess that Loris himself knew before he came to treat with us; if he hadn't, he wouldn't have snatched up the needler Generalissimo Oosik offered to Councillor Potto and begun firing. He understood Generalissimo Siyuf well enough to realize that she would have him executed on some pretense, and knew he had his life to lose like any other man. In the event, he lost it sooner; but he had the satisfaction of a combatant's death, which may have meant something to him."

"One of those women shot him?"

Maytera Marble's voice reached them out of the darkness, spectrally reminiscent of old Maytera Rose's. "Yes. I watched it. I saw him fall."

Silk told her, "I've been expecting you to join us, Moly. I would have invited you, but I wasn't sure where you were, and it wouldn't do to go stumbling around waking up people."

"Certainly not, Patera."

Nettle said, "I'm glad you're here, Maytera. I want to ask something. Everybody says we run things in Trivigaunte. The Rani's a woman and so's Generalissimo Siyuf. I saw her. So who were the women that Willet let in, the ones that shot Councillor Loris? Why did they take orders from him?"

Maytera Marble sniffed. "You've a great deal to learn, Nettle. Doesn't Horn do what you tell him, sometimes, even when he doesn't want to?"

"I don't believe I can improve on that," Silk said, "but I'll enlarge upon it a trifle. They are spies, of course—agents of the Rani's, as Hossaan himself is. I'm reasonably sure that they're Vironese as well. Hossaan has told me that he and Doctor Crane were the only Trivigauntis in the ring they built up here, and I believe he was telling the truth."

Horn began another question, but Silk stopped him. "I ought to tell you that before I went into the tunnels by the lake I saw someone ahead of me. Later I saw footprints, and still later I came across the body of someone who Hammerstone told me had been a woman."

"Don't even talk about that place," Nettle said, "every time I hear about it, it sounds so awful."

"It is. But if I may talk about the dead woman, I would imagine she traveled here from Trivigaunte from time to time, probably in the guise of a trader. Chenille carried messages to a woman in the market, and the dead woman I found may well have been the same person. Hossaan wouldn't have counted her as a part of Doctor Crane's ring, since she wasn't subject to Doctor Crane's orders. I'd imagine she stayed here no more than a few weeks—a month at most—when she came."

"Does anybody know about him?" Nettle inquired. "About Hammerstone? Is he, you know, all right?"

Maytera Marble murmured, "You want to know if I'm a widow so soon. I don't know, but I doubt it. He was away searching for materials when Willet and his women came in, but he might have saved us all if he'd been there. He would certainly have saved Patera Incus and me, and the daughter we had begun to build, if he could."

Horn said, "There were two hundred Trivigauntis coming, Maytera. Patera had me out in the street watching for them. They would've killed Hammerstone, unless he gave up."

"We'll never know." Maytera Marble seated herself beside Nettle.

"He may rescue you still," Silk told Maytera Marble. "He may well rescue us all. From what I've seen of him, he will surely try, and that worries me—but I'd like to return to Nettle's question.

"Because women have more power than men in Trivigaunte, Nettle, most people would expect that most or all of the Rani's agents would be women—that's as good a reason for employing men as I can think of. But it would be natural for male agents from Trivigaunte to recruit women here. Women would be more sympathetic to their point of view— Hyacinth said something like that when we first met—and men from Trivigaunte would naturally seek out courageous, assertive women like the ones among whom they had lived at home.

"We all tend to generalize too much, I'm afraid. If most augurs are pious and naïve, for example, we imagine that every augur is, though if we were to reflect we would see immediately that it cannot be true. In the same way, there are bound to be bold men in Trivigaunte and brave and forceful women here—in fact there is a fine example of the latter sitting with us now. As for those women following Hossaan's instructions, it really doesn't matter if they were Vironese or Trivigauntis. If they wouldn't obey, they would have been of no value to Doctor Crane and Hossaan, and would have been eliminated long ago."

"I want to ask about something else, Caldé, but I'm afraid Maytera will be mad at me."

"That's the risk you run, Nettle dear."

Horn said, "Tell me and I will."

"No. If those women could spy and shoot a councillor, I can do this. Caldé, I was listening at the door. Maytera caught me and made me quit, but when she went to work on her child again I came back."

"I'm not angry," Maytera Marble told her, "but you should be angry with yourself. It was wrong, and you knew it."

Silk said, "It hardly matters now."

"Yes, it does. Because I heard something right at the end, and it's why I got up when I heard you talking to Horn. You—you just . . . Gave up. The councillor they shot? Loris? He was talking about giving away slug guns. . . ."

"And I said that we could discuss terms later. That we surrendered."

"Uh-huh."

Horn objected, "We were winning. Everybody said so."

"Horn, he said *they* were, because the farmers would fight the Trivigauntis and they'd have to leave. Then the Caldé said all right we give up, we'll settle the arrangements when we've got more time. Only Maytera said he had to be caldé, because if he wasn't it wouldn't mean anything."

"Patera Silk has never been vindictive, dear."

"I know, Maytera, and I know that word, but I don't know what you mean by it. Didn't you want to kill the councillors, Caldé?"

"Of course not. As far as our insurrection is concerned, what I've always wanted to do is end it. I want peace, and a reunited Viron. Echidna ordered Maytera Mint to destroy the Ayuntamiento and return the city to Scylla. Haven't you ever thought about what that last instruction meant, Nettle?"

"Not enough, I guess."

"Then think now." Silk's fingers groped for his ambion. "Returning to Scylla means returning to our Charter. Scylla wrote it, and no quantity of prayers and sacrifices would be a convincing demonstration of loyalty as long as we violate it. The Charter demands an Ayuntamiento. Did you know that?"

Horn said, "I did, Patera."

"From that, it's clear Echidna does not want us to do away with the institution of the Ayuntamiento. There can be nothing wrong, surely, with a board of advisors elected at three-year intervals, which is what the Ayuntamiento is intended to be—a council of experienced men and women to whom the caldé can turn in time of trouble. Echidna was demanding that the present and quite clearly illegitimate Ayuntamiento be dissolved, a demand entirely in harmony with her implied demand that our government return to the Charter.

"That being the case, the way to peace was clear, as I had seen from the beginning. I would remain as caldé as long as the people wanted it. I could declare the present Ayuntamiento ended, announce an election, and urge everyone to support the surviving members of the previous Ayuntamiento. Those who still favored their cause would vote for them as well, and they would be reelected. Would have been, to be realistic."

"You sound so sad, Caldé." Nettle shivered, snuggling against Horn. "It might happen yet."

"Yes, it may. I was thinking of the time at Blood's when Councillor Loris presented a list of demands to Moly and me."

"Absurd demands," Maytera Marble declared.

"Extreme demands, certainly. He wanted hostages from the Rani, and he would have put Generalissimo Oosik and the other high-ranking officers on trial. I defied him."

"You offered to resign, too," Maytera Marble said. "You were very brave, Patera."

"I was very stupid, very tired, and very frightened. If I hadn't been, I would have realized that the thing to do was to agree, stop the fighting, and go to work on the details. Have you ever talked with the clerks in the Juzgado, Nettle?"

"No, Caldé."

"I have. I made it a point to, because I knew Hyacinth's father was a head clerk; she hates him, yet she will always be his daughter. I located him, and while we were talking about reforming the Fisc he said that the devils are in the details."

Silk chuckled, cheered by the memory. "Later, one of the officers of the Fisc made the same remark; and I recalled what we were taught in the schola—that the malice of devils is such that they destroy even evil people. My teachers didn't really believe in them, as Patera Pike did; but I believe what they said was true, and that what Hyacinth's father and the official from the Fisc said was true as well.

"All right, let the Ayuntamiento accommodate the devils. Peace would mean that nine-tenths of Siyuf's horde could go home. Thousands of innocent women would be spared horrible deaths in the tunnels, we could buy enough food for those who remained here, and the Ayuntamiento's chief weapon would be snatched from its hands—let it give our farmers slug guns, those guns would only make us stronger."

"You were going to win by giving up?"

Silk shook his head. "No one wins by giving up, Nettle, though many fights are not worth winning. I was going to gain what I wanted—peace—by persuading my enemy that he gained by letting me have it, which happened to be the truth. I still hope to do it, though the prospect isn't bright at the moment."

Horn said, "General Mint and Colonel Bison got away. So did Generalissimo Oosik." Nettle added, "The fat councillor did, too, I think. Is there going to be peace now because of what you said?"

"I don't know, but I doubt it." Silk sighed. "It will depend mostly on the Trivigauntis; and as long as they hold us, Generalissimo Oosik and General Mint are liable to regard them as enemies as bad as the Ayuntamiento, if not worse."

Maytera Marble sniffed. "I don't see why they want us."

"His Cognizance is fond of giving short and long answers," Silk told her. "In this case, he'd probably say that the short answer was that Siyuf has a bad conscience. She came to Viron as an ally, ostensibly, but with the secret hope of making it dependent upon Trivigaunte—a servant city."

"Did she actually say that, Patera?"

"Of course not; but she was quick to believe that we were plotting against her, and people who always suspect they're being cheated are generally trying to cheat. When General Mint and Patera Remora tried to treat with the Ayuntamiento, Siyuf feared we'd come to an agreement unfavorable to Trivigaunte. By taking our Juzgado, she showed clearly that she intended to govern Viron. Today—though that's yesterday now, I suppose—I made the mistake of telling Councillor Loris that he and Potto could confer in person with us, since that was what they wanted. I thought it was safe, because Hossaan would report everything we said to Colonel Abanja, and I was resolved to say nothing that Siyuf could object to."

"I don't think you did, Caldé, except there at the end."

"Thank you. There at the end it no longer mattered. Horn and Mucor had told me the Trivigauntis were on their way, and I knew I'd overplayed my hand just by letting the councillors into the Caldé's Palace. Unfortunately, Hossaan overplayed his as well. If he and his spies had simply kept us from leaving until the troopers arrived, something might have been gained. I doubt it, but it might have been. As things are, a great deal has been lost—peace first of all. Peace is always a great deal, but now it's more urgent than ever, because of Pas's threat."

Silk wiped his eyes. "Having saved our manteion, I tried to save Viron and the whorl, Nettle; and now all I can do is sit here crying."

"That's a awfully big job for just one man, Caldé, saving the whorl. Do you really think Pas is going to destroy us?"

As if he had not heard her, Silk said, "We were talking about those who escaped, and no one mentioned Oreb. Did he get out? Did anyone see him?"

A horse voice croaked, "Bird here!"

"Oreb! I should've known. Come down here."

Wings beat in the darkness, and Oreb landed with a thump.

"His Cognizance reminded me once that there are people who love birds so much they cage them, and others who love them so much they free them. Then he said that Echidna and the Seven were people of the first kind, and Pas a person of the second kind. When I bought Oreb, he was in a cage; and when I freed him I smashed that cage—never thinking that it might have seemed a place of refuge to him."

Horn said, "I never thought of the whorl being a cage."

"I never had either, until the Outsider showed me what lies outside it."

"Maybe Auk and Chenille can steal General Saba's airship, Caldé, and take Sciathan back to Mainframe like he wants."

"Good man," Oreb informed them. "Man fly."

"He is, Oreb, in both senses, I believe. So is Auk, and even Chenille is a very competent person in her way. But to tell you the truth I have no confidence in them at all when it comes to this—less than I would have in Potto and Spider, if anything. Frankly, I've never imagined that there was any way to get Auk and his followers to Mainframe other than getting General Saba and her crew to fly them there.

"That was another reason for wanting peace, and in fact it was the most pressing one—as long as there was war, Siyuf would want to keep the airship here. It couldn't be used in the tunnels, of course, but eventually the Ayuntamiento would have to send troops to the surface if it hoped to win, and the airship would be a terrible adversary.

"With the war ended, it might—I say might—have been possible to persuade her to do what we wanted. Now we'll have to wait for it to end, I'm afraid, or at least for Pas to do whatever he plans to do first to drive humanity out. I can think of a dozen possibilities, none pleasant."

Silk awaited another question, but even Oreb was silent. At length he said, "Now let's sleep if we can. We'll have a trying day tomorrow, I'm afraid."

"Ah—Caldé?" Remora's nasal voice floated out of the darkness.

"Yes, Patera. I'm sorry we woke you. We tried to keep our voices down."

"I have listened with great, um, edification. Sorry I did not wake sooner, eh? But there is one, um, point. Eland, eh? I knew him. You said—ah—"

"I said I had a vague description of his killer. Vague from our point of view, anyway. I believe it was Hossaan, whom you may have met as Willet, my driver. I won't tell you at present how I obtained it. Let us sleep, Patera."

"Good girl," Oreb confided.

"Add cot end add word," Tick commented sleepily from his place at Hyacinth's side.

Staring up at the still-distant airship, Silk clenched his teeth, determined equally that the icy wind that whipped his robe would not make them chatter and that the airship would not make him gape, though so immense a flying structure seemed less an achievement than a force of nature. Ever so slowly, it edged its vast, mummy-colored bulk across the gray midday sky, lost at times among low clouds dark with snow, always reappearing nearer the winter-wet meadow where he and his companions waited under guard.

Maytera Mint's grip on his arm tightened, and she uttered a sound like a raindrop falling into a scrub bucket, then another, and another. He turned from his contemplation of the airship to her. "Why are you making that noise, Maytera?"

Hyacinth whispered, "She's crying. Let her alone."

"Wise girl!" Oreb approved.

"You won't be able to take your bird, Caldé." Dismounting and dropping her reins, Saba strode over to them, her porcine face sympathetic and severe. "I'm sorry, but you can't." She indicated Hyacinth with her riding crop. "You had some sort of animal too, girly. Where is it?"

"A c-catachrest," Hyacinth told her through chattering teeth. "I gave him a little of my food this morning and sent him away."

Silk said, "You'll have to leave, Oreb. Fly back to the place where you were caught if you can."

"Good Silk!"

"Good bird too, but you must go. Go back to the Palustrian Marshes, that's where the man in the market said you came from."

"Bird stay," Oreb announced, then squawked and took wing as Saba cut at him with her quirt.

"Sorry, Caldé, I didn't try to hit it. Have a nice breakfast?"

"Baked horse-fodder," Hyacinth told her.

"Horde bread, you mean. We turn little girls like you into troopers with it."

Silk said, "I had assumed that we would be questioned by Generalissimo Siyuf."

Behind him, Incus began, "We are holy *augurs*. You *cannot* simply—" He was jointed by Remora, and Remora by Spider.

"Quiet!" Saba snapped. "I'll have the lot of you flogged. By Sphigx, I'll flog you myself!" She counted them, her lips twitching. "Eight, that's right."

She raised her voice. "You're going up in my airship. The caldé said he'd like to see it, and he's going to. So are the rest of you, as soon as they drop the *'ishsh*. We're taking you home so the Rani and her ministers can have a look at you, but anybody who gives us trouble might not get there. She might sort of fall off first. Understand? If you—if . . ."

Seeing Saba's eyes sink and grow dull, Silk took his arm from Hyacinth's shoulders. "Can you and I walk a step or two, General? I'd like a word with you in private."

Saba's head nodded like a marionette's. "I've been in here all morning, Silk. She thinks you won't come back."

"I see." He drew Saba aside. "But she isn't going to kill us, or she wouldn't have threatened to. I'm not worried about myself, Mucor; the Outsider will take care of me in one way or another. I'm worried about Hyacinth, and about you."

"Grandmother will take care of her, Silk."

"At the moment, Hyacinth's taking care of her; but no

doubt you're right. With your grandmother gone, however, there's no one to take care of you."

Saba laughed, a mirthless noise that made Silk shudder even as he worried that the watching troopers had heard it. "I'm going with you, Silk, way up in the air. The man who broke his wings is there already."

"You can't! Can't you understand? You absolutely cannot!" Assistant Day Manager Feist trotted at Sand's side, snapping and yelping.

"It's right up there, Sarge." Hammerstone waved toward the sentries before Siyuf's door. "See the twist troopers? Got to be it." The "Twist troopers" in question were moving the safety catches of their slug guns to the FIRE position.

Ignoring them, Sand grasped the front of Feist's tunic and separated his highly polished shoes from Ermine's three-finger-thick stair runner. "You say we can't go barging in, right?"

Feist gasped and choked.

"Fine, we've got it. So you're going first. You've got to talk your way past those girls and get inside."

Sand paused at the top of the stair, displaying Feist to the sentries while covering them with his slug gun, gripped in one hand like a needler. "When you get in, tell the Generalissimo we got big news to trade real cheap, and if—"

The intricately-carved sandalwood door of the Lyrichord Room had opened; a tall and strikingly handsome brunette in a diaphanous gown peered out. "Hi. You want to see Generalissimo Siyuf?"

"You got it, Plutonium." Sand strode toward the door, as an afterthought tossing Feist over the ornate railing. "You tell her the First Squad, First Platoon, Company 'S,' Army of Viron's here. You got all that?"

The handsome young woman nodded. "Close enough, Soldier. I'm Violet."

"Sergeant Sand, pleased. You tell her we won't take much of her time and we aren't asking much, and she'll be shaggy glad she talked to us."

"Wait a minute, she's getting dressed." The door closed.

"What do you think?" Slate asked Hammerstone. "She goin' to see us?"

"One way or the other," Hammerstone told him; almost too swiftly for the eye to follow, his hands shot out, grasped the barrels of the sentries' slug guns, and crushed them.

At length, when repeated knockings had produced no result, Maytera Marble's friend Scleroderma employed the butt of her new needler to pound the rearmost door of the Caldé's Palace. A second floor window flew open with a bang, and a cracked male voice called, "Who's there? Visitor? Want to see the Caldé? So do I!"

"I'm here to see Moly," Scleroderma announced firmly. "I'm going to. Is she all right?"

"Mollie? Mollie? Good name! Fish name! Relative of mine? Don't know her! Wait."

The window slammed down. Scleroderma dropped her needler into the pocket of her winter coat, drawing the coat so tightly about her that for a moment it appeared buttonable.

The door flew open. "Come in! Come in! Cold out there! In here, too! Wall's down! Terrible! No Mollie. You mean Mucor? She's here, skinny girl! Know her?"

"I certainly do, she's Moly's granddaughter. Maybe—"

"Won't talk," the lean old man who had opened the door declared. "Asked about Mollie. She talk to you? Not to me! Upstairs! Want to see her? Maybe she will!"

Scleroderma, whose weight gave her a pronounced aversion to stairs, shook her head emphatically as she pushed the door shut behind her. "She'll catch her death up there, the poor starved little thing. You bring her down here right away." Waddling after him through the scullery and into the kitchen, she called to the old man's fast-vanishing back, "I'll build a fire in the stove and start her dinner."

High above the Trivigaunti airship, Oreb eyed the cage-like enclosure swinging below it. The question, as Oreb saw it, was not whether he should rejoin Silk, but when. It might be best to wait until Silk was alone. It might also be best to find something to eat first. There was always food at the big house on the hill, but Oreb had a score to settle.

Bright black eyes sharper than most telescopes examined the good girl pressing herself against Silk without result, then scanned the orderly rows of pointed houses. The target sighted, Oreb began a wingover that quickly became a dive.

"You," Pterotrooper Nizam told her new pet, "are going to have to be as quiet as a mouse in this barracks bag."

"Ess, laddie."

"As quiet as *two* mice. As soon as we get aboard—"

A red-and-black projectile shot between them with a rush of wind and a hoarse cry. The new pet bared small teeth and claws in fury. "Add, add word! Laddie, done by scarred."

Sand's soldiers filled the Lyrichord Room's luxurious sellaria with polite clankings as Siyuf returned his salute. "I have hear of you, Sergeant. Why do you come?"

"You got a couple prisoners—" he began.

"More than this."

"Two I'm talking about. This's Corporal Hammerstone."

Hammerstone stiffened to attention.

"He's married, only you got his wife and his best buddy. We want 'em back, and what we got to tell you's worth ten of 'em. So here's what I say. We tell you, and we leave it up to you, sir. If you don't think it's worth it, say so and we'll clear off. If you do, give 'em back. What do you say?"

Siyuf clapped her hands; when the monitor appeared in her glass she said, "Get Colonel Abanja.

"To begin, Sergeant, I do not know that I hold the wife or the friend of this soldier. Violet my darling, bring for me the list that was last night from Colonel Abanja."

Violet grinned and winked at Hammerstone. "Sure thing."

"The wife, the friend, they are soldiers also?"

Hammerstone said, "No, sir. My wife's a civilian. Her name's Moly. She's no bigger'n you, sir, maybe smaller. My friend's a bio, a augur, His Eminence Patera Incus. People think he's the coadjutor. Really he's the Prolocutor, only people don't know yet."

The monitor's face gained color, reshaping itself to become that of Siyuf's intelligence officer.

"There is here too much of warlockery, Colonel. You see here soldiers, marvels we should have in museums but here fight us, and for us also. They are come to offer a bargain. Am I not a woman of honor?"

Violet nodded enthusiastically and Abanja said, "You are indeed, Generalissimo."

"Just so. I do not cheat, not even these soldiers. So I must know. Do we have the holy man Incus? Violet, my darling, read the names. How many now, Colonel?"

"Eighty-two, sir. There were some other holy men besides the caldé, and I suppose this might be one of them." Abanja leafed through papers below the field of her glass.

Leaning over Violet's shoulder, Hammerstone pointed with a finger thrice the size of hers.

"I don't really read so good," she whispered. "What's that second word? It can't— Sweetheart, there's a Chenille in here. Is that the Chen we know?"

Abanja looked up. "The paramour of the Vironese who was plotting to steal our airship, sir. She was seated across the table from me at that dinner at the caldé's residence."

Hammerstone said, "It says, 'Maytera Marble a holy woman,' on here, sir. That's my wife, Moly. Patera's here, too. You got them all right."

"Then you must give me your information," Siyuf told Sand. "If it is worth their freedom, I will free them as soon as I can. I do not say at once. At once may not be possible. But as soon as is possible. You do not betray your city when you do this?"

Sand shook his head. "Help it, is what we figure. See, if you're smart you'll let the caldé go when we tell you. And with us, it's him. He's the top of the chain of command, and we know you got him."

"Sir, the airship. . . ." Abanja's face was agitated.

Siyuf motioned her to silence. "We speak of that later, Colonel. First I must learn what this soldier knows."

She turned back to Sand. "I will release your caldé, you say. I do not say this. With regard to Caldé Silk, I give no promise. You do not bargain for him. I notice this."

"Because we know you wouldn't, sir. You'd say you were going to keep him, and dismissed. But you'll let him go if you're smart. It'll be better for us and better for you, too. You're going to, is what we think. Only we want to see to it Hammerstone's wife and his buddy get loose too."

Sand hesitated, glancing at Abanja's face in the glass, then back to Siyuf. "The insurrection's over. That's what we're here to tell you, sir. Give us your word on Moly and Patera What'shisname—"

"Incus," Hammerstone prompted.

"And Patera Incus, and we'll give you the details. Have we got it?"

"I will release both as soon as I am able. Have I not said? Bring to me the image of the sole great goddess, and I swear on it. There is not one here, I think."

"Your word's good enough for us, sir." Sand glanced at Hammerstone, who nodded.

"All right. You want me to tell you, or you want to ask questions, sir?"

"First I ask one question. Then you tell, and after I ask more if I wish. When I am satisfied, I give the order, and if there is a place to which you wish them brought, we will do it. But not more than a day's travel."

Hammerstone said, "The Caldé's Palace. That's where me and Moly have been living." Shale asked, "You got any problem with that, sir?"

"No. This is within reason. My question. You say I will let go your caldé, the head of your government. I do not think so, so I am curious. Why do you say this?"

" 'Cause out of all the people you got to deal with here, he's the one that likes you the most," Hammerstone told her. "I know him pretty well. Me and Sarge picked him up one time on patrol, and I shot the bull with him before he gave me the slip. Then too, I been living in his palace like I said, and I heard a lot from Moly."

"I helped Councillor Potto interrogate him the next time we got him," Sand said, "so I know him pretty well too. He's big for peace. He was trying to stop the insurrection before you got here."

For a second or more, Siyuf studied Sand as if she hoped to find a clue to his thoughts in his blank metal face. "You have kill this man Potto. After, I suppose? This Mint tells. But you have not kill him well. He is now back."

"I been dead too," Sand told her, and Violet gasped. "I could give you the scoop on that, but it'd take a while."

"Rather I would hear of the end of the insurrection. This you proposed."

"Good here. Last night there was a confab at the Caldé's place. None of us were there, but we heard from General Mint. Your people tried to grab everybody, only four made it out, and Councillor Loris is *K*. The ones that gave you the slip was her and Colonel Bison, and the Generalissimo and Councillor Potto."

"I know of this." Siyuf delivered a withering glance to Abanja's image in the glass.

Schist said, "Tell her about surrendering, Sarge. That's pretty important."

"Yeah, he did. The caldé did. Maybe you don't know that, sir. It was before your people came in."

Siyuf nodded. "Colonel Abanja have report this. She has had an informant in your caldé's household, a most praiseworthy accomplishment."

Abanja said, "Thank you, Generalissimo."

"So the four that got clear put their heads together, see? Our generalissimo, he'd come in a Guard floater, and they piled in and took off, Councillor Potto too. Naturally he said, well, your caldé's called quits so we're in charge again. Councillor Loris's dead so I'm the new presiding officer. You're working for me, and if you do what I say maybe I won't shoot you."

Schist interjected, "He figured they all had it coming, I

guess. What we figure is, not just them. He'll probably stop
Sarge's works real good."

Violet said, *"Ah!"* and Siyuf laughed. "Shadeup, after so
long a night. Potto is not friend to this soldier who not one
month past shoot him. Potto has the . . . What is this word?"

"He'll have it in for him."

Sand nodded. "But he can't hand out anything that I can't
take. I been dead already, just like I said. You want to talk
about me, or you want to hear the rest?"

Hammerstone said, "They went around quite a bit, to hear
Colonel Bison tell it. Only there was one thing they didn't
have any trouble with. Tell 'em, Sarge."

"You foreigners, sir." Sand leveled his huge forefinger at
Siyuf. "Councillor Potto's mean as a bad wrench, and he
hates you worse'n dirt in his pump. General Mint, she hates
Councillor Potto, but you're number two on her list."

"She is the central, to be sure. The sole woman." Siyuf
looked thoughtful. "Colonel, what is it you say of this?"

In the glass, Abanja's image shrugged. "It doesn't run
counter to any information I have, Generalissimo."

"You have leave off two, Sergeant. What of those?"

"I didn't leave 'em out, sir," Sand protested, "I hadn't got
to 'em yet. Colonel Bison's General Mint's man. If she says
spit oil, he says how far?"

"I grasp this. Proceed."

"We haven't seen Generalissimo Oosik, but Corporal Slate
here chewed things over with his driver this morning, the one
that brought him and got them clear. Tell her, Slate."

"He brought a slug gun to the meetin', sir," Slate began.
"That's what his driver says, 'n he says he don't usually have
nothin' but a needler 'n his sword, see? So who was that for?
Then when they was talkin' in back—you know how them
armed floaters are laid out, sir? There's no wall or nothin' between the seats up front and the back, so he tuned in. General
Mint said somethin' about how Councillor Loris was the head
of the Ayuntamiento, and it was Generalissimo Oosik that said
he was dead. He thinks maybe Generalissimo Oosik did it
himself, he seemed so happy about it."

Sand looked from Violet to Abanja, then at Siyuf. "Only Councillor Potto's got it in for him, and he knows it. He was like a brigadier back before the insurrection, so he had to be one of the Ayuntamiento's floor bolts. But when Caldé Silk came along, he went over right away and got made head of the whole host of Viron. He knows Councillor Potto, so he's got to know how pissed off he is about that."

Siyuf, who had been slouching in her chair, straightened up. "You desire me to set free your caldé to save your Viron, so much is plain. I do not care about your Viron."

Violet said, "I do, a little. Besides, I know his wife."

"You're thinking it's going to go back the way it was," Sand told Siyuf. "Them in the tunnels and us on top. Stuff it. Like we say, there's one thing they're together on."

He paused and Abanja said, "That we must return to our own city, I'm sure. He's probably right, Generalissimo."

"I am, only you're not. What they're saying, all four of them, is that they can't let you go back. Or won't. To start off, they don't think you'll go."

Sand wanted for Siyuf to speak, but she did not.

"So they're thinking let's take care of this, wipe 'em out— that's you, sir—before they can get reinforcements from Trivigaunte."

Hammerstone declared, "The caldé wouldn't do that, or I don't think so, sir. They're getting set now, getting General Mint's troopers together again, and lining up the Guard and getting the Army into position. If we weren't detached, we'd be with it this minute. You got maybe a day, maybe two. But if you let the caldé go, he'll put a lid on it."

"You are wise," Siyuf said. "I agree. Colonel Abanja, you have our friend Caldé Silk? Bring him to my Juzgado, I meet him there. This holy woman Marble, and the holy man, also. Saba's airship have not depart?"

"I'm afraid it left an hour ago, Generalissimo," Abanja sounded regretful. "I'll contact General Saba on the glass, however, and convey your request that she return to Viron."

Hammerstone edged closer, his hard features and scratched paint incongruous among so much satin, porcelain, and polished rosewood. "We don't want a request. We want a order. Tell them to turn around!"

"This I cannot do," Siyuf explained. "When the airship has leave Viron, it come under control of our War Minister in Trivigaunte. She will send it back, I think, when I ask."

"Get her now. Tell her!"

"This I cannot either. Monitor, this is sufficient of Abanja. She know what she is to do."

Siyuf turned back to Sand and Hammerstone. "Abanja must speak to General Saba, then Saba to our War Minister. While they speak I must make prepares for this attack. It may be we attack first. This we see."

As Abanja's face faded to gray, Violet murmured, "I'd help if I could, only—"

"Sure, Plutonium." Slinging his slug gun, Sand stooped, grasped an astonished Siyuf about the waist, and tossed her headfirst onto his broad steel shoulder. "You come too. You can keep her company."

Shale caught Violet's arm. "You make one more for us to trade, see? That don't ever hurt."

Sitting crosslegged on one of the ridiculous bladders that served as mattresses aboard the airship, Silk found it almost impossible to remain upright without holding onto the swaying, whispering bamboo grill that substituted for a floor. "You're wonderfully cheerful," he told Auk. "I admire it more than I can say. Cheerfulness is a sacred duty." He swallowed. "A cheerful agreement with the will of the gods is a—a—"

"I been sick already," Auk told him. "Had the dry heaves, too. Worst thing since I busted my head down in the tunnels."

The Flier smiled impishly. "I heard no cheerful agreement to the wishes of Mainframe at that time, however. Cursing is not a new thing to me, and my own tongue is a superior vehicle to this Common Tongue we speak. But never have I heard curses such as that."

Face down and miserable behind Auk, Chenille muttered, "Just don't talk about it, all right?"

"I do not. Instead I talk of cursing, a different thing. Should

I say in this Common Tongue, may your pubic hair grow longer than your lies and become entangled in the working of a mill, it is but laughable. In my own tongue, it soars to the sun and leaves each hearer awed. Yet the cursing of Auk was new to me, grand and hideous as the birth of devils."

Silk managed to smile. "I have been sick, actually. I was sick in the cage that swings so horribly in the wind, and we were so tightly packed into it that I couldn't help soiling myself and Hyacinth, and Patera Remora, too; they bore it with such fortitude and good will that I felt worse."

Hyacinth smiled as she sat down beside him. "You didn't get a whole lot on me, but you filled up one of his shoes. If you're feeling better now, you should take a look around. Gib showed me, and it's pretty interesting."

"Not yet." Silk found his handkerchief and wiped his nose.

"It's not like the Juzgado at all, no bars on the windows."

"Sure." Auk winked. "We can climb right out."

"I opened one and looked outside. Not long, because it's so cold. I wish you could see better through the white stuff."

"That's sheep's hide stretched and scraped till it's real thin," Auk told her. "When you get it the way you want it, you rub fat on it, and it lets the daylight in. They use it in the country 'cause they can make it themselves, but glass costs. It's a lot lighter, too, so that's why they got it here.

"See, Patera, even with this as big as it is, everything's got to be real light, 'cause it's lifting the guns and those charges they blew up the Alambrera with, and food and water, and palm oil for the engines. That's going to make it easy for us."

"To do what?"

Gib sat down so violently that Silk feared the grill would give way. "To hook it, Patera. We got to. Only I wish I had Bongo here. He'd be abram about this place."

Chenille groaned. "You're all abram. Me, too."

"This ain't bad," Auk told her. "See, Patera, after they loaded us on in the city, it had to go northeast to get you, louse-wise into the wind. It was doing this." He illustrated with gestures. "We all got pretty sick. Only now—"

"I did not," Sciathan objected. "I am accustomed to the vagaries of winds."

"Me neither," Hyacinth told Auk. "I never have been."

"You weren't on it then. This is nicer, 'cause there's a north wind and we're heading south. That's why you can't hear the engines much. They don't have to work hard."

"We're out over the lake," Hyacinth told Silk, who felt (but did not say) that it would be a blessing if the airship crashed into the water.

"Thing is, Patera, Terrible Tartaros is setting this lay up for us. It's like we got somebody inside. The fat councillor said they'd do it in a month, remember? Then I said I got the best thieves in the city, we can do it quicker. I was thinking two or three weeks, 'cause we'd have to get clothes like these troopers' and get pals up so they could pull up the rest—"

Spider joined the group around Silk, sliding across the woven bamboo as he shook his head.

"You got a better way? Dimber here. I don't say mine's best, just that's how I was thinking. The queer was it'd have to be mostly morts, likely all morts. Wouldn't be rum, finding morts that wouldn't up tail if there was a row up here."

"We'd be too sick." Chenille sat up, pale under her tan.

Silk began, "If this is indeed the hand of Tartaros—"

"Got to be. What I was saying, I was figuring maybe three weeks, and the fat one maybe a month. Then Upstairs here says we only got a couple days."

Sciathan nodded.

"Tartaros heard it and he says, Auk needs a hand. Willet, you tell the Trivigauntis Auk's knot's going to be at the Cock. They nab us and haul us up. How long was it? Under a day. So right there's the difference between a god and a buck like me. Twenty-one to one."

For a moment there was silence, filled by the distant talk of the other prisoners, the whispered complaints of the bamboo, the almost inaudible hum of the engines, and a hundred nameless groanings and creakings. Silk said, "They have slug guns, Auk. And needlers, I suppose. You—we—have nothing."

"Wrong, Patera. We got Tartaros. You watch."

Chenille stood up; sitting at her feet, Silk found himself a trifle shocked by her height. She said, "I'm feeling better, I guess. Want to show me around, Hy? I'd like to see it."

"Sure. Wait till you look outside."

He made himself stand. "May I come? I'll try not to . . ." He groped for words, reminding himself of Remora.

"Puke," Chenille supplied.

"See their beds?" Hyacinth kicked the side of a bladder. "There's four rows, and twenty-five in a row, so this gondola's meant for a hundred pterotroopers. Gondola's what you call this thing we're in, Gib says."

Silk nodded.

"Look through the floor and you can see the guns. Their floor's got to be solid, I guess, so it's iron or anyhow some kind of a metal. There's three on each side, and the barrels stick out through those holes. That's why it's so cold here, it comes up through the floor."

"How do you get them open?" Chenille was wrestling with the fastenings of a port.

Silk rapped the wall with his knuckles. "Wood."

"You've got to pull out both pins, Chen. You're right, they're wood, bent like on a boat, but really thin."

Chenille slid back the frame of greased parchment to reveal what looked like a snow-covered plain bright with sun.

"There's another gondola ahead of ours," Hyacinth told her, "and two in back. You can see them if you stick your head out. I don't know why they don't just have one big, long one."

"It would break, I imagine," Silk told her absently. "This airship must bend a good deal at times." He looked out as she had suggested, peering above him as well as to left and right.

"Remember when we were up in the air in that floater? I was scared to death." Her thigh pressed his with voluptuous warmth, and his elbow was somehow pushing her breast. "But you weren't scared at all! This is kind of like that."

"I was terrified." Silk backed away, fighting with all his strength against the thoughts tugging at his mind.

Chenille put her head through the port as he had; she spoke and Hyacinth said, "Because we're blowing along, or that's what I think. Going with it, you can't feel anything."

Chenille retreated. "It's beautiful, really beautiful, only I can't see the lake. You said we were over it, but I guess the fog's too thick. I was hoping to see the place Auk and me bumped out to, that little shrine." She turned to Silk. "Is this how the gods see everything?"

"No," he said. The gods who were in some incomprehensible fashion contained in Mainframe saw the whorl only through their Sacred Windows, he felt sure, no matter what augurs might say.

His sweating hands fumbled the edge of the open port.

Through Windows and the eyes of those whom they possessed, although Tartaros could not even do that, Auk said; born blind, Tenebrous Tartaros could never see.

Over the snowy plain the long sun stretched from Mainframe to the end of the whorl—a place unimaginable, though the end of the whorl must come very soon.

Through Sacred Windows and other eyes, and perhaps through glasses, too. No, certainly through glasses when they chose, since Kypris had spoken through Orchid's glass, had manifested the Holy Hues in Hyacinth's glass while Hyacinth slept.

"The Outsider," he told Chenille. "I think the Outsider must be able to see the whorl this way. The rest of the gods can't—not even Pas. Perhaps that's what's wrong with them." A shoelace had knotted, as it always did when he tried to take off his shoes quickly. He jerked the shoe off anyway.

Hyacinth asked, "What are you doing?"

"Earning you, I hope." He pulled off his stockings and stuffed them into the toes of his shoes, recalling the chill waters of the tunnels and Lake Limna.

"You don't have to earn me! You've already got me, and if you didn't I wouldn't charge you."

He had her, perhaps, but he had not deserved her—he despaired of explaining that. "Doctor Crane and I shared a room at the lake. I doubt that I've mentioned it."

"I don't care what you did with him. It doesn't matter."

"We did nothing. Not the way you mean." Memories flooded back. "I don't believe he was inclined that way; certainly I'm not, though many augurs are. He told me you'd urged him to give me the azoth, and said something I'd forgotten until now. He said, 'When I was your age, it would have had me swinging on the rafters.' "

Hyacinth told Chenille, "Half the time I don't understand a thing he says."

She grinned. "Does anybody?"

"One does, at least. I looked out the window of that room just as we've been looking out this opening." Silk put his foot on its edge and stepped up and out, holding the upper edge to keep from falling. "I was afraid the Guard would come."

He had feared the Civil Guard, and had been willing to try to pull himself up onto the roof of the Rusty Lantern to escape it; yet very little had been at stake: if he had been taken, he would have been killed at worst.

The roof of the gondola was just out of reach; but the side slanted inward, as the sides of large boats did.

Much, much more was at stake now, because Auk's faith might kill them all. How many pterotroopers were on this airship? A hundred? At least that many, and perhaps twice that many.

Hyacinth was looking out at him, saying something he could not understand and did not wish to hear; her hand or Chenille's grasped his left ankle. Absently, he kicked to free it as he waited, gauging the rhythm of the airship's slight roll.

Auk and his followers would wait, biding their time until shadelow probably, if shadelow came before the airship reached Trivigaunte—break the hatch that barred them from its body, climb the rope ladder through the canvas tube that he could just glimpse, and strike with a rush, breaking necks and gouging out eyes. . . .

At the next roll. It was useless to wait. Hyacinth would have called for help already; Auk and Gib would grapple his legs and pull him inside.

He jumped, caught the edge of the top of the gondola, and

to his delight found it a small coaming. In some remote place, someone was screaming. The noise entered his consciousness as he scrambled frantically up the clinker-laid planks, hooking his leg over the coaming when the slow roll favored him most.

A final effort, and he was up, lying on the safe side of the coaming and almost afraid to look at it. Rolling onto his back put half a cubit between him and the edge; he pressed his chest with both hands and shut his eyes, trying to control the pounding of his heart.

Almost he might have been on top of Blood's wall, with its embedded sword blades at his shoulder. Almost, except that a fall from Blood's wall would have been survivable—he had survived one, in fact.

He sat up and wiped his face with the hem of his robe.

How foolish he had been not to take off his robe and leave it with his shoes! The gondola had been cold, the draft from the port colder still; and so he had kept his robe, and never so much as considered that he might have lightened himself by some small amount by discarding it. Yet it was comforting to have it now, comforting to draw its soft woolen warmth around him while he considered what to do next.

Stand up, though if he stood he might fall. Muttering a prayer to the Outsider, he stood.

The top of the gondola was a flat and featureless deck, painted mummy-brown or perhaps merely varnished. Six mighty cables supported the gondola, angled out and stabbing upward into the airship's fabric-covered body. Forward, the canvas tube snaked up like an intestine; aft was a hatch secured with lashings, a hatch that would return him to the gondola—that would, equally, permit those inside it to leave. Once again he pictured the stealthy advance and wild charge, a score of young pterotroopers dead, the rest firing, disorganized at first.

Soon, shouted orders would render them a coherent body. A few Vironese would have weapons by then, and they might kill more pterotroopers; but they would be shot down within a minute or two, and the rest shot as well. Auk and Chenille and Gib would die, and with them Horn and Nettle and even poor Maytera Marble, who called herself Moly now. And not long after that, unless he and Hyacinth were lucky indeed—

"Hello, Silk."

He whirled. Mucor was sitting on the deck, her shins embraced by her skeletal arms; he gasped, and felt the pain of his wound deep in his chest.

She repeated her greeting.

"Hello." Another gasp. "I'd nearly forgotten you could do this. You did it in the tunnel, sitting on the water—I should have remembered."

She bared yellow teeth. "Mirrors are better. Mirrors scare more. This isn't, is it? I'm just here."

"It was certainly frightening to hear your voice." Silk sat too, grateful for the chance.

"I didn't mean to. I wanted to talk to you, but not where there were so many people."

He nodded. "There would have been a riot, I suppose."

"You were worried about me with so many people gone. My grandfather came to see if I was all right. The old man and the fat woman are taking care of me. He wanted to know where Grandmother and the little augur went, and I told him."

My grandfather was Hammerstone, clearly; Silk nodded and smiled. "Does the old man have a beard and jump around?"

"A little beard, yes."

Xiphias in that case, not His Cognizance; no doubt the fat woman was a friend of Xiphias's, or a servant.

"I've been eating soup."

"That's very good—I'm delighted to hear it. Mucor, you possessed General Saba, and there's something that you can tell me that's very, very important to me. When does she expect us to arrive in Trivigaunte?"

"Tonight."

Silk nodded, he hoped encouragingly. "Can you tell me how long after shadelow?"

"About midnight. This will float over the city, and in the morning they'll let you down."

"Thank you. Auk intends to try to take control of this airship and fly it to Mainframe."

Mucor looked pleased. "I didn't know that."

"He won't be able to. He'll be killed, and so will others I like. The only way that I've been—" He heard voices and paused to listen.

"They're in there." Mucor looked over her shoulder at the dangling canvas tube.

"Going down into the gondola? Can they hear us?"

"They haven't."

He waited until he heard the hatch thrown back. "What do they want?"

"I don't know."

His forefinger traced small circles on his cheek. "When you go, will you try to find out, please? It may be important, and I would be very, very grateful."

"I'll try."

"Thank you. You can fly, I know. You told me so in that big room underground where the sleepers are. Have you been all over this airship?"

"Most of it, Silk."

"I see. The only way that I could think of to stop Auk from trying to take it and being killed was to disable it some way— that was why I climbed up here, and you may be able to tell me how to do it. In a moment I'm going to try to tear the seam of that tube and climb up."

"There's a trooper up there."

"I see. A sentry? In any case, I must find a way to open the seam first. I should have gotten new glasses; I could have broken them and cut it with a piece of glass. But Mucor," Silk made his tone as serious as he could to emphasize the urgency of his request, "you've given me another way now, at least for the time being. Will you possess General Saba again for me?"

She was silent, and as seconds crept by he realized that she had not understood. "The fat woman," he said, but Mucor would surely confuse that with the woman Xiphias had found to care for her. "The woman that you frightened in the Caldé's

Palace. She spilled her coffee, remember? You talked to me through her before Hyacinth and I went into the cage."

"Oh, her."

"Her name is General Saba, and she's the commander of this airship. I want you to possess her and make her turn east. As long as it's going in the direction that Auk—"

Mucor had begun to fade. For a second or two a ghostly image remained, like a green glimmer upon a pool; then it was gone and he was alone.

Condemning himself, he rose again. There had been half a dozen things—eight or ten, and perhaps more—he should have asked. What was taking place in Viron? Was Maytera Mint alive? What were Siyuf's plans? The answers had melted into the fabled city of lost opportunities.

He walked forward to the tube and examined it. The canvas was thinner than he had feared, but looked strong and nearly new. His pockets yielded only his new prayer beads and a handkerchief, the only items that his captors had let him retain. He detached an arm of Pas's voided cross and tried to tear the canvas with it, but its sharpest corner slipped impotently along the surface. Many men, he reminded himself angrily, carried small knives for just such occasions as this— although any such knife would presumably have been taken from him.

Even if he had possessed a knife, there was a sentry at the top of the ladder. If he was able to poke a hole in the canvas and enlarge it enough to climb through, he would almost certainly be captured or killed by that sentry when he emerged from the tube. Saba had no doubt worried that her prisoners might break one of the hatches; but a single pterotrooper there would be able to hold her position until she exhausted her ammunition, and her shots would have brought reinforcements long before then. Saba's prisoners had not escaped through either hatch—not yet. But Saba's logic confined him as though he had been its object.

Shaking his head, he crossed the deck of the gondola to the nearest cable. Woven of many ropes, it was as thick as a young tree, and its surface was rougher than the bark of many.

Still more significantly, its angle, here where it was bent through a huge ringbolt, slanted noticeably off the vertical.

Removing his robe, he put it over his shoulder and tied it at his waist. Once he had finished praying and begun to climb, he found it relatively easy; as a boy he had climbed trees and poles far more difficult. The key was to fix his eyes on the surface of the cable, never stealing even a glance at the snowy plain of cloud so achingly far below.

He had boasted of his climbing to Horn, while conceding only that he had climbed less adroitly than a monkey; it was time to make good that boast. . . .

Gib missed the companionship of his trained baboon— what would Bongo think, if Bongo could see him crawling upward with chattering teeth and sweating palms! Could baboons laugh?

The airship was, just possibly, turning ever so slightly to its left. To look down was death, but to look up?

The whir of the engines sounded louder, but of course he was somewhat nearer them. He reminded himself sharply that he had not yet climbed far. . . .

The airship's southward course must necessarily have put its long axis across the great golden bar of the sun. If he looked up—if he risked it, and it was not much risk, surely, he might be able to catch sight of the sun to one side of the vast hull from which the gondola hung. . . .

Momentarily, he halted to rest the aching muscles in his thighs, and glanced upward. Scarcely ten cubits overhead, the cable entered the monstrous belly of the airship proper; beyond the opening, he glimpsed the beam to which it was attached.

"Done try, laddie."

"Tick!" Hyacinth stared, blinking away tears. "Tick, how in the whorl—"

Auk handed him to her. "Came in through the window, didn't you, cully? A dimber cat burglar, ain't you?"

"My see, wears she putty laddie?" Tick explained. "An Gawk sees, hue comb wit may. Den my—add word!"

" 'Lo, girl." Flapping in advance of Silk, Oreb ignored the little catachrest. " 'Lo, Auk."

Auk swore. Hyacinth dropped Tick (who landed on his feet) and Silk embraced her.

To him, so lost in the ecstasy of her kiss that he scarcely knew that her right leg had twined about his left, or that her loins ground his, Horn's distant shout meant less than nothing.

"So what?" Auk inquired from the West Pole. *"Let 'em come."*

After what seemed an eternity of love, something tapped Silk's arm and Hyacinth backed away.

"Caldé Silk!" The harsh voice belonged to a gaunt, hard-faced Trivigaunti officer of forty or more; he blinked, certain that he should recognize her.

"You're Caldé Silk. Let's not waste time in evasions."

"Yes, I am." She had clicked into place in his memory, her hand around a wineglass, her back straight as a slug-gun barrel. "Major Hadale, this is my wife, Hyacinth. Hyacinth, my darling, may I present Major Hadale? She's one of General Saba's most trusted officers. Major Hadale consented to join me for dinner Thelxday, before we were reunited."

Oreb eyed Hadale apprehensively. "Good girl?"

The major herself addressed the lieutenant on her right. "You were in here an hour ago looking for him. Are you saying he wasn't here then?"

"No, sir." The lieutenant's face was set like stone. "He was not. I'm familiar with his appearance, and I examined every prisoner in this gondola. He was not present."

Hadale turned to a trooper with a slug gun. "How long have you been on post?"

Silk began, "If I may—"

"In a moment. How long, Matar?"

The trooper had stiffened to attention. "Almost my whole watch, sir."

Auk spoke into Silk's ear; but if Silk heard him—or anything—he gave no indication of it. "You're going to ask her if anyone left this gondola," he told Hadale. "She'll say no, and then I suppose you'll call her a liar, or the lieutenant will. Can't we—"

"Before we came down here I asked if she'd seen anybody," Hadale interrupted. "She said she did. She saw a Vironese holy man. He went down into this gondola, and he had an order from General Saba that let him. Is that right, Matar?"

"Yes, sir."

Silk fished a folded paper from his pocket. "Here it is. Do you want to see it?"

"No!" Angrily, Hadale took it from him. "I want to keep it. I intend to. Caldé, you were careful to remind me that I've been your guest. You welcomed me and fed me well. That puts me in an uncomfortable position." She glanced at the crowd that had formed around them. "Get out of here! Go to the other end of the gondola, all of you."

Auk smiled and shook his head. Sciathan tugged the sleeve of Silk's robe. "Now you wish it? If not, you must stop it."

"You're right, of course." Silk raised both hands. "Auk! All of you! Go to the other end. You're very brave, and there are only three of them; but there are at least a hundred others on this airship." He took Hyacinth's hand.

"Go 'way!" Oreb seconded him.

Maytera Marble added her voice to theirs, the crisp tones of a teacher bringing her classroom to order. "Hear that bird? He's a night chough, sacred to Tartaros. Trust Tartaros!"

"*I* speak for the *gods.*" Incus stood on tiptoe, making wide gestures. "We must *obey* the caldé, whom the *immortal* gods have chosen for all of us."

"Thank you," Silk told the little Flier. "Thank you very much. Moly—thank you. Thank you, Your Eminence."

Hadale exhaled, a weary sigh that recalled Maytera Marble. "And I thank you, Caldé. They wouldn't have succeeded, but there would've been a lot of killing. By Scarring Sphigx, I don't like this! A few days ago, we were drinking toasts."

"I like it less," Silk told her. "I propose that we put an end to it. May I speak with General Saba?"

Hadale shook her head. "Lieutenant, you and Matar go

over there and keep an eye on those people. They may try to jump you. Shoot if they do."

Silk watched them go. "I'd imagine you've got a glass on this airship. If you won't let me speak with General Saba, may I use it to speak to your generalissimo?"

"No." Hadale paused to listen. "We just lost an engine."

"The second one," Hyacinth told her. "That was what Auk whispered to my husband, that the first one had stopped. I've been paying attention to them ever since."

"Auk's the man who was talking to my wife and me when you came," Silk explained. "I apologize for not introducing you."

"I should be in the cockpit, they'll be going crazy up there. Caldé, are you doing this?"

"Good man!" Oreb assured Hadale. "Good Silk!"

She gave him a look intended to fry him. "Your bird's an oracle of Tartaros, so if he says you're good that settles it. Don't you know that many of us don't believe in Tartaros, Caldé? We have a faction that teaches that Sphigx is the only true god, and Pas and the rest are just legends. A lot of us believe it."

Silk nodded, looking at the dangling ladder behind her. "I can sympathize with that—no doubt it's nearer the truth than many of our beliefs. May I offer a suggestion, Major?"

"I've got one, too, but let's hear yours. What is it?"

He showed her his hands. "We're unarmed. You may search us if you wish; and we won't attack you—we'll swear to that by Sphigx or any other god you choose. If you were to hand your needler to Hyacinth or me, we wouldn't employ it against you—though of course I'm not asking you to do anything of the kind. That said, I suggest we go to the place from which this airship is commanded. Where the tiller is, or whatever you call it. Is that the cockpit?"

Hadale nodded, her eyes suspicious.

"First, because we'd like to see it—that's a selfish reason, I admit, but we would. Second, because they may need you there, you're clearly anxious to go, and we can talk there as well as anywhere. Third—"

Hadale pointed to the dangling ladder. "That's enough. All right. You two first, and stay in front."

"So," Siyuf began as she sat down in the wooden chair the round-faced stranger pulled out for her, "are we today at war? I hope you are lose, General Mint." Without evident curiosity, her quick, dark eyes surveyed the spartan room, and the snow-splotched drill field and leaden sky beyond its windows.

Oosik nodded as he took his seat. "That was a point we planned to discuss, Generalissimo. Events have overtaken us."

"Trivigaunte declared war on Viron an hour ago," Maytera Mint said briskly. "We feel we owe it to you to explain the situation. Our caldé thinks you care nothing for the lives of your troops. He's told me so. I'm doing something here that's quite foreign to me, I'm assuming he's wrong. If he isn't, no harm will be done by this meeting. If he is," she smiled, "some good may come of it. Are your troopers' lives precious to you?"

The elevation and decline of Siyuf's epaulets was scarcely visible. "Valuable is certain. Precious we must speak about, I think. Do you know how greatly I have desire to meet you, Mint? Do they tell this? Is Bison to sit in one of these empty chairs? He know of this."

A new voice exclaimed, "So do I! I vouch for her, my dear young general. She's expressed the wish many times."

Siyuf turned to the fat man who had come in. "You I know from a picture. You are Potto of the Ayuntamiento, that would make war on my city. You have win, I think, if we are at war."

Potto sat gingerly, unsure of the strength of his chair. "If only a declaration were all it took!"

"I'm Councillor Newt," the round-faced stranger explained, "The newest member of the Ayuntamiento." He offered his hand.

She accepted it. "I am your prisoner Siyuf."

"Not a badly treated one, I hope."

Potto giggled. "A very well treated one, so far, Cousin.

Since you're a councillor now, I've appointed you an honorary cousin. Do you mind?"

Oosik cleared his throat. "Perhaps I should outline the entire situation, Generalissimo."

"We are at war, you say. I believe this. I therefore give my name and rank. These alone, no other fact. Do you desire to exchange me? I will go."

Maytera Mint said, "We do, very much."

"Then I will fight you, after. It is to be regretted, but it is so. You cannot make me answer your questions—"

Potto giggled again.

"No more can I make you to answer mine. I ask anyway. Do you fight me together, Mint? Or do you fight each other also? When I return to my horde, it would be good that I know this."

"Viron's reunited. It's been our caldé's dearest wish, and I'm delighted to say we've realized it."

Potto rocked with mirth. "Wait till he finds out we're on the same side! I can't wait to see his face."

"He'll be radiant with joy. If you understood him as I do, you'd know it." Maytera Mint spoke to Siyuf. "Let me explain, because all this hinges on your understanding what your troops are up against. We've not only made peace among ourselves, but given the city a new government. There are two main provisions to our agreement. One is that ours is a Charterial government, which means there must be a caldé and an Ayuntamiento. We agree mutually that Caldé Silk is—"

"My prisoner," Siyuf interrupted.

"Hardly." Oosik leaned forward, his elbows upon the old deal table, his bass voice dominating the room. "He may be a prisoner of your city. We don't know that yet. It is one of the things we need to discuss."

Siyuf looked back to Maytera Marble. "You wish to tell me of the Charter of your city, before this man have interrupt you. I find this of interest."

"I think it's vital. If we're to secure the favor of the gods, we have to govern according to the Charter they gave us. We've been trying from the start. Now we've succeeded."

"I would ask who it is who rule this government, but you say Silk, who is not here. Who is commander here? You?"

Maytera Mint shook her head. "In military affairs, my own superior, Generalissimo Oosik. In civil, Councillor Potto, the Presiding Officer of the Ayuntamiento."

"In this case you are not needed," Siyuf told her, and turned to Newt. "Neither you, I think. Yet both sit at this table where is one chair more. You take our custom that each bring a subordinate? Is that the explanation I require? You for Potto, Mint for Oosik, Violet for me, perhaps? I do not think this I have say."

"I'm breaking in," Newt told her. "I'm the new boy." He sounded anything but humble.

"I'm here," Maytera Mint explained, "because we think you may listen to a woman when you won't really hear a man."

Oosik rumbled, "You've the quickest mind I know. You are present because we are likely to succeed because you are here."

"I'm less apt to kill him, too," Potto confided.

"He's only joking," Newt assured Siyuf.

"Not, I hope. You are a new councillor, you say. Where is it they find you?"

Maytera Mint said, "In the Juzgado. Councillor Newt was a commissioner there, the one who bought supplies for the Caldé's Guard, made out the payroll, and so forth." She paused.

"When I began, when Echidna called me her sword, I thought all we had to do was fight. I'm learning that fighting is the smallest part of it, and in some ways the easiest."

Smiling, Siyuf nodded.

"Quite often it's the other things that count most. You have to get supplies to the people who need them, and not just ammunition but food and bedding, and warm clothes. At any rate, part of our agreement was an acknowledgment by all of us that the Charter demands an Ayuntamiento."

Potto made her a seated bow.

"But not *just* an Ayuntamiento, an elected one with a full

compliment of councillors. We can't hold elections because of the state things are in, so we've promised them after a year of peace. Meanwhile the present members will continue to serve, with Councillor Potto as Presiding Officer. New councillors are to be appointed as necessary by the caldé, or in his absence by a de facto board of those who have his confidence. It consists of the current Ayuntamiento, including Councillor Newt now, with Generalissimo Oosik, His Cognizance, and me. I wanted a woman councillor—"

"You will not have her," Siyuf put in. "They are all men."

"So we appointed Kingcup. She's not here because she's out explaining all this to our people. I felt we needed—" Maytera Mint groped for words. "An ordinary woman with extraordinary gifts. Kingcup's from a poor family, but she built a successful livery stable from scratch, so she's used to managing. Besides, she's the bravest woman in Viron."

Oosik muttered, "No one but you would say that, General."

She brushed the compliment aside. "So Kingcup for the people and Newt for the Juzgado."

"With such as these you prepare to fight me," Siyuf mused, "but I am not there. This is sad. I beat you, I think. Does my General Rimah beat you also? I do not know. She is a good officer. You ask of love for my horde. Why is this?"

"Because we hope that you will want to preserve it," Oosik told her, "as I want to preserve the Guard. There has been some skirmishing already. If we fight in earnest, your horde will be destroyed and my Guard decimated." Maytera Mint added, "To say nothing of what will happen to our city," and Oosik nodded.

"We wish victory. None but cowards count life more high."

Maytera Mint started to speak, but Oosik silenced her with a gesture. "I am confident General Rimah is an able officer. You're not the sort to tolerate anything less. There is a gulf, however, between an able officer and an exceptional leader. The ranks sense it at once, and the public almost as quickly. I will not ask if you care about your troops. We're too close for that, you and I, so close I can hear my own voice in everything you've said. You long for victory, and you know, as I do, that it would be more probable if you were in command of your troops. Wouldn't you agree that for any other—"

Potto interrupted. "A subject of the Rani's."

"That for another citizen of your city," Oosik continued, "To prevent you from resuming your place would be treason? It is not an idle question."

"You think someone does this? I wish to know."

"Let me." Maytera Mint's small, not uncomely face shone with energy and resolve. "You want to fight me, Siyuf, because of what you've heard about me. I don't want to fight you, and in fact it's the last thing I want. I want peace. I want to end this foolish fighting and let everybody in our city and yours go back to their proper lives. But it's been clear ever since your spies tried to arrest us that as long as you have our caldé there can be no peace. I'm going to assume you understand that, because if you don't there's no use talking."

"I am captive also." Siyuf touched her chest.

"Exactly! You've saved me a lot of time. We've got you, but in a very important way we don't want you, since your city will fight to get you back. Clearly the sensible thing is to exchange you for our caldé. Peace would be possible then, but if we still couldn't make peace, you and I would be fighting each other, which is what you want. Now if—"

Siyuf made a quick motion, the gesture of one accustomed to instant obedience. "I have pledged to your Sand that I will free Incus the holy man and Marble. She is your friend?"

"Yes, she is." Maytera Mint glanced at Oosik, but he did not speak. "You cheated Sergeant Sand and Corporal Hammerstone. You know you did. You knew those prisoners were already on your airship when you promised to let them go."

"Over this we fight a duel, perhaps, if I am free. It may still be so. I did not know, Mint. If you have deal with Saba and her airship as I, you know that what is to be at shadeup may not be until midday, or not this day or the next. Let me go. I get them again and free them. Caldé Silk also."

For a second or two Maytera Mint studied her with pursed lips. "All right, I'll accept that. I apologize."

Potto tittered.

"But your airship doesn't seem to have reached Trivigaunte yet. Does that bother you?"

Siyuf shook her head. "Tonight, or I think the morning."

Oosik rumbled, "Suppose I were to say tomorrow afternoon, Generalissimo. Your knowledge, I contend, is not so deep as you pretend. Tomorrow afternoon!"

Siyuf shrugged. "If you say. Perhaps."

"In that case I proffer a further supposition. Not before shadelow next Phaesday. What would you say to that?"

"That you are a fool. The airship could be here once more in such a time."

"Just so." Oosik wound his white-tipped mustache about his finger. "We have contacted Trivigaunte by glass, Generalissimo. We have spoken to your Minister of War. We have explained how things stand here, and offered to exchange you for Caldé Silk."

"They won't," Newt declared. "Won't do it or even talk about it, by Scylla! We invite your comments."

"I offer what is better. Let me speak with her."

Potto roared, slapping his thigh. "This is too, too rich! My dear young General, you're not even smiling. How do you do it?" He turned back to Siyuf, speaking across the empty chair. "You already have, and it didn't help a bit."

"I have not. Abanja for me, perhaps."

Maytera Mint said, "We think it's politics. By we I mean Generalissimo Oosik and I. The internal politics of your city. We'd like confirmation of that, and some suggestions about what to do about it."

"If this you say is true . . ." Siyuf shrugged again.

Oosik muttered, "Every city has its feuds, Generalissimo."

"Mine also. Our War Minister, you do not say her name. This is Ljam? A scar here?" Siyuf touched her upper lip.

Newt and Maytera Mint nodded.

"This is not possible. My city have politics, as your generalissimo say. Feuds, plottings, hatreds. Of these very many. But Ljam is with me most near. If I fail here she fail also. You understand? Lose her ministry, perhaps her head."

Oosik regarded Siyuf through slitted eyes. "You're saying it is impossible for her to betray you, Generalissimo?"

"She cannot unless she is betray herself!"

Potto sang, "I told you! I told you!"

"He thinks your airship's wrecked, or it's gone off course somehow." Maytera Mint looked somber. "Naturally they won't say so, and Generalissimo Oosik and I thought it was more likely they were playing some game, though Councillor Potto received a report implying it's gone. Now it seems he must be right. This is truly unfortunate."

"But we're going to let you go anyhow," Potto told Siyuf. "Isn't that nice of us?" He bounced from his chair and went to the door calling, "You can send them in!"

It was opened by a soldier; and Violet and a second Siyuf entered, Violet with her arm linked with the second Siyuf's. She stared at the first in open-mouthed amazement.

"You'll have to go now, my dear young strumpet," Potto told her. "We don't want you, though I'm sure many do. Have a seat, Generalissimo. I'll be with you in a half a moment."

"I am to sit beside this bio?" the second Siyuf inquired. "This I do not like. You say you send me to my horde, I think. When is it you do this?"

"You'll escape," Newt explained to the first Siyuf. "Or rather, she will."

"Too much warlockery for me." Hadale dropped into one of the cockpit's black-leather seats. "Too much in your city, and too much on our airship now that you're here. People at home say you're all warlocks, but I discounted it. I should have tripled everything. You're a warlock, Caldé, and I'd call you the chief warlock if I hadn't met the old man who sat between our generalissimo and General Saba."

"She refers to His Cognizance," Silk told Hyacinth; awed and delighted, he tried to stare at everything at once. "Like a conservatory . . ."

Oreb croaked "Bad thing" as Tick squirmed in Hyacinth's grasp. "Add word, dew!"

"Three engines gone." Hadale peered morosely through the

nearest rectangle of glass at the parting clouds and the rocky sandscape that they revealed. "What do you want? Surrender? I'll shoot you first and take my chances with the desert."

"Then we don't want it," Hyacinth declared.

"We don't in any case," Silk said, "and I'm no warlock; the truth is that I'm hardly an augur any more—I certainly don't feel like one."

"General Saba told me the other day that you read about our advance in sheepguts. Do you deny it?"

"No, though it isn't true. Denying it would waste time, so you may believe it if you like. There are five engines still in operation. Is that enough to keep us in the air?"

The navigator looked up from her charts, then returned to them; Hadale pointed to the ceiling. "None are needed to keep us up, the gas does it. Are we going to lose all our engines?"

Silk considered. "I can't promise that. I hope so."

"You hope so."

"No shoot," Oreb advised Hadale nervously. "Good man."

"It was what I intended." For a moment, Silk allowed his eyes to feast on Hyacinth's loveliness. "The risk that gave me most concern was that Hyacinth might be killed as a result of what I was doing; I hoped it wouldn't happen, and I'm very glad it won't. I betrayed my god for her—I was horribly afraid that it would recoil on me, as such things do."

She brought his hand to the soft warmth of her thigh. "You betrayed the Outsider for me? I'd never ask you to do that."

Hadale turned to the pilot, "We've still got five?"

The pilot nodded. "Can't make much headway against this wind with five, though, sir."

Hyacinth asked, "Aren't we going south anyway? Isn't the wind blowing us south to Trivigaunte? Somebody said something like that."

"It's blowing us south," Hadale told her bitterly, "but not to Trivigaunte. We turned east for about an hour before the first one quit."

"Veering north-northwest, sir," the pilot reported.

Having freed himself from Hyacinth's grasp, Tick stood on

his hind legs to pat Hadale's knee. "Rust Milk, laddie. Milk bill take hit hall tight."

"He says you can trust my husband," Hyacinth interpreted. "He's right, too, and I don't think you ought to pay too much attention to what my husband says about betraying a god. He—oh, I don't know how to explain! He's forever blaming himself for the wrong things. He's sorry for holding me too tight when I wish he'd hold me tighter. See?"

"Your catachrest's an oracle of our goddess, so I have to trust him implicitly. Is that it?"

"I didn't say that." Hyacinth sat down. "I guess I would have, though, if I thought you'd believe it. Maybe it's right, and she isn't telling us."

"Hat's shoe!" Tick exclaimed.

Silk smiled. "I take it that General Saba's no longer in charge. Where is she?"

"In her bunk, with three troopers to watch her. I won't ask how you drove her mad. I'm sure you wouldn't tell me."

"I didn't." He leaned over the crescent-shaped instrument panel for a better view of the desert below. "I arranged for her to be possessed, that's all. You saw the same thing at our dinner. Are you in charge now? There's no one over you?"

"The War Minister. In a moment I'm going to have to report this situation to her."

"No talk," Oreb advised.

"By 'this situation' you mean—"

"Three engines out. I've told her about Saba turning east already. I had to. I was hoping you'd agree to repair the engines before I had to report them, too. That's why I let you come up here. Will you?"

"I can't." Silk took the seat next to Hyacinth's. "Nor would I if I could. We'd be back where we began, with Auk's people trying to seize control, and everyone—all of us, I mean—dying. I said I betrayed the Outsider because that was how I felt—"

"Wind's due west now, sir," the pilot reported.

"Course?"

"East by south, sir. We might try dropping down."

"Do it." Hadale considered. "A hundred and fifty cubits." She turned back to Silk. "You were afraid we'd crash. We may. It's dangerous to fly that low in weather as windy as this. If a downdraft catches us, we could be finished. But the wind won't be as strong down there."

Hyacinth gasped, and Silk said, "I can feel the airship descend. I rode in a moving room once that felt like this."

"You want to go east. That was how you had General Saba steering us."

He nodded, and smiled again. "To Mainframe. Auk wants to carry out the Plan of Pas, and the Outsider wants it, too, which is why I felt I was betraying him when I did what I did to your engines. But letting Auk try to take your airship wouldn't have achieved anything, and this was the only way I could think of to prevent him."

"So now that we don't have enough engines to fight the wind, you're working your magic on that."

Silk shook his head. "I can't. All that I can do is pray, which isn't magic at all, but begging. I've been doing it, and perhaps I've been heard."

He drew a deep breath. "You want your engines back in operation, Major. You want to preserve this airship, and to deliver me to your superiors in Trivigaunte; the rest of your prisoners don't matter greatly, as you must know. I do."

Slowly, Hadale nodded.

"We can do all that, if only you'll cooperate. Take us to Mainframe, as Pas commands and the Outsider wishes. Auk and his people can leave the whorl and thus begin carrying out the Plan. Hyacinth and I will return—"

"Shut up!" Hadale cocked her head, listening.

The pilot said, "Number seven's quit, sir." The absence of all emotion in her voice conveyed what she felt.

"Take her up fast. Just below the cloud cover."

Hyacinth asked Silk, "Won't the wind be stronger there?"

Hadale was on her feet, scanning the desert below. "A lot stronger, but I'm going to set her down and try to fix the engines. Even if we can't, we won't be blowing farther from

Trivigaunte. We want a big level stretch to land on, and an oasis, if we can find one."

"No land!" Oreb advised sharply; Hyacinth began, "If you'll go to Mainframe like he—"

Hadale whirled. "He can't fix them. He admits it."

Silk had risen, too; almost whispering, he said, "You must have faith, Major."

"All right, I've got faith. Slashing Sphigx, succor us! Meanwhile I need a place to set us down on."

"I said I couldn't repair your engines. I said it because it's the truth. I should have added—as I do, now—that if only we were doing the gods' will instead of opposing it, a way to repair them—"

"Sir!" The pilot pointed.

"I see them. Can you get us over there?"

"I think so, sir. I'll try."

Silk leaned forward, squinting. Hyacinth said, "Something like ants, but they're leagues and leagues away."

"That's a caravan," Hadale told Silk, "could be one of ours. Even if it isn't, they'll have food and water, and a few of us can ride to the city to guide a rescue party."

"I just hope they're friendly," Hyacinth murmured.

Rubbing her hands, Hadale looked ten years younger. "They will be soon. I've got two platoons of pterotroopers on board."

Chapter 15

To Mainframe!

"Silk say." Settling on Auk's extended wrist, Oreb whistled sharply to emphasize the urgency of his message. "Say Auk!"

"All right, spill it."

Matar prodded Auk's ribs with the muzzle of her slug gun. "The lieutenant says for you to stop leaning out of this port. She's afraid you'll jump out."

Auk withdrew his head and arm. "Not me. I could, though. With our gun deck—that what you call it?"

Both Matar and Chenille nodded.

"Shaggy near on the ground like this, it's maybe eight cubits. That's sand down there, too, so it'd be candy."

Matar was studying Oreb. "Where did you find that bird? I thought your caldé had it."

"Girls go," Oreb reported hoarsely. "Say Auk."

"He just flew down and lit on me," Auk explained. "Me and him's a old knot." Gently, he stroked Oreb with his forefinger.

Chenille told Matar, "We were together down in the tunnels under our city. It was pretty rough."

"It *was,* my daughter." Incus joined the group. "It was *there,* however, that *I* received the divine *favor* of Surging *Scylla,* our patroness."

From her seat at the front of the gondola, the lieutenant called, "What are you talking about back there?"

"Tunnels, sir." Matar was a lean young woman two fingers smaller than most.

"There," Incus elucidated, "I learned to load and *shoot* a needler." He approached the lieutenant, his plump face wreathed in smiles. "It is an *accomplishment* of which very few augurs *indeed* can boast. I had a most excellent *teacher* in my faithful *friend* Corporal Hammerstone."

"Girls go," Oreb repeated. "Camels. Girl take."

"Matar!" the lieutenant called. "Get over here." Matar hurried to obey.

Maytera Marble caught Auk's sleeve. "There's something else," she whispered. "That little cat creature Patera's wife had is back."

Auk nodded absently. "He's got word from Silk, I'll lay."

"Something about milk and mammals," she explained, "and strong twine off caramels. I can't quite make out what it's so excited about. Gib has it."

"That's camels in a caravan," Auk said under his breath. "I saw 'em, and I saw troopers going after 'em. Now I got to take the dell and her jefe before that flash little butcher does it and nabs the credit."

The flat crack of a needler came from the front of the gondola; a woman screamed.

Silk had been watching two distant Trivigauntis probe the desert sand for soil with enough cohesion to hold a mooring stake. As the faint thuddings of the heavy maul reached the cockpit, he turned to the pilot. "Could we take off without untying those ropes?"

"The mooring lines?" The pilot shook her head.

"That's unfortunate. It might have saved lives." He sat down beside Hyacinth again and took her hand, listening to the moan of a winter wind that raised sand devils in the distance.

"We ought to have half a dozen more," the pilot told him. "We will, too, pretty soon. We use twenty-four at home."

"You have five already." The number suggested Hyacinth's five fingers; Silk raised them to his lips, kissing them and the cheap and foolish ring that had been the only ring they had. His padded leather seat lifted sharply beneath him, a forceful upward push like that of Blood's floater rising from the grassway. "Feel that?" the pilot said.

Hyacinth pointed. "Something flashed way over there." She swung wide the pane they had opened for Tick.

"Don't do that," the pilot told her. "We've got plenty of cold air in here already."

Silk put his own finger to his lips. Almost beyond the edge of hearing, faint, irregular booms filled the intervals between the blows of the maul. "They're firing," he informed the pilot. "I know the sound from the fighting in our city."

Then the gondola heaved beneath them again, faster than the moving room had ever moved, and wilder even than Oosik's armed floater—rocked and shook them as it soared into the air.

Nearer than the besieged caravan, a slug gun boomed, loud among the gondola's tormented creaks and groans. Reeling, the pilot jerked out her needler. Hyacinth knocked it from her hand and rammed both thumbs into her eyes, kicking savagely at her knees until both she and the pilot fell.

"What are you doing?" Auk inquired.

"Dropping ballast." Silk pointed. "If you'll look down there, you should see something like smoke falling from under the rear gondola."

Auk thrust his head and shoulders through the opening left by a shot-out pane of glass. "Yeah."

"That's desert sand," Hyacinth explained. "They started shoveling more on as soon as we got down, and the pilot told us about it. You can make this go up with the engines, or pull it down with them. That's what we did when we landed. But if you want to fly high up for a long while, the easiest way's to drop sand like he's doing."

Chenille said, "This floor's about level now."

Silk nodded, pointing toward the bubble in a horizontal tube on the instrument panel.

Auk took the seat nearest him. "If you want me to, I can get somebody else to do this. Even that pilot. I'd have one of ours sit here to watch her."

"She's blind," Silk told him. He threw a lever on the instrument panel. "Hyacinth blinded her. I saw it."

"She's just got sore eyes, Patera. She'll be dandy."

Hyacinth sat on Silk's left. "You like this, don't you?"

"I love it—and I'm terrified by it at the same time. I'm afraid I'm going to kill us all; but the pilot or another Trivigaunti might do so intentionally, and I certainly won't. But . . ." His voice trailed away.

"Even if we had a pilot we could trust, you'd want to."

He cleared his throat. "We do have a pilot we can trust—me. I'm not very experienced as yet, but there must have been a time when that woman wasn't either."

Chenille sat down next to Hyacinth. "You poke her glims?"

Hyacinth nodded. "She was going to shoot us, Chen."

"No shoot!" Oreb sailed into the cockpit.

"Right," Hyacinth told him. "That's what I thought, but we had shooting anyway when Auk's culls fought it out with the troopers watching the general."

"Only Patera's still sort of bothered by what you did to her. I can tell."

Silk glanced at Chenille. "Am I so transparent as that?"

"Sure." She grinned. "Listen, Patera. Do you think us dells at Orchid's were always really polite? Do you think we always said please and thank you, and excuse me, Bluebell, but that gown you've got on looks a whole lot like one of mine?"

"I don't know," Silk admitted. "I would hope so." From his shoulder, Oreb eyed him quizzically.

"You think I'm rough because I'm big, and you think those dells from Trivigaunte are because they don't wear makeup, and they had needlers and slug guns. I never had to fight a lot at Orchid's because I was the longest dell there. You know where Hyacinth comes on me?"

"I believe I do, yes."

"Without those heels she always wears, the top of her head doesn't even hit my shoulder. She's beautiful, too, like you always say. The whole time she lived there, she was the best-looking dell Orchid had, and Orchid would tell you so herself. You know who looks the most like Hy now? It's Poppy, and Poppy looks like Hy about as much as a sham card looks like a lily one. You know how that is? They look the same till you look hard, but when you do you know it's not even close. The gold in the sham one looks brassy, and it feels greasy. You look at Hy, at her eyes and nose. Look at her chin. Just look! The first couple weeks I knew her I couldn't see her chin without feeling like a toad in the road." The huskiness that affects women's voices when they speak of matters of genuine importance entered Chenille's. "Poppy's cute, Patera. Hy's real gold."

"I know."

"So just about everybody hated her." Chenille coughed. "I nearly did myself. The second or third day—"

"Second," Hyacinth interjected.

"She came to the big room with a mouse under both eyes. Orchid threw a fit. But you know what?"

Silk shook his head; Hyacinth said, "That's plenty, Chen," and he swiveled his seat to face Chenille. "Please tell me. I promise you that I won't hold it against her, whatever it is."

"No talk," Oreb croaked.

"I was going to tell you what happened next, but I'll skip it. She doesn't want me to, and she's probably right. Only she learned fast. She had to, or she'd of been killed. A couple days after that I saw a dell shove her, and Hy tripped her and wapped her with a chair. A lot of the other dells saw it too, and they left her alone. Are you wanting to ask something?"

Silk said, "No."

"I kind of thought you were, that you were about to ask me if Hy and I ever got into it."

Hyacinth shook her head.

"If I could've worn her clothes, maybe we would. Or if she could've worn mine. We weren't a knot, either, I'd be lying if I said we were. For one thing, she wasn't there long enough. I didn't like her a whole lot, even, but there were things I liked about her. I told you one time."

Auk said, "Sitting in that thing they got for the grapes back at your manteion, Patera. I was there."

Silk nodded. "Yes, I remember. I could tell you what you said, Chenille, almost word for word—not because my memory's remarkable, but because Hyacinth is so important to me."

He turned away to scan the instrument panel and the cloud-smeared sky, then turned to Auk. "As a favor, would you please bring Sciathan?"

"Sure." Auk rose. "Only I got to talk to you about those engines, see? I need you to tell me what you did to 'em, and if we're going to lose any more."

"I'll get him," Hyacinth said, and left the cockpit before Silk could stop her.

Chenille leaned nearer Silk. "She thinks you ought to be proud of her. I do too."

He nodded.

"Only you're not, and it hurts. The first time you saw her she had an azoth, and you had to jump out the window to get away. Isn't that right? Moly told me."

"It was terrifying," Silk admitted. Although he was not perspiring, he wiped his face with the hem of his robe. "The azoth cut through a stone windowsill. I don't believe I will ever forget it."

Auk said, "You think she was just some village chit after that, Patera?"

"No. No, I didn't. I knew exactly what she was."

He was silent then until Sciathan came into the cockpit and bowed, saying, "Do you desire to speak to me, Caldé Silk?"

"Yes. Have you flown an airship like this one?"

"Never. I have flown with my wings many times, but we crew have nothing like this save the *Whorl* itself, and that is flown by Mainframe, not by us."

"I understand. Just the same, you know a great deal about updrafts and downdrafts and storms; more than I'll ever learn. I've been flying this airship since a gust dispatched for our benefit by Molpe—or the Outsider, as I prefer to believe—returned us to the air. Now I want to leave the controls for a while. Will you take my place? I'd be extremely grateful."

The Flier nodded eagerly. "Oh, yes! Thank you, Caldé Silk. Thank you very much!"

"Then sit here." Silk left his seat, and Sciathan slid into it. "There are no reins, nor is there a wheel one turns, as there is in a floater. One steers with the engines. Do you understand?"

Sciathan nodded, and Auk cleared his throat.

"A west wind is carrying us toward Mainframe. We could fly faster, but it may be wise to conserve fuel. These dials give the speeds of all eight engines; as you see, four are no longer operating."

As quickly as he could, Silk outlined what he had learned of the functions of the levers and knobs on the panel; as soon as the Flier seemed to comprehend, Silk turned to Auk. "You wanted to know what I did to the engines. I did very little. I climbed up there into the cloth-covered body."

Auk said, "Sure. I knew you must of."

"Most of the space—it's enormous—is occupied by rows of huge balloons. There are bamboo walkways and wooden beams."

"I been on some."

"Yes, of course; you'd have had to in the fighting. What I was going to say is that there are tanks and hoses, too. I'd found a clamp, a simple one such as a carpenter might use."

Silk paused to glance at the bird on his shoulder. "It was then that Oreb joined me; I'd just picked it up. Anyway I put it on a hose, I suppose a fuel hose, and screwed it closed as tightly as I could. I doubt that it stopped the flow entirely, but it must have reduced it very considerably. It shouldn't be hard to find when you know what to look for."

Auk rubbed his chin. "Don't sound like it."

"For my conscience's sake, I should tell you that I lied to

Major Hadale—or anyway, I came very close to lying. She asked whether I could repair the engines; and I said, quite honestly I believe, that I could not. One speaks of repairs when a thing is broken. To the best of my knowledge, the engines we've lost aren't; but if they were, I wouldn't have the faintest notion how they might be repaired—thus I told her truthfully that repairing them was beyond my power. It was not a lie, though I certainly intended it to deceive her. If I'd said I might be able to set them in motion again, she would have had me beaten, I imagine, to compel me to do it."

Without turning toward them, Sciathan nodded vigorously.

"I'll ask Patera Incus to shrive me later today. Will you excuse me now? I . . . I would like very much to be alone."

As he left the cockpit, Auk told his back, "Get him to tell you how he charmed the slug gun."

A flimsy door of canvas stretched over a bamboo frame was all that separated the cockpit from a narrow aisle lined with green-curtained cubicles. Hearing a familiar voice, Silk pushed aside the curtain on his right.

The cubicle seemed overfilled by a bunk, a small table, and a stool; Nettle occupied the stool, holding a needler, and Saba smiled in a way that Silk found painful from the bunk.

"Poor girl," Oreb muttered.

Silk traced the sign of addition in the air. "Blessed be you, General Saba, in the Sacred Name of Pas, Father of the Gods, in that of Gracious Echidna, His Consort, in those of their Sons and their Daughters alike, in that of the Overseeing Outsider, and in the names of all other gods whatsoever, this day and forever. So say I, Silk, in the name of their youngest, fairest child, Steely Sphigx, Goddess of Hardihood and Courage, Sabered Sphigx, the glad and glorious patroness of General Saba and General Saba's native city."

"Gracious of you, Caldé. I thought you'd come to gloat."

Nettle shook her head. "You don't know him."

"I came—or at least I left the cockpit—to escape my friends," Silk told Saba. "I had no more than stepped out when I heard you and looked in. 'When neither our fellows nor our gods spoil our plans, we spoil them ourselves.' I read that when I was a boy, and I've learned since how very true it is."

Nettle said, "She was telling me about Trivigaunte, Caldé. I don't think I'd want to live there, but I'd like to see it."

"We go in for towers." Saba smiled. "We say it's because we build such good ones, but maybe we build good ones because we build so many of them. Towers and whitewash, and wide, clean streets. Your city looks," she paused, searching for a telling word, "squatty, like a camp. Squatty and dirty. I know you love it, but that's how it looks to us."

Silk nodded. "I understand. The interiors of our houses are clean, I believe, for the most part; but our streets are filthy, as you say. I was trying to do something about it, and a great many other things, when I was arrested."

"Not by me," Saba told him. "I didn't order it."

"I never thought you did."

"But you were talking to the enemy without telling us. If—" Saba's voice broke, and Oreb croaked in sympathy.

"We each have our sorrows." Silk let the green curtain fall behind him. "I won't ask you to palliate mine, but I may be able to ease yours. I'll try. What were you about to say?"

"I started to say I'd put in a word for you back home, that's all. Because we'll get you again when we get back this airship. If Siyuf's not running your city yet, she soon will be." Saba chuckled wryly. "Then I remembered where I stand. I'd forgotten, talking to this girl. I'm the general who went crazy and turned the airship east when it ought to have been headed home. That's what Hadale told them at the Palace, that I'd gone crazy. They'll think it was treachery and she was covering for me."

"You weren't insane," Silk told her. "You were possessed by Mucor, at my urging. You were possessed in the same way at my dinner. Others must have told you about it—Major Hadale, particularly, since she is your subordinate."

"I didn't want to hear it. Is Hadale your prisoner too?"

Silk shook his head. "She left the airship with most of your pterotroopers to capture a caravan. That let Auk and Gib and their friends overcome the rest."

Nettle held up her needler. "We fought too, Horn and me both. We'd fought hoppies already for General Mint, but a lot of Auk's people had never fought before. Hardly any of the women." To Saba she added, "Your pterotroopers were good, but our hoppies were better. You couldn't panic them."

"I'm sure you acquitted yourself creditably," Silk told her. "I, unfortunately, did not. Hyacinth knocked a needler from the pilot's hand and subdued her. I picked it up and held it, feeling an utter fool. I couldn't fire for fear of hitting Hyacinth, and with the needler in my hand I couldn't think of anything else to do. Then someone back here started shooting. Slugs came into the cockpit, and it was only by the favor of a god that all three of us weren't killed."

Silk paused, reflecting. "Have I thanked you, General, for your obvious goodwill? I should, and I do. I'll see to it that you're not mistreated, of course."

Saba shrugged. "That man Auk said I could stay in here, which was nice of him. Those were my jailers that almost shot you. I like this girl better."

She fell silent, and Silk found himself listening to the hum of the engines.

"My pterotroopers fought alongside Mint's when we were the only Trivigauntis in Viron, Caldé. We fought beside your Guard to get you out of that place outside the city, too. If I said I was planning to put in a good word for you already when we left Viron, would you believe it?"

"Of course."

"I wasn't, but I should have been. I was thinking about covering my own arse, as if that mattered."

"Don't torment yourself, General, I beg you." Silk pushed back the curtain that served the cubicle as a door. "In the second gondola there was a hatch toward the rear that opened onto the roof. Is there a similar hatch here?"

"Sure. I'll show you, if it's all right with her."

"That won't be necessary." Silk stepped back and let the curtain fall.

A rope ladder rolled and tied at the ceiling marked the hatch. Pulling a cord released the ladder. The light wooden hatch was held shut by a simple peg-and-cord retainer. Silk removed the peg, threw back the hatch, and climbed out onto the open, empty deck.

With a glad cry Oreb left his shoulder, racing the length of the gondola, shooting ahead of the airship until he was nearly lost to Silk's myopic vision, wheeling and soaring.

More circumspectly, Silk followed until he stood at the gondola's semicircular prow, the toes of the scuffed old shoes he had never found time to replace hanging over the aching void. He looked down at them, seeing them as if he had never seen them before, noting as items new and strange small cracks in their leather, and the ways in which the shoes had shaped themselves to his feet. Beside his left shoe there was a brass socket set into the deck. Presumably a flagpole would be put in it when the airship took part in military ceremonies in Trivigaunte.

Even more probably, similar sockets ringed the entire deck. Light poles would support railings of rope, used perhaps when dignitaries stood where he was standing now, bemedaled women in gorgeous uniforms waving to the populace below. It was even possible that the Rani herself had stood upon this very spot.

He recalled then that he had wished for flags to be raised on this airship to signal the approach of Siyuf's horde. The signalmen (who would more plausibly have been signal-women) would have kept watch from here with telescopes, would have run their flags up one of the immense cables from which the gondola hung. Below them—

Some minute motion of the gondola, some response to a tiny variation in the wind, nearly caused him to lose his balance; he came very close to putting his right foot forward to regain it, and would have fallen if he had, ending the persistent pain in its ankle.

It would not have been such a bad thing, perhaps, to have fallen. If one did not dread death, it would be an experience of unparalleled interest; to fall from such a height as this, a height greater than that of the loftiest mountain, would provide ample time for observation, prayer, and reflection, surely.

Eventually his body would strike the ground, probably in some unpeopled spot. His spirit would return to the Aureate Path, where once he had encountered his mothers and fathers; his bones would not be found—if they were found at all—until Nettle's children were grown. To the living he would not die but disappear, a source of wonder rather than sorrow. All men died, and all died very quickly in the eyes of the Outsider. Few died so well as that.

He peered upward to study the Aureate Path as it stretched before the airship's blunt nose, and again felt himself—very slightly—lose balance. If his parents waited there for him, they were not to be seen by the eyes of life.

One father had been Chenille's father as well. He, Silk, who had possessed no family save his mother, had gained a sister now. Although neither Chenille nor Hyacinth nor any other woman could take his mother's place. No one could.

Recalling the unmarked razor he had puzzled over so often, he fingered his stubbled cheeks. He had not shaved in well over a day; no doubt his beard was apparent to everyone. It was better, though, to know to whom the razor had belonged.

He looked down at his shoes again. Beneath them, Sciathan sat at the controls, steering a structure a hundred times larger than the Grand Manteion with the touch of a finger. There was no Sacred Window on the airship—that would have been almost impossible—but there was a glass somewhere. Idly Silk found himself wondering where it was. Not in the cockpit, certainly, nor in Saba's cubicle. Yet it would almost have to be in this gondola, in which the Rani's officers ate and slept, and from which they steered her airship. Perhaps in the chartroom; he had climbed to this deck from that chartroom without seeing it—but then he had been occupied with his thoughts.

Too much so to do anything to relieve Saba's depression. Yes, too self-centered for that. Saba and her pterotroopers might be outnumbered at present, but—

Hands upon his shoulders. *"Don't jump, Caldé!"*

He took a cautious step backward. "I hadn't intended to," he said, and wondered whether he lied.

He turned. Horn's pale face showed very clearly what Horn thought. "I'm sorry I frightened you," Silk told him, "I didn't know you were there."

"Just come away from the edge, please, Caldé. For me?"

To soothe Horn, he took a step. "You can't have been up here when I came—I would have seen you. You weren't on the roof of our old gondola either, because I looked back at it. Nettle told you I asked about a hatch, of course."

"A little farther, Caldé. Please?"

"No. This is foolish; but to reassure you, I'll sit down." He did, spreading his robe over his crossed legs. "You see? I can't possibly fall from here, and neither can you, if you sit. I need someone to talk to."

Horn sat, his relief apparent.

"When I was in the cockpit, I wanted to leave it in order to pray—that was what I told myself, at least. But when I was up here alone and might have prayed to my heart's content, I did not. I contemplated my shoes instead, and thought about certain things. They weren't foolish things for the most part, but I feel very foolish for having thought so much about them. Are you going with Auk when he leaves the whorl? That's what he's going to do, you know. The Crew, as Sciathan calls the people of his city, have some of the underground towers Mamelta showed me—intact underground towers—and they're going to give Auk one. I forget what Mamelta called them."

"You never told me about towers, Caldé."

Silk did, striving unsuccessfully to make his description concise. "That isn't all I can recall, but that's all that's of importance, I believe; and now that you mention it, I don't think I've ever told anyone, except for Doctor Crane while we were fellow-captives, and Doctor Crane is dead."

"I never even got to see him," Horn said. "I wish I had because of the way you talk about him. Is the underwater boat like this airship?"

"Not at all. It's all metal—practically all iron, I'm certain.

There's a hole at the bottom, too, through which the Ayuntamiento can launch a smaller boat. You'd think that would sink the big one, wouldn't you? But it didn't, and we got away through that hole, Doctor Crane and I." Silk paused, lost in thought. "There are monstrous fish in the lake, Horn, fish bigger than you can imagine. Chenille told me that once, and she's quite correct."

"You wanted to know if I was going with Auk. Nettle and me, because either way we'd do it together."

"Yes, of course."

"I don't think so. He hasn't asked us, but I don't think Nettle would want to if he did. There's my father and mother back home, and my brothers and sisters, and Nettle's family."

"Of course," Silk repeated.

"I like Chenille. I like her a lot. But Auk's not what I call a good man, even if Tartaros did choose him to enlighten. You remember what I told you about him that time? He's still the same, I think. The people he's got with him aren't much better, either. He calls them the best thieves in the whorl, did you know that, Caldé? Because of stealing this airship."

"They're not all thieves," Silk said, "Though Auk may like to pretend they are. Most are just poor people from the Orilla and our own quarter. I doubt that many real thieves have the sort of faith something like this requires." He fell silent, by no means sure that he should say more.

"What is it, Caldé?"

"I doubt that all of them will go. Chenille will, I think, though she would be a wealthy woman in Viron; but I wouldn't be in the least surprised to see more than a few of the others hold back."

"You're not going, are you, Caldé?"

Silk shook his head. "I would like to. I don't believe Hyacinth would, however; and these are Auk's people when all is said and done. Not mine."

"Then Nettle and me will come home with you and Hyacinth. Moly wants to go back, too. She wants to find her husband and get back to building their daughter. And there's Patera Incus and Patera Remora."

Silk nodded. "But we will not be numerous enough to keep the Trivigauntis we have on board from reclaiming their airship, even so. Had you thought of that, Horn? Not unless a great many of Auk's followers desert him at the last moment. It had just occurred to me when you laid hold of my shoulders."

Horn frowned. "Can we leave the Trivigauntis in Mainframe, Caldé? I can't think of anything else we can do."

"I can. Or at least, I believe I have, which gave me a very good reason not to step off the edge. Perhaps I needed one more than I knew." Noticing Horn's expression, he added, "I'm sorry if I distress you."

Horn swallowed. "I want to tell you something, sort of a secret. I haven't told anybody yet except Nettle. I know you won't laugh, but please don't tell anybody else."

"I won't, unless I believe it absolutely necessary."

"You know the cats' meat woman? She comes to sacrifice just about every Scylsday."

Silk nodded. "Very well."

"She likes Maytera. Moly, I mean. She came to see her one time at the palace. I wouldn't have thought she'd walk all the way up the hill, but she did. They were sitting in the kitchen, and the cats' meat woman—"

"Scleroderma," Silk murmured. His eyes were on the purple slopes of faraway mountains. "It's a puffball—it grows in forests."

"She was the one that held General Mint's horse for her before she charged the floaters in Cage Street," Horn continued. "She told Moly, and naturally Moly wanted to know all about it, so they talked about that and the fighting, and how Kypris came to our manteion for the funeral. Then she said she was writing all about it, writing down everything that had happened and how she'd been right in the middle of all the most important parts."

Silk tried not to smile, but failed.

"So she wants her grandchildren to be able to read about everything, and how she met you when you were just out of the schola, and how she walked up to the Caldé's Palace and they let her right in. I thought it was pretty funny too."

"I think it heart-warming," Silk told him. "We may laugh—I wouldn't be surprised if she laughed herself—and yet she's right. Her grandchildren are still small, I imagine, and though they've lived in these unsettled times themselves, they won't remember much about them. When they're older, they'll be delighted to have a history written by their own grandmother from the perspective of their family. I applaud her."

"Well, maybe I should of thought like that too, Caldé, but I didn't. To tell the truth, I got kind of mad."

"You didn't play some trick on her, I hope."

"No, but I started thinking about what had happened and if she'd really been in the middle like she said. Pretty soon I saw she hadn't at all, but you'd been there more than anybody, more even than General Mint. And what Scleroderma said about meeting you when you got out of the schola? Well, I met you then too. You used to come into our class and talk to us, and naturally I'd see you helping Patera Pike at sacrifice. So I decided I'm going to write down everything I can remember as soon as I get some paper. I'll call it Patera Silk's Book, or something like that."

"I'm flattered." This time Silk succeeded in suppressing his smile. "Are you going to write about this, too? Sitting up here talking to me?"

"Yes, I am." Horn filled his lungs with the still, pure air. "And that's another reason for you not to jump off. If you did, I'd have to end it right here." He rapped the deck with his knuckles. "Right up here, and then maybe I'd wonder a little about why you did, and then it would be over. I don't think that would be a very good ending."

"Nor would it be," Silk agreed.

"But that's the way you were thinking of ending it. You were standing too close to the edge to of been thinking about anything else. What's the trouble, Caldé? Something's—I don't know. Hurt you somehow, hurt you a lot. If I knew what it was, maybe I could help, or Nettle could."

Without rising, Silk turned away; after a moment, he slid

across the varnished wood so that he could let his legs dangle over the edge. "Come here, Horn."

"I'm afraid to."

"You aren't going to fall. Feel how smooth the motion of the airship is. Nor am I going to push you off. Did you think I might? I won't, I promise."

Face down, Horn crept forward.

"That's the way. It's such a magnificent view, perhaps the most magnificent that either of us will ever see. When you mentioned your class, you reminded me that I'm supposed to be teaching you—it's one of my many duties, and one that I've neglected shamefully since you and I talked in the manse. As your teacher, it's my pleasure as well as my duty to show you things like this whenever I can—and to make you look at them as well, if I must. Look! Isn't it magnificent?"

"It's like the skylands," Horn ventured, "except we're a little closer and it's daytime."

"A great deal closer, and the sun has already begun to narrow. We haven't much time left in which to look at this. A few hours at most."

"We could again tomorrow. We could look out of one of those windows. All the gondolas have them."

"This airship may crash tonight," Silk told him, "or it may be forced to land for some reason. Or the whorl below us might be hidden by clouds, as it was when I looked out of one of the windows earlier today. Let's look while we can."

Horn crept a finger's width nearer the edge.

"Down there's a city bigger than Viron, and those tiny pale dots are its people. See them? They look like that, I believe, because they're staring up at us. In all probability, they've never seen an airship, or seen anything larger than the Fliers that can fly. They'll speculate about us for months, perhaps for years."

"Is it Palustria, Caldé?"

Silk shook his head. "Palustria doesn't even lie in this direction, so it's certainly not Palustria. Besides, I think we've gone farther than that already. We were hoisted up early this morning, and we've been flying south or east ever since. A well-mounted man can ride there in less than a week."

"I've never seen off-center buildings like those," Horn ventured. "Besides, there aren't any swamps. Everybody says Palustria's in the middle of swamps."

"They've turned them into rice fields, or so I'm told—if not all of them at least a large part of them, no doubt the part closest to their city. Their rice crop's failed this year because of the drought. They say it's the first time the rice crop's failed in the entire history of Palustria." For a while Silk sat in silence, staring down at the foreign city below.

"Can I ask you something, Caldé?"

"Certainly. What is it?"

"Why isn't it windier up here? I've never been up on a mountain, but Maytera read something about that to us one time, and it said it was real windy just about all the time. Looking down, it seems like we're going fast. It's not taking us very long at all to go over this, and it's big. So the wind ought to be in our faces."

"I asked our pilot the same thing," Silk told him, "and I was ready to kick myself for stupidity when she told me. Look there, up and out, and you can see one of the engines that's still running. Notice how slowly it's turning? You can almost make out the wooden arms; but when the engines were going fast, those were just a blur, a shimmer in front of each engine."

"Like a mill."

"Somewhat; but while the arms of a windmill are turned by the wind, these are turned by their engines to create a wind that will blow us wherever we wish. They're making very little wind at present—just enough to keep us from tumbling about. We're being carried by a natural wind; but because we're blown along by it, like a dry leaf or one of those paper streamers the wind tore off our victory arch, it seems to us that the air is scarcely moving."

"I think I understand. What if we turned around and tried to go the other way?"

"Then this still air would at once become a gale."

The smooth wooden deck on which Silk was sitting tilted, seeming almost to fall away from under him.

"*Patera!*"

He felt Horn clutch his robe. The sound of the remaining engines rose. "I'm all right," he said.

"You could've slid off! I almost did."

"Not unless the gondola were to slope much more steeply." A vagrant breeze ruffled Silk's straw-colored hair.

"What happened?" From the sound of Horn's voice, he was far from the edge now, perhaps halfway to the hatch.

"The wind increased, I imagine. The new wind would have reached our tail first; presumably it lifted it."

"You still want to die."

The plaintive note in Horn's voice was more painful than an accusation. "No," Silk said.

"Won't you tell me what's wrong? Please, Caldé?"

"I would if I could explain it." The city was behind them already, its houses and fields replaced by forbidding forests. "I might say that it's an accumulation of small matters. Have you ever had a day when everything went amiss? Of course you have—everyone has."

"Sure," Horn said.

"Can you come a little closer? I can scarcely hear you."

"All right, Caldé."

"I also want to say that it has to do with the Plan of Pas; but that isn't quite right. Pas, you see, isn't the only god who has a plan. I've just understood this one, perhaps while I was still in the cockpit, as it's called, guiding this airship and thinking—when I didn't have to think much about that— about Hyacinth's overpowering our pilot. Or perhaps only when I was talking with General Saba, just before I came up here. It might be fair to say that I understood in the cockpit, but that the full import of what I had understood had come only when I was talking with Nettle and General Saba."

"I think I get it."

"On the other hand, I could say that it was about facts that the Outsider confided on my wedding night. You see, Horn, I was enlightened again then. Nothing I learned at the schola had prepared me for the possibility of multiple enlightenments, but clearly they can and do take place. Which would you like to hear about first?"

"The little things going wrong, I guess. Only please come back here with me, Patera. You said it was hard to hear me. Well, I can hardly hear you."

"I'm perfectly safe, Horn." Silk discovered that he was grasping the edge of the deck; he forced himself to relax, placing his hands together as if in prayer. "We might begin anywhere, but let us begin with Maytera Marble. With Moly, as she asks us to call her now. Do you think her name was really Moly—Molybdenum—before she became a sibyl? Honestly."

"That's what she says, Caldé." Horn was moving closer; Silk heard the faint scrub of his coat and trousers against the planking.

"I don't. She hasn't told me she's lying, but I hope she will soon."

"I—I don't think so, Caldé." Horn's tones grew deeper as he asserted his opinion. "She's really careful about that kind of thing."

"I know she is. That's why it's such a torment to her. I'm going to ask Patera Incus to shrive me. I hope that it will lead her to ask him—or Patera Remora, though Incus would be better—to do the same."

"I still—"

"Why are there so few chems now, Horn? There the Plan of Pas has clearly gone awry. He made them both male and female, and clearly intended them to reproduce and so maintain their numbers—perhaps even increase them. Let us assume that he peopled our whorl with equal numbers of each sex, which would seem to be the logical thing for him to do. What went wrong?" It was becoming colder, or Silk more sensitive to the cold. He drew his thick winter robe about him.

"I don't know, Caldé. The soldiers sleep a lot, and naturally they can't, you know, build anybody then."

"Ours do, at least. Most of the soldiers in most other cities are dead. Most have been dead for a century or longer. Pas should have made female soldiers, like the troopers from Trivigaunte. He didn't, and that was clearly an error."

"You shouldn't say things like that, Patera."

"Why not, if I think them true? Would Pas like me better if I were a coward? Some male chems were artisans and farm laborers, from what I know of them, and a few were servants—butlers and so forth. But most were soldiers, and the soldiers fought for their cities and died, or slept as Hammerstone did. The female chems, who were largely cooks or maids, wore out and died childless. Nearly every soldier must have courted a cook or a maid, three hundred years ago. And nearly every such cook and maid must have loved a soldier. How likely is it that such a couple would be reunited by chance after centuries?"

"It could happen." Horn sounded defiant.

"Of course it could. All sorts of unlikely things can, but they rarely do. Something has been troubling her ever since she and Hammerstone were married, and I believe I know what it is. Let's leave it at that."

"Even if you're right," Horn said, "That's not a very good reason to want to die."

"I disagree, but let's move on. In the cockpit, I realized that Chenille and Hyacinth had fought when both of them were at Orchid's—she was the woman who paid for the funeral at which Kypris spoke to us, not that it matters. My sister—"

"I didn't know you had a sister, Caldé."

Silk smiled. "Forget I said that, please; it was a slip of the tongue. I was about to say that Chenille blacked Hyacinth's eyes, which isn't surprising since she's considerably larger and stronger. Nor do I blame her. If Hyacinth has forgiven her, and she clearly has, I can do no less. But they lied about it, both of them, and I found it very painful. I can't prove they lied, Horn; but if you'd been there, you would have caught the lie just as I did. Hyacinth identified an incident to which Chenille was about to refer before Chenille specified it. That could only mean that Chenille was much more closely involved than she pretended."

A wide river dotted with ice divided the forest below. Silk

leaned forward to study it. "You'll say that what I've told you is not a good reason to die. Again, I disagree."

"Caldé . . . ?"

"Yes. What is it?"

"You don't look like her. Like Chenille. She's got that red hair, but it's dyed. Underneath her hair's dark, I think. Your eyes are blue, but hers are brown, and like you said she's real big and strong. You're tall and pretty strong, but . . ."

"You need not proceed, Horn, if it embarrasses you."

"What I mean is she'd be a lot like Auk if she was a man. You'd be a better runner, but—but . . ."

"We are alike in certain ways, I suppose."

"That's not it." Horn was less at ease than ever. "Since you've been caldé everybody talks about the old one. Then last night before those women came you were talking about his will. Nettle told me, and this's her idea, really. He said he had an adopted son, and this son was going to be the next one. What Nettle says is he didn't say to make it happen, he just said it would. Is that right?"

Silk nodded. " 'Though he is not the son of my body, my son will succeed me.' "

"Chenille's his real daughter, Nettle told me that too. And you're the next caldé. So if she's your sister—"

"We will go no further with this, Horn. It has nothing to do with our topic."

"All right. I won't tell anybody."

"There are so many lies in the whorl that it's not likely anyone would credit you if you did. May I instance one more? Hyacinth subdued our pilot, Hyacinth alone. I mentioned it."

"Yes, Caldé."

"I've been trying to think of an enlightening analogy for you, but I can't. Suppose I were to say that it was like seeing Patera Incus overpower Auk. The analogy would be flawed because I've never supposed that Patera Incus could not fight, only that he would fight badly. I had imagined Hyacinth would be helpless in the face of violence; she spoke of taking fencing from Master Xiphias once, yet I never . . ."

"I can't hear you. Can't you turn around this way?"

"No. Come closer." Silk found Horn's hand and drew him nearer the edge.

"Nobody thought you could fight either, Caldé."

"I know, and they had almost convinced me of it. That was a part of the reason I broke into Blood's—I needed to prove I wasn't the milksop everyone took me for. Nor was I, though I was badly frightened most of the time."

"Maybe that's how Hyacinth felt about the pilot." Greatly daring, Horn sat up, his legs stretched before him and his feet on the edge of the deck. "Hyacinth's real girly when you're around. We got lots of it this morning. She smiles whenever you look at her and holds on like she can't stand up. She wants you to like her. Caldé, you know that big cat Mucor's got?"

Silk was staring down at a mountain valley, following the snowy rush of a young river over red stones. "You mean Lion?"

"I don't know the name, but Lion sounds like a boy. This was a girl cat, I think, kind of gray, with long pointed ears and a little short tail. I saw it one time when I brought up Mucor's dinner. It really liked her. It would rub up against her and smile. Cats can smile, Caldé."

"I know."

"It kept putting its paw in Mucor's lap so she'd pet it, but it wasn't too sure about me. It showed me its teeth, pulling its lips back without making any noise. I was pretty scared."

"So was I, Horn. I shot two of those horned cats once; I'm very sorry for that now." Silk leaned forward again. "Look at that cliff, Horn. Can you see it?"

"Sure, I saw it just a minute ago. I don't think I could climb it, but I'd like to try." Horn made himself speak more loudly. "I know what Hyacinth seems like to you, Caldé, but she seems a lot like Mucor's cat to Nettle and me. She's respectful to Moly, though."

Silk glanced over his shoulder. "You're right, there is a great deal of good in Hyacinth, though I would love her even if there were none."

Horn shook his head. "I was going to say she sort of hits it off with Hammerstone. He can be awful rough."

"Yes, I'm well aware of it."

"He likes Moly and Patera Incus, so he's nice to them. But he treats Nettle and me like sprats, and with other people he's like Auk. Hyacinth won't give him half a step, and once when she got mad she called him all kinds of names. I thought I knew all those. I learned most of that stuff when I was little, but she had some I never heard. If the pilot pulled a needler on Mucor, what do you think her cat would do?"

"Come here," Silk told him. "Sit with me. Are you afraid I'll take you with me if I jump? I'm not going to, and I'd like you beside me."

"I'm still pretty scared."

"You would have climbed that cliff, given the chance. You would be no more dead falling from here."

"All right." Gingerly, Horn edged forward until his legs dangled over the abyss of air. Oreb settled on his shoulder.

"As I said, I've neglected my duty to teach you. Now I can actually show you part of the Plan. I find it enlightening, and you may, too. See the city ahead? The mountains we crossed isolate it from the west. Soon we'll see what isolates it from the east; and if we were to turn north or south, we'd come upon barriers there as well. Some are more formidable than others, of course."

"Their houses are like people, Caldé. Look, there's Pas, with the two heads. Even the little ones are like people lying down, see? The thatch makes it look like they've got blankets."

"Good place." Oreb bobbed on Horn's shoulder.

"It is," Silk agreed, "but if we weren't used to seeing Pas pictured like this, we'd think this image the more horrible— and it is horrible—for being so large. I won't ask if you've lain with a woman, Horn; it's too personal a matter to broach save in shriving, and I know you too well to shrive you. Should you wish to be shriven, I hope you'll go to Patera Remora."

"All right."

"I had not until my wedding night. Indeed, it remains my only such experience. You needn't tell me that Hyacinth has lain with scores of men. I knew it and was acutely conscious of it; so was she. I can't say what our experience meant to her, and perhaps it meant little or nothing. To me it was wonderful. Wonderful! I came to her as one starving. And yet—"

Still very frightened, Horn jerked his head. "I know."

"Good. I'm glad you understand. There was a taint that came from neither Hyacinth nor me, but from the act itself. After two hours, or about that, I rested. We had done what men and women do more than once, and more than twice. I was happy, exhausted, and soiled. I felt that Echidna, particularly, was displeased; and I doubt that I would have had the courage if I had not rejected her in my heart after her theophany. You were there, I know."

Horn nodded again. "She's a very great goddess, Caldé."

"She is. Great and terrible. It may be that I was wrong to reject her—I won't argue the point. I only say that I had, and felt as I did. As I've said, the Outsider enlightened me a second time then. I won't tell you all that he told me—I couldn't. But one thing was that he created Pas. The Seven, as everyone knows, are the children of Pas and Echidna; it had never occurred to me to wonder whence they themselves came. Why do you think Pas built barriers between our cities, Horn?"

The sudden question caught him off guard. "To keep them from fighting, Caldé?"

"Not at all. Not only do they fight, but he knew that they would; if he hadn't, he wouldn't have provided them with armies. No, he erected mountains and dug rivers and lakes so they could not combine against him. More specifically, so they couldn't combine against Mainframe, the home he was to set over them."

"Did the Outsider tell you that, Caldé?"

Silk shook his head. "Hammerstone did, and Hammerstone is right. The Outsider, as he showed me, has no reason to fear our leaguing against him. We've done it innumerable times, just as we betray him daily as individuals. His fear—he is afraid for our sake, not his own—is that we may come to love other things more than we love him. When I was at your manteion on Sun Street, foolish people used to ask me why Pas or Scylla permitted some action that they regarded as evil, as if a god had to sign a paper before a man could be struck or a child fall ill. On my wedding night, the Outsider explained why it is that he permits what people call evil at all—not this theft or that uncleanness, but the thing itself. It serves him, you see. It hates him, yet it serves him, too. Does this make sense to you, Horn?"

"Like a mule that kicks whenever it gets a chance."

"Exactly. That mule is harnessed like the rest and draws the wagon, however unwillingly. Given the freedom of the whorl—and even of those beyond it—evil directs us back to the Outsider. I told you I rejected Echidna; I thought I did it because she is evil, but the truth is that I did it because he is better. A child who burns its hand says the fire's bad, as the saying goes; but the fire itself is saying, 'Not to me, child. Reach out to him.' "

"I think I see. Caldé, I'm getting pretty cold."

"Fish heads?" Oreb inquired.

Silk nodded. "We'll go in soon, so you and Oreb will be warm and can get something to eat; but first, have you been looking at our whorl, Horn? This is winter wheat below us, I believe. See how the sunlight plays on it, how it ripples in the wind, displaying every conceivable shade of green?"

"You still haven't told me—maybe I shouldn't ask you—"

"Why I was tempted to jump? It's obvious, isn't it?"

Oreb squawked, "Look out!"

Already, Horn was sliding from the edge of the deck; the face he turned toward Silk displayed Mucor's deathly grin.

"You know where Silk is?" Auk stepped into the cockpit and shut the flimsy door behind him.

Sciathan pointed to the ceiling, his urchin face all sharp *V*'s. "Upstairs, which is what you call me. I saw shoes and stockings, and the legs of trousers at the top." He gestured toward the slanted pane before him. "The trousers were black, the shoes and stockings the same, the legs too long for the smallest augur. The tallest, I think, would not do this."

"They ain't there any more." Auk bent, craning his neck to peer upward. "I ought to tell you, too. Number Seven ought to work if you start it."

Sciathan flicked two switches and nodded appreciatively as a needle rose. "You have removed his clamp."

"There was more to it than that. We're working on Number Five now. They got 'em out on booms, see?"

"I have observed this. In a moment I shall tell you what else I have observed."

"Only you can haul the booms in to fix the engines. It's a pretty good system. We had to yank the heads and beat on the pistons some, but we didn't hurt 'em much. What'd you see?"

"Another seated beside Silk. It is hazardous to sit thus."

"You said it."

"The other was almost chilled . . ." Sciathan paused, his head cocked. "Caldé Silk comes now to General Saba's cabin. I hear his voice."

Leaving the cockpit, Auk saw that Saba's curtain was drawn back. Silk stood where it had hung, and a perspiring Horn had crowded into the cubicle beside Nettle.

"—don't know how to put this, exactly," Silk was saying. "I ought to have given that more thought while I was up on the roof a moment ago." He glanced over his shoulder. "Hello, Auk. I'm glad you're here; I was going to send Nettle for you. We're about to return her airship to General Saba."

Oreb bobbed in assent as Auk stared.

"I don't mean, of course, that we're not going to take you to Mainframe—you and Sciathan, and the rest. We are. Or rather, she is; Hyacinth and I will accompany her, with Nettle, Horn, His Eminence, Patera Remora, and Moly."

Saba grinned at Auk. "I don't understand this either, but I like it."

"Of course you do," Silk told her, "and so will Auk. We all should, because it will help every one of us."

He turned back to Auk. "A small ceremony at which you

return General Saba's sword might be appropriate. Would you like that?"

Auk shook his head.

"It wasn't taken from her, in any event. It's still in that box at the foot of her bed, she tells me."

Nettle displayed her needler. "Can I put this up?"

Auk snapped, "Keep it!"

"A very small ceremony, then—here and now. Would you get out your sword for me, General? I'll give it to Auk, who will give it back to you. You should wear it thereafter. It will hearten your troopers, I'm confident."

Auk declared, "We're not giving the slug guns back."

"Not now, at least. That will depend upon whether there are arms on the craft the Crew provides you, though I imagine there will be."

Horn mopped his forehead. "Nobody understands this except you, Caldé."

"It's simple enough. Neither General Saba nor I desire a war between Viron and Trivigaunte. We Vironese have seized this airship, the pride of its city."

Horn looked to Nettle, who said, "They'd seized *us.*"

"Exactly. Another reason for war, which General Saba and I wish to prevent. The solution is obvious—our freedom for the airship."

"We're free now!"

"Nobody can be truly free without peace. Consider the alternative. When we returned to Viron, Generalissimo Siyuf would try to recapture this airship by force, while General Mint and Generalissimo Oosik tried to prevent her; it would cost five hundred lives the first day—at least that many, and perhaps more."

Saba told Nettle, "You're going to have to wait a little before you get a tour of Trivigaunte. When he wanted to know if I'd take you home if I got my airship back, I was too surprised to say anything. But I will, and let Auk here and the rabble we loaded first out at Mainframe, if that's what he wants." She bent over her footlocker. "Some of you are afraid

I'm going to cross you. All of you, except your caldé, most likely."

Auk grunted.

She straightened up, holding a sharply curved saber with a gem-studded hilt. "This is the sword of honor the Rani awarded me last year, and I'm proud of it. Maybe I haven't worn it as much as I ought to for fear something might happen to it."

Oreb whistled, and Nettle told Saba, "It's beautiful!"

Saba smiled at Auk. "The girl let me keep it. I told her about it, and she said leave it where it is, Auk won't mind."

He muttered, "I'd like mine back. That Colonel's got it."

"If you come back with us, I'll try to get it for you."

"No cut!" Oreb hopped from Silk's shoulder to Saba's to examine the sword more closely.

She drew it and took a half step backward, holding it at eye level with both hands grasping the blade. "By this sword I swear that as long as Caldé Silk's on my airship, I'll do whatever he tells me, and when I land him and his friends at their city it will be as passengers, and not prisoners."

Silk nodded. "On the terms you have described, General, we return command to you."

"You're going to let me talk to the Palace on the glass and tell them what we're doing?"

"If you choose to. You are in command."

Saba lowered her sword. "Then if I break my oath, you can take this and break it."

She led them through the gondola to the airy compartment from which Silk had climbed to the deck. It held cabinets, a sizable table, and two leather seats; there was a glass on the wall, next to the door. "This is the chartroom," Saba told Silk, "The nerve center of my airship, where our navigational instruments and maps are. There's a speaking tube that runs through officers' quarters to the cockpit. Do you know about those? Like a glass, but only to the one place and all you can do is talk."

"This's where you ought to be," Auk said, but Silk shook his head.

Saba pointed. "Right up there's the hatch. We go up to take the angle between the ship and the sun, mostly. Now it should be zero." She swallowed. "I'll check it as soon as I talk to the Palace."

Horn touched Silk's arm. "Don't go back, Caldé. Please?"

Auk asked, "You were up there, huh? Somebody nearly got killed is what I heard."

"He was going to jump off," Horn told Auk. "I grabbed him and I guess I got him back, only I don't remember, just sort of wrestling, and the roof gone, and music." Puzzled, he stared at Silk. "Someplace down there was having a concert, I guess."

"I saw the evil in the whorl," Silk explained. "I thought I knew it, when I actually had no idea. A few days ago, I began to see it clearly."

He waited for someone to speak, but no one did.

"An hour ago, I saw it very clearly indeed; and it was horrible. What was worse was that instead of focusing on the evil in myself, as I should have, I gave my attention to the evil in others. I would have told you then that I saw a great deal in Horn, for example. I still do."

"Caldé, I never said—"

"That was utterly, utterly wrong. I don't mean that the evil isn't there—it is, and it always will be because it is ineradicable; but seeing it alone, not merely Horn's evil but everyone else's too, did something to me far worse than anything Horn himself would ever do, I'm sure—it blinded me to good. Seeing only evil, I wanted with all my heart to reunite myself with the Outsider. That would itself have been an evil act, but Horn saved me from it."

"I'm so glad." Nettle looked at Horn with shining eyes.

"Just by coming up on the roof of this gondola, really. For Horn's sake, I won't go there again, though it's such a marvelous thing to stand in the sky smiling down at the whorl that I find it difficult to renounce it; merely by standing there, I came to understand how Sciathan feels about flying."

Auk cleared his throat. "I want to tell you about that clamp.

All right if I do it now, before she talks to 'em back in Trivi-gaunte?"

"You found it, I assume."

"Yeah, only that wasn't a fuel hose. It was a lube hose."

Saba's eyes opened wide. *"What!"*

Auk ignored her. "The clamp cut the flow to where they got hot and seized. It didn't show on the gauge up front 'cause it just measures tank temperature. The tank was all right and the pump was running, but there wasn't much getting through. We got Number Seven busted loose, and maybe we can fix the rest."

"They'll never be as good as they were." Saba sounded disgusted.

"They weren't anyhow," Auk told her. "I made a couple little improvements already."

Oreb eyed them both. "Fish heads?"

"I feel the same way myself," Silk announced. "If I'm to live after all, I'd like something to eat."

Saba stepped to the glass and clapped; it grew luminous, as the monitor's gray face coalesced. At once dancing flecks of color replaced it—peach, pink, and an ethereal blue that deepened until it was nearly black.

Silk fell to his knees; for him the sunlit chartroom and its occupants vanished.

"Silk?" The face in the glass was innocent and sensual, preternaturally lovely. "Silk, wouldn't you like to be Pas? We'd be together then . . . Silk."

He bowed his head, unable to speak.

"They can scan you at Mainframe. As I was scanned, Silk, with him. He held my hand. . . ."

Silk found that he was staring up at her; she smiled, and his spirit melted.

"You'll go on with your life. Silk. Just as it is. You'd be Pas too. And he would be you. Look . . ."

The face lovelier than any mortal woman's dispersed like smoke. In its place stood a bronze-limbed man with rippling muscles and two heads.

One was Silk's.

Chapter 16

EXODUS FROM
THE LONG SUN

They floated in an infinite emptiness lit by a remote, spool-shaped black sun: Sciathan the Flier, Patera Incus and Patera Remora, the old woman who called herself Moly, Nettle and Horn, the calde's wife, and the calde. The shrinking red dot that was the lander winked out.

"Good-bye, Auk my noctolater." The speaker seemed near, though there was a note in his voice that had traveled far; it was a man's voice, deep, and heavy with sorrow.

"Good-bye, Auk," Silk repeated; until he heard his own voice, he did not realize he had spoken aloud. "Good-bye, sister. Good-bye, Gib. Farewell."

Maytera Marble murmured, "Heartbroken. Poor General Mint will be simply heartbroken."

"He goes to a better place than any you have seen."

"I *disliked* him, though the harlot *Chenille* was not devoid of *pre-eminent qualities. Notwithstanding,* I feel *bereft . . .*"

So softly that Silk supposed that only he could hear her, Hyacinth inquired, "Is that where? Those little dots?"

"To one or the other," the god replied. "The blue whorl or the green. Auk's lander cannot carry them to both."

"Auk—ah. Devoted to you, eh? As we, um, all. He was, er, reformed? Devout. If you are not, um, hey?"

There was no reply. The distant sparks faded. Hyacinth gripped Silk's arm, pointing to the black, spool-shaped sun behind them, from which light streamed. "What *is* that? Is it— is it . . . ? The lander came out of it."

"That is our *Whorl.*" Sciathan wiped his eyes.

"That little thing?"

Already the little thing was fading; Silk relaxed. "You liked Auk, didn't you? So did I. If I live as long as His Cognizance, I won't forget meeting him in the Cock, sipping brandy while I tried to make out his face in the shadows."

"When I saw Aer die, I did not weep. That pain was too deep for weeping. Auk is not dead, but no one will call me Upstairs any more. I weep for that."

"Wish that he stated, um, unequivocally, eh?" Remora had already activated his propulsion module and was drifting toward the circular aperture. "Is—um—Great Pas satisfied? Is this adequate? Sufficient?"

Silk and Hyacinth followed him. Silk said, "If he were, we Cargo would return to our herds and fields. Auk has bought us a brief respite, that's all. Pas will not be satisfied until the last person in the whorl has gone. It has served its purpose."

They emerged into the penumbra, shade that seemed blinding light after the darkness. "I don't see how Tartaros showed us the whorl from outside," Hyacinth murmured. "There can't be an eye out there, can there?" When Silk did not reply, "I don't like not walking. My thighs are getting fat, I can feel it."

Maytera Marble overtook them. "They can't be, dear, you don't eat anything. I'm worried about you."

"I don't like people seeing up my gown, either. I know it sounds silly, but I don't. Every time I feel like somebody's looking up there my thighs swell up and never go back down."

"There is no *up,*" Incus called as he accelerated toward them, "nor is there *any down.* All is a realm of *light.*"

"The, um, deceased." Remora glanced back at him, vaguely worried. "How shall we explain that, Your Eminence? The, um, faithful, eh? They expect the—ah—dear decedent."

"Do you desire a visitation by your dead?" Sciathan asked.

Silk said firmly, "No." Hyacinth's jaw dropped, and for a moment her sculptured face looked foolish.

Silk decelerated to allow Sciathan to catch up. "I speak only for myself. I've met mine, and know and love them. The temptation to rejoin them would be too great. I know your offer was well intended—but no, I do not."

"There is no physicality," the little Flier explained. "Mainframe recreates them and beams the data to one's mind."

"Moly, would you escort Hyacinth back to the airship for me, please? I have to confer with Sciathan." Silk took the Flier's arm.

Horn asked, "Can we come?" Silk hesitated, then shook his head; Oreb launched himself from Horn's shoulder to flap after them upside down.

One by one the pilot was testing the engines; Horn counted as each coughed, roared to life, and declined to a hum.

Nettle asked, "Aren't you going to knock?"

He would have preferred that she do it, but could not say so. "What on?"

"On the frame, I guess. They're pretty solid."

Silk pushed the curtain to one side as Horn raised his fist. "Hyacinth isn't here. Were you looking for me?"

Both nodded.

"Very well, what can I do for you?"

Horn cleared his throat. "You promised me you wouldn't go up on the roof again, Caldé. Remember?"

"Of course. I've kept my promise."

"Me and Nettle have been up there," Horn said, and Oreb applauded with joyful wings.

Nettle said, "It's not scary when you can float." Her eyes appealed to Horn, who added, "We want you to go up with us."

"You're releasing me from my promise?"

Horn nodded. "Yeah."

"Say *yes,* Horn." Silk looked thoughtful. "You bear the repute of your palaestra."

"Yes, Caldé. Caldé, is Patera Remora really going to be our new augur?"

"No." Absentmindedly, Silk glanced around the cubicle for his propulsion module before remembering that he had returned it. "He cannot become your new augur, since he is augur there already. He'll take up his duties when we get home. How do you keep from floating away? That might not be frightening, I'll allow; but I would think it serious."

"Bird save!"

"Yes, if I'm adrift you must tow me to safety."

"There's supplies in the last gondola," Horn explained as Silk pushed off from the doorway. "We found a coil of rope in there. The table in the chartroom's bolted down, so we tie onto the legs."

"It's better than having that thing on your back," Nettle told Silk. "You just float around without having to worry about anything. When you're tired of it, you pull yourself in."

Horn added, "But I don't get tired of it."

"There's something you want me to see." They had floated through the officers' sleeping quarters; Silk stopped, bulging the canvas partition, and opened the door to the messroom.

"Just—just everything you can see from out there."

"Something to ask, in that case."

In the chartroom, Silk knotted the finger-thick line about his waist in accordance with Horn's instructions and pushed off from the table, out through the open hatch.

The airship had revolved, whether from the torque of its engines or the pressure of some passing breeze, until Mainframe stood upright as a wall, its black slabs of colossal mechanism jutting toward them and its Pylon an endless bridge that dwarfed the airship and vanished into night.

Horn gestured. "See, Caldé? We don't have to sit on the edge, but we can go over there if you want to. Way, way down you can see the Mountains That Look At Mountains, I guess. It's kind of blue at first, then so bright you can't be sure."

Nettle emerged from the hatch. "I still don't understand what Mainframe is, Caldé. Just all those things with the lights running over them? And why do they have roofs here if it can't rain? How would they get the rain to come down?"

"This is Mainframe," Silk told her. "You are seeing it."

"The big square things?"

"With what underlies its meadows and lawns; Mainframe is dispersed among them all. Imagine millions of millions of tiny circuits like those in a card—billions of billions, actually. The warmth of each is less than the twinkle of a firefly; but there are so many that if they were packed together their own heat would destroy them. They would become a second sun. As things are it is always summer here, thanks to those circuits."

"That's what you call the little wiggly gold lines in card?" Nettle inquired. "Circuits? They don't do anything."

"They would, if they were returned to their proper places in a lander. We will have to return some ourselves soon."

Horn was watching Silk narrowly. "Did Sciathan tell you all that?"

"Not in so many words, but he said enough to let me infer the rest. What was it you wanted to ask?"

"A whole bunch of stuff. You know, Caldé, for my book. Is it all right if I call you Caldé?"

"Of course. Or Patera, or Silk, or even Patera Caldé, which is what His Cognizance calls me. As you like."

"I heard Chenille tell Moly that when she was Kypris she made you call her Chenille anyway. It must have seemed funny."

Nettle said, "I'm not writing a book, Caldé, but I've got stuff I want to ask, too. I'm helping Horn with his, I guess. I'll have to, probably. Did you make the dead people come back and talk to us like they did?"

"Mainframe did that, Nettle." Silk smiled. "Believe me, I'm unable to compel it to do anything. I asked Sciathan to ask it on our behalf, but he explained that it was unnecessary. Mainframe knows everything that takes place here; as soon as I formulated my request, Mainframe took it under consideration. I'm delighted that it was granted, immensely grateful."

"But not back home." Nettle waved vaguely at the deck some ten cubits below. "It doesn't hear everything there."

"No, it doesn't; but it discovers more than I would have believed. Since Echidna's theophany, I've assumed the gods knew only what they saw and heard through Sacred Windows and glasses, which seems to be very near the truth. Those are Mainframe's principal sources, too; but it has others—the Fliers' data, for example."

Horn said, "I've got a tough one, Caldé. I'm not trying to show you up or anything."

"Of course not. What is it?"

"Tartaros told Auk the short sun whorl would be like ours, only there wouldn't be any people, or no people like us. Auk told Chenille, and I asked her. She said it means there'll be grass and rocks and flowers, only not like we're used to. Why is that?"

Nettle shook her head in disbelief. "That's not hard at all. Because Pas picked them out for us to make it easy."

"Or difficult," Silk muttered.

"I don't understand."

"Suppose there were no plants or animals—we'll leave the rocks aside. Auk's lander is stocked with seeds and embryos, as you saw. He'll be able to grow whichever ones he wants; and if the whorl he chooses had none of its own, those would be the only plants and animals with which he would have to deal. As things are, he'll have a much more interesting time of it—as well as a much harder one."

The hum of their engines deepened, and the three of them drifted toward the prow of the second gondola until the ropes that united them with the first were taut. "We're under way," Horn announced. Oreb agreed: "Go home!"

"As soon as we're gone, I don't think I'll believe I was here." Nettle sighed. "Grandma came for a talk. I said stay with me and we'll take you back, but she said she couldn't."

"Patera Remora's mother came to see him," Horn told Silk.

"He's been smiling at everybody. He told her he had his own manteion now, and he'd sacrifice and shrive and bring the Peace, and wouldn't have to work in the Palace any more. And she said it's what she'd wanted for him all the time."

"Hyacinth's mother visited her, too."

Nettle looked surprised. "I didn't think her mother was dead, Caldé."

"Neither did Hyacinth."

Hand over hand they pulled themselves forward again, until they were standing on the deck, although standing very lightly; Silk freed himself from the loop of rope.

Nettle said, "Caldé, you never did answer my question about the roofs. And I wanted to know why the shade's so close here, and we can't see the sun."

"The Pylon makes it," Horn declared, "or anyhow it shoots it into the sky. Isn't that right, Caldé? Then the sun burns it but instead of smoke it turns into air. If the Pylon didn't shoot out more, the shade would burn up and there'd be daylight all the time. Only Mainframe would fry, because it's so close. The sun starts at the top of the Pylon and goes all the way to the West Pole."

"Long way," Oreb elaborated.

"We, too, have a long way to go," Silk said, addressing neither Horn nor Nettle, "but at last we've begun."

"I understand about the roofs now," Nettle said.

He looked around at her. "Do you? Tell me."

"We used to go to the lake every summer when I was little. Then . . . I don't know, something happened, and it seemed like we never had enough money."

"Taxes went up after the old caldé died," Horn told her. "They went up a lot."

"Maybe that was it. Anyway, one year when I was nine or ten we waited till everybody else had gone home, and went when it was cheaper, and after that we never went any more."

Silk nodded.

"It would be nice, sometimes, in the afternoons, and we'd swim, but it was pretty cold in the morning. One morning I got up when everybody else was still asleep and walked to the lake just to look at it. I think I knew this was the last year, and we wouldn't come any more. Maybe we were going home that day."

"This isn't about roofs," Horn said; but Silk put a finger to his lips.

"The lake was all covered with ghosts, white shapes coming up out of the water and reaching for the air, getting bigger and stronger all the time. I was thinking about ghosts a lot then, because Gam had, you know, gone to Mainframe, the one I talked to today. We were supposed to say she was in Mainframe, but we didn't think it meant anything. Aren't you going to say that it wasn't really ghosts, Horn?"

He shook his head.

"It wasn't, it was fog. There was an old lady fishing off the pier, and I guess she liked me because when I asked she said there was water in the air over the lake, and when it got cold enough it came together and made tiny little drops that take a long, long while to fall, and that was what you saw. I'd never wondered where fog came from before then."

"Fog good."

"That's right, you're a marsh bird. Don't they come from Palustria, Caldé? The swamps around there?"

Silk nodded. "I believe so."

"What I was going to say was that the fog got thicker and thicker that day, and got everything wet. So if they have a lot of fogs here . . . We're not hardly there, though, any more. But you know what I mean. Only you wouldn't want it inside, so you'd have roofs, and they do."

Horn said, "The fountains get the grass wet, too, like it does at home on a windy day. It's not as much as you'd think, because there's a thing that sucks in air at the bottom and takes the water out for the pump. If they shut that off, it would water everything."

Silk tossed aside his rope and watched it settle to the deck. "We have weight once more."

"Yeah, I know. I mean yes."

"I should consider this better before I speak, Horn, but I find it exhilarating. When we arrived and could float—could fly, after a fashion, after Sciathan secured propulsion modules for us—I found that exhilarating as well. I'm contradicting myself, I suppose."

Horn looked to Nettle, who said, "I don't think so."

"It's not easy for me to sort out, and even less easy for me to explain. Sciathan is a Flier, in love with flight and pardonably proud of his wings and his special status among the Crew. Until we got here, I was confident that I understood his feelings."

Horn looked puzzled. "Everybody flies here, Caldé."

"Exactly. They have to, and we flew in the same way. Or floated. *Floated* may be the better term. It's easy, so much so that all three of us floated here without modules; but we floated under a lowering shade that never brought night or rose to bring a new day."

"It's getting to be daylight here." Horn gestured toward the sky-filling brown bulk of the airship.

"We've reached the foothills of the Mountains That Look At Mountains," Silk said, "and if we had tried to float this far, we'd have settled to the ground. But Sciathan flies over these hills, and across the mountains, too—or soars from valley to valley, if he chooses."

"Bird fly!"

"Yes. Sciathan flies like Oreb here, or the eagle that brought down poor Iolar. I had a taste of that when I piloted this airship." For a moment Silk's smile was radiant.

Saba's head emerged from the hatch. "Hello, Caldé! Going to take a reading?"

"I wouldn't know how."

She swung herself easily onto the deck. "I do, and I've got the protractor so I can show you. It's early yet, but I wanted to climb up here while it didn't take so much lifting." She chuckled. "I heard you talking about flying. I command a thousand pterotroopers, but I can't fly like they do. Neither could you, we're both too heavy. Even this girl would have to lose a little to be much good."

"I was about to explain to Horn and Nettle that while wings are wonderful—and they are, truly, truly wonderful—feet are wonderful too. Doctor Crane, if he were still alive, could amputate my legs, and then I'd be light enough to fly the way your troopers do, and perhaps even as Sciathan does; but as much as I envy them, I wouldn't want him to. It would be marvelous to fly as they do, so it's not surprising that we envy them; but imagine how much someone without legs must envy us."

"I don't have to imagine. Some of my dearest friends have lost their legs."

Horn asked, "Are you going to be pilot some on the way back, Caldé? You like it so much I think you ought to. You were good at it, too."

Saba said, "For somebody without training, he was better than good. He'll be taking over in four hours."

Horn looked relieved.

"When we're past the mountains," Silk told him, and walked forward to the prow of the gondola.

Saba trotted after him. "I wouldn't do that, Caldé. We still haven't got all the altitude we want, and mountains can give you some tricky winds."

"I'll be fine; but you must remain where you are."

Behind Saba, Nettle called, "Horn's afraid you're going to jump, Caldé. That's all it is."

"I'm not."

"When General Saba said you were going to be the pilot, he felt a lot better, because he thought you wouldn't want to miss it. We both did."

Looking down upon the green and rising slopes far below, where hillside meadows yielded to forested heights, Silk smiled. "You don't have to worry. I love life and Hyacinth too much to jump. Besides, if I jumped I wouldn't be able to wrestle with your questions, Nettle—though that might be good for both of us. Have you more?"

"I was going to ask you about the mountains." Timorously, she edged past Saba to grasp Silk's hand. "It scares me to look at them. You know how lampreys look in the market? Those round mouths with rings and rings of teeth? These look like that to me, under us and up in the skylands too. Only a million times bigger."

"Were you going to ask me why they exist? Because Pas built them to guard Mainframe; but that's sheer speculation. I don't know any more than you do."

"If anybody lives there. And—and why there's snow on the tops. The tops are closer to the sun, so they ought to be warmer."

"I don't believe that the sun heats air," Silk told her absently, "not much, and perhaps not at all. If it did, the sun's heat couldn't reach us. If you think about it, you'll soon realize that sunlight doesn't illuminate air either; we could see air if it did, and we can't."

Behind Silk, Horn said, "No kind of light does then."

"Correct, I'm sure. The warmth of the sun heats the soil and the waters, and they in return warm the air above them. Up here where there are only widely separated peaks, the air must be cold of necessity. Hence, snow; and in the Mountains That Look At Mountains, snow has weight enough to fall."

Silk paused, considering. "I never asked Sciathan who lived in the mountains, or whether anyone did. I've seen no cities, but I would think a few people must, people who fled the cities or were driven out. It must be a wild and lawless place; no doubt many like it for just that reason."

From the hatch Hyacinth called, "Silk, is that you?" and he turned to smile at her.

"I've been looking all over for you, but nobody'd seen you. Oh, hello, General." As gracefully as ever, Hyacinth stepped from the ladder onto the deck. "Hi, sprats. Got a better view from up here? It's bigger, anyway."

"You can leave me to my own devices now," Silk told Horn.

It was snowing in Viron, a hard fall that converted misery to unrelieved wretchedness, snow that rendered every surface slippery and made every garment damp, and rushed into Maytera Mint's eyes each time she faced the wind.

"We have done what we can, My General." Under stress

of weather, the captain stood beside, not before, her. Both had their coat collars turned up against the wind and cold; his uniform cap was pulled over his ears like her striped stocking cap, his right arm inadequately immobilized by a bloodstained sling.

"I'm sure you have, Colonel. They'll start dying in a few hours, I'm afraid, just the same."

"I am not a colonel, My General."

"You are, I just promoted you. Now show me you deserve it. Find them shelter."

"I have tried, My General. I shall try again, though every house in this quarter has been burned." He was not a tall man, yet he seemed tall as he spoke.

That about the houses had been unnecessary, Maytera Mint thought, and showed how tired he was. She said, "I know."

"This was your own quarter, was it not? Near the Orilla?"

"It was, and it is."

"I go. May I say first that I would prefer to fight for you and the gods, My General? Viron must be free!"

She shivered. "What if you lose that arm, Colonel?"

"One hand suffices to fire a needler, My General."

She smiled in spite of her determination not to. "Even the left? Could you hit anything?"

He took a step backward, saluting with his uninjured arm. "When one cannot aim well, one closes with the enemy."

He had vanished into the falling snow before she could return his salute. She lowered the hand that had not quite gotten to her eyebrow, and began to walk among the huddled hundreds who had fled the fighting.

I would know every face, she thought, if I could see their faces. Not the names, because I've never been good with names. Dear Pas, won't you let us have even a single ray of sun?

Children and old people, old people and children. Did old people not fight because they were too feeble? Or was it that they had, over seventy or eighty years, come to appreciate the futility of it?

Something caught at her skirt. "Are they bringing food?"

She dropped to one knee. The aged face might almost have been Maytera Rose's. "I've ordered it, but there's very little to be had. And we've very few people we can spare to look for it, wounded troopers mostly."

"They'll eat it themselves!"

Perhaps they will, Maytera Mint thought. They are hungry, too, I'm sure, and they've earned it. "Somebody will bring you something soon, before shadelow." She stood up.

"Sib? Sib? Mama's over there, and she's real cold."

She peered into the pale little face. "Perhaps you could find wood and start a fire. Someone must have an igniter."

"She won't . . ." The child's voice fell away.

Maytera Mint dropped to one knee again. "Won't what?"

"She won't take my coat, Maytera. Will you make her?"

Oh, my! Oh, Echidna! "No. I cannot possibly interfere with so brave a woman." There was something familiar about the small face beneath the old rabbit-skin cap. "Don't I know you? Didn't you go to our palaestra?"

The child nodded.

"Maytera Marble's group. What's your name?"

"Villus, Maytera." A deep inhalation for words requiring boldness. "I was sick, Maytera. I got bit by a big snake. I really did. I'm not lying."

"I'm sure you're not, Villus."

"That's why she won't, so tell her I'm well!" The small coat stood open now, displaying what appeared to be an adult's sweater, far too large.

"No, Villus. Button those again before you freeze." Her own fingers were fumbling with the buttons as she spoke. "Find wood, as I told you. There must be a little left, even if it's charred on the outside. Make a fire."

As she stood, the wind brought faint boomings that might almost have been thunder. Distant, she decided, yet not distant enough. It probably meant the enemy had broken through, but it would be worse than futile for her to rush back knowing nothing. Bison would send a messenger with news and a fresh horse. These two . . . "Are you all right?" ·

"We'll keep." An old man's voice, an old man with his arm

around a woman just as old. The old woman said, "We're not hurt or anything." "We been talking about that." (The man again.) "We'd stay warmer moving around." "We were pretty tired when we got here."

"I'm trying to get you some food," Maytera Mint told them.

"We could help, couldn't we, Dahlia? Help pass it out, or anything you want done."

"That's good of you. Very good. Do either of you have an igniter?"

They shook their heads.

"Then you might look for one, ask other people. I set a little boy to gathering fuel a moment ago. If we could build a few fires, that would help a great deal."

"All this burned." The old man made an unfocused gesture with his free hand. "Should be coals yet." His wife confirmed, "Bound to be, snow or no snow." "I smell smoke." Sniffing, he struggled to stand, and Maytera Mint helped him up. "I'll have a look," he said.

Here I am, Maytera Mockorange. I am the sibyl I dreamed of becoming, moving among sufferers and helping them, though I have so little help to give.

She visualized Maytera Mockorange's severe features. The girl who would soon assume the new name *Mint* had yearned for renunciation and pictured herself walking through the whorl she would give up like a blessing; Maytera Mockorange had warned her of missed meals and meager food, of hard beds and hard thankless work. Of year after year of loneliness.

They had both been right.

Maytera Mint fell to her knees with folded hands and bowed head. "Oh Great Pas, O Mothering Echidna, you have given me my heart's desire." A feeling she had never known thrilled her: her body alone knelt in the snow; her spirit was kneeling among violets, baby's breath, and lily-of-the-valley, in a bower of roses. "I have won life's battle. I am complete. End my life today, if that is your pleasure. I shall rush into the arms of Hierax exulting."

"We tried, Maytera."

It had been a woman's voice to her left, and its words had not been addressed to her. To another sibyl then? Maytera Mint got to her feet.

"Cold," the woman was saying, *"and there's not a scrap of flesh on her poor bones."*

Three—no, four people. Two fat people sitting in the snow, with a starved face between the round, ruddy ones. The figure in black bending over them was the sibyl, clearly. What had been that young one's name? "Maytera? Maytera Maple? Is that you?"

"No, sib." She straightened up, turning her head farther than seemed possible, eyes glowing in a tarnished metal face. "It's me, sib. It's Maggie."

"It—it—I—oh, sib! Moly!" And they were hugging and dancing as they had on the Palatine. "Sib, sib, SIB!"

Another distant boom.

"Moly! Oh, oh, Moly! May I call you Maytera Marble, just once? I've missed you so!"

"Be quick. I'm about to become an abandoned woman."

"You, Moly?"

"Yes. I am." Maytera Marble's voice was firm as granite. "And don't call me Moly, please. It's not my name. It never was. My name's Magnesia. Call me Maggie. Or Marble, if it makes you happy. My husband will—never mind. Have you met my granddaughter, sib? This is she, but I don't think she'll talk right now. You must excuse her."

"Mucor?" Maytera Mint knelt beside the emaciated girl. "Our caldé described you to me, and I'm an old friend of your grandmother's."

"Wake up." Mucor's pinched face grinned without meaning. "Break it." There was no hint of intelligence in her stare. She said nothing further, and the silence of the snow closed about them until the fat woman ended it by saying, "This's my husband, General. Shrike's his name."

"Scleroderma! Scleroderma, I didn't recognize you."

"Well, I knew *you* right off. I said that's General Mint and I held her horse when she charged them on Cage Street, I did, and if you'd gone like you ought to you'd know her too."

The fat man tugged the brim of his hat.

"I went up to the Caldé's Palace to see Maytera, only she wasn't home and half the wall down, so I've been taking care of her granddaughter ever since, poor little thing. Did those bad women carry you off, Maytera? That's what I heard."

"You'd better call me Maggie," Maytera Marble said, and pulled her habit over her head.

"Maytera!"

"I am not a sibyl any more," the slender, shining figure declared. "I have become an abandoned woman, as I warned you I would." She dropped the voluminous black gown over Mucor's head, and pulled it down around her. "Put your arms into the sleeves, dear. It's easy, they're wide."

"There was an old man that helped me with her," Scleroderma explained, "but he went to fight, then the bad women came and we had to scoot."

If it had not been for the shock of seeing Maytera Marble nude, Maytera Mint would have smiled.

"I think it means he's dead, but I hope not. Aren't you cold, Maytera?"

"Not a bit." Maytera Marble straightened up. "This is much cooler and more comfortable, though I'm sure I'll miss my pockets." She turned to Maytera Mint. "I've been consorting with other abandoned women, a dozen at least. I'm afraid it's rubbed off."

Maytera Mint swallowed and coughed, wanting to bat the snowflakes away, to sit down with a mug of hot tea, to awaken and find that this lithe pewter-colored creature was not the elderly sibyl she had thought she knew. "Did they capture—"

With nimble fingers, Maytera Marble wound the long top of Maytera Mint's blue-striped stocking cap about her neck like a scarf. "This way, dear, then you won't be so cold, that's what it's for. You tuck the end in your coat." She tucked it. "And the tassel keeps it from coming out. See?"

"These women!" Maytera Mint had spoken more loudly than she had intended, but she continued with the same vehemence, telling herself, I *am* a general after all. "Are you referring to enemy troopers or Willet's spies?"

"No, no, no. Dear Chenille, who's really quite a nice girl in her way, and the caldé's wife. She's no better than she ought to be if you know what I mean. And the women our thieves brought. They were more interesting than the poor women, though the poor women were interesting too. But the thieves' women didn't mind taking their clothes off, or not very much. Dear Chenille actually enjoys it, I'd say. Her figure's prettier than her face, so I find it understandable."

Scleroderma said, "So's yours, Maytera," and her husband nodded enthusiastically.

Another explosion punctuated the sentence. Cocking her head, Maytera Mint decided it had been nearer than the last; there had been something portentious about the sound.

". . . Cognizance told us," Scleroderma finished.

Maytera Mint asked, "Did you say His Cognizance?" Then, before anyone could answer, put her finger to her lips.

The stammering popping reports seemed to come from above her head. They were followed after an interval by the remote crash of shells.

"What is it, General?" Scleroderma asked.

"I heard guns. A battery of light pieces. You don't often hear the shots, just the whine of the shells and the explosions. These are near, so they may be ours."

Maytera Marble took Mucor's hand and got her to her feet. "Will you excuse us? I want to take her to the fire."

"Fire?" Maytera Mint looked around.

"Right over there. I just saw it. Come along, darling."

Scleroderma and Shrike were getting to their feet as well, not swiftly but with so much effort, scrambling, and grunting that they gave the impression of frantic action.

The messenger should be here by now, Maytera Mint told herself, and stepped in front of Scleroderma. "You said His Cognizance was here? You must tell me before you go. But before you do, have you seen a mounted trooper leading another horse?"

Scleroderma shook her head.

"But His Cognizance was here?"

The fat man said, "Stopped an' had a chat, nice as anybody.

I wouldn't of known, only the wife, she knows all that. Goes twice, three times most weeks. Just a little man older'n my pa. Had on a plain black whatchacallit, like any other augur." He paused, his eyes following Maytera Marble and Mucor. "Crowd around any harder, an' they'll shove somebody in."

"You're right." Maytera Mint trotted through the snow to the fire. "People! This little fire can't warm even half of you. Collect more wood. Build another! You can light it from this one." They dispersed with an alacrity that surprised her.

"Now then!" She whirled upon Scleroderma and Shrike. "If His Cognizance is here, I must speak to him. As a courtesy, if for no other reason. Where did he go?"

Shrike shrugged; Scleroderma said, "I don't know, General," and her husband added, "Said we'd have to leave this whorl, then the caldé come an' got him. First time I ever seen him."

"Caldé Silk?"

Scleroderma nodded. "He didn't know *him* either."

The Trivigauntis had released their prisoners, as General Saba had promised; no other explanation made sense, and it was vitally important. Maytera Mint looked around frantically for the messenger Bison would surely have dispatched minutes ago.

"He was lookin' for the caldé," Shrike explained, "only it was Caldé Silk what found *him.*"

"There aren't as many as there were." Maytera Mint stood on tiptoe, blinking away snow.

"You told 'em to go find wood, General."

"General! General!" Beneath the shouted words, she heard the stumbling clatter of a horse ridden too fast across littered ground. "This way!" She waved blindly.

Scleroderma muttered, "Just listen to those drums. Makes me want to go myself."

"Drums?" Maytera Mint laughed nervously, and was ashamed of it at once. "I thought it was my heart. I really did."

Through the snow, Bison's messenger called, *"General?"*

She waved as before, listening. Not the cadent rattle of the thin cylindrical drums the Trivigauntis used, but the steady *thumpa-thumpa-thump* of Vironese war drums, drums that suggested the palaestra's big copper stew-pot whenever she saw them, war drums beating out the quickstep used to draw up troops in order of battle. Bison was about to attack, and was letting both the enemy and his own troopers know it.

"General!" The messenger dismounted, half falling off his rawboned brown pony. "Colonel Bison says we got to take it to 'em. The airship's back. Probably you heard it, sir."

Maytera Mint nodded. "I suppose I did."

"They been droppin' mortar bombs on us out of it all up and down the line, sir. Colonel says we got to get in close and mix up with 'em so they can't."

"Where is he? Didn't you bring a horse for me?"

"Yes, sir, only the caldé took it. Maybe I shouldn't of let him, sir, but—"

"Certainly you should, if he wanted it." She pushed the messenger out of her way and swung into the saddle. "I'll have to take yours. Return on foot. Where's Bison?"

"In the old boathouse, sir." The messenger pointed vaguely through the twilit snow, leaving her by no means certain that he was not as lost as she felt.

"Good luck," Scleroderma called. And then, "I'm coming."

"You are not!" Maytera Mint locked her knees around the hard-used pony, heedless of the way the saddle hiked her wide black skirt past her knees. "You stay right here and take care of your husband. Help Maytera—I mean Maggie—with the mad girl." She pointed to the messenger, realizing too late that she was doing it with the hilt of her azoth. "Are you certain he's in the boathouse? I ordered him to stay back and not get himself killed."

"Safest place, sir, with them bombs droppin' on us."

A floating blur resolved itself into two riders in dark clothing upon a single white horse. A familiar voice shouted, "Go! Follow that officer—he'll take you to shelter. Get away from that fire!"

The voice was Silk's. As she watched in utter disbelief, he

galloped through the fire. For a moment she hesitated; then the boom of slug guns decided her.

"I like this part though," Hyacinth whispered, hugging Silk tighter than ever, "just don't let it trot again."

He did not, but lacked the breath to say so. Reining up, he shielded his eyes with the right hand that snatched at the pommel whenever he was distracted; the group he had glimpsed through the snow might be a woman with children, and probably was. Gritting his teeth, he slammed his heels into the white gelding's flanks. It was essential not to trot—trotting shook them helpless. More essential not to lose the stirrups that fought free of his shoes whenever they were not gouging his ankles. The gelding slipped in the snow; for an instant he was sure it would fall.

Behind him, Hyacinth shrieked, *"Up, stand up! That way!"* She sounded angry; and briefly and disloyally, he wished that she possessed the clarion voice that Kypris had bestowed upon Maytera Mint—though it would have been still more useful to have it himself.

"My Caldé!" A snow-speckled figure had caught the bridle.

"Yes, what is it?"

"All are within, My Caldé. They are gone. You must too, before you die."

He shook his head.

"But a few remain, I swear. I shall send them. You must compel him, Madame."

Then the captain was running and the gelding trotting after him, and they were being shaken as if by a terrier.

"Here is the entrance, My Caldé. I regret I cannot assist you and your lady to dismount."

Too shaken even to think of disobeying, Silk slid from the gelding's back and helped Hyacinth down. The captain pointed to a deep crater almost at his feet; its bottom gleamed with greenish light.

Too sharply for comfort, Silk recalled the grave he had been shown in a dream. "We got to ride on a deadcoach the first time," he told Hyacinth. It was difficult to keep his voice casual. "That was a lot more comfortable, but there was dust instead of snow." She stared at him.

"You must climb down." The captain pointed again. "The climb is somewhat difficult. Several have fallen, though none were injured seriously." He produced a needler, fumbling the safety with his left thumb.

Silk said, "You're about to join the fighting."

"Yes, My Caldé. If you permit it."

Silk shook his head. "I won't. I have a message for you to give to General Mint. Do you know where Hyacinth and I are going?"

"Into this tunnel below the city, My Caldé, to preserve yourself for Viron, as is proper."

Hyacinth smoothed her gown. "We're supposed to leave the whole whorl with thousands and thousands of cards. If we get to whatever it is, we'll be rich." She spat into the snow.

"I've taken all the funds I could out of the fisc," Silk explained, "and His Cognizance has emptied the burse—the Chapter's funds. I'm telling you this so you can tell General Mint what's become of us, and what's happened to the money. Do you know which Siyuf you're fighting?"

A voice called, "*Caldé!*"

"Is that you down there, Horn?"

"Yes, Caldé." Horn climbed toward him, his feet loosening stones that rattled down the slope to fall into the tunnel.

"Go back down," Silk told him.

"My Caldé, we have been so fortunate as to chance upon this refuge opened for the defenseless by the enemy's bombs. I thank the good gods for it. You and your lady must employ it as well. Her airship cannot but see the fire."

Horn caught Silk's hand and joined them.

"As for this boy," the captain finished, "I shall procure a weapon for him."

"If we're going we'd better go," Hyacinth declared.

"You inquire concerning the two Siyufs, My Caldé. I have heard only rumors. Are they true?"

"I spoke to General Mint on a glass before we returned,"

Silk told him. "One of the councillors—Tarsier, I imagine—has altered a chem to look like Siyuf. She was supposed to mend relations between Trivigaunte and Viron, or see to it that the Trivigauntis lost if she could not. She appears to have chosen to occupy Siyuf's place permanently and conquer Viron for herself instead. Generalissimo Oosik has freed the real Siyuf in the hope—"

The final words were lost in an explosion. Silk found himself half in the crater, with Horn beside him and Hyacinth clinging and sobbing. After a few seconds he managed to gasp, "That was too near. Near enough to ring my ears."

"Where's the captain?" Horn asked. From the bottom, Nettle shouted, *"Horn!"*

"I don't know." Silk raised his heat to look around. "I can't see him, or—are those horses?"

"Our horse." Hyacinth staggered but managed to stand. "It must have been killed."

"Unless the captain mounted it and rode away. In either case, we'd better go."

She glared at him; then turned abruptly and slid down the slanting wall of the crater, pushing past Nettle and vanishing into the tunnel.

Horn caught Silk's arm. "You were sort of waiting here with the captain, Caldé. Like you didn't want to."

"Because I wasn't sure all the people who fled the battle had gotten inside."

Silk coughed and spat. "That explosion blew dirt into my mouth. I suppose it was open, as it usually is—I shouldn't talk so much. At any rate, I wanted to tell him I was resigning my office, and General Mint is to succeed me. Don't feel you have to chase after him with the message."

Nettle called, "I'm going inside with Hyacinth. Are you coming?"

"In a minute," Horn told her. "No, Caldé, I won't. But I promised His Cognizance I'd find you and bring you down there, and I'm going to as soon as . . ." He paused, shamefaced.

"What is it, Horn?"

"It's a long way, he says, to the big cave where the people are asleep in bottles, and when we get there we'll have to wake them up. Maybe we'd better get going."

"No, Horn." With the air of one who intends to remain for some time, Silk seated himself on the edge of the crater. "I asked Mucor to awaken the strongest man she could find and have him break the cylinder before the gas inside it killed him. If I could break one with Hyacinth's needler as easily as I did, I'd think a very strong man might break one from within with his fists. They'll be coming to meet us—or at least I hope they will—and may be able to show us a shorter route to the belly of the whorl, where the landers are."

He studied Horn with troubled eyes. "Now, why did you stop me from following Hyacinth? What is it?"

"Nothing, Caldé."

Like noisy spirits, troopers on horseback thundered past, their faces obscured and their clothing dyed black by the snow.

"Those were Trivigauntis, I believe," Silk said. "I don't know whether that's good or bad. Bad, I suppose. If I say it myself—tell you what I believe you were about to say—will you at least confess I'm right?"

"I don't want to, Caldé."

"But you will, I know. You were going to tell me why you and Nettle took me up on the roof of the gondola, where General Saba and Hyacinth joined us, pretending that they hadn't—"

"I was going to tell you about falling off the time before, Caldé. You said you tried to kill yourself and I stopped you, but it was the other way. I started to slide off on purpose. I don't know what got into me, but you grabbed me. You were just about killed too, and now I remember. I'd be dead if it weren't for you."

Silk shook his head. "If I hadn't acted foolishly, you wouldn't have been in danger at all; I provoked your danger and very nearly occasioned your death."

He sighed. "That wasn't what you came so close to telling me, however. Hyacinth had been in General Saba's cabin, though both pretended they had not been together. The walls of those cabins are cloth and bamboo, and you and Nettle were afraid I'd overhear them and realize they were doing the things that women do, at times, to provide each other pleasure."

Seeing Horn's expression, he smiled sadly. "Did you think I didn't know such things occur? I've shriven women often, and in any event we were taught about them—and worse things—at the schola. We're far too innocent for our duties when we leave it, I'm afraid; but our instructors ready us for the whorl as well as they can." He looked down at the object that Horn was offering him. "What is that?"

"Your needler, Caldé. It used to be the pilot's, I guess. Hyacinth knocked it out of her hand, you said, and you picked it up. You must have left it there in the cockpit, because the Flier found it there and gave it to me."

Silk accepted it, tucking it into his waistband. "You want me to kill Hyacinth with it. Is that the plan?"

"If you want to." Wretchedly, Horn nodded.

"I don't. I won't. I'm taking this because I may need it— I've been down there, and I may have to protect her. Haven't I told you about that?"

"Yes, Caldé. On the airship, for my book."

"Good, I won't have to go over it again. Now listen. You feel that Hyacinth has betrayed me, and unnaturally. I want you to at least consider, as I do, that Hyacinth herself may feel differently. Isn't it possible—in fact, likely—that she feared that General Saba might regain her airship in fact as well as in name? That in that case it would be well for us—for Hyacinth and me, and every Vironese on board—if she were as friendly toward us as we could render her?"

Horn nodded reluctantly. "I guess so, Caldé."

"Furthermore, Hyacinth knew that I meant to return General Saba's airship when we returned to the city. May not Hyacinth have considered that General Saba might at some future date be a good and strong friend to Viron?"

Through the break in the tunnel wall, Hyacinth called, "Aren't you coming down?"

"Soon," Silk told her. "We're not finished here."

"Caldé, she's the one dropping mortar bombs on us. General Saba is. That's her up there in the airship right now."

"It is indeed; but she's dropping them because she's been ordered to, as any good officer would. I doubt very much that Hyacinth cherished any hope of suborning General Saba from her duty; but there are many times when an officer, particularly a high-ranking one, may exercise discretion. Hyacinth tried, I believe, to do what she could to make certain any such decisions would favor us—more specifically, my government."

"But we're going. You said so on the airship, and before we found this way, we were going to have to walk all the way to the Juzgado. On the Short Sun Whorl, it won't matter whether General Saba likes us or not, will it?"

"No. But Hyacinth could not have known aboard the airship that we would be leaving this soon, and she may even have hoped that we would not leave at all. I think she did."

"I see." Horn nodded; and when Silk did not speak again, he said, "Caldé, we'd better go."

"Soon, as I said. There's one more thing—no, two. The first is that whatever that act might mean to me, or to you, or even to General Saba, it meant next to nothing to Hyacinth; she has performed similar ones hundreds of times with any number of partners. With Generalissimo Oosik, for example."

"I didn't know that."

"No. But I do—he told me. When she had to leave the house of the commissioner who had obtained her from her father—I don't even know which it was—she lived for a time with a captain. Eventually they quarreled and separated."

"You don't have to tell me all this, Caldé."

"Yes, I do. Not for your book—which you will probably never complete or even begin—but for guidance in your own life. Who was that captain? Would you care to guess?"

Horn shook his head.

"I think I can. He was very formal with her, but I saw his eyes—particularly when he stopped our horse. I don't believe he meant much to her; he was a protector and provider when she needed one. She meant a great deal to him, however—no doubt she always will."

Horn whispered, "She's climbing back up," and pointed.

Silk scrambled halfway down the crater to meet and assist her. "I won't say I'm not delighted to see you—I'm always overjoyed to see you, Hyacinth, you know that. But Horn and I were about to join you down there."

Entering the crater from the tunnel, Nettle called, "You wouldn't believe all the people down here, Caldé. Half the quarter. Marrow the greengrocer, and Shrike the butcher, and even the new augur that was with us on the airship. Moly's here, and he's making her wear his robe. The Prolocutor made everybody sit down."

Horn offered his hand to Hyacinth, and the other to Silk. "My mother, and my brothers and sisters. That's what I care about, only . . ." Something caught in his throat. "Only that sounds like I don't care about my father."

"But you do," Hyacinth muttered. "I know how it is."

"Yeah, I guess so. He made me work in the shop every day after palaestra, and—and we'd fight about that, and lots of other stuff."

"I understand."

"I'm the oldest," Horn said, as though that accounted for everything.

Silk called, "If half the quarter's down there, what about our manteion? The congregation, I mean, the people who came to sacrifice on Scylsday and the children from the palaestra?"

"They're just about all here," Nettle told him. "Not some of the men, they're off fighting for General Mint. But, oh, Goldcrest and Feather and Villus, and my friend Ginger. Wait, let me think. Teasel is, and her sisters and brothers and her mother. And Asphodella and Aster. And Kit—he's Kerria's little brother, and she's there too. And Holly and Hart. He's wounded. And the cats' meat woman, and that old man that sells ices in the summer, and a whole lot more."

Silk nodded, then smiled at Hyacinth. "I've done it—saved it from the dissolution of the whorl. Or at least I will have when we reach the new one. I was to save our manteion; and that is the manteion, all of those people coming together to worship. The rest was trimming, very much including me."

Hyacinth could not look at him.

"When you came back up, I was explaining to Horn that in the end it is only love that matters. The Outsider once told me that though he's not Kypris, she cannot help becoming him. The more she becomes a goddess of love in truth, the more they will unite—it was before we met in Ermine's by the goldfish pool." He smiled again. "Where Thelx holds up a mirror."

Hyacinth nodded; and Horn saw that her eyes were filled with tears. He asked, "Did you really see him there, Caldé? The Outsider?"

"Yes, in a dream, standing upon the water. I had only this left to say, Horn, and there's no reason I shouldn't say it now, or that Hyacinth and Nettle shouldn't hear it. It is that love forgets injuries. I know that Hyacinth would never betray me, just as you know that Nettle would never betray you; but if she did—if she did a thousand times—I would still love her."

Almost violently, Hyacinth pushed herself away from the crater. "I can't listen to any more of this. I don't want to, and I won't." She stood up.

Silk said, "Then let us go," and began to climb down to the break in the tunnel wall.

"I'm not going!" Hyacinth shouted. Her lovely face was savage. "You told me about that place, and I've seen it, and it's horrible! All the landers are broken, you said, not like Auk's, and you're just hoping to fix them. And you're giving up the whole *city!*" She turned and dashed away, vanishing in the swirling snow before she had taken five strides.

Silk tried to scramble back, but in his haste set off a slide that carried him almost to Nettle, who followed him when he began to climb again.

When he reached the surface and started after Hyacinth, Horn and Nettle went with him. A bomb burst near enough to shake the earth beneath their feet, and he stopped. "You have to go, both of you, and you must go together."

His eyes flashed even in that snowy twilight. "Nettle, do you understand? Do you, Horn? I'll find her, and enough cards to repair another lander. Get down there, find His Cognizance, and tell him. We'll meet you at the landers, if we can."

Nettle took Horn's hand, and Silk said, "Make him go. By force, if you must." He offered her his needler, but she drew her own, the one that had been Saba's. He nodded, put his back in his waistband, and disappeared into the snow like a ghost. Overhead, the harsh voice of his bird sounded again and again: *"Silk? Silk? Silk?"*

For a score of poundings of their hearts, Nettle and Horn stood together, staring after him and wondering what the future held for them; until at length they smiled as one, she gave him Saba's needler, and hand-in-hand they returned to the crater and scrambled down to the opening that a bomb had made in the tunnel wall, and went into the tunnel, where Horn's mother was waiting for them.

MY DEFENSE

With the account you have now read, I had intended to con-
clude *The Book of Silk*, for we never saw him again. I am
adding this continuation in response to criticisms and questions directed to us by those who read the earlier sections, sections which Nettle has corrected, and transcribed in a hand
clearer than mine.

Many of you urge me to tell the story in my proper person,
relating only what I saw, and in effect making myself my own
hero. I reply that any of you might write such an account. I
invite you to do so.

My purpose is not (as you wish) merely to describe the way
in which we who were born in Viron reached Blue, but to re-
count the story of Patera Silk, who was its caldé at the time
we left and was the greatest and most extraordinary man I
have known. As I have indicated, I had planned to call my account *The Book of Silk*, and not Starcrossers' Landfall or any
of the other titles (many equally foolish) that have been suggested. In the event, it has become known as *The Book of the
Long Sun*, because it is much read by young people who do

not recall our Long Sun Whorl, or were born after Landing Day. I do not object. You may call it what you wish as long as you read it.

To our critics, I say this: Patera Silk was personally known to Nettle and me; I recall his look, his voice, and his gait to this day, and when young I was punished for imitating him too well, as you have read. Nettle knew him as well as I.

We knew Maytera Marble (who also employed the names Moly, Molybdenum, Maggie, and Magnesia, the last being her original name) at least as well. Until we reached our teens, she was our instructress in the palaestra on Sun Street, as Maytera Mint and Maytera Rose were subsequently. Silk loved her and confided in her; in fact, I have often thought that she had been given the child she longed for, although she was not conscious of it. She in turn confided in us during the time we worked in the Caldé's Palace under her direction, during the time we were together on the airship, and during our passage through the abyss, and here on Blue. To prevent confusion, I have called her Maytera Marble throughout my account. There was never a more practical woman, nor a better one.

On the flight to Mainframe, we had many opportunities to see and hear Auk, though he was not generally communicative. Chenille, with whom we had worked at the Caldé's Palace, often spoke of him as well. Silk did not, as some readers assume, confide to us the content of Auk's shriving, although he told me that he had shriven him upon meeting him in the Cock. That Auk had kicked a man to death was known throughout the quarter, and it seems probable that it was one of the offenses of which he was shriven. Chenille confided to Nettle that he had struck her on two occasions, and described them.

More than one reader has taxed me with whitewashing Auk's character. It is more probable that I have painted it too dark; I disliked him, and even after so many years have found it hard to treat him fairly. As I have tried to make clear, he was a big man and an extremely strong one, far from handsome, with a beard so heavy that he appeared unshaven even when he had just shaved; although he was said to be courageous and a free spender, few besides Silk, Chenille, and Gib ever spoke well of him.

If I found it hard to be fair to Auk, I found it harder still to be fair to Hyacinth, whose extraordinary beauty was at once her blessing and her curse. She had little education, far too much vanity, and a savage temper. When Nettle was present, she displayed herself to me, posing, bending over to exhibit her décolletage, raising her skirt to adjust her hose, and so forth. In Nettle's absence, she cursed me if I so much as glanced at her. She saw all human relationships in terms of money, power, and lust, and understood Silk less well than Tick understood her.

Very few of us, I would say, have known such a woman as General Mint; and it is almost impossible to convey an accurate impression of her to those who have not. She was small, with a smooth little face, a sharp nose, and a dart of brown hair that divided her forehead almost to the eyebrows. In conversation her voice was the soft and timorous one we recalled from her classroom; but when the need for quick, decisive action arose, the little sibyl was cast off immediately. Her glance was fire and steel then, and at the sound of her voice wounded troopers who had seemed too weak to stand snatched up weapons and joined the advance. Unless restrained by her subordinates, she led her troops in person, striding boldly ahead of the boldest and never slackening her pace as she shouted encouragement to those behind her. If it had not been for Bison and Captain Serval, she would certainly have been killed by the second day.

As a tactician, she understood better than most the need for a simple workable plan which could be put into effect before conditions changed; that and the astounding loyalty she inspired were the keys to her success. Although she is better known as General Mint, I have titled her Maytera, just as I have referred to her sib as Maytera Marble throughout my account. Fewer than I had expected have found fault with Silk's assertion that she took her warlike character from the Goddess of Love, although it seems implausible to me. Nettle suggests that many women, thus inspired by love of their city and their gods, might exhibit the same dauntless courage. Certainly love will face the inhumi at midnight, as we say now.

Although neither of us spoke to Blood, both of us saw and heard him when he visited the manteion, and saw him and Musk when they offered their white rabbits. Blood's conversations with Silk and Maytera Marble were detailed to us by them; they, I would guess, saw more good in him than Nettle or I would have.

Neither of us ever saw Doctor Crane, but Maytera Marble had met him and liked him, as Silk had. Chenille, who had known him intimately, said that he looked on injury and illness as a butcher looks on pigs and steers; and I have tried to convey something of that. From what Silk said of him, he believed in Sphigx no more than any other god, and had her reality been proven to him, he would only have turned from ridiculing those who credited it to ridiculing her.

I have taken Incus's character from Remora's description and our own observations during the flight to Mainframe. He was physically unimpressive, and perhaps for that reason frequently impelled to assert his importance, but not lacking in courage. On the airship I watched him "enchant" a slug gun by slipping his finger behind the trigger, then snatch it from the trooper as she struggled to fire it.

Many readers have demanded that I include an account of our passage through the tunnels to the lander and our flight through the abyss. Again I invite them to pen their own, as Scleroderma did. (Her grandson has it and permits visitors to copy it.) I intend to say no more here than is necessary to illuminate the character of the inhumu Nettle and I knew as Patera Quetzal, His Cognizance the Prolocutor of Viron. No doubt many will object to my writing *character* in such a context, urging that a monster of that kind can no more have character than a hus; but those who trap hus and tame them have told me they differ at least as much as dogs.

To us Quetzal was not an inhumi, but a venerable old man, wise and compassionate, Silk's supporter and steadfast friend. When Nettle and I returned to the tunnel it was to him that we brought Silk's message. When they had heard it, many wanted to return to the surface to look for Silk and help him search for Hyacinth. Quetzal forbade it, pointing out that it was contrary to Silk's own instructions, and led us down the tunnel in the direction of the lake.

Then I remembered something that Remora had told me on the airship: how Quetzal had vanished when Spider forced him into the cellar of Blood's ruined villa. When we had walked a long way down the tunnel and even the hardiest had grown weary, and Quetzal himself had fallen behind nearly all of our straggling company, I was able to ask about it.

"Walk beside me, my son." He put a hand on my shoulder; I recall how light and boneless it felt through the thin jacket I wore, as if he had laid a strip of soft leather beside my neck. "I can't keep up any more. Will you support me? You're young and strong. Patera Caldé likes you, did you know that?"

I said I hoped he did, and that he had always been kind to me.

"He likes you. He speaks of you warmly, and of you, my child. You're both good children. Good children, I say. But men and women with children are children to me. No fool like an old man! You women are wiser when you're old, my child. You're grown, both of you. I doubt you know it, but you are."

We thanked him.

"I can hardly get along. Like the fat woman. Can't leave her, can we? Can't leave them back there, and she's too heavy to carry." He was wearing an ordinary augur's robe; but he bore the baculus, his rod of office, which he used as a staff.

I said that we would have to stop soon for Scleroderma's sake, and many others, and offered to go ahead if he would tell me what to look for.

"I want you to sleep, my son." He seemed to suck his gums and reconsidered. "No, to keep watch. Can you stay awake?"

I assured him that I could.

"Good. Someone must, and I can't. I'm always nodding off, ask young Remora. I can't keep up this pace myself, but I have to keep urging everybody to walk faster. What tricks the gods play! Have you a weapon, my child?"

Nettle shook her head; I explained that she had brought a needler from the airship but had given it to me, and offered to return it to her.

"Keep it. Keep it! You'll need it when you stand guard." He turned his head. He had a long and very wrinkled neck that would have betrayed his true nature at once had I known then of the hooded inhumi. As it was, I was suddenly frightened because there was nothing of warmth or kindness in his look. It was as though I were seeing a mask, or the features of a corpse propped erect. He said, "You won't shoot me, will you?"

Naturally I assured him that I would not.

"Because I'll walk. I always do. They see me around the Palace all night long. They say it's my spirit, that I step out of my skin and walk all night. Do you believe it, my child?"

Nettle nodded. "If Your Cognizance says so."

"I don't." I had the impression that he was leaning most of his weight upon my shoulder, yet he was certainly not heavy. "Never believe such stuff. I can't sleep, and so I wander about dazed and tired, that's all. My son, would you tell those in front to go faster? I haven't the breath."

I shouted, "His Cognizance says we must walk faster!" or something of the kind.

"Thank you. Now we can stop. Let the fat woman and her man catch up." He turned, motioning to them urgently.

Nettle whispered, "We're in danger down here. We must be, or he wouldn't be in such a hurry."

She had spoken in my ear, and I myself had hardly heard her, yet Patera Quetzal (as I thought of him) said, "We are, my daughter, but I don't know how much. When you don't know, you have to act as though it were great."

Wishing to return to my question, I asked him, "Were you in very much danger from Spider, Your Cognizance?"

He shook his head, not as a man does, turning it from side to side, but swaying it while holding it nearly upright. "From him? None. No, a lot, since he would have wasted my time. I'd a lot to do, so I left." He laughed, an old man's high-pitched cackle. "Vanished in the darkness. Is that what young

Remora told you? He told somebody that, I know. Want to know how to do it?"

He turned his back and raised his black robe to cover his head, standing with his hands and the baculus out of sight in front of him. That stretch of tunnel was as well lit by the creeping green lights the first settlers brought as any, yet he seemed almost to have disappeared, baculus and all. I said, "I see, Your Cognizance. I mean, I don't."

Scleroderma and her husband caught up with us then, she waddling very slowly and dolefully, he limping in a way that showed how his feet hurt. Nettle told them that Quetzal was worried about them.

"I'm worried about him," Scleroderma said, and holding onto her husband and me as though we were a couple of trees lowered herself to the shiprock floor and kicked off her shoes. Her husband said, "You sprats walk too fast. How's His Cognizance supposed to keep up?" He sat down beside his wife and pulled off his as well.

Recalling that Quetzal had been concerned for their safety, I motioned for Nettle to sit and sat down myself. Scleroderma said accusingly, "I heard you yell at them in front, trying to get them to go faster."

I explained that Quetzal had instructed me to, and Nettle asked, "Where is he? He was here with us a minute ago."

"Up ahead," Shrike told her. "Haven't seen him in a quite a while."

We rested for perhaps an hour, during which Nettle and I worried that we were becoming permanently separated from the rest. For a long way, however, it was impossible for our route to diverge from theirs; the tunnel ran nearly straight, slanting gently, and in fact pleasantly, downward. At length we came upon a side tunnel; but we found a note there signed by Hart, saying that His Cognizance had instructed him to write it, that they would follow the main tunnel, and that anyone who found the note was to leave it to direct others.

After another half league or so, we heard a baby crying and faint snores; and soon we caught up with our friends from the quarter and my mother, brothers, and sisters, all of them sound asleep. Scleroderma and her husband lay down at once, and I got Nettle to lie down as well, telling her to sleep if she could. She had no more than pillowed her head on my jacket than she was sleeping as soundly as Scleroderma.

I sat down, took off my shoes and rubbed my feet, and tried to decide what I ought to do. I had promised Quetzal I would stay awake, and I recalled very clearly what Silk had told me about the dog-like creatures the soldiers called *gods* and the convicts *bufes*. But I was tired and hungry, and longed to rest; and though Quetzal had asked me to protect the company, which by then numbered more than four hundred, he had said nothing about anyone's protecting me while I slept an hour or two.

After turning the matter over for what seemed a very long while in the dilatory fashion in which I weigh problems when I'm fatigued, I decided I would watch faithfully until someone woke, charge him or her to take my place, and sleep myself.

Then it almost seemed that I was asleep already, because it seemed that I could hear the soft sigh of wings, as if a big owl were flying along the tunnel a considerable distance from where I sat. I sat up straight and listened with all my might, but heard nothing more. Soon afterward, it struck me that Quetzal had said he often had difficulty sleeping. Thinking he might watch for me if he were wakeful, I stood up and padded among the sleepers looking for him; but he was not there.

I cannot describe the consternation I felt. Over and over I told myself that I must surely be mistaken, that someone had lent him a blanket or coat that covered his black robe; and so I peered into the same faces that I had peered into a few minutes before, until I sincerely believe that I could have described everyone present and said where each of them lay. We had among us a dozen infants, a large contingent of children, and a good many women; but not more than forty men, including Patera Remora and Shrike. I told myself very firmly then that a woman or even a girl could guard us as well as I could. She would only have to wake me if danger threatened.

Eventually it occurred to me to ask myself what Silk would have done in my situation. Silk would have prayed, I decided, and so I knelt, folded my hands and bowed my head, and implored the Outsider to take pity on my plight and cause one at least of those sleeping around me to wake up, very carefully specifying that a woman or a girl would be entirely acceptable to me.

When I raised my head, someone was sitting up in the midst of the sleepers; when I saw her dark and deathly eyes, I knew at once the mocking fashion in which the Outsider had answered my prayer. "Mucor," I called softly. "Please come over here and talk to me."

Her face floated upward like a ghost's and seemed almost to drift along the tunnel; she was wearing a sibyl's black gown.

"Mucor," I inquired, "where is your grandmother? She was here before." Very tardily it had occurred to me that Maytera Marble rarely slept, and would be the ideal person to relieve me so that I could.

"Gone," Mucor said. I expected to get nothing more out of her, having learned at the Caldé's Palace how seldom she spoke. But after a few seconds she added, "She went with the man who isn't there."

It was encouraging, but there seemed little use in asking who the man who wasn't there was. I asked instead if she would send her spirit to learn where her grandmother was and whether she was in need of help. Mucor nodded, and we sat side-by-side in silence for what I felt sure was at least a quarter hour. I was nearly asleep when she said, "She's carrying him. Crying. She'd like somebody to come."

"Your grandmother?"

I must have spoken more loudly than I had intended, because Nettle sat up and asked what was wrong.

Mucor pointed down the tunnel, saying, "Not far."

Nor was she. We had hardly lost sight of our friends when we met Maytera Marble, more or less dressed in an augur's robe so long it swept the tunnel floor, with Quetzal in her arms. Her face could not display emotion, as I have tried to make clear; but every limb expressed the most heart-rending anguish. "He's been shot," she told us. "He won't let me do anything to stop the bleeding." Her voice was agonized.

As slowly as a flower's, Quetzal's face turned toward us; it was terrible, not merely swollen or sunken, but misshapen, as if death's grip had crushed his chin and cheekbones. "I am not bleeding," he said. "Do you see blood, my children?"

I suppose we shook our heads.

"You can't stop my bleeding if I'm not bleeding."

I offered to carry him, but Maytera Marble refused, saying he weighed nothing. Later I was to find that she was not far wrong; I had lifted younger brothers who weighed more.

Nettle asked who had shot him.

"Troopers from Trivigaunte." He tried to smile, achieving only a grimace. "They're down here now, my child. They were digging trenches east of the city looking for a tunnel near the surface, and found one. They think Silk's with us." He gasped. "But they'd try to stop us anyway. Sphigx commands it."

I said, "We have to do the will of Pas."

"Yes, my son. Never forget what you just said."

By that time we had nearly reached the sleepers. Nettle ran ahead and woke up Remora, knowing that where there is no doctor an augur makes the best substitute; but Quetzal would not let him see his wound. "I'm an old man," he said. "I'm ready to die. Let me go fast." Yet he did not die until the following day, when we had begun to cross the abyss.

Remora brought him the Peace, and when it was over Quetzal gave him his gammadion, saying, "Your turn now, Patera. You were cheated by Scylla, but you'll have to guide the Chapter in the Short Sun Whorl."

(So it came to be. Although there are many other holy men here, His Cognizance Patera Remora heads what people from other cities call the Vironese Faith. I am adding this note because I know that not all of my readers came from Viron, and as Nettle's copies are themselves copied, still more will be unfamiliar with the Chapter.)

But I am running ahead of my account. When Quetzal

would no more answer our questions than permit us to treat his wound, we asked Maytera Marble what had happened.

"I was lying awake," she said, "Thinking things over. How we'd seen Mainframe, and about dear Chenille and Auk, and Patera Silk and Hyacinth. Wondering, too, whether my husband was still alive, and, well, various things.

"I saw His Cognizance get up and start down the tunnel, so I told Mucor not to worry, I'd be back soon, and went after him and asked where he was going. He said he was afraid there might be danger ahead, so since he couldn't sleep he was going to see. I said he shouldn't risk himself like that, that he should send Macaque or one of the other boys."

She broke down at that point, sobbing uncontrollably, and cried for so long that many of her listeners left to talk among themselves; but Nettle and I stayed, with Remora, Scleroderma, and a few others.

When she had regained her self-possession, she continued, "I wanted him to send someone else. He ordered me to go back, and I said thanks be to Pas that I'm a laywoman now and don't have to obey, because I'm not going to let you run off alone like this, Your Cognizance, and get killed. I'm going with you. He said he knew these tunnels because he'd come down here alone to make the Ayuntamiento talk to him when they didn't want to, and he knew the dangers. But I wouldn't leave."

Nettle said, "This isn't your fault, Maggie. I don't know how it happened, but I know you, and it can't be." The rest of us seconded her.

Maytera Marble shook her head. "After we'd walked a long, long way we came to a crossing where four tunnels met. I asked which way we were going, and he said he was turning right, but I had to go back. Then he went into the right-hand tunnel. It was the darkest, the one he went into was. I followed him, and for a little while I saw him up ahead, but he wouldn't slow down. We were both practically running. Then I really did run as fast as I could, but I lost sight of him. I walked on and on, and there were these tunnels off to the side but I always kept to the one I was in. Then there was a big iron door and I couldn't go any farther, so I went back. I got to the place—"

She choked and sobbed. "Where the tunnels crossed, and I could hear him walking. Not the way he had been when I'd been following him, but slowly, stumbling every step or two. He was a long way off, but I had good ears and I gave them to Marble."

Nettle looked puzzled; I signaled her not to speak.

"So I ran some more." Maytera Mint looked up at us, and it seemed worse to me than any weeping that her eyes were not full of tears. "He'd fallen down when I got there. He was bleeding terribly, like the animals do after the augur pulls his knife out, but he wouldn't let me look at it, so I carried him."

We ourselves carried him after that, carrying him in our arms like a child because we had no poles from which to make a stretcher. He directed us, for he knew where the Trivigauntis were, and down which tunnel the sleepers were coming.

(I will say nothing of our brush with the Trivigauntis; it has been talked about until everyone is tired of listening. Shrike, Scleroderma, and I had needlers, as did certain others. Scleroderma risked her life to get our wounded to safety; and as the fighting grew hotter, she was wounded and wounded again, but she continued to nurse us when her skirt was stiff with her own blood.

(She has been dead for years now; I very much regret that it has taken me so long to pay her this well-deserved tribute. Her grandchildren are very proud of her and tell everyone that she was a great woman in Viron. Nobody in Viron thought her a great woman, only a short fat woman who trudged from house to house selling meat scraps, an amusing woman with a joke for everyone, who had dumped a bucket of scraps over Silk while he sat with her on a doorstep because she felt he was patronizing her. But the truth is that her grandchildren are right, and we in Viron were wrong. She was a very great woman, second only to General Mint. She would have ridden with General Mint if she could, and she fought the Guard in Cage Street and nursed the wounded afterward, and fought fires that night when it seemed the whole city might burn. In the end, she and Shrike lost their home and their shop, all that they possessed, to the fire that swept our quarter. Even then, she did not despair.)

Quetzal had brought hundreds of cards from the Burse. He had already entrusted most of them to Remora, and he gave him the rest when we reached the landers. Some of us had thought that he had refused to have his wound bandaged for fear his cards would be stolen, but when they had been turned over to the sleepers, he still refused.

With the sleepers, we filled two landers. It was thought best to have some of them on each, because they knew much more about their operation than any of us did. As has been told many times, the monitor who controlled our lander appeared in the glasses, displayed Blue and Green to us, and asked which was our destination. No one knew, so we consulted Quetzal, although he was too weak almost to speak.

He asked to be carried to the cockpit, as we called that part of our lander which Silk had called the nose. The monitor there displayed both whorls to him, as it had to Remora, Marrow, and me; and he chose Green, and choosing died. Remora then personally carried his body back to the small sickbay; it was no easy task, because our engines were firing as never before, not even when we had left the Long Sun Whorl. As it chanced, there was a glass in this sickbay, I suppose to advise those who cared for the sick.

There was a woman named Moorgrass on board whose trade it had been to wash the bodies of the dead, and perfume them, and prepare them for burial. Remora asked her to wash and prepare Quetzal's, and Maytera Marble and Nettle volunteered to help her. I shall never forget their screams.

We did not know then that the inhumi live on Green, nor that they fly to Blue when the whorls are in conjunction, nor that they drink blood, nor even how they change their shapes. Or in fact anything about them. Yet everyone who saw Quetzal's body was deeply disturbed; and Marrow and I urged that we come here to Blue instead of going to Green as he had advised.

Remora heard us out; but when we had finished, he affirmed his faith in Patera Quetzal, whose coadjutor he had been for so many years, and declared that we would remain on the course he had recommended. It was not until three days later, when it had become apparent to anyone who went into the cockpit, that we were really on course to Blue, that we learned that the monitor had overruled him. No one questions its decision now.

Here I close my defense, having (as I hope) satisfied the demands of my critics. Whether I have or have not, having compromised my principles more than I wished, I repeat that I set out to tell Silk's story, and no other.

It may be that he is dead, having been killed in the Long Sun Whorl. It may also be that he and Hyacinth later boarded a lander that carried them to Green, and died there.

But it also may be that he is still alive, and in my heart I feel that he is, either in the Long Sun Whorl or—as I hope— on another part of this Short Sun Whorl we call Blue. The years will have changed him as they change all of us; I can only describe him as he looked on that overheated summer afternoon when he snatched the ball from my hand as I was about to score, a man well above average height, with a clear, somewhat pale complexion, bright blue eyes, and straw-colored hair that would never lie flat. A slender man, but not a slow or a weak one. He will have a scar upon his back where the needle left it, and may have faint scars on his right arm, left by the beak of the vulture Mucor called the white-headed one.

My own name is Horn. My wife Nettle and I live with our sons on Lizard Island, toward the tail, where we make and sell such paper as this. We will be grateful to anyone who brings us word of Patera Silk.

AFTERWARD

Horn wiped the point of his quill with a scrap of soft leather and corked the ink that he and his wife had concocted from soot and sap, pushed back his chair, and stood. It was done. It was done at last, and now perhaps the ghost of the boy he had been would leave him in peace.

Outside, the short sun's fiery rim had touched the sea. A golden road—an Aureate Path—stretched westward across the whitecaps toward a new Mainframe that almost certainly did not exist. He walked to the beach where Hoof and Hide were playing and asked where Sinew was.

"Hunting," Hide declared; Hoof added, "Over on the big island, Father." Hoof's wide, dark eyes showed plainly how deeply he was impressed.

"He should be home by this time."

Nettle called from the kitchen window as he spoke.

"Go inside." When the twins objected, he gave each a push in the direction of the sturdy walls.

From the summit of the tor, he had a clear view of the strait. Still, a half minute passed before he could be certain of the coracle, lifted upon distant waves only to vanish from sight.

Night had come already to the eastern sky, scattering the short suns of other whorls across its black velvet. Soon Green would rise, almost a second sun, yet baleful as a curse; it had brought a succession of storms and monstrous tides—

There!

Horn watched and waited until he was sure the faint gleam was actually moving against its glittering backdrop. Within that point of light he had been born, and had grown almost to manhood. Within that point of light Sinew had been conceived, in all probability, in the Caldé's Palace. It did not seem possible.

Almost too quickly to be noticed, something dark flitted between Horn and the whorl that had been his; and he shuddered.

TOR
BOOKS The Best in Science Fiction

MOTHER OF STORMS • John Barnes
From one of the hottest new nanes in SF: a shattering epic of global catastrophe, virtual reality, and human courage, in the manner of *Lucifer's Hammer*, *Neuromancer*, and *The Forge of God*.

BEYOND THE GATE • Dave Wolverton
The insectoid dronons threaten to enslave the human race in the sequel to *The Golden Queen*.

TROUBLE AND HER FRIENDS • Melissa Scott
Lambda Award-winning cyberpunk SF adventure that the *Philadelphia Inquirer* called "provocative, well-written and thoroughly entertaining."

THE GATHERING FLAME • Debra Doyle and James D. Macdonald
The Domina of Entibor obeys no law save her own.

WILDLIFE • James Patrick Kelly
"A brilliant evocation of future possibilities that establishes Kelly as a leading shaper of the genre."—*Booklist*

THE VOICES OF HEAVEN • Frederik Pohl
"A solid and engaging read from one of the genre's surest hands."—*Kirkus Reviews*

MOVING MARS • Greg Bear
The Nebula Award-winning novel of war between Earth and its colonists on Mars.

NEPTUNE CROSSING • Jeffrey A. Carver
"A roaring, cross-the-solar-system adventure of the first water."—Jack McDevitt

---